Meadowlark

Carolyn Lampman

RCP
RED CANYON PRESS

Like **Carolyn Lampman**
on Face Book
Visit my website
www.carolynlampman.org

Meadowlark

Printed in the United States of America

Formatting: Wild Seas Formatting
(http://www.WildSeasFormatting.com)

Published by
RED CANYON PRESS
4530 W. Mountain View Dr. Riverton, WY 82501

Dedication

To Kathy, who introduced me to Garrick and helped me understand how hard it was for him to say *"Jeg elsker deg"*.

A special thanks to Louie for the poem and to Jeri for the title.

A meadowlark's song
Given freely to the wind,
Drifts easily with the breeze
Undisturbed by fence post
Or man's clink and clank.

Unlike mine,
An easy song
Which needs not be understood
To feel its enjoyment.

And, this by pen,
A much too complicated
Thank you
For the all-out effort
Of a small yellow-bellied bird.

Louis R. Lampman

Chapter 1

South Pass City, Wyoming Territory, 1870

Becky was out of options, and she knew it. With the last of her money gone, it was only a matter of time until hunger drove her down to Beer Garden Gulch in search of a job in one of the saloons. It was stupid to wait any longer hoping for a miracle. Cameron wasn't coming back.

She kicked a small rock into the creek and glanced down the street. There was already music and raucous laughter coming from the saloons. It wasn't even dark out and business was booming. Obviously, the owners would be too busy to talk to her now. Morning would surely be better.

With a relieved sigh, Becky sat down on a pile of sluice box tailings. There was no guarantee anybody down there would hire her anyway. No one else in town had. Too young, they said, or not enough experience. She'd heard that some of the hurdy gurdy girls were almost as young as she was. Maybe it wouldn't matter that she was tall and gangly with too much hair and not enough chest as her father always said.

Cameron hadn't minded. In fact, he'd made her feel beautiful and loved right up until he'd walked out of her life. Becky's father had said Cameron Price played her for a fool, taking what he wanted and never giving her another thought after he rode away. As the months passed and no word came, it began to look as though her father were right.

"Oh, Cameron," she whispered into the twilight, "Would it have made any difference if you'd known about your son?"

Her hands moved over her softly rounding stomach. Within a month she wouldn't be able to hide it anymore, and they wouldn't even let her work in a brothel. Becky's lips twisted at the irony: too young to work, but old enough to have a baby.

Maybe her father wasn't far wrong when he called her a stupid little slut. His words and the hard slaps that followed were etched indelibly into her mind. Afterward, he'd gone to work his shift in the mine and had never returned.

Becky closed her eyes and tried to conjure some regret for her father's death. There was none. It had been over a month, and she still couldn't mourn him.

Her stomach rumbled painfully. Another night without food. She was almost used to it by now. With a deep sigh, Becky opened her eyes and watched the brilliant reds and golds of the sunset fade into cool, concealing darkness as the sun dipped below the hill.

The cold dampness of the ground beneath her began to soak through her skirt, but she ignored the discomfort as she savored the spring evening. The pungent, rich soil and the smell of wood smoke covered the other, less pleasant odors of man. Crickets chirped in the nearby grass, and an owl called to its mate over the roar of the swollen creek.

At last, some of the lights began to wink out. It was late, and people were staggering home to bed. Though the saloons and bawdy houses would keep going until dawn, there was almost total silence in the city of tents that made up a good portion of South Pass City. It was time to find a place to sleep.

Becky rose and walked to the edge of the creek. The spring run-off was at its highest. The placer miners had been watching it for days, anticipating the new gold it would wash out of the hills. She looked down at the normally insignificant stream that now roared by with awesome power. An entire tree rolled by, bobbing in the turbulent waters.

Suddenly, the ground crumbled under her feet, and she slid down into the icy stream. The water choked off her scream as it closed over her face. Then her head collided with a solid object, and her thoughts sank into blessed darkness as she surrendered to the flood.

"A bottle of Redeye, Sam," Garrick told the bartender, then glanced around the brightly lit room. As a casino and a brothel, The Green Garter was the best South Pass had to offer, but for some reason, watching the miners gamble away their pitifully small wages irritated him this evening. He'd been one of their number often enough, but tonight it seemed a pathetic waste of time.

With a sigh, Garrick turned back to the bar, slid a few coins across its shiny surface to Sam, and picked up the bottle. As he pulled the cork out with his teeth and poured the deep amber liquid into a glass, he imagined how aghast his mother would be to see him doing such a thing. The thought of Minnesota brought the usual pang of homesickness, and he lifted the glass to his lips in irritation. He gulped down the raw whiskey and grimaced as the fiery brew burned its way to his stomach. It tasted worse than usual and did nothing to relieve his loneliness.

"Hello, Swede." A husky feminine voice cut into his thoughts. "Aren't you going to give my dealers a chance to win back some of that money you walked out of here with last night?"

Garrick glanced down at the brassy redhead and smiled. "Not tonight, Angel. I have a feeling the cards wouldn't fall my way."

Angel snorted. "That'd be a first! Never seen anybody with luck like yours." She gave him an appraising look. "What's eatin' you, anyway? That scowl would curdle milk."

"Bored I guess. Care for a drink?"

Angel glanced at the bottle in front of him and made a face. "No thanks. Rotgut whiskey ain't my idea of a good time. Don't remember it being yours either."

"Not usually, but we ran short of black powder, so I don't have to work tomorrow."

"You planning on getting drunk?"

"I was, but if you won't join me..."

She laughed and patted his arm. "If it's company you want, I may have just the ticket. A new girl came in on the stage today. Calls herself Collette, though she ain't any more French than Sam." Angel nodded toward a sultry dark-haired beauty at the end of the bar. "Be glad to introduce you."

Garrick let his gaze roam over the curvaceous brunette, wondering how he'd managed to miss her before. Almost as if she felt his gaze, Collette glanced up, wet her lips, and smiled seductively.

"What do you think, Swede? Want to see if she can wipe that frown off your face?"

He shrugged. "Might as well." Maybe Collette was what he needed.

"Hello," he said when she sidled up to him.

"Hello yourself." Collette ran her hand up his arm. "I just love big men."

"I'll let you two get to know each other," Angel said, walking away. "Take good care of Swede, Collette, he's one of my best customers."

"Don't you worry, Miss Angel. I'll take excellent care of this one." Collette let her fingers wander down the massive chest. "Tell me, Swede, are you big all over?"

He let a slow smile cross his face. "Only one way to find out."

Three quarters of an hour later, Garrick buttoned his coat against the chill outside and collected his bottle of whiskey. Collette had been all he could wish for, yet, if anything, he felt worse than he had before.

He went outside and took a deep breath of the crisp mountain air. There was a tang of spring on the breeze tonight, almost like home. Garrick turned his steps toward the creek. Maybe a walk would clear his head and chase away the blue devils that plagued him.

From the corner of his eye he caught a movement far up the bank. Peering through the darkness, he saw a shadowy figure walk toward the edge of the creek, apparently contemplating the rushing water as he was. Whoever it was, he hoped their thoughts were more pleasant than his.

As he watched, Garrick was startled to see the stranger stop on the very edge of the bank.

Didn't they realize how dangerous the creek was this time of year? Garrick was beginning to wonder if he should call out a warning when, to his utter horror, the other person went down and was swallowed up by the flood. Shock held him immobilized for a blink of an eye. Then he was shrugging out of his coat and pulling off his boots as he scanned the stream for some sign of the stranger.

At last, he spotted a flash of white up stream. Quickly judging where the current would carry its burden, he stepped into the frigid water. Garrick's breath seemed to catch in his lungs as the icy wetness struck his legs.

It took all of his strength to withstand the force of the water as it sucked and pulled at him like a living thing. Searching frantically for another glimmer of white, Garrick wished his eyes could pierce the blackness of the water. But he could see nothing as he battled his way to the middle of the stream.

All at once, something hit him, and he went down. Some instinct made him reach out and his hands encountered the unexpected texture of cloth. As he grabbed the body inside the clothing, he let himself be taken downstream until he had a firm hold. By the time his head broke the surface the third time, he had the other person locked against his body with one arm.

Pulling great draughts of air into tortured lungs, he struck out for the edge of the stream. Though Garrick was a strong swimmer, his skills were nearly useless in the rush of water that swept them along.

Instead of fighting the current, he moved with it, working steadily closer to the bank. At last his knee struck solid ground, and he scrambled up the muddy bank where he collapsed on the shore. Panting for air, he lay there for a moment holding the stranger against his chest as he fought the blackness that threatened to overwhelm him.

Gradually, Garrick's vision cleared, and he gently rolled his burden to the ground. As he blinked the water out of his eyes, he glanced down at the thin body and long skirt and his eyes widened in surprise. *A woman!*

He felt for a pulse along the delicate neck. A slight fluttering against his fingers reassured him. Garrick leaned down and put his cheek next to her nose. There was no movement against his skin, no stirring of air. She wasn't breathing.

With a sense of urgency, he turned the woman to her stomach and straddled her hips. Alternately pushing on her upper back and pulling on her elbows, he attempted to force the water from her lungs. Push... Pull...Push...Pull. Garrick kept repeating the motions, over and over, never admitting the possibility that his efforts might be wasted. At long last, she choked as water came rushing from her mouth.

Relief rolled through him. Garrick moved to the side as she coughed and gasped, trying to catch her breath. At last, the spasms stopped, and he pulled her into his arms. "It's all right, little one," he murmured as a whimper escaped her lips. "You're safe."

A deep voice like melted honey flowed over Becky. She opened her eyes and looked up into the kind face of an angel. Never had she seen such hair, so pale it seemed to glow in the moonlight. She reached up and tried to touch it.

"Where do you belong?" he asked.

"With angels?" she whispered hopefully, then sank into sweet, dark oblivion.

Chapter 2

"Angel's? You're from The Green Garter?" Garrick thought he knew all of Angel's girls pretty well, but he didn't remember seeing this one before. What was she doing out this time of night when she should be working?

A sudden breeze reminded him of how wet they both were. Whoever the woman was, he needed to get her warmed up and soon. Garrick thought longingly of the coat he'd left on the bank of the creek. Unfortunately, it was a good three hundred yards up stream somewhere with his boots and most of a bottle of whiskey.

He climbed wearily to his feet, picked up the girl, and turned toward The Green Garter. It would be useless to go to his tent, where it wasn't much warmer than outside.

Though slender, she was obviously quite tall and no featherweight. As he carried her slung over his shoulder, Garrick lost count of the times he had to stop and rest before they reached The Green Garter.

Loud music and laughter coming through the double swinging doors brought him to a halt. Angel wouldn't thank him for bringing a nearly drowned girl in the front door during her busiest time. He stumbled around to the back and made his way to the storeroom where he laid his burden on the floor and looked around for something to cover her with. There was nothing.

Briefly cursing Angel's efficient housekeeping, he turned and walked down the short hallway.

At the door that led to the casino, he stopped. If he walked in soaking wet with no boots on, he was bound to stand around answering a lot of questions while the girl lay freezing on the cold floor of the storeroom. With a brief grin, he opened the door slightly then slammed it. The sound was loud enough to be heard above the din but probably wouldn't be noticed by many.

Garrick crossed his arms and settled back against the wall to wait. Angel would be here soon, ready to do battle with whoever had the audacity to enter her private domain.

Within minutes, the door burst open, and Angel was there, her eyes snapping with fire. "Swede! What in blue blazes do you think you're doing?" she demanded.

"I need to talk to you privately."

"Well, this is a damn funny way to—" Her voice faltered. "For God's sake, you're soaking wet! What the hell is going on?"

Garrick glanced over Angel's shoulder at the gun-toting bartender standing protectively behind her. "I'll explain as soon as we're alone."

"It's all right, Sam," she said, lifting her hand and waving him away. "I'll take care of this. You can go back to the bar."

"Are you sure?"

"Yes, yes, I'm sure. I have nothing to fear from Swede. She closed the door behind Sam. "Now, what's this all about?"

"I just pulled one of your girls out of the creek."

"What?"

"She almost drowned. In fact, I thought I'd lost her for a while."

"All my girls are working, Swede."

He shrugged. "She said she lived here."

"Where is she?"

"In your storeroom."

With a swish of taffeta, Angel walked down the hall to the small room where the girl lay unconscious. She knelt down and brushed the wet strands of hair back from the girl's face.

"Well I'll be damned. It's Fenton White's daughter."

Garrick looked over Angel's shoulder. "So you do know her.

"Not really. I've seen her around a little. Her father had a bad habit of getting drunk and busting up whatever place he was in. She usually came and got him before he did too much damage. Nobody cried much when he died a couple of months ago."

Garrick rubbed his chin. "I wonder why she said she belonged here."

"Who knows? Doesn't have any family that I know of, poor girl. Maybe she was going to ask me for a job." Angel stood and dusted her hands briskly. "We've got to get her warmed up, or she'll catch her death. I have an empty room upstairs if you want to bring her along."

With a nod, Garrick picked up the unconscious woman again and followed Angel up the back stairs. He laid his burden on the bed in a room he'd never seen before and looked around in surprise. It was very different from the other upstairs rooms in The Green Garter.

Totally devoid of the opulence that characterized the rest of the establishment, it would have fit more easily into a genteel home than a notorious brothel. There was a large bookcase along one wall filled with many well-worn volumes. An over-stuffed chair was placed in comfortable proximity to the pot-bellied stove in which Angel was building a fire. Cheerful calico curtains at the single window went with the brightly-colored rug on the polished wood floor and with the hand-made quilt on the bed. There was a homey, welcoming feel about the tidy little room.

"You needn't look like that," Angel snapped, slamming the stove door. "This is my room, and I like it this way."

"Actually, I like it a whole lot better than the others." Garrick smiled down at her as she stomped to the bed and began to undo the girl's buttons. "To tell you the truth, it suits you."

"Humph, don't try to bamboozle me. You're shocked as hell!" She gave a fatalistic shrug. "As a matter of fact, it does suit me — far better than the rest of this place. You're the only man besides Sam that's ever been in here, so forget you ever saw it."

"It's already forgotten."

"Good. Keep it that way." As she slid the wet dress off the girl's shoulder, she suddenly stopped and gave him a sharp look. "I can handle this myself. You go change your clothes before you catch pneumonia." She turned back to her task. "But get back here as soon as you can. The girl shouldn't be left alone, and I can't spare anyone to sit with her."

Without a word, Garrick turned on his heel and left. When he returned half an hour later, his charge was tucked into bed and sleeping soundly.

"It's about time," Angel said, rising from the chair by the bed as he let himself in.

"Sorry, I had to get my coat and boots from the creek bank."

"And I have work to do," Angel grumbled. "Your friend hasn't moved much, but at least she's warmed up some." She nodded toward a decanter and a glass on the table next to the bed. "Give her some brandy if she wakes up."

"I'll try, though I'm not much of a nurse maid."

"And you think I am?"

He grinned at her. "I think you have a lot of talents you don't share with the world." Ignoring the disgusted sound Angel made, Garrick glanced longingly at the bookshelf. "Mind if I borrow a book? I haven't had anything but the *South Pass News* to read in a long time."

Angel raised her eyebrows. "Well, well, I'd never have figured you for a reader."

"I could say the same for you."

"Good point." She walked to the door. "Read anything you like. Just make sure you put it back on the shelf when you're done. I'll see you about dawn."

Awareness came to Becky slowly. There was a sound, an ominous crackling close at hand that Becky couldn't identify at first. When she did, there was an instant recoil in her gut.

Fire! She was dead, and her bright-haired angel had only been an illusion. Afraid to open her eyes, Becky lay still as she gradually became aware of a variety of sensations. A slight odor of flowers in the air...the ground soft and warm beneath her...the unexpected rustle of a page turning...None of it made any sense.

Cautiously, she opened her eyes, and her confusion intensified. She lay on a bed in a comfortable room, the kind she remembered from her childhood. The fire didn't burn in the deepest pits of hell as she had supposed, but in an ordinary pot-bellied stove. It was the sight of the stove that suddenly brought it all together. Closing her eyes, she made a small noise in the back of her throat. She was still alive.

"You're awake." A deep melodious voice from the other side of the bed startled Becky. Her eyes popped open, and she turned to look.

It was the angel! No, not an angel, she corrected herself, a man...a lying, hurting, deceitful, man.

"Drink this." He poured something into a glass, then slipped his arm around her back and held the beverage to her lips.

Taking a swallow, Becky came straight up in bed, coughing and choking as the liquid fire burned its way down her throat.

"Easy now," he said, patting her back with a huge hand. "Brandy is meant to sip, not gulp."

When she finally caught her breath, she glared up at him with reproachful eyes. "Brandy!"

"It's a restorative. You nearly drowned."

"Who are you?"

"They call me Swede." After easing her back against the pillow, he set the glass on the small table.

A Swede. Well, that explained the white-blond hair. Becky watched as he rose to his feet, her eyes widening in amazement as he crossed the room. He was huge! The easy swing of his walk struck a chord of memory, and she realized she'd seen him striding down the muddy street of South Pass more than once. She'd noticed him because he was so tall. "Where am I?"

"Angel's," he said over his shoulder as he squatted down in front of the stove with a poker.

"Where?"

"Angel's. You know, The Green Garter."

"You brought me to a brothel?" Becky wondered why she was so dismayed when she'd planned on doing the same thing herself. It seemed that thinking about it and doing it were very different.

The note of panic in her voice surprised him. "You said you lived here." He closed the stove and rose to his feet. "I asked where you belonged, and you said with Angel."

She did have a vague recollection of saying something about angels. "Why did you save me?"

"You fell into the creek. If I hadn't been there, you'd have drowned."

Becky turned away. "It might have been better if you had just let me go."

"What?" Garrick was shocked.

"Drowning would be less painful than starving." She rubbed her hand across the blanket. "It was an option I hadn't even thought of. I think I might like it better than becoming a saloon girl."

"A saloon girl! Surely there are plenty of other jobs around South Pass City."

"Not for me." Becky shook her head. "Nobody would hire me. They all said I was too young. Of course, they'd throw me out as soon as they found out about the baby anyway. I won't even be able to work in a place like this for very long."

"Baby? You have a child?"

"No, but I soon will have."

"You're expecting?"

"Expecting, in a family way, pregnant, whatever you want to call it."

"What about the father?"

She bit her lip as an image of Cameron flashed through her mind. "He's gone. I thought of going somewhere else and pretending to be a widow. The farthest I could get on the money I had was Miner's Delight, and I don't think twelve miles would be far enough."

Silence fell between them. Becky closed her eyes, seeking solace in oblivion as sleep overtook her once more.

Thunderstruck by the turn of events, Garrick came back to the bed and sat down. His book lay forgotten on the washstand as he mulled over the new information, approaching it from all angles.

Two things were abundantly clear no matter how he looked at it. He had saved two lives instead of one, two lives that might still be lost unless she found some way to support herself.

Suddenly, he wondered if finding a solution for this woman and her child might begin to atone for the black shadow that lay in his past. Would salvaging two lives make up for the loss of one?

It was nearing dawn when Becky awoke once more. He was still there, the blond giant with the beautiful voice. Somehow, she thought he'd be gone once he learned of her shame. Her own father had turned his back on her, why wouldn't a stranger?"

"Would you like a drink?"

"No, thanks." Becky remembered the brandy with a shudder. "Did you spend the whole night in that chair?"

"I was thinking."

"Must have been some problem!"

"Bad enough you thought drowning sounded like a good idea."

"Oh."

Unbelievably, he smiled, not a false tinny smile but one that lit up his whole face. "I came up with something I'm sure you never considered."

"What?"

"We can get married."

Chapter 3

"Swede's waiting for you downstairs," Angel said from the doorway.

Becky turned away from the window where she'd been basking in the mid-day sunshine. "I'm ready."

"Good, because he seems kind of fidgety."

"Oh dear." Becky paled at the thought of making him angry. With a quick glance in the mirror, she hurried past Angel and out into the hallway.

"You don't need to look like that. He isn't going to bite you."

Becky didn't bother explaining being bitten was the least of her worries. Bitter experience had taught her the folly of keeping a man waiting. It was a lesson she had no intention of forgetting.

As she rushed down the stairs, she was barely aware of her opulent surroundings. She had eyes only for the man at the bar trading small talk with the bartender.

He glanced up at her arrival and straightened in surprise as she came to a halt in front of him.

Slightly breathless, she dropped her gaze to the floor. "Sorry I took so long," she murmured. Nervously, she waited for him to say something. After several long moments of silence, she looked up.

Becky was very tall herself, but the top of her head only came to his chin. She had the unfamiliar sensation of feeling small as she looked up at him. There was no clue of what he was thinking as he watched her impassively.

For the first time, she realized his eyes were a pale aquamarine. The blue-green color reminded her of frigid water beneath a thin shell of ice in the winter. His thick, white-blond hair added to the illusion of cold.

"You planning on standing here all day?" Angel asked.

Garrick tore his eyes away from his prospective bride to look at Angel. "No, and we'd better get going. Would you mind coming with us? We'll need a witness."

"A witness? For what?"

"For our wedding."

"Your wedding!"

Garrick smiled at Becky. "Angel seems to have developed a habit of repeating everything I say."

Becky looked away in confusion. The words were teasing, but she didn't want to do the wrong thing and make him mad.

"I thought you didn't know her," Angel said.

"I do now."

Angel gave a crack of laughter. "I'll be damned, Swede. You're the last person I'd expect to be swayed by a pretty face. All right, I'll go with you, but don't be surprised if the new Justice of the Peace won't let me in her house. It's the disadvantage of letting women hold public office, you know. They're a trifle skittish around my kind."

"I hadn't thought of that. If you'd rather not go—"

"I don't mind, but your bride might," Angel said. "Mrs. Morris will probably think this little chick is one of mine."

Becky shook her head. "It doesn't matter to me what she thinks. I...I'd like you to come. You're the only friend I have."

Angel gave her an odd look but didn't dispute Becky's claim of friendship.

"Let's go, then," Swede said. He self-consciously offered each lady an arm and escorted them out the door. "We may be a little crowded, but at least we won't have to walk in all this mud."

Becky felt a flash of disappointment as Swede led her to the dilapidated black buckboard sitting in front of The Green Garter and helped her up. She had always imagined going to her wedding dressed in a beautiful gown of white satin and riding in a shiny new buggy, the envy of all who saw her.

Staring at the peeling paint of the buckboard, she suddenly realized the enormity of what she was doing. A few hours ago, it had seemed a heaven-sent solution to her problems, a way out of the impossible situation she'd landed herself in. Now she wasn't so sure. By marrying Swede, she was sacrificing everything she had ever dreamed of.

An image of Cameron with his debonair charm and heart-stopping good looks rose in her mind. Irritated with herself, Becky pushed the thought away. She'd given up the right to dreams when she'd gotten pregnant. Instead of finding fault with Swede and their arrangement, she should be thanking her lucky stars.

Crammed together on a seat that was meant for two, the trio headed down the street to Esther Morris's home. Becky was uncomfortably aware of the long muscular thigh pressed against her own and the huge hands gripping the reins. The thought of those same fingers knotted into a fist made her shudder. She would have to be very careful around this man.

"Listen," Angel said suddenly, "a meadowlark!"

Becky and Garrick both looked at her questioningly as the bird's warbling call filled the air.

"Look over your shoulder when a meadowlark sings," Angel quoted the old saying. "Long life, love, and good luck it brings."

Garrick and Becky glanced back at the street behind them. It was filled with men, horses, and mules battling the quagmire of mud and animal droppings that made the thoroughfare difficult to navigate. Nothing new there.

As they turned back around, their eyes met. Garrick raised an eyebrow and smiled down at her. "Maybe he's wishing us good luck."

"Or telling us we're lucky we don't have to walk," Becky said, returning his smile.

"Whatever he's saying, I'm glad to hear him," Angel put in. "If the birds are back, that means spring is finally here. Winters in South Pass City are entirely too long to my way of thinking."

"Ja, it is always that way in the mountains," Garrick said as he pulled to a halt in front of a well-kept cabin at the end of the street. "Here we are."

He jumped to the ground and lifted Becky down from the buckboard.

She instinctively put her hands on his shoulders to catch her balance. Even through the heavy flannel of his shirt, she could feel the thick muscles moving beneath her fingers. A curious jolt ran through her at the unexpected contact. Once again, she was reminded how large and powerful he was. She tried to put it from her mind as Swede helped Angel alight.

Esther Morris herself opened the door, and it was all Becky could do not to gape in surprise. For the second time in less than thirty minutes, she felt dwarfed. The woman had to be at least six feet tall and none too slender.

Right now, she was listening patiently as Garrick explained why they had come. When he finished, her rather stern face broke into a smile.

"A wedding. How delightful. Please come in and make yourselves comfortable. It won't take me a minute to get ready." If she recognized Angel, she didn't mention it. Angel was still a bit wary but relaxed her defensive stance as she muttered something about feeling like a midget.

To the rest of the world, Esther Morris was a celebrity, for she was the first female justice of the peace in the entire country. She was said to have been instrumental in pushing the world's first women's suffrage bill through the territorial legislature and had already gained the reputation for making just decisions.

To Becky, she would always be the woman who quite cheerfully bound two strangers together for life.

"You're my first wedding," she said as she came back into the room a few minutes later thumbing through a book. "It will be a pure pleasure to do this. Now let's see, it should be right...Ah, here it is. If the bride and groom will please join hands."

Most of the ceremony passed in a blur as Mrs. Morris read the ritual. Becky responded at the appropriate times with little enthusiasm. She was surprised when Mrs. Morris called Swede, "Garrick Swenson." How strange to be marrying a man without even knowing his name!

She looked up at him, and he squeezed her fingers reassuringly. Her hand felt lost in Swede's hard, callused palm, and yet his touch was as gentle as though he held a delicate piece of porcelain.

"And now the ring..." Mrs. Morris looked at Garrick expectantly.

There was an uncomfortable pause as Garrick realized with all his other plans he'd forgotten to get a wedding ring. Then suddenly, he smiled and pulled a rawhide thong from around his neck. Dangling at the end of it was a silver ring, which he removed and placed on Becky's finger. It still held the warmth of his body, branding her skin, tying her to him. A few more words, and the wedding was over.

There was a moment of discomfort as Mrs. Morris gave him permission to kiss his bride. With an apologetic look, Garrick leaned down and brushed his lips across Becky's.

The touch was brief and not unpleasant, but it brought Becky to earth with a jolt. As her husband, he'd certainly expect her to share his bed. Her mind flashed back to the intimacy she'd shared with Cameron. She swallowed nervously, wondering if she'd be able to do those things with a total stranger.

Within a very short time, the three were back outside and loaded into the buckboard. All too soon, they dropped Angel off at The Green Garter. For the first time all day, Becky and Garrick were alone.

Garrick looked down at the woman beside him, sensing her nervousness but unsure what to say. He slapped the reins against the horse's back, and they started down the street. "I'm sorry about the ring."

"What?"

"The ring. I forgot to get one."

"Oh." For the first time she glanced down at the ring on her hand. It was made from a horseshoe nail, cleverly bent into a circle and fused together. Burnished by years of wear, it shone in the sunlight like the finest silver. "This one is fine. It fits pretty well."

"My grandfather made it."

"Oh," she said again, unable to think of anything else. Silence fell between them as he maneuvered the horse and buckboard around the worst of the potholes and mud puddles in the street.

"Where are we going?" she asked after a few minutes.

"Home."

"Where is that?"

"Just out of town. I bought out a miner who decided it was time to move on. Sold me everything for a grubstake and my tent." He looked down at her. "Did you want to stop and pick up your things first?"

"There's nothing to pick up. I sold it all." She searched her mind for something else to say, to fill the uncomfortable void. "Was the horse part of the deal?"

"Ja."

"She looks fat and healthy."

"Her owner said he was pretty sure she'll foal in the fall. Her name's Sophie."

The mare's ears twitched at the sound of her name, and Becky smiled. "Hello, Sophie."

Garrick followed the road to a small aspen grove, then turned down a faint track that was hardly more than a trail. They bounced along through the trees until they came to a small cabin.

Garrick's heart sank. With all his other preparations he hadn't had time to come out and examine his purchase. It looked as if it had been abandoned. The front door was open, hanging by a single leather hinge. There was a hole where the window should have been, offering a glimpse of the dismal interior.

He hadn't expected it to be perfect, but it appeared much worse than he'd imagined. "Wait here," he said as he tied the reins to the brake lever and jumped down. At the doorway, he stopped and stared at the mess in dismay. The floor was covered with dirt and debris, and light showed through numerous holes where the chinking had fallen out of the walls. A bunk sagged against the wall, and a rickety table stood in one corner next to the fireplace.

"Is something wrong?" Becky asked, joining him in the doorway. "Oh, my."

"The miner I bought it from said it was in good shape. I'd hate to see something that he thought needed some work."

"It has four more-or-less solid walls and a roof. To most miners this is a palace."

"Maybe, but it's no place for a woman."

"Oh, I don't know." Becky stepped over the threshold and looked around. "I've lived in a lot worse. Other than a little dirt, it's not bad."

"It could use a few repairs."

"I suppose." She moved across the room to a large wooden box by the fireplace. "I wonder what's in here. Oh, look, pots and pans!"

Garrick watched her for a moment as she dug out a battered collection of blackened cooking utensils. Her delight was obvious. With a shake of his head, he went back to the buckboard. Any other woman he knew would have been in tears.

By the time Becky had dug clear to the bottom of the wooden box and rearranged it to her satisfaction, Garrick had replaced the missing leather hinge on the door. She watched as he turned his attention to the bunk.

Apparently, he was a man of action and few words. Beyond his observation about the cabin's state of disrepair, he had said nothing. Instead, he'd gone out to the buckboard, retrieved a hammer from his things and gone to work.

By now, Becky's father would have somehow decided it was all her fault and wouldn't have hesitated to take out his frustration on her. Swede hardly seemed concerned by the inconvenience. Even now, trying to support the sagging bed frame with his shoulder as he worked on the leg, his face was calm, his temper apparently unruffled.

"W-would you like some help?" Becky asked timidly. "I could hold that up for you."

Garrick glanced up in surprise. "All right," he said after a moment as he shifted the side rail off his shoulder. "Hold it right here."

Obediently, Becky knelt by the bed and put her hands under the board. With a barely perceptible nod of approval, he went back to work. As the light reflecting off her wedding ring caught her eye, Becky suddenly realized this was the bed she would have to share with him. Though it was certainly big enough for two people, it would be crowded when one of them was the size of her new husband.

"Did you find anything interesting?" his voice broke into her thoughts.

"What?"

"In the box. Were there any surprises?"

"Not really, though there were a few things I didn't recognize. I think they might be for setting pans on in the fireplace, but I'm not sure. I've never cooked in a fireplace before."

"I'm sorry there isn't a stove."

"It doesn't matter. I haven't ever cooked on one of those either. We never had anything but a campfire."

As he glanced over his shoulder at her in surprise, she hastened to add, "But I'm sure it won't be that difficult to learn to use the fireplace." Looking away from his gaze, Becky mentally cursed her unruly tongue. He probably thought she'd starve him to death before she learned the proper way of it.

When he said nothing, Becky wondered uncomfortably if he was already regretting the generous impulse that had led to their marriage. Stiffening her spine, she vowed he would never have cause to look back on this day and be sorry he'd tied himself to her.

"That should do it," Garrick said a few minutes later as he finished reinforcing the board she was holding. He stood and looked around as he reached down to give her a hand up. "It may be a while before this place is livable."

Putting her hand in his, Becky smiled up at him shyly as she climbed to her feet. "I don't know, I think it's...oh..."

Becky forgot what she was saying as her ears started ringing, and Swede's face swam in front of her eyes. Unable to focus, she felt her body sway before she pitched forward into darkness.

Chapter 4

"Rebecca? Can you hear me? Rebecca, open your eyes!"

Becky heard the vaguely familiar voice through the rushing noise in her ears, but she couldn't remember who it belonged to. Her mind felt stiff and awkward, almost as though it were stuffed with cotton. Gradually, though, her senses began to clear, and she opened her eyes. "Becky," she said as Swede's face came into sharp focus.

"What?"

"Nobody calls me Rebecca anymore."

"Are you all right?"

Becky suddenly realized she was lying half on his lap, her upper body supported by his arms as he watched her with concern.

"What happened?"

"You fainted."

"I did?" She struggled to sit up as hot embarrassment stained her face. "How silly of me. I must have stood up too fast."

"When was the last time you ate?"

"I don't know. Yesterday maybe."

"When?" he asked again, his voice firm.

Becky hung her head. "Three days ago."

"Good Lord, why didn't you say something?"

"I d-didn't want to bother you."

"Don't you think it bothered me to have you faint in my arms?"

"I'm sorry. I didn't know I'd faint," she said in a small voice. "I ran out of money, and there wasn't anything else to sell except...myself." Her voice sank to a whisper. "I was trying to get the courage to ask for a job in Beer Garden Gulch when I fell into the creek."

Garrick's chest tightened. He felt stupid for not realizing the truth when she told him drowning was a kinder death than starving. "Why didn't you eat at Angel's this morning?"

"Nobody was even awake until just before you got there this afternoon."

"Stop looking so guilty. It's more my fault than yours." He sighed, then gave her a slight smile. "I'm kind of hungry. What do you say we go back to town and have supper?"

"Shouldn't we do a little more work here first?"

"Nope." He shook his head decisively. "It's our wedding day, and we should be celebrating."

"I-I hadn't thought of that."

"Neither had I until just now." He stood and scooped her up in his arms. "It's good luck for the groom to carry the bride over the threshold. I suppose it works just as well going out as in," he said as he ducked through the doorway.

Becky had the irrational desire to lay her head on his shoulder as he carried her to the buckboard and deposited her on the seat. The big Swede had shown more kindness in the few hours they'd been acquainted than her father had in the all the years she'd lived with him. For the first time in a very long time, she began to feel safe.

They went to the Sherlock Hotel for supper. Garrick ordered a huge meal, and Becky tried not to wolf it down. She didn't think any food had ever tasted quite so wonderful. Fighting the urge to eat like a pig, she went slowly and was careful to stop before she made herself sick.

Garrick studied her across the table. Gone was the slightly pathetic waif he'd pulled from the creek. The huge brown eyes, thick dark hair, and pert little nose were still the same, but, somehow, she'd been transformed into a lovely woman. Becky didn't have the classically pretty features that inspired poets and artists; hers was the sort of earthy beauty that made a man's blood run hot in his veins and his breath catch in his throat. That she seemed innocently unaware of her allure only added to her appeal.

He wondered about the man who had tasted her charms. Had he loved her, whispering sweet promises he couldn't keep? Or had he been drawn by her beauty, seduced her uncaringly, and then walked away?

Satisfied at last, she looked up from her meal and caught him staring at her. Blushing slightly, she smiled. "A penny for your thoughts."

Figuring she wouldn't appreciate observations about her appeal or questions about the baby's father, he racked his brain for an acceptable topic. "Why doesn't anyone call you Rebecca anymore?"

"My grandmother was about the only one who ever did. It was her name, you see. After she died, my mother would call me Rebecca Anne when she was mad at me, but the rest of the time I was Becky."

He smiled. "Rebecca Anne, I like that. My father called my mother Anna occasionally. It was his nickname for Alaina."

"Alaina? That doesn't sound much like a Swedish name."

"She's Irish."

Becky looked surprised. "You must resemble your father then. No one would think you were anything but pure Swedish."

"I do, but he isn't Swedish either."

"He isn't?"

"Nope, not a drop of Swedish blood in him." Garrick grinned. "My family is Norwegian."

"What? Then why do they call you Swede?"

He shrugged. "I don't know. I guess all Scandinavians look and sound pretty much the same to the rest of the world. The crew boss called me Swede when I worked on the railroad. I never corrected him, and it just sort of followed me to South Pass."

"Well, I think it's ridiculous. I'm going to call you by your given name and that's that." She gave her head a decisive nod to emphasize her point. After a moment, she looked at him. "It is Garrick, isn't it?"

He laughed, the deep, rich sound turning heads and bringing smiles to the faces of the other diners. "*Ja*, my name is Garrick, though nobody has called me that for so long I may not answer to it. How did you know it anyway?"

"The same way you found out mine was Rebecca. Mrs. Morris called you that at the wedding."

They smiled at each other, both suddenly much happier about the bargain they'd made.

"Are you finished?" Garrick asked, nodding toward her plate.

"Hmm? Oh, yes. I couldn't eat another bite."

"Good. What would you like to do now?"

"We could go back to the cabin," she said uncertainly.

Garrick smiled. "We could, but I have a better idea. There's a troupe of actors in town putting on a play at the Variety Theater. Would you like to go?"

"Oh, could we? I've never been to a real play before."

"And I've never been to one in South Pass City."

Becky's delight at the promised treat was like a warm glow inside Garrick as he paid for their dinner and took a room at the hotel for the night. Noting Becky's wistful look when the clerk mentioned the bath down the hall, Garrick paid the extra four bits for her to use it.

He knew his poker winnings wouldn't last long if he continued to spend so recklessly, but Becky's look of pleased surprise was worth every penny. After escorting his new wife to the room, he left her to take her bath in private and took his belongings back out to the cabin. As he drove down the rutted trail, it occurred to him that his bone-deep loneliness of the night before was gone.

Becky luxuriated in the first hot bath she'd had in years. Though she knew her time was limited, she couldn't resist the self-indulgence of washing her hair with the fresh-smelling soap. She didn't even care that it would still be wet hours later. Trying not to wish she had clean clothing to put on, she dressed and was ready to go by the time Garrick returned.

Justin T. Franklin and his world-renowned acting troupe were far from the best that had ever graced the boards of South Pass's theater, but Becky was enchanted. It didn't matter that the leading lady had a tendency to forget her lines and the villain had a suspiciously unsteady gait. The play held her spellbound, and she was sorry when the final curtain fell.

She chattered happily all the way back to the hotel, reliving the entire performance in minute detail. Adjusting his stride so she didn't have to run to keep up, Garrick listened with half an ear. He was pleased with her obvious delight, but his mind had already turned to the night ahead. Though they'd exchanged vows, and he'd given her his ring, he was pretty sure they weren't really married.

Right now, she seemed reconciled to their situation, but after her baby was born she might feel differently. Becky was young and bound to fall in love someday. When she did, she'd want her freedom. Even if the marriage was legal, they could get it annulled easily enough if they never consummated their union. The important thing now was for her to feel safe and secure by thinking their marriage was real.

Garrick needed to come up with a plausible reason for not sleeping with her. It shouldn't be too difficult. Many women were intimidated by the size of him, and he could tell his new wife was one of them. He'd seen the fear in her eyes. Listening to her talk, he wondered if nervousness might have something to do with her nonstop conversation. By the time they reached the hotel, he was sure of it.

"...and I hope we're done with snow for the year," Becky was saying. "Of course, that's the problem with living in the mountains like this. Spring comes so late that—"

"Becky, I would never hurt you."

She glanced at his face in shock. "Wh-what?"

"I said I wouldn't hurt you, and I won't. You don't have to be afraid of me."

"I-I'm sorry if it seems that way." She dropped her gaze. "I'm just very tired." When she realized what she'd said, her face turned a dull red.

"We don't have to make it a real marriage tonight," he said gently.

"I-I don't mind."

"This time yesterday we didn't even know each other, and we're still practically strangers. We both need time to adjust."

She looked up at him questioningly and was surprised to find gentle understanding in his eyes. "Thank you," she whispered.

"You take the bed. I'll sleep on the floor."

"That hardly seems fair. You paid for the room."

Garrick smiled as they climbed the stairs. "Sleeping on the floor won't bother me. I'm used to the ground."

"So am I."

"Then you'll enjoy a nice soft bed."

"I slept in one last night while you sat on a chair."

"Most beds are too short for me anyway." Garrick opened the door and stepped aside for her to enter.

She looked at the tiny room doubtfully. An iron bedstead was pushed up against one wall, while a chest of drawers with a mirror and a washstand took up most of the other. She'd forgotten how small the room was. The distance between them was barely big enough to walk in. "There isn't enough room for you down there. We'll have to share the bed."

For a moment, he was tempted, then cool reason returned, and he shook his head ruefully. "I don't think so."

"Then I'll take the floor."

"No, you won't. You'll sleep in the bed, and that's final."

"And where are you going to sleep, under the bed?" After a moment she sighed. "I just don't see that we have much choice. Either I sleep on the floor, or we share the bed."

He looked from the floor to the bed and back again. She was right. There was no way he'd fit in that small space. "All right, have it your way then. I'll be back in about half an hour or so."

Without another word, he turned on his heel and left.

It took Garrick somewhat longer than he'd expected to discover his supply of black powder had arrived and to have it delivered to the mine. When he tracked down Ox Bruford, the freighter was already involved in a poker game and not interested in leaving. Though Garrick finally managed to get the mule skinner to cooperate, Ox complained good-naturedly all the way out to the mine about friends who took unfair advantage.

By the time they had unloaded the kegs of powder and Garrick had made his way back to the Sherlock, Becky was sound asleep. He stood looking down at her for a few minutes before blowing out the lantern and stripping down to his long underwear.

As quietly as possible, Garrick crawled into bed and settled down to sleep. The bed was too short, and the soft warm body next to him far too enticing. Still, with his lack of sleep from the night before, it wasn't long before he started to relax.

Just as he was beginning to drift off, he heard a soft noise from the other side of the bed. Turning his head toward the sound, he listened intently until it came again. With a grin, he settled back down and closed his eyes. There was something strangely endearing about a woman who snored.

Chapter 5

"Garrick?" Becky sat up in bed and looked around the room. He was gone. Except for a dent in the pillow next to her, he might never have been there. Thinking he'd probably gone outside to the privy, she scrambled out of bed and dressed hurriedly.

Half an hour later she was pacing the limited floor space of the tiny room in agitation. Where was he? Time passed, and still he didn't come. At last, Becky could stand the waiting no longer.

Downstairs, the desk clerk greeted her with a smile. "Good morning, Mrs. Swenson. Your husband left you a note."

She was startled to hear herself addressed as Mrs. Swenson. "Oh? When did he leave?"

The clerk shrugged. "In time for the day shift."

"I see. Thank you." Feeling rather silly, Becky took the note and walked over to the window. Of course he'd have gone to work. Why hadn't she thought of that?

The strong, heavy lines on the paper reminded her of him. Though she was not a very accomplished reader, she was able to figure out most of his message. He'd left her money in...something...and wanted her to buy...bread? *What in the world?*

After struggling with Garrick's note for several minutes, she finally decided he wanted her to eat breakfast and then pick up supplies. It made sense.

It only took a few minutes to go back upstairs and locate the money he'd left in the dresser. There was a great deal, more than she'd ever had to spend before. For once, she'd be able to buy a few luxuries like coffee, maybe even some sugar.

After a leisurely breakfast, Becky went to the nearest mercantile. Within a short time, she emerged armed with those items she considered indispensable for cleaning. The storekeeper had offered to drop off the supply of food staples on his way out of town later, and she'd accepted gratefully. As she walked the quarter of a mile to the cabin, she felt more optimistic than she had in a long time. Life no longer looked quite so hopeless.

Garrick couldn't afford to be distracted. A dozen lives, including his own, depended on his ability to concentrate on the task before him. Usually, it wasn't a problem, but today a pair of velvety brown eyes kept intruding as he carefully measured out the exact amount of black powder needed for a charge.

He'd awakened at first light, his body responding uncomfortably to the feminine warmth pressed against him. Stifling a groan, he regretfully untangled himself and crawled out of bed before he gave in to temptation.

As he pulled on his clothes, he studied his wife. For the first time, he wondered how old she was, not more than twenty, certainly. She was little more than a child who had lost a lover, then her father, and finally bound herself to a total stranger.

Garrick reached into his pants pocket to pull out his rapidly dwindling roll of bills. He peeled off a couple, and then glanced down at Becky. She'd never really been given the chance to leave South Pass, to make a new life for herself somewhere else. After a moment, he divided the roll in half and placed part of it in the dresser drawer. He really didn't want her to go, but he had to give her the option.

Telling himself it was the only honorable thing to do, Garrick borrowed a pen and paper from the desk clerk downstairs. After telling her where he'd left the money, and urging her to get breakfast, he told her to do whatever she wanted with the rest. Then he gave the note with the clerk and left quickly before he had a chance to change his mind.

All day, he'd regretted his generous impulse. She had no reason to stay, and he'd given her a small fortune to take with her if she wanted to leave. By the time his shift was finally over, Garrick was convinced he was the biggest fool around.

Though he was expecting it, the hotel clerk's revelation that Becky had left after breakfast and not returned was like a hammer blow. Uncertain why her defection should bother him so much when they were virtual strangers, Garrick went to the stable to collect the horse and buckboard. He might as well pick up his things from the cabin and come back to town for the night. Maybe a game of poker at The Green Garter would lift his spirits.

The ride out to the cabin was a gloomy one. When he arrived, he ducked through the open door and came to an abrupt halt. He looked around the room in amazement. All the dirt and grime was gone. The walls and floor had a freshly scrubbed look; a few wet spots even remained on the floorboards. The battered collection of pots and pans sat on the hearth, gleaming in the firelight as a pot of beans bubbled invitingly over the fire. It must have taken hours to remove the accumulation of soot that had covered them.

The sound of splashing water outside caught his attention. He stepped back through the door just as Becky upended a bucket of water into a barrel that sat at the corner of the house.

"Oh," she said, looking up. "You startled me."

"What are you doing?"

Becky's welcoming smile faltered. "I-I was just filling the water barrel."

"Not anymore, you aren't," he said gruffly as he took the bucket from her hand and walked toward the creek.

Becky watched him leave with confusion. She knew that curt sound in a man's voice. It meant he was angry for some reason, and he didn't even know she'd spent all the money he'd given her yet. Wondering what else she could have done wrong, she went inside and immediately realized the pans were still stacked on the hearth. She'd left them there after she scrubbed out the storage box, waiting for it to dry. It was just the sort of untidiness her father had always berated her for.

With a sinking feeling in her middle, Becky hurried over to the fireplace and started stuffing the pans into the box. That's what came of trying so hard to make things nice for him. She'd done the best she could, and it wasn't good enough. What had made her think it would be?

By the time Garrick finished filling the water barrel, Becky had mixed up a batch of corn bread and was putting it among the coals to bake. Forcing herself not to look up, she pulled the hot embers up around the dutch oven. "Supper will be ready pretty soon."

"Good." Garrick could tell she was unhappy, and he was pretty sure he knew why. He just didn't know how to say he was sorry for putting her through all this. His tongue felt as though it was stuck to the roof of his mouth.

As the silence stretched out unbearably, Becky stood up and nervously wiped the spotless mantle with a rag. "I'm sorry I didn't have everything finished when you got here," she finally blurted out.

"What?"

"The house was a mess, supper wasn't ready." Her voice quavered. "I didn't even have the water barrel filled."

Her words hit Garrick like jagged pieces of metal. In two steps, he was at her side. Feeling like a complete fool, he laid his hand on her shoulder. "Becky— "

"I wa-anted to have it all finished wh-en...you got here. I spent all your money and supper isn't ev-even done."

"Don't cry." Her sobs tore at Garrick's heart as he pulled her into his arms. Not sure what to do, he patted her back clumsily. "I never expected you to do all this," he said at last. "You shouldn't even be here."

That got her attention. "W-why not?" she asked, pulling away from his shoulder with a sniff.

"The place is falling apart. You can see daylight through the walls in a dozen places, the window's broken, there's no furniture, and the roof probably leaks." He glanced around ruefully. "In fact, there isn't much right with it."

"Oh, but you're wrong," Becky said, wiping her eyes. "Look at the floor."

Garrick glanced at his feet and then back to her face. "What about it?"

"It's wood, not dirt, and only a few of the boards are warped. The walls are solid, so we can replace the chinking and mend the roof." Then Becky grabbed his hand and pulled him over to the window. "Listen."

Obediently, Garrick strained his ears. "I don't hear anything."

"That's right. Other than an occasional boom from one of the mines, I didn't hear much all day. If I didn't know South Pass City was less than half a mile away, I'd think this was an isolated mountain cabin."

"And that pleases you?"

"Very much." She smiled. "When high water is over, the creek in back will even be fairly clean because we're upstream from town. There isn't much mining going on above us either, so if we let the water set for a while in the water barrel, it should be safe to drink."

"I'll admit I'm impressed," Garrick said, looking around. "You've got it looking much better than I would have ever imagined possible in such a short time."

"Then you're not mad anymore?" Becky's voice was barely more than a whisper.

Garrick gave her a startled look. "I never was."

"You sounded like it when you had to finish filling the water barrel."

"I wasn't happy to find you doing it, but I wasn't mad at you."

"Why didn't you want the barrel filled?"

"It has nothing to do with the water barrel. You shouldn't be lifting heavy buckets, or chopping wood, or doing anything that could hurt your baby."

"Oh."

"Promise me you'll leave things like that for me to do."

"A-all right," Becky said. Nobody had ever worried about her like that before. It seemed like almost everything this man did was a new experience for her. As she watched him dig through the pile of his belongings he'd dropped off the day before, she wondered if she'd ever learn to understand him.

"Here," he said, pulling out a canvas bag and handing it to her. "I'll be right back."

When Becky opened the bag, she discovered two tin plates and the flatware to go with them. There was only a single cup, but at least they wouldn't have to eat out of the pans with their fingers.

By the time the cornbread was done baking, Garrick had returned with two pieces of a thick log. Both were more or less flat on either end and stood about two feet high. Becky was puzzled until he upended them next to the table and covered each with one of his shirts.

"They won't be the most comfortable stools around, but they'll work until I can build some chairs."

"You can do that?" Becky looked surprised as she set the table.

Garrick shrugged. "My father made all our furniture."

"Was he a craftsman?"

"No, a farmer, but working with wood was something he always loved."

"Were you close to him?"

Garrick smiled softly as he looked into the distant past. "*Ja*, we were very close."

"When did he die?"

"Last I heard, he was still alive." Abruptly, he turned away and walked to the fireplace. "Are the beans done?"

"I-I think so."

"Good. Let's eat."

The first meal they shared in their new home was far from exciting, but the food was plentiful and filling. Beyond cutting her apology short and telling her he didn't mind that she had spent all the money he'd given her, Garrick had very little to say. He was more inclined to eat than talk, and Becky was beginning to find his long silences less unnerving. In fact, she was more disturbed by sharing the single cup with him. There was something oddly disquieting about drinking from it moments after his lips had touched the rim.

After supper, Becky washed the dishes while Garrick dug out his lantern and a large square of canvas he'd used as flooring in his tent. After cutting it in half, he covered the window with part of it and rigged a curtain across one corner of the room with the other.

Becky watched silently as he made up her bed on the bunk then spread his own bedroll in front of the fireplace. She was glad he was being so considerate but couldn't help wondering how long it would be before he wanted to share a bed the way they shared the cup.

As the days went by, life settled into a routine. Every morning, Garrick left for work right after breakfast and returned at the end of his shift twelve hours later. He spent the evenings building furniture while Becky sewed, and a quiet camaraderie began to develop between them. Though their marriage of convenience wasn't without its bumps, they were, for the most part, satisfied.

When Garrick taught her how to drive the buckboard, Becky was delighted. She'd grown up accepting boredom and loneliness as a way of life; now she reveled in the freedom the buckboard gave her. During her daily excursions, Becky talked to Sophie as she would a friend. The horse always swiveled her ears toward the sound as though she were listening intently.

More and more frequently, Becky found herself telling Sophie about the confusing feelings Garrick aroused in her. The memory of the solid comfort of his body the time he'd held her in his arms and his many kindnesses lay soft and warm in her mind. It wasn't love, for the hot thrills Cameron's touch had evoked weren't there. Still, the thought of sleeping with her new husband wasn't the least bit repulsive. Perhaps her father had been right about her, after all.

Chapter 6

"Supper's on, Garrick."

"Be right there." Garrick sank his ax into the chopping block and picked up an armload of split wood to take into the cabin. Maybe he'd get lucky and they'd have something different to eat tonight.

In the month and a half that he and Becky had been married, the meals had never varied. Supper was always cornbread and beans and breakfast was cornmeal mush. She'd faithfully sent cold beans and corn bread every day for lunch until he told her he really didn't have time for a mid-day meal.

Garrick ducked through the door and dumped the wood into the wood box. As he glanced toward Becky, who was cheerfully setting supper on the table, his heart sank. Beans.

With an inward sigh, he rolled up his sleeves and poured hot water into the washbowl. In spite of her unimaginative cooking, he was well satisfied with his young wife. She kept the cabin spotless and never complained about anything. He didn't even mind her cheerful chatter, which seemed inexhaustible. If he occasionally wished for a little peace and quiet, he reminded himself how lonely he'd been before she came into his life.

"How was your day?" she asked over her shoulder.

"Fine."

"I finished sewing your new shirt this afternoon."

"Thanks."

Becky resisted the urge to slam the pan of cornbread down on the table. If she told him she'd spent the afternoon running naked through the streets of South Pass City he'd probably just arch one of those darn eyebrows of his and say, "Oh?"

A sudden knock on the door startled them both. Their gazes met in a look of mutual surprise. There had never been a visitor in all the time they had lived there. "Who do you suppose that is?" Becky asked, heading for the door.

When she opened it, she was confronted by a complete stranger. He was tall and broad, with dark hair and bright green eyes that widened when he saw her. "Good evening, ma'am," he said, whisking his hat from his head. "I was told I might find Swede here."

"Ox!" Garrick greeted their visitor with obvious pleasure as he dried his neck with a towel. "What brings you out here?"

"I need to talk business with you."

"We were about to sit down to supper," Becky said. "Would you like to join us?"

Ox's face split into a delighted grin. "I sure would, ma'am. I never turn down a home-cooked meal."

"Hope you like beans," Garrick couldn't resist saying as his friend came inside. "This is my wife, Becky. Becky, Ox Bruford."

"How do you do?"

"It's a real pleasure, ma'am, a real pleasure."

Becky blushed slightly and moved away to set another place at the table. Thank goodness Garrick had thought to buy more dishes.

"Holy hell, Swede," Ox said in an undertone. "Where did you find her? She's plumb beautiful."

"It's a long story."

"And you never were one for talking a man's leg off," Ox said with a grin. "Danged if that ain't one I'd like to hear, though." He let out a soundless whistle, as Becky turned sideways to set the table. Her pregnancy was obvious. "Son of a gun, Swede. You don't waste any time, do you?"

Garrick shrugged. "Some things come naturally."

Becky gave a sigh of relief at the sound of Ox's delighted laughter. Apparently, she'd done the right thing inviting the man to dinner. She hadn't been sure.

Ox Bruford turned out to be as garrulous as Garrick was quiet. He spent the entire meal telling stories of his travels, and Becky listened with real interest. When supper was over, she regretfully cleared the table so the two men could talk.

"You hear about the Indian trouble out at Fort Stambaugh?"

Garrick nodded. "I heard there'd been a few skirmishes. Why?"

"The colonel ordered an escort for all wagons for the next few months, at least until the Sioux go to their winter hunting grounds. That means we won't be able to come in as often. I need to know how much black powder you're going to need to hold you over just in case."

"Did you talk to Tom Ryan?"

"Yup, and he said to ask you and Klynton since you'd be using it."

"How long do you figure it might be between deliveries?"

"Hopefully not more than a few weeks, but you'd better be prepared for a month."

Garrick rubbed his chin thoughtfully as he pondered the question. "Better get me a dozen kegs, then. I don't want to run short. You'll have to ask Klynton about the nitro."

"He's going to have to make special arrangements for that with somebody else. I wouldn't touch it for half the gold in the Carissa. Well, guess I'd best get on back to town." He stood and flashed Becky a grin. "Thanks for supper, ma'am. Those were damn...uh...I mean dang good beans."

"Thank you, Mr. Bruford. I hope you'll come again." Her words were for Ox, but her gaze never left Garrick.

"Take care of yourself," Garrick said, walking their guest to the door, "and I'll see you in a few weeks."

"Yup, thanks again for supper. Good night."

Garrick knew Becky was unhappy about something, but he didn't have a clue what. No doubt she'd tell him soon enough.

He didn't even glance at her as he went to the corner and picked up the seat of the rocking chair he was working on. He didn't have to; he was aware of her with every fiber of his being, just as he always was. God help him, but she seemed to grow more beautiful with each passing day.

Nights were the best...and the worst. Becky always waited until the lantern was out and she thought he was asleep before she prepared for bed. The first time she'd stepped out from behind the canvas curtain dressed in a voluminous nightgown, with her hair in a long thick braid, Garrick thought his heart would stop. Unaware of how transparent the firelight made the cotton, she'd moved freely through the cabin, doing little womanly things before she went to bed.

It had become a ritual that Garrick looked forward to every night. Sometimes, she would sit and brush her hair until it crackled; other times she'd only wash her face and hands, but it was always intensely satisfying to watch her from his darkened corner. Even her impending motherhood didn't make her less desirable. In fact, the softly rounding contours stirred unfamiliar feelings within him that were more difficult to deal with than lust.

Now, Garrick waited patiently for the storm to break over his head. It was the way his father had always dealt with his mother's volatile Irish temper, working quietly at some task until she finally blew up and told him what was bothering her. He'd sit contritely listening to her tirade then smooth her ruffled feathers with good calm Norwegian logic. Though Garrick's mother often complained that her husband didn't fight fair, it seemed the best way to deal with an angry woman.

Garrick could tell Becky's anger was simmering just below the surface as she slammed the dishes in and out of the dishwater. It wouldn't be long now. He braced himself.

But nothing happened. Finally, he chanced a glance in her direction and was appalled to see tears sparkling in her eyes. "What's wrong?"

"What's wrong?" she repeated, glaring at him. "Nothing's wrong. I just found out my husband has the most dangerous job in the world, and he never told me. Why should I be upset?"

"What are you talking about?"

"You're a powder man, aren't you?"

"Yes, but I use black powder, not nitroglycerine like Ace Klynton does. The way I do it, my job isn't any more dangerous than any other."

"Oh, no. You just blow things up. If you use too much powder, or too short a fuse, or somebody sneezes at the wrong time, you're either blown to smithereens or buried under several tons of rock. There's nothing dangerous about that."

Garrick was incredulous. "You're mad because I'm a powder man?"

"No, I'm mad because you never told me. But then I guess that shouldn't come as a surprise. You never tell me anything. We've lived together for six weeks, and we're still total strangers."

"We are not."

"Oh no? I don't know one thing about you that I didn't find out the first day."

Garrick felt a spark of anger. "That's not true."

"It is too. I couldn't even get you to tell me if you wanted me to make you a new shirt."

"I bought that material for you and the baby."

"But did you tell me that? No. You just brought it in and dropped it on the table. I was supposed to figure out what you wanted on my own."

"What did you want me to do," he asked, rising to his feet and glaring back at her, "give you detailed instructions?"

"I want you to talk to me once in a while."

"I talk to you."

"Yes, one word at a time. Don't you understand, Garrick? You never tell me anything. I don't even know if you like me."

That hurt. He'd shown her how much he liked her in a dozen different ways. Didn't she realize all the things he did around the cabin were for her? He felt the irrational desire to hurt her back. "How can I tell you anything when you never shut up long enough to listen?" he asked.

"Maybe I would if you'd tell me what's going on inside your head."

"You don't want to know what I'm thinking."

"Try me."

"All right," he said, crossing the room to her. "Sometimes I think I'll go crazy if I don't have some peace and quiet. I detest cornmeal mush, and I'm so sick of beans and corn bread that I could throw up."

As he advanced, Becky backed away until she stood cringing against the wall. The stark terror in her eyes infuriated him even more. He braced his hands on either side of her head and leaned over her. "And most of all," he said in a dangerously soft voice, "I hate the way you act when I get close to you."

As he moved to grab his hat off the mantle, she instinctively covered her face and ducked away with a whimper of fear.

"You don't need to worry, Madam Wife," he said with dry emphasis. "I won't touch you." He took a dozen steps and went out, slamming the door behind him.

With a sob, Becky slid to the floor. Why, oh, why hadn't she just left well enough alone? Suddenly, she realized how she must look to him, tall and gangly, her body distorted and swollen with another man's child. No wonder he hadn't ever wanted to share her bed. He couldn't even stand the thought of touching her.

Worst of all was the knowledge that she'd been making a complete fool of herself, and he knew it. Shame flooded her as she thought of the many times she'd unobtrusively leaned closer to him to catch the scent of wood, leather, and an indefinable something that was uniquely Garrick. When she'd touched his hand or brushed against him just to feel his solid warmth, he'd been aware of what she was doing and had been repulsed by it.

Tears came, and sobs of anguish racked her body. After everything he'd done for her, saving her life, giving her a real home, chinking the walls, mending the roof, building chairs, chopping wood, she couldn't even cook him a decent meal. She was a dismal failure as a wife. Right now, he was probably on his way to the saloon just as her father used to do when she'd made him mad, and the thought scared her half to death.

"Swede, long time no see!" Angel's obvious pleasure at the sight of him went a long way toward soothing Garrick's hurt feelings. "The little wife finally let you out of the house?"

"You could say that."

"Well, I'm glad to see you at my place again. Can I buy you a drink?"

"No, thanks. I work tomorrow."

"So, marriage hasn't changed you after all."

"It hasn't made me stupid, if that's what you mean." Garrick gave her a sardonic smile. "That happened last time I was in here and decided to get drunk."

"Ah. So, the newlyweds had a little lovers' spat, did they?" When Garrick's only reply was a glower, Angel laughed. "What you need is a good game of cards and a little appreciative female companionship."

"That's why I'm here."

"There's an empty chair right over there at Molly's table. Just go easy on the house, will you?"

"I will as soon as you go easy on your customers."

It was an old joke between them, and Angel wrinkled her nose at him before she wandered off to circulate among her other clientele.

As usual, the cards took his full concentration. Garrick loved to manipulate them, to figure the odds, and to read the other player's expressions. He was unbeatable at Blackjack, but tonight he settled for five-card stud. He played steadily for several hours, winning more than he lost, but never really relaxing and enjoying himself.

Images of Becky kept tumbling through his mind. In retrospect, it seemed as if she had invited Ox Bruford, a total stranger, to stay for supper very quickly, then she'd hung on his every word. But her own husband, who had never been anything but kind to her, she cowered away from in fear.

"Hello, Swede," said a sultry feminine voice as long fingers ran through the hair on the nape of his neck.

Garrick looked up into Collette's smoky gray eyes. Here was a woman who wasn't afraid of him. In fact, she found him appealing. He could see it on her face as she sat down on his lap and undid the top button on his shirt.

"What do you say, Swede, shall we slip upstairs and let them play this hand without you?"

"I can't leave," he said with a smile as he put an arm loosely around her waist. "I'm winning."

"Then I'll be your prize, and you can collect me," she murmured as she put her arms around his neck and kissed him deeply.

With her stomach tied in knots, Becky lay in bed waiting for Garrick to come home. Hours passed, and she finally fell into a fitful sleep. She jerked awake at the sound of the door opening. Praying that feigned sleep would be enough to protect her, she closed her eyes and waited.

She heard him walk up to her bed and stop. It was impossible not to flinch when his fingers unexpectedly touched her cheek, but she covered her reaction by shifting slightly as though moving in her sleep. After several long minutes, he gave a deep sigh and moved away to get his bedroll.

In horrified agony, Becky turned her face to the wall, and shoved her fist up against her mouth to stifle any sound that might escape. Though she had been dreading the familiar heavy odor of whiskey, and the beatings that frequently came with it, she discovered the smell of another woman's perfume was much, much more painful.

Chapter 7

"Sorry, ma'am, The Green Garter ain't open till later."

"Good, because I'm here to see Miss Angel," Becky said.

"We don't need any more girls right now," the bartender said, staring pointedly at her stomach.

Becky gripped her bag a little tighter. "That's not what I've come to see her about. Could you please tell her Rebecca Swenson is here? She'll remember me."

Sam looked her up and down, then shrugged and disappeared into the back of the casino.

Feeling very much out of place, Becky waited nervously for Angel to appear. When the door at the back finally opened, what she heard didn't sound promising.

"And I tell you I don't know a Rebecca anything. Probably just somebody looking for a handout." With a swish of taffeta, Angel came through the door. When she saw who her visitor was, the expression on her face was anything but welcoming. Her gaze dropped to Becky's stomach. "So that's why he married you, the damned noble fool. And I'll bet it isn't even his."

Becky straightened angrily. "My baby is none of your business."

"That's right, honey, and the problems between you and your husband aren't either. So, if you've come to tell me I should have thrown him out last night, you can just turn your tail around and march right out of here."

"He came here?" It was out before Becky could stop it and sounded pathetic even to her own ears.

Angel's eyes narrowed suspiciously. "Just what the hell do you want?"

"I-I need your help."

"Huh, and if I was stupid enough to help you out today, you'd be looking down your nose at me just like all the other self-righteous biddies tomorrow."

"I'm hardly in the position to look down my nose at anybody. I came here because I thought you were my friend."

Angel snorted. "What gave you that idea?"

"You gave me a place to stay and were a witness to our wedding."

"I did that for Swede, not you."

"This is for him, too." Becky looked her squarely in the eye. "What can it hurt to listen?"

Angel hesitated for a moment. "All right, I'll listen, but that's all I'm promising. Now, what is it you want?"

"I want to learn how to cook."

There was a moment of stunned silence, then Sam and Angel both broke into laughter. "Honey, I think you're confused. This is a whorehouse, not a restaurant."

Becky blushed. "I know that, but there are five...girls, and you two. That makes seven people who have to eat. Somebody around here must know how to cook."

"Even if we do have a cook, why should I take her away from her duties to teach you?"

"Oh, I'm not asking you to do it for nothing. I may not know how to cook, but I can sew." She reached into her bag, pulled out the shirt she had made for Garrick, and handed it to Angel. "If you'll let your cook teach me, I'll do all your mending."

Angel examined the shirt. It was well made, the tiny stitches on the cuffs and collar nearly invisible. A closer look at Becky's dress showed that it had been mended many times, yet, unless one really looked, it was impossible to tell. Torn clothing was one of the hazards of Angel's business. A good seamstress could save her a fortune, especially one who didn't cost her anything.

"All right. It's a deal, but you'll have to take your lessons when it's convenient for us. If something comes up, and I need you out of here, you're gone. Is that understood?"

Becky nodded.

"Does Swede know about this?" Angel asked.

"No, and I'd appreciate it if you wouldn't tell him."

Angel shrugged. "As I said before, the problems between you and your husband are none of my affair. You can start tomorrow."

"D-do you think your cook could maybe take a few minutes to show me something I can fix for supper tonight?" Becky asked.

Angel raised an eyebrow. "Are you that desperate?"

"If I try to feed my husband beans and cornbread one more time, he'll probably throw me out."

"Or come back here and break my bank," Angel said. "All right, I suppose I can take time to show you how to make biscuits."

"You?"

"As a matter of fact, I'm a damn good cook."

Becky smiled. "I knew this was the right place to come."

Angel made a disgusted sound as she turned and led the way to the kitchen. "Just be sure you use the back door from now on. I don't want my place to get a bad name."

An hour later, Becky emerged happy and relieved. Not only did she have a bag full of biscuits, she was pretty sure she'd made a new friend. Though Angel was surly on the outside, she was a patient teacher and had a good sense of humor. Best of all, her perfume was distinctly different from what Becky had smelled on Garrick the night before.

Garrick took his time getting home. He knew he was being a coward, but he'd made a terrible mess of things. So much for using his father's technique on Becky. It might have worked if he hadn't inherited his mother's temper. Over the years, he'd become so adept at holding it in check that he tended to forget how explosive it was and how often it had gotten him into serious trouble.

It wasn't until Collette had tried to seduce him last night that it suddenly hit him how badly he'd blundered. No wonder Becky had shrunk away from him; anybody would have. He was three times her size and raging at her like a lunatic. She probably had a point, too. He did have a habit of keeping his thoughts to himself instead of speaking them aloud.

The minute he realized what he'd done, he sent Collette on her way, gathered up his winnings and headed for home. Becky was asleep when he got there, but he'd been unable to resist touching her. No matter how badly he'd hurt her, he'd been paid back in full when she jerked away. Even in her sleep she was afraid of him.

Awake before dawn, he'd snuck out of the house rather than face her rejection again. It wasn't until later that it occurred to him she probably thought he'd never come home at all.

Becky visibly sagged with relief when he came through the door. He'd never been this late before, which probably convinced her all the more that he wasn't coming back. "Supper will be ready in a few minutes if you want to wash up."

"I'm sorry I'm late."

She just shrugged as though it didn't matter before getting the plates and silverware out of the storage box.

"I stopped at the mercantile on the way home." He set a package down on her bed.

"Oh?"

"I bought some cloth for you to make yourself some new dresses and clothes for the baby."

She looked up in surprise. "You didn't have to do that."

"I figured you'd be needing them soon, and you used up most of the rest."

"Thank you." Becky finished setting the table before opening her package. Tears stung her eyes, for he'd bought not one but three different fabrics.

Silence filled the cabin as he rolled up his sleeves and poured water into the washbowl. Without Becky's cheerful chatter, the quiet seemed oppressive rather than peaceful. Garrick searched his mind frantically for something to say as he sat down. Guilt lay heavy on his soul but not nearly as much as when he realized how nervous she was. Garrick closed his eyes and swallowed hard. She seemed afraid to put supper on the table.

"I hope you like venison," she said shyly. "It's all they had at the butcher shop."

Garrick's eyes popped open. He looked first at the meat and golden-brown biscuits on the table and then up at Becky's hopeful face.

"I love venison," he lied.

She smiled tremulously. "Good."

The meat was burnt on one side, the biscuits stone cold, but Garrick ate as though it were the best meal he'd ever had. "That was delicious."

"No, it wasn't. But it's a start. Food is so expensive in mining camps; we never had money enough for anything but beans and corn meal. I just got so used to them I never thought about cooking anything else. I'm sorry."

"No, Becky, I'm the one that's sorry. You were right about me, you know. I don't talk much."

"And I talk too much." She looked down at her hands. "My father used to tell me to shut up all the time. I should have realized you were just too nice to say anything."

"That isn't true. I didn't mean those things I said. I have a terrible temper."

"No, you don't. You're the most even-tempered person I ever met in my life. The fight was my fault; I started it. Papa always said I was mean-spirited. He frequently told me I was the worst person in the world to live with."

Garrick wondered what kind of man would say such a thing to his own daughter. "Tell me about your father," he said.

Becky shrugged. "There's not much to tell. He drank too much and worked too little."

"How did he die?"

"He fell down a winze and drowned."

"A winze?"

"It's a shaft drilled in the floor of the mine to collect ground water and keep the tunnels from flooding."

"I know what a winze is. How did he manage to fall into one?"

"He was drunk, as usual. I thought that's what you were going to do last night but you didn't, did you?"

"I don't drink when I work the next day."

"I'm glad." At least going to another woman wouldn't leave him dangerously unable to do his job. Becky rose to her feet and started to clear the table.

Garrick watched her, thoughtfully. "You're not, you know."

She looked over her shoulder curiously. "Not what?"

"Hard to live with, and you're not mean-spirited."

"Maybe you just bring out the best in me."

They both smiled, each pleased at the reconciliation, but achingly aware something sweet and wonderful had been lost.

Over the next few weeks, Becky's cooking skills gradually improved, though there were times when Garrick wondered why he'd ever been so stupid as to complain about the beans. The day she forgot the baking powder and her biscuits came out so hard he couldn't even bite into them, he thought he was in real trouble.

Close to tears, Becky watched him struggle with one for several minutes, then suddenly remembered Angel's advice: *Everybody makes mistakes. The trick is to figure out a way to make it work anyway. When that isn't possible, make a joke.*

Becky leaned her elbows on the table and put her chin on her hands. "Would you care for a pick with your biscuit?" she asked casually.

Garrick looked startled for a moment, and then he grinned. "No thanks, I'll just use my hammer."

After that, her culinary errors became a joke, and Becky discovered her husband loved to tease. It took some getting used to, for there had been very little humor in her life, but she found she rather liked it. Usually, her threat to dig out the beans and corn meal would bring profuse apologies and exaggerated pleas for forgiveness.

Garrick tried to talk more and Becky less. If they weren't always successful, at least each knew the other was attempting to change.

Becky spent two hours every morning at The Green Garter mending piles of scandalous clothing. The cooking lessons would start as soon as Angel came down and usually lasted until early afternoon. The two women soon became fast friends, though Angel still tended to be cynical about it.

As life settled into a pleasant routine for Becky, she suddenly realized she wasn't spending hours thinking about Cameron anymore. A different face, one that would be described as strong rather than handsome, invaded her thoughts regularly. Garrick's rather plain features weren't dazzling like Cameron's, but more and more often his honey-butter voice made her insides flutter, and his smile filled her with pleasure.

It was Garrick who occupied her mind today as she searched for wild onions. Mindful of the Indian threat, she stuck to the top of the hill where she could see everything for miles. It would be virtually impossible for anyone to sneak up on her. Even though her advancing pregnancy made her clumsy and slow, she was close enough to the Carissa Mine that she could get there if she saw any sign of Indians.

Figuring the Carissa at her back was protection enough, Becky scanned the other three directions repeatedly as she wandered the crest of the hill. Though she never forgot the danger, her thoughts were elsewhere.

She was haunted by enticing images of water droplets sparkling on muscular forearms as Garrick washed for supper, and strong hands caressing the sleek wood of a chair rocker as he smoothed and shaped it. It was bad enough that her stomach had a habit of lurching in the oddest way as she watched Garrick do the most commonplace tasks. Last night, she'd nearly dropped the plate she was washing when he stepped out from behind the canvas curtain wearing only his britches and suspenders.

Fresh from the bath, with his wet hair curling against his neck and the lantern light playing across the broad muscles of his chest and arms, he'd been breathtaking, a golden giant. Watching him shave had been one of the most erotic experiences of her life. Though she felt like a voyeur, she hadn't been able to tear her eyes away. Even now, she was feeling uncomfortably warm just thinking about it.

Suddenly, the lilting song of a meadowlark sounded nearby. Remembering what Angel had said, Becky glanced over her shoulder—and gasped in dismay. Behind her, huge black clouds roiled upwards from the horizon. The turbulence of the thunderheads was frightening, but not nearly as much as the dark curtain at the bottom of the storm that was moving toward her at a terrifying pace. The constantly blowing wind was so common here; Becky hadn't noticed it had risen, and now it was whipping at her skirts.

The Carissa was the closest shelter, and she started toward it, fighting desperately against rapidly increasing wind. She had only gone a few feet when a flash of white light exploded against the metal roof of The Carissa. With the horrible crash of thunder rolling around her in deafening waves, Becky turned and ran.

She headed for the brow of the hill, lightning popping all around her. Town looked impossibly far away, and she knew she'd never reach it in time. Her breath was coming in gasping sobs, but she kept moving. The wind howled around her, filling her eyes with dirt and trying to tear her clothes from her back.

The rain began to fall, huge ice-cold drops that immediately turned the trail under her feet to mud. At the bottom of the hill, she tripped and fell. Cursing her awkward body, she clambered to her feet, only to fall again several feet farther on.

Suddenly, Garrick was there, coming out of the storm to lift her off her feet and into the safety of his arms just as the hail hit.

Chapter 8

"Keep your head down," Garrick yelled above the storm.

Becky didn't have to be told twice as the hard pellets of ice began to bombard them. She buried her face against his shoulder and wrapped her arms around his neck.

He headed for the only cover around, a large boulder several yards away at the bottom of a dry creek bed. By the time they reached its feeble protection, the hail had increased to marble-sized stones and was falling in sheets. Garrick put Becky next to the rock, then wrapped himself around her, shielding her body with his.

Even crushed beneath his bulk, she knew the punishment he was taking and tried desperately to think of a way to protect him. She wasn't even aware of the sobs that wracked her body as the hail pounded the man above her.

A lifetime of agony passed, then gradually the hail turned back to rain, torrents of it. Suddenly, Becky realized it presented a new danger and began to struggle. "We've got to move, Garrick."

"What?" With his senses dulled by the beating he had just taken and the cold that filled him with lethargy, he didn't understand her concern.

"We're too low. It's going to flood." Already the water was flowing through the bottom of the gulch they were in. She tugged at him. "Get up."

"Flood?"

"Yes. For God's sake, move."

He rose stiffly to his feet and reached out to help her up. Becky grabbed his hand and started to clamber up the side of the small gully, pulling him along. He caught her urgency at last. Climbing up the embankment, he grabbed her around the waist and set her on her feet at the top.

"Up the hill, Garrick," she urged. "We'll be safe there."

They struggled about halfway up the hillside and then turned to watch as the once dry creek bed below them rapidly filled with water.

"Look at that!" Garrick said as the boulder disappeared from sight. "If we hadn't moved when we did..."

"That's why they call them flash floods. They're especially dangerous in the mountains. We lost our tent in one after a storm like this once. Come on, let's get back to town before we freeze to death."

By the time they reached the first buildings, the street had turned into a sea of mud, and they were both near the end of their endurance. In spite of his size and strength, Garrick was in worse shape. He had his arm around Becky to help her along, but the farther they went the more she supported him. Becky knew they'd never make it all the way home.

The rain was still pouring down when they staggered through the front door of The Green Garter. It was afternoon, but the downstairs was already doing a brisk business. Becky felt helpless as a dozen pairs of curious eyes turned her way.

"Damn, it's Swede," said a masculine voice from among the onlookers. Suddenly, they were surrounded by concerned miners. Nervously, Becky stepped closer to Garrick. As she felt the violent, uncontrolled shivering of his body, she knew he was in trouble. Where was Angel?

Just as Becky was beginning to panic, Angel came through the crowd. Her expression changed from mild curiosity to alarm when she saw who was dripping all over her floor. "My husband needs help," Becky said, mindful of Angel's edict that she never show any recognition of their relationship in public. "We got caught in the hail storm."

"Can't let Swede get sick," said a heavily bearded man, stepping forward to support Garrick on the opposite side. "He's the best powder man around. Nobody else in this town I want to trust my life to." There was a murmur of agreement from the crowd.

"I have an empty room upstairs I suppose he could have," Angel said, as though she begrudged its use.

Becky had been around the other woman enough to realize Angel's brusque manner covered a very real concern for the man she called Swede. Not for the first time, she wondered if Angel's feelings for Garrick were warmer than friendship.

Within a few minutes, Becky found herself and her husband in the bedroom she had inhabited before. Its rather plain decor still surprised her. Somehow, she'd expected the rooms in a brothel to be more decadent.

"This will help, but it won't be enough," Angel said as she finished kindling a fire in the pot-bellied stove. "I'll go get water for a hot bath."

"You have bath water ready?"

A brief smile crossed Angel's face. "You forget where you are. Some of my customers prefer a bath to a bed. We have to be prepared for anything." She chuckled as Becky's face turned a bright red. "What an innocent you are."

"Leave her alone, Angel," Garrick said from where he lay face down on the bed, his voice shaking with cold. "Becky's only been in a place like this once. She doesn't have the slightest idea what goes on here."

Becky thought of the skimpy costumes she mended every day and the stories she sometimes overheard the girls tell each other. Her eyes met Angel's.

The older woman just grinned and winked. "You both better get out of those wet clothes. I'll be back directly."

Becky turned her attention to her husband. His skin had turned a mottled blue, and his teeth were chattering uncontrollably. "She's right, Garrick. You've got to get those wet clothes off. Can you sit up?"

With a groan, he rolled onto his side and swung his legs over the edge of the bed. "Can't seem to think straight," he mumbled.

"It's the cold. Here, let me help you." She pushed aside the big hands that fumbled with his buttons. Though her own fingers weren't much warmer, she had better luck, and it wasn't long before his shirt hung open clear to his waist. Becky chattered nervously as she pulled out his shirttail and unfastened his suspenders. Though she knew she was babbling, the intimate contact was too unnerving to endure in silence.

"The wild onions were for stew, but I guess—Oh, Garrick!" Her monologue came to an abrupt halt as she peeled off the wet shirt, exposing his back for the first time. There wasn't a square inch that wasn't covered with welts and bruises. Tears gathered in her eyes as she gazed at him in horror. The pain must be excruciating.

Just then, Angel stepped back into the room and came to a halt. "Are you ready— Good Lord, Swede, your back's a mess."

"It must be. My wife is speechless." A slight smile took the sting from his words. "Don't worry, Becky, it only hurts when I breathe."

Only Angel saw the sheen of tears in Becky's eyes and knew how badly the sight of her husband's mangled back was affecting her. Garrick's attempt to joke about it was clearly falling on deaf ears.

"Can't say I blame her. It isn't real pretty. First things first," Angel said briskly as she lay a comforting hand on Becky's shoulder. "I'll give you some laudanum, then we'll get you warmed up."

After Angel gave Garrick the promised painkiller, she and Becky pulled a huge hipbath from behind the screen. Angel poured the first two buckets in just as a knock at the door heralded the arrival of two more. "Best get him out of those pants," she said to Becky as she opened the door and traded buckets with Sam.

Becky felt her face go fiery red. There was no way Garrick's cold-stiffened fingers could manage the buttons on his pants. Their eyes met, hers mortified, his full of entreaty. In that second, Becky realized Garrick didn't want Angel to know theirs was not a marriage in the full sense of the word. Swallowing hard, she stepped forward and reached for the top button, her eyes locked on the non-threatening plane of his stomach.

"If you'll get the buttons, I can manage the rest," he whispered in her ear. She nodded almost imperceptibly.

As her fingers slid the first button through the fabric, Becky tried not to notice the thin line of hair that slid enticingly down his belly. Embarrassment coupled with her cold, clumsy hands made the chore nearly impossible, but at last it was finished. As she turned away in relief, she was aware of an odd feeling of breathlessness and the rapid beating of her heart.

"Here, put this on," Angel said, thrusting a nightgown into her hands. "You're not in much better shape than Swede is. I've sent for Dr. Caldwell to take a look at both of you."

"Both of us? But I'm fine," Becky protested.

"Maybe," Angel said, giving Becky's stomach a meaningful glance, "but there's no sense in taking any chances, is there?"

"No, I guess not." In spite of her objections, Becky was grateful to step behind the screen and peel off her wet dress. Though the rain had washed most of the mud away, the garment was torn and bedraggled. The nightgown felt deliciously warm and dry against her chilled skin. She was pleasantly surprised to find it as modest as something she herself might own.

By the time the doctor arrived, Angel had left to go back to work and the laudanum was beginning to take effect on Garrick. He was pleasantly drowsy through most of the examination, and sound asleep by the time it was over. Dr. Caldwell gave Becky some salve for Garrick's back and a small bottle of laudanum for pain.

Then he turned his attention to her. It was the first time she'd ever been examined, but the gentle doctor soon put her at ease. "This young fella's none the worse for wear," he said as the baby moved beneath his hand.

71

"Everything seems to be fine, but if you have any cramping or back pain, let me know."

"Can you tell when it will be born?" Becky asked shyly, hoping the question wouldn't show her ignorance but unable to resist asking.

"Oh, I'd say we've got a month or so yet," he said as he packed up his medical bag. "Is that about what you had figured?"

"About."

"When the time comes, just send your husband for me. I've brought many a wee one into the world. Meanwhile, Swede should be fine in a couple of days. Just make sure you put salve on those bruises twice a day."

"I will, and thank you, Dr. Caldwell."

"Don't mention it."

Becky sat thinking after the doctor left. A month. It seemed awfully soon. Would she know what to do when the time came? This was when she missed having a mother the most. There was no one she could ask. Maybe if there had been, she would have known what caused babies before Cameron led her down the path to destruction.

"Doc says it might be best if you two stay here tonight," Angel said as she came back into the room with two more steaming buckets of water.

"Oh, no. We'll be in the way."

"Actually, I won't need this room till morning, and Doc thinks there's still a small chance you could lose your baby."

"But he said—"

"Now, don't get excited. He figures everything's all right, he just thinks you ought to be where someone can keep an eye on you." She dumped the water into the tub and glanced at Garrick who was dead to the world. "Besides, I don't think you'll be moving him anytime soon."

"Oh, Angel, you're always so good to us."

"Huh, nothing good about it. I don't want to lose my seamstress."

Becky just smiled and went to put more wood in the stove.

Chapter 9

Garrick hurt. His back felt as though every square inch was covered with cuts and bruises, which probably wasn't far from the truth. Resisting the urge to groan, he opened his eyes, and then blinked in surprise. He'd died and gone to heaven. Less than five feet away sat Becky, dressed only in a cotton nightgown, leisurely brushing her damp, waist-length hair.

He swallowed hard. Watching the ritual in the light of day was far different from watching it by the glow of the fireplace. The movement of her arm pulled the material tight against her breast, causing the shadow of a nipple to appear then disappear. Garrick closed his eyes and stifled another groan. He was wrong; this wasn't heaven, it was hell! A heartbeat later, his eyes popped open again. Whatever it was, he wasn't going to miss a second of it.

It was obvious Becky's thoughts were far away as she reached back to pull a section of hair over her shoulder. Closing her eyes, she dreamily ran the brush through it with long, slow strokes.

Garrick gazed longingly at his wife while his stomach did somersaults. She had to be the most beautiful woman in the world. The longer he lived with her, the more fascinated he became and the more difficult it was to maintain his distance.

Becky leaned over and swept her hair forward to brush it from underneath. Garrick smiled as it touched the floor in front of her. Rapunzel had always been his choice when his mother let him pick the story she'd tell.

"Where the hell do you think you're going?" The menacing words came through the wall as a drunken miner crashed into the door of their room. The brush dropped to the floor with a clatter as Becky ducked and instinctively covered her head with her hands.

While Garrick looked on in astonishment, Becky glanced at the door, then visibly relaxed when a feminine voice spoke soothingly to the man, and they moved off down the hall. She took a deep breath and closed her eyes in relief. It was obvious the incident had shaken her.

"Your father beat you, didn't he?" Garrick asked in a horrified whisper.

Becky jumped at the sound of his voice and looked his way with huge eyes. Then, with an inarticulate cry, she covered her face with her hands and let her hair fall around her like a protective shield.

Heedless of his own pain, Garrick rose from the bed and crossed the short distance to kneel beside the chair. "Becky, don't. I'm sorry; I shouldn't have asked."

"My f-father said I was evil."

"Oh, Becky." Garrick put his hand on the back of her neck and pulled her head forward to rest against his shoulder. "That's not true. I never met anyone less evil in my life."

"He used t-to try and beat it out of me wh-when he got drunk. I hated him."

Garrick's grip tightened as he felt the bile rise in his throat. The man must have been a monster. "Becky, your father was sick. The things he did were not your fault, even if he said they were. You weren't evil to hate him.

Anyone would." He rubbed his other hand comfortingly across the top of her back. "I can't imagine you doing anything really bad."

"I got pregnant."

"Not by yourself." Crooking a finger under her chin, he raised her face and smiled down into her eyes. "If there were anything wrong with you, I'd have noticed it in the four months we've lived together. All I've seen is a woman who does everything she can to please me."

Becky sniffed. "I don't deserve you, Garrick."

"And I don't deserve you," he said softly, tracing the line of her jaw with his thumb. The blue-green of his eyes seemed to darken as his hand continued to caress the sensitive skin.

For a magic moment, Becky thought he was going to kiss her. With lips slightly parted, she waited breathlessly, her heart pounding in anticipation.

He glanced away as a chunk of wood shifted in the stove, and the spell was broken. "I'd better let you finish drying your hair," he said, dropping his hand.

Becky suddenly realized that she was wearing a thin nightgown, and Garrick was dressed only in the blanket Angel had given him to wrap around his waist. She could feel the heat of a blush climb to her face.

It wasn't difficult for him to figure out what was going through her mind as she ducked her head in embarrassment. With an inward sigh of regret, Garrick rose to his feet. "I'll get out of your way."

Becky finished drying and braiding her hair in record time. Knowing Garrick was watching made her strangely self-conscious, though it had never bothered her at home. Of course, he'd never touched her bare skin before. The feel of his fingers against her cheek lingered as a sweet memory.

She went behind the screen to put on the robe Angel had lent her. Taking a deep breath, she stepped nervously around the edge of the screen. Though Garrick lay on his stomach with his eyes shut, she could tell he wasn't asleep by the tension in his face. "The doctor gave me this salve for your bruises," she said.

"I don't want it."

Becky smiled slightly at the almost petulant tone of his voice. "He said I was to apply it twice a day."

"It won't make my back feel better."

"I don't know if it will or not," she said, "but it shouldn't make it any worse."

"Do I have any choice in this?"

"No," Becky said as she dipped her fingers into the salve and gently applied it to the back of his shoulder. "I always tried to think of something pleasant when I'm sick or hurt. My favorite was the last picnic my mother and I went on before she died. We packed a big lunch and went down to the river. Mama had borrowed a rowboat from a friend of hers so we could row out to the island. It was wonderful. No matter how bad I feel, the memory of that day makes me feel better. Surely there was a special day like that for you."

"How did your mother die?"

"Smallpox. I had it too, but I survived. About all I remember is my aunt telling me Mama was gone and that everything in our house would have to be burned. At the time all I could think about was how awful I felt and how it didn't matter because I was probably going to die too."

"Then your father brought you west?"

"No, I never even knew I had a father until later. I'm not sure my parents were ever married. She didn't take his name."

"Then how did you wind up with him?"

Becky sighed as she leaned across him to reach the other side of his back. "I don't really know. He just showed up one day. I think my aunt must have sent for him. She had six children of her own and didn't need another one. Besides, she and my mother were only stepsisters, so we weren't really kin. I don't think my father was pleased to have a seven-year-old tagging along, but he did take me with him. Mining camps were better than an orphanage."

The image of her instinctive reaction to the loud voice in the hall crossed Garrick's mind, and he wasn't so sure. As her fingers gently spread the soothing salve over his hurts, he couldn't help thinking there had been no one to do that for her. No one had been there for her for a very long time.

"It's not a day," he said suddenly. "It's a place."

"What?"

"The memory that makes me happy is my grandfather's shop. I loved to go there when I was a boy. He was a blacksmith."

"A Norwegian blacksmith?"

"Why not? Norwegians use as much metal as anyone else," Garrick said. "Actually, though, this was my grandfather O'Brian. I never knew my father's father."

Becky glanced down at her hand. "He made this ring, didn't he?"

"For my tenth birthday. I wore it until I couldn't even get it on my little finger any more. He taught me how to work the bellows as soon as I was big enough, and I was at the forge before I turned thirteen."

"I was never inside a blacksmith's shop. What's it like?"

"You've never been in a smithy?"

"I never had a reason to go to one. Besides, not many mining camps are as big as South Pass City."

"My grandfather's smithy was in the middle of town..."

As Becky listened to Garrick's enthusiastic description, she was pleased to feel the muscles under her fingers relax. Hers were doing the opposite. The combination of his skin under her fingers and that beautiful masculine voice was doing strange things to her insides. How she wished she could affect him the same way.

With a flash of annoyance at herself, Becky dismissed the thought. How could he find her attractive when she was roughly the shape of a barrel? She put the lid on the jar of salve and set it aside before moving to the unoccupied side of the bed. With a pillow between her back and the headboard, she settled down to listen. In the four months they'd been together, Garrick had never said so much all at once. Blacksmithing was obviously more than just a fond memory.

"You really loved it, didn't you?" she asked when he finally stopped talking.

"We both always thought I'd take over his shop when I was old enough."

"Why didn't you?"

There was a long moment of silence before he spoke, his voice filled with deep regret. "I got stupid and threw away my chance."

"Couldn't you still do it?"

"No. It's years too late."

"You're sure?"

"*Ja*, I'm sure," Garrick said with a touch of irritation.

Becky lapsed into silence. She knew from experience that Garrick's accent became pronounced when his emotions were close to the surface. It always seemed to happen when she asked about his past. Strangely enough, everything she knew pointed to a happy childhood. So why didn't he want to talk about it?

"I never thanked you for saving me today," she said, moving on to a safer topic. "I wouldn't have made it without you."

He smiled up at her. "I headed home early today. When the thunder started, I looked up and saw my wife dodging lightning. What were you doing up there, anyway?"

"Looking for wild onions. I wanted to make a stew for supper."

"Wild onions! In September? They don't grow after —" He stopped in mid-sentence to stare at her.

"What's wrong?" she asked uneasily.

"Your stomach," he said in a shocked voice. "I thought I saw it move."

Becky giggled. "You don't need to look like that. It's just the baby."

"But the whole thing shifted."

"I know. Here, give me your hand." She placed it on the mound of her abdomen and held it there. "He's pretty active today."

"It's hard," he said in surprise. "I thought it would be soft." Just then the baby gave a powerful kick and Garrick's eyes widened. "It kicked me!"

"Isn't it something?"

"*Ja*, it's wonderful." As he felt it move once more, the baby suddenly became real to Garrick. He lay there for several minutes reveling in the unexpected sensations as the activity continued beneath his hand. For the first time, Becky and her baby became separate entities.

Garrick's expression of incredulous delight gave Becky a strange feeling of warmth as she gazed down at him. She resisted the urge to lift her hand and run her fingers through his white-blond hair. What had she done to deserve him?

At last he raised his eyes to hers. "I never knew," he said simply. "Thank you."

In that instant, Becky realized something completely unexpected had happened; she'd fallen in love with her husband.

Chapter 10

"What do you mean you're not going to vote?" Angel asked, staring at Becky accusingly. "You can't just turn your back on our first election. The women of Wyoming are the only ones in the world with the right to vote. You're going to go to the polls if I have to drag you down there."

Becky shook her head. "No, Angel, you don't understand—"

"I don't care what your excuse is; it's not good enough. You have an obligation to women everywhere to stand up and be counted." Suddenly Angel's eyes narrowed. "It's Swede isn't it? He won't let you vote."

"Oh, no. He's never said a word. I can't vote because I'm not old enough."

"Good Lord." Angel glanced first at Becky's swollen midsection, and then at her face. "How old are you?"

"Seventeen."

"Jesus!"

"That ain't so young," said a woman Becky knew only as Molly. "I'd been working almost four years by the time I was that age."

"And my ma had two youngun's," put in another.

"I know, I know, I just thought Becky was older. All right, ladies, we'd best get moving. I want to be back before the shift changes at the mines, and we may run into trouble." Angel glanced at Becky. "You sure you'll be all right here by yourself?"

"What could happen to me here?"

Angel gave a snort. "If you don't know, I'm sure as hell not going to tell you. Sam's out front. If you need him, just holler."

Becky grinned as Angel marched the other five women out the door. In spite of her profession, Angel was a dyed-in-the-wool suffragette. Seeing it as her patriotic duty to get as many women as possible to the polls, she had spent the entire week before the election organizing all the less than respectable ladies of South Pass City. The women who worked in the brothels, saloons, and dance halls were all going to vote at the same time, and heaven help anyone that questioned their right to do so. Becky almost wished she could go along to watch, but she knew Garrick would never approve of her associating with the so-called soiled doves. With a sigh, she turned back to the dress she was mending.

At the thought of Garrick, her smile deepened. There had been a subtle change in their relationship in the week since the hailstorm. Though neither had said anything, there was a new closeness between them, a warmth that hadn't been there before.

She still faithfully spread the salve over Garrick's back twice a day, though most of the soreness was long gone. If she was very careful and used it sparingly, there was enough for several more days. Rubbing her hands across the broad expanse of muscles and skin was a delight she wasn't going to give up until she had to. Best of all, Garrick didn't seem to mind. In fact he—

KA-*BOOM*!"

For an instant, Becky sat paralyzed in her chair as the explosion rattled the windows of The Green Garter. Then, with a cry of anguish, she jumped to her feet and ran out into the street. She all but collided with a man who was running toward the mines.

"What happened?" she yelled.

"Don't know, but that wasn't a normal blast. Nobody in his right mind would use that big of a charge."

"Do you know which mine?" Becky asked, franticly grabbing his sleeve as he started to move away.

"It sounded like either the Goulden Curry or the Garfield, but it could have been any of them on that side of town."

A second explosion rent the air. Though it was more muted than the first, it was no less ominous. With a choked cry, Becky lifted her skirts and headed for the mines as fast as she could.

South Pass City's main street never seemed so long. Slowed by her cumbersome body, Becky was still some distance away when her fears were realized. The crowd was gathered outside the entrance of the Goulden Curry, not the Garfield. She knew Garrick was there somewhere deep in the bowels of the earth, probably at the center of the explosion.

Dr. Caldwell was already at the mine entrance, kneeling next to the bodies of three men when Becky arrived. Two were covered with a piece of sacking and the third seemed to be unconscious as the doctor tended him.

"Have you seen my husband, Dr. Caldwell?" Becky asked desperately.

"No," he said, glancing at the shrouded bodies. "But in this case, that's good news."

Two men emerged from the mine carrying a third. "There's still three men down there, and one of the main timbers is broken. The whole thing's going to crash down any minute. We'll need help if we're going to get them out.

"I'll go."

Glancing over her shoulder, Becky was surprised to see Ox Bruford striding through the crowd. She hadn't even known he was in town. Half a dozen others stepped forward. There was no shortage of men willing to risk their lives to save the trapped miners.

"No." Ox held up a hand. "The more we take in, the less chance we have of getting everyone out safely. Three of you come with me. The rest of you find something to shore up that broken beam."

"You may need my help." Dr. Caldwell stood up and shrugged out of his coat. "If someone could keep an eye on this man..."

Becky knelt down next to the unconscious miner. "What do you want me to do?"

"Just watch him. If he starts to choke, roll him on his side."

"Doctor," Becky said, looking up at him beseechingly, "my husband — "

"I know. We'll do everything we can."

With that he was gone. Becky swallowed hard to keep the tears at bay.

"I'm alive?"

Becky looked down at her patient in surprise. Though one eye was completely swollen shut and the pupil of the other seemed oddly large, the man was obviously awake.

"Pete?" The miner who had just come from the mine spoke before Becky had a chance to answer. "Are you all right?"

"My head feels like it's been stomped into the ground, and I can't move my right arm or leg."

"What the hell happened?"

"Blasting oil. That danged fool powder man dropped a whole vial into a keg of powder."

"Jesus. There won't hardly be enough left to bury."

"If they even find him."

"Noooooo!" As the full impact of the men's words hit, Becky gave in to the blackness that rose up to engulf her.

"Wake up, dammit." Angel's voice penetrated the curtain of darkness surrounding Becky's mind. "We don't have time to waste on a silly female who doesn't know any better than to faint. There are wounded men here."

Becky opened her eyes and stared up into her friend's face.

"That's better." Angel's disapproving words were at odds with her look of relief. "Now, pull yourself together. They're starting to bring the men up out of the mine."

"Oh, Angel, they said —"

"It wasn't Swede."

"What?"

"The shift was changing. The accident happened outside with the powder man from the second shift. Swede's blasting crew were the only ones left in the mine. They were just about ready to set off the charges like they do at the end of every shift."

"But there were two explosions."

"The first one somehow triggered the second. Jack was down in the mine, but he wasn't real sure what happened. They heard the explosion, and the next thing he knew Swede was tearing fuses out of the drill holes. Must have missed one."

Becky's eyes filled with tears. "Then he could still be hurt or dead."

"Maybe, but it isn't going to do a bit of good for you to cry. If he's hurt, the last thing he needs to see when he comes out of that mine is you bawling your eyes out." Angel stood and reached down to help Becky up. "There'll be plenty of time for tears later."

Becky wiped her eyes then got to her feet. "How do you know what happened?"

"The men told me."

"When?"

"While you were out cold. I heard the explosions and knew there was big trouble, so I hotfooted it up here as fast as I could. Got here just in time to pick you up out of the dirt."

"There they are," someone shouted, and Becky held her breath, almost afraid to hope. One of the rescuers stumbled out with a man slung over his shoulder. Following close behind came two more men carrying another between them on a blanket as the doctor supported the man's bloodied arm. There was no sign of Ox Bruford or Garrick.

Becky hurried to the doctor's side. "Did you see my husband?"

He looked at her indecisively for a moment then nodded.

"Is he...is he hurt?"

"Only a few minor cuts and bruises."

"Then why didn't he come out with the others?"

Dr. Caldwell avoided her eyes. "We're going to get him out."

"He's trapped somehow, isn't he?"

"No, not exactly."

"For God's sake, Dr. Caldwell, I'm his wife. I have the right to know."

For a long moment she didn't think he was going to answer, then he sighed. "The explosion cracked one of the main beams, and there wasn't anything down there to prop it up to keep it from breaking."

"And...?"

"And Swede's down there holding it up with his bare hands."

Chapter 11

Garrick felt like an utter fool. Anybody with any intelligence would have gotten out of this hellhole when they had the chance. No sane man would have stepped under a cracked beam and tried to hold it together. As if to remind him of his folly, the timber above him groaned and a spattering of dirt fell around him.

"We're gonna die, ain't we, Swede?" The whispered voice was filled with pain.

A single glance down at Amos's broken body and Garrick knew he'd done the only thing possible. There was no way he could have left his men behind. "Don't worry. The mine's just settling. It always does that after a blast," he said quietly, wondering how long it would be before they were buried under several tons of rock.

"Do you think Jack and the others made it out?" Amos asked.

"Probably. Can you see Pierre?"

"Kinda. He's over by the wall, but I can't see him real well. He ain't movin'." Amos was quiet for a long moment before he spoke again. "Dammit, Swede, this is all my fault. If I hadn't dropped that lamp, the fuses wouldn't have fired."

"That lamp hit the floor when you did. You didn't cause the blast that knocked everybody down. Besides, if I'd been quicker, I'd have gotten the fuses all pulled loose."

Silence fell between them. Garrick hoped Amos had slipped into unconsciousness. His pain must be excruciating.

Unfortunately, it left Garrick alone with the growing ache in his arms. He knew it was only a matter of time before his strength gave out. There was always the possibility the cracked beam would hold, but it wasn't likely. He wondered if the lantern would go out before the roof caved in.

Garrick conjured the image of Becky. Not only was the thought of his wife much more pleasant, he wanted her vision to be foremost on his mind when death came. Now he wished he'd told her how he felt about her, and how she'd brightened his life. He'd wanted to a hundred times but couldn't seem to find the words.

Suddenly, he caught the glimmer of light far down the tunnel. Was it his imagination or a rescue party? A second later, the sight of Ox Bruford's familiar form filled him with hope. Maybe, just maybe...

The beam gave another ominous groan just as the four men reached him. All of them looked up at the cracked timber then down at Garrick.

"Jesus, Swede, what the hell are you doing?"

"Unless you want the whole mountain to come down on us, Ox, you'd better lower your voice," Garrick whispered. "Amos is pretty bad, Doc, but better check Pierre first. He's over against the wall. Don't know if he's alive or not."

It only took a glance for Dr. Caldwell to see Pierre was beyond help. With a regretful sigh, he turned away and went to Amos. At least this one had a chance.

"We sent some men to get something to hold the beam up, Swede," Ox said. He looked up at the heavy timber and shook his head. "I see it, but I don't believe it. What were you thinking?"

"I obviously wasn't thinking at all," Garrick said dryly. "Better get those men out of here while you still can."

Dr. Caldwell worked quickly. Within a very few minutes they rigged a sling between two of the rescuers to carry Amos out.

"I'll get him," the third man said, nodding toward Pierre. All of them avoided looking at Garrick. There was nothing any of them could do. No one was tall enough to help hold the beam.

"Don't jostle him anymore than you can help," Dr. Caldwell cautioned as they lifted Amos from the floor and started down the tunnel. His moan of pain was nearly drowned out as the beam shifted with an ominous crack.

"Get the hell out of here," Garrick said urgently as a nearly unbearable weight settled against his hands. There was no longer any doubt about whether it would stay up without his support.

"I'm not going anywhere until we get you out of here," Ox said stubbornly, as the other men disappeared from sight.

"Don't be...a fool...Bruford. My wife..." Garrick said, gritting his teeth. "Promise me...promise you'll take care of her."

Ox started to deny the need for such a promise then nodded. "I will."

"Find...out...where that...damn support...is."

They both knew there was no way the rescuers would get there in time, but it was easier to pretend.

"I'll be right back," Ox promised, knowing he'd probably never see his friend again.

Ox was almost out of sight when Garrick felt the beam shift in his hands. "Run for it," he yelled as his reflexes took over.

Becky was staring at Pierre's mangled body in horrified disbelief when an ominous rumble filled the air. "*Garrick!*" she screamed as a cloud of dust belched out of the mine entrance.

Without a thought, she turned and ran toward the opening. Someone grabbed her and stopped her flight before she could reach her destination. "Let me go!" she screeched, trying to twist loose from the arms that restrained her.

Angel held on tightly but did nothing to calm Becky. She just stood there staring at the empty blackness of the mine. "Dear God," she whispered, "not both of them."

An eternity passed. The men around them were still deciding what to do when two dust-covered figures stumbled out of the mine coughing and choking.

"Jesus, Swede," Ox said, wiping dirt out of his eyes. "How did you move so fast? I was halfway out when you yelled. The next thing I knew, you were right beside me."

"Long legs."

"You're one hell of a runner."

"You didn't do so bad yourself."

Suddenly, Becky was in Garrick's arms sobbing against his chest, and everything else ceased to matter.

"Oh, Garrick," she cried, her hands clutching the back of his shirt as though she were afraid he might disappear. "I was so scared."

"Shhh, little one, it's all right." Garrick closed his eyes and pulled her closer as he savored the feel of her in his arms. He hadn't expected to ever experience it again. The world ebbed and flowed around them, but they paid no attention as they clung to each other.

"What happened in there, Swede?"

Garrick opened his eyes and looked down at Tom Ryan, the owner of the Goulden Curry mine. "We'd just finished tamping in all the powder cartridges..."

Becky listened with growing horror as Garrick described the events that had taken place in the mine below. She kept her arms around her husband with the side of her head pressed against his chest where she could hear the steady beat of his heart and assure herself that he was somehow miraculously still alive.

"...but I'm not sure what started it. You talked to Klynton yet?"

"He's dead," Tom Ryan said. "Seems you were right about the blasting oil being too unstable to use safely."

"So, the nitroglycerin finally did him in." Garrick sighed. "He was so sure he could handle it."

"At least the tunnel isn't blocked. The sides caved in, but the roof held."

Garrick stared at him for a moment in stunned disbelief, and then gave a derisive laugh. "That explains how I was able to hold that beam up so long. I thought it was pretty amazing."

"Who knows? If you hadn't been there it might have shifted differently."

"How are my men?"

"Pierre Françoise is dead, Amos Peterson has two broken legs and may lose his arm. Everybody else is all right."

Garrick closed his eyes and swallowed hard.

"You did all you could," Becky said softly.

"I know, but they were my responsibility."

"We were lucky, Swede. Fifteen minutes earlier or later, there would have been a whole shift down in the mine," Tom Ryan said, gripping his shoulder. "Take your wife and go home, Swede. You both look about done in."

"If you're sure you don't need me."

Tom Ryan shook his head. "You've done more than your share already.

After a quick good-bye to Ox and Angel, they headed home. Garrick said little on the way, and for once even Becky was disinclined to talk. All she could think about was how close she had come to losing him. One moment of carelessness, not even his own, and he'd almost died.

Becky glanced up at his strong profile. For some reason she couldn't fathom, Garrick seemed to put everyone else first, even if it meant putting his life on the line. Even when he'd married her, he'd sacrificed himself to solve her problem.

Today he'd risked death twice, both times without even thinking about it. With a flash of insight, she realized he would always be that way. The inherent risks of his job made it that much worse. Every time he went down in that mine, he was in danger.

When they arrived home, Becky put water on to heat, and Garrick was soon relaxing in a hot bath. If only the memories of the day could be soaked away as easily as the dirt and sore muscles.

Supper was a silent meal. Garrick was grateful until he noticed Becky wasn't eating. There was nothing wrong with the food, but she just kept pushing it around her plate.

"Are you feeling all right?" he asked with concern.

"Fine."

"Is the baby moving around a lot?"

She smiled at that. Garrick's growing fascination with the baby endeared him to her even more. "No, he's pretty calm right now."

"Oh."

Silence fell again as Garrick went back to his meal. Watching him across the table, Becky had a sudden need to touch him, to assure herself that he was truly all right. "I can put the salve on your back right after supper. Then you can go to bed."

"That sounds fine."

As soon as the meal was finished, Garrick removed his shirt and lay down on the bed while Becky went to get the salve. She settled herself next to him and began to smooth the substance over his skin. The muscles under her fingers were curiously knotted. It hadn't occurred to her that he might be suffering physical discomfort other than the various cuts she had already doctored on his face and hands.

"Would you like me to rub your shoulders?"

"Mmmhuh. With his eyes closed and his chin propped on his folded arms, Garrick felt the bone-deep weariness ease beneath Becky's healing touch. If he couldn't forget the horrors of the day, at least there was a feeling of peace here at home. A soft thump on his ribs where Becky leaned against him brought a smile to his lips. It was pretty hard to be despondent with Becky and her baby around.

He wasn't even aware of the tears that filled Becky's eyes or the knot that blocked her throat. The image of Pierre Françoise's mutilated body was impossible to forget as she massaged her husband's strong, healthy back.

Much later that night, shadows shifting across his face awakened Garrick. It took a few seconds to realize what had disturbed him. From his usual place near the hearth, he could see Becky clearly outlined by the moonlight streaming in through the open shutter. There was something about the way she was standing there staring out into the night that sent a wave of alarm rippling through him.

In a moment, he had slid out of his bedroll and slipped on his pants. He walked barefoot and shirtless across the floor to stand behind her. "Are you all right?"

"No," she said without turning, "I'm not."

"Is it the baby?"

"No."

"Then what's wrong?"

"I don't want you to go down into that mine again."

"What?"

"I can't take it anymore, Garrick."

"But I'm a powder man. I can't do my job without going into the mine. Measuring the charges is only part of it. I have to tell my crew where to drill the blasting holes. They need me right there to—"

"Garrick," she said softly, "I want you to think about quitting your job."

He was stunned. "Are you crazy?"

"I know it's a lot to ask but —"

"A lot to ask! It's my life. I learned how to work explosives during the war, then spent four years using that knowledge on the Union Pacific before I even came to South Pass City. I was one of the best; I still am."

"But for how long?" She finally turned to him, her swollen eyes clearly visible in the bright moonlight. She'd obviously been crying most of the night. "You almost died today."

"It was a freak accident."

"I know, and it wasn't even your fault, but three men are dead and another is probably crippled for life. It was a miracle you weren't hurt." She crossed her arms in front of her body and rubbed her elbows. "You threw that miracle away when you grabbed the broken beam. I don't know another man in the world who would have done that. It was extremely brave, a truly noble thing to do, but it was also incredibly stupid."

Her words were like shards of glass driven into his pride. Couldn't she see he'd done the only thing he could? Didn't she know how much it hurt him to see his men dead and wounded because he wasn't fast enough? "What do you want from me?" he asked angrily.

"I want to know you'll be there tomorrow and the day after. I can't stand the thought of you dying in some foolish act of heroism."

"I can't change what I am, Becky."

"Does being a powder man really mean so much to you?"

"With Klynton gone, Mr. Ryan is already short one powder man." He shrugged. "Besides, it's all I know."

"Couldn't you learn something new?" she asked. "Nobody pans the creek here. Maybe you could build a sluice box and—"

"You *are* crazy. Even if there were any gold here, which I doubt, it would probably take both of us all day every day just to get enough so we could buy food."

"I wouldn't mind."

"Well, I would. Besides, in another month it'll be winter. How do you propose to support us then?"

"I don't know. Maybe I could take in sewing."

"Oh, that's a great plan," he said sarcastically. "And you could do laundry in your spare time."

"Actually, it's a pretty good idea," Becky said, warming to her theme. "Angel seems pleased enough with my work. Maybe she'd..." Becky's voice trailed off as she realized she'd given away her secret.

"What work is that?" Garrick's voice was quiet, but Becky wasn't deceived. He was furious.

"It's just...I only..."

His huge hands closed around her upper arms as he leaned forward until their noses were almost touching. "What kind of work?" he repeated ominously.

"I...I've been doing their mending."

"Whose?"

"A-Angel's and her g-girls, but I only go in the morning."

"*What*! You go to The Green Garter?"

"Well, yes...but there's no reason for you to be upset."

"No reason? My wife spends every morning in a brothel and I'm not supposed to be upset!"

"You don't understand."

"You're right, I don't." He thrust her away and stomped over to where his shirt hung on the wall. "If you needed more money, you should have told me."

"But it wasn't —"

"No wife of mine is going to work," he said, shoving his arms into the shirtsleeves. "Especially not in a brothel!" He grabbed his boots and headed for the door.

"Garrick, where are you going?"

"Out!"

"You're running away again, just like you did last time."

"No, I'm doing the only thing I can. I've never beat a woman in my life, and I don't want to start now."

"This isn't about me, Garrick."

He turned to look at her with one eyebrow raised superciliously. "It's not?"

"No." Becky gripped her hands behind her back to give herself courage. There was too much at stake to let him leave without resolving this. "I don't want to be a widow, Garrick. If I have to sit here every day and worry about whether you're going to make it home again, I'll go crazy. I can't survive married to a man who flirts with death for a living."

He stared at her angrily for a moment then turned to go.

"Garrick, don't you dare leave without answering me."

As he stopped in the open doorway, Garrick suddenly remembered how he'd held onto the image of Becky when he thought he had only moments to live. He glanced over his shoulder and gritted his teeth against the stricken look on her face. He wanted to make her happy, but she asked too much. "*Jeg elsker deg*," he muttered in Norwegian.

"What does that mean?"

"You don't want to know," he said, then walked out into the night.

Chapter 12

Garrick was so angry that he was a hundred yards from the house before he realized he was barefoot. Feeling foolish, he pulled on his boots and buttoned his shirt. He hadn't even thought to grab his coat, and the walk to town in the cold mountain air didn't improve his humor any. By the time he reached The Green Garter, he was in a thundering rage.

His entrance into the casino caused quite a stir. The story of his bravery down in the mine had grown to astounding proportions. The fact that it was well after midnight and most of the patrons were drunk added to the mystique of his heroism. No one seemed to share Becky's belief that it had been a stupid thing to do.

If he hadn't been so angry, their adulation would have gone a long way toward soothing his wounded feelings. As it was, the crowd around him only irritated him further as he searched the room for Angel. He finally located her dealing Blackjack at a table in the back. Shedding his admirers like an unwanted garment, he stalked to her corner.

"I want to talk to you, Angel."

"Talk away," she said, shuffling the cards.

"This needs to be discussed in private."

Angel was surprised. She'd never seen him angry in all the time they'd been friends, but he most definitely was unhappy about something. "Can't it wait?"

"No."

"All right," she said with a shrug. "Take over for me, Collette."

Collette nodded and took Angel's place at the table. Garrick ignored the obvious invitation in her smile as she sat down.

Angel led the way to her office and shut the door behind them. "What the hell is this all about, Swede?"

"Why didn't you tell me my wife was working for you?" he asked.

"Ah, so that's it." She sat down behind her desk and smiled. "I knew you'd be madder than blue blazes when you found out."

"That doesn't answer my question."

Angel leaned back in her chair. "She asked me not to. Besides, I figured you'd make her quit as soon as you found out."

"If you knew I wouldn't like it, why did you encourage her to come here?"

"Your wife and I have a business arrangement. It has nothing to do with you."

"Everything my wife does is my business."

"Wake up, Swede. This is 1870. In case you missed it, women in this territory now have the right to vote and own their own property. Your wife doesn't need your permission to work."

"This is no place for someone like Becky."

"She sews here, Swede, nothing more. If you're worried about who she'll run into, don't. There's never any customers around that time of day, and she has very little contact with the girls."

"But why did she come to you if she needed more money?"

Angel laughed. "I see your wife didn't explain our little arrangement to you. There's no money involved. She does our mending, and I'm teaching her how to cook."

"To cook!"

"That's right." She sighed. "And to be honest, Swede, I think she's lonely."

"Lonely?"

"Why is that such a surprise? You work a twelve-hour shift. She hasn't got anybody else to talk to."

"But why here?"

"Who else does she know? Her father certainly didn't have any friends." She eyed him shrewdly. "There's more to this than Becky coming here every day, isn't there?"

"She wants me to quit the mine."

"Do you blame her? You're all she's got, Swede, and you damned near died today."

"She said I was stupid."

Angel arched an eyebrow. "Did she?"

"No, not really" he admitted. "She said what I did today was stupid. Becky doesn't seem to understand I didn't have any other choice."

"Maybe she does, and that's why she feels the way she does. She knows you'll always walk straight into danger without a second thought. Look, Swede, Becky's only seventeen, but she's already lost both parents and the man who fathered her baby."

"What makes you think I'm not the father of her baby?

Angel gave a snort. "This is me you're talking to, Swede. I can count, and I know damned well you never set eyes on her before you pulled her out of that creek."

She rose and walked to the door. "Better give it some thought, Swede. What's more important, your job in the mine or that sweet little lady you married?"

Garrick was pensive as he followed her back into the casino. As usual, Angel was dead right. Becky meant far more to him than being a powder man. If the truth were known, after today, he didn't care if he never saw the inside of a mine again. He'd probably be having nightmares about it for years to come. But what else could he do? He'd been working with explosives since he was eighteen and had never even thought of doing anything else. Nor were there many jobs that paid as well.

Leaning against the bar, he surveyed the room broodingly. There must be something he could do. All at once, he straightened as an idea sprang into his head. A slow grin spread across his face. There *was* something he knew as well as explosives. In fact, he had a real talent for it. With a new lightness in his step, he crossed the room to an empty chair at Collette's blackjack table.

Garrick didn't come home that night, and Becky died a thousand deaths waiting for him. Over and over, she reproached herself. She should never have made such an unreasonable demand on him. What had she ever given him in exchange for all he'd done for her? As usual, she'd let her emotions rule her head, and now she was paying the price. All night long, she pictured him in the arms of another woman. She agonized until dawn when her exhaustion won out, and she finally fell asleep.

It seemed as though she had only been asleep a few minutes when she awoke to the sound of singing. Becky sat up and rubbed her eyes. It had to be Garrick; there was no mistaking that golden voice, but she'd never heard him sing before. The slightly bawdy tune seemed out of character for him, too.

"...Sooo don't turn your back on a—" The song came to an abrupt halt as Garrick stepped inside and found his wife still in bed. He frowned when he saw the swollen bloodshot eyes and rumpled bedclothes. "Are you all right?"

"Just fine!" she snapped, irritated by his obvious good humor when she had just spent an interminable night feeling rotten. She was instantly remorseful. It was her short-tempered demands that had driven him away in the first place. "Why do you ask?" she asked in a milder tone.

"I've never known you to sleep this late before."

"What time is it?"

"Almost nine."

Nine!" Becky practically jumped out of bed. With a blanket draped around her shoulders, she hurried behind the canvas curtain to get dressed. When she emerged a few minutes later, Garrick was hunkered down next to the fireplace pouring cornmeal into a pan of boiling water.

"You seem happy this morning," she said, vowing she would not ask him where he'd spent the night if it killed her.

"I am."

"Aren't you going to work today?"

"I quit."

"What!"

"I just got done talking to Mr. Ryan."

"You did?

"*Ja* and he wished me luck."

"But what's he going to do for a powder man?"

"Jack's almost ready to take over. I can finish teaching him everything he needs to know by the time they get the mine opened up again."

"That's only one. I thought he needed two."

Garrick looked up. "Changed your mind about me being a powder man?"

"N-no, I was just curious."

"How about some breakfast before you leave for Angel's?"

Becky stared at him in astonishment. "Garrick, what's going on?"

"I had a long talk with Angel last night," he said, stirring the cornmeal. "She convinced me there's nothing wrong with you going there."

"What are you going to do?"

"While you're at Angel's? Sleep. I didn't get any last night."

"That's not what I meant."

"I know." He peered into the pan. Apparently satisfied with the contents, he set it on the hearth and removed the coffee pot from the fire. "Where's the molasses?"

"Are you still mad at me?" Becky asked as she took the molasses off the shelf and handed it to him.

"No."

"Then why won't you tell me what you are planning?"

"Because I'm not sure it's going to work out. If I can manage what I have in mind, I won't have to work as a powder man any more. If I don't..." He shrugged. "Tom Ryan said I could always have my job back."

"Can't you tell me?"

"No, I want it to be a surprise." He stood up. "Shall we eat?"

"I thought you hated cornmeal mush."

He grinned. "I do, but it's the only breakfast I know how to make."

Becky spent the whole morning pondering Garrick's strange mood. On the one hand, she'd never seen him so happy, but he also seemed nervous, almost apprehensive about whatever he was planning to do. She sat in her usual chair at The Green Garter trying to puzzle it all out as she sewed.

Beyond admitting she'd talked to Garrick, Angel had said little. If she knew what he was doing, she wasn't about to share that information with Becky.

"And I still say he's just like any other man."

Tucked away in her corner by the pantry, Becky was partially hidden from the two women who entered the kitchen. She looked up when she heard the venomous tone in Molly's voice. Becky didn't know Molly's companion, though she'd seen her a few times, but Angel's girls never fought with each other. They knew better.

"That's because he's never picked you." The other woman smiled complacently as she walked over to the stove and poured herself a cup of coffee. "He likes his women with a little more meat on their bones."

"You mean fat?"

The brunette's eyes narrowed menacingly, then she shrugged and smoothed her manicured hand down over the lush figure beneath her wrapper. "You're just jealous."

"He's married, Collette."

"So what? He spent the night with me." She took a sip of coffee and gave Molly a sly look. "And he told me he'd be back tonight. No wife can give him what I can."

Molly laughed. "That's probably true, but not many men want the pox. Just joking," she added hastily as Collette's lips thinned and her fingers curled into claws. "Most wives don't enjoy sex, so she's probably glad."

"Well, I hope she appreciates the special attention I give her husband as much as he does. There aren't many around like Swede. He kept me awake for hours." Collette smiled maliciously as she heard the shocked gasp behind her.

A moment later the back door slammed, and Collette laughed. "What a little fool."

"You know, you really are a bitch, Collette. She ain't never been nothin' but nice to any of us. If Angel knew about this little scene you just set up, she'd skin you alive."

"But she's not going to find out, is she, Molly? Because if she does I'll tell her all about that nasty little opium habit you have."

Molly sighed. "No, I won't tell her. I still don't see why you're doing this."

"Because every time Swede has a fight with his wife, he comes here. She'll probably rip his head off over this."

"He still won't sleep with you."

"If she pushes him hard enough, he will."

"You're crazy," Molly said as she walked out of the room.

"We'll see," Collette said with a sly smile. "We'll see."

Becky ran blindly down the street. A sharp pain in her side made her slow down, but it was nothing compared to the ache in her heart. No wonder Garrick had been so happy this morning. He'd spent the night with the luscious Collette.

Almost before she realized it, Becky found herself at home. Though Garrick was almost certainly still asleep, she didn't want to have to face him just yet. Like a small, wounded animal, she crept into the shed out back and sobbed her woes out against Sophie's neck.

At last, her tears spent and her emotions drained, Becky fell asleep on the fragrant pile of hay. That's where Garrick found her when he came to feed the horse several hours later.

"Becky? What are you doing out here?"

"Oh." She sat up and looked around in confusion. "I guess I must have fallen asleep."

"Are you all right?"

"Yes, I—" Becky gasped in surprise as he effortlessly lifted her to her feet.

He held her there and gazed down at her with a worried frown on his face. "You look tired."

"I...I didn't sleep very well last night."

"Because of the accident at the mine or our fight?"

"Both." Her lip quivered. "Oh, Garrick, I'm so sorry. I had no right to place such impossible demands on you."

He put his arms around her and pulled her close. "You had every right, Becky. You're my wife. How can I know how you feel about something if you don't tell me?"

"But you were so angry."

"I know. My temper is a flaw I inherited from my mother. I can't promise I'll agree with everything, or even that I'll discuss it calmly, but I'll never hurt you."

Becky thought of Collette's self-satisfied smirk and wondered what he considered *hurt*. "Can't you at least tell me what you're doing?"

He hugged her tighter and smiled down at the top of her head. "I'm trying to make a business out of the one natural talent I possess."

"And what is that?"

"You'll just have to wait and see. Trust me, Becky."

In spite of what she'd heard in Angel's kitchen, she found that she did trust him; clear through supper and right up to the moment when he told her he was leaving and not to wait up. With a sunny smile and a cheerful wave, he was gone, and Becky's world caved in around her.

By ten-thirty, having exhausted all the excuses she could think of for staying up, Becky undressed for bed. It looked as if this was going to be another all-nighter for Garrick. She wanted to cry but was beyond it. There were only so many tears a person could shed within a twenty-four-hour period, she thought as she pulled the pins from her hair, and she'd already used up her allotment.

Usually the rhythmic strokes of the brush calmed her, but not tonight. At twenty strokes, she thought about how happy Garrick had been when he returned home this morning. By forty-five, she was hearing Collette's sultry voice assuring Molly he would be back tonight. At seventy-five, Becky found herself wondering what Collette's perfume smelled like. When she hit ninety-eight, she threw the brush down and went to get dressed.

The full moon gilded the streets of South Pass City in silver, but Becky hardly noticed as her steps took her unerringly to The Green Garter. Maybe he wasn't even there. At this time of night, he was almost certainly in a saloon or casino, but it wasn't necessarily The Green Garter. There were twenty-eight of them in town.

From long habit of searching for her father, Becky looked through the door without entering. A simple once-over had saved her a lot of time and embarrassment in the past. She saw Garrick almost immediately, sitting at a table with a hand of cards laid face up in front of him. He was smiling lazily up at Collette who stood close by. As Becky watched, the scantily-clad temptress ran her long fingers possessively down the side of his face and bent down to kiss his ear.

With a gasp of horror, Becky flung herself away from the doorway and pressed her back up against the outside wall of The Green Garter. Had she had the nerve to peek through the door again, she'd have seen her husband shake off Collette's unwanted attentions as the dealer weighed out his winnings in gold dust.

Swallowing against the bile that rose in her throat, Becky closed her eyes and concentrated on staying upright.

"Hello."

The deep masculine voice startled Becky. She opened her eyes and found herself looking up into the brilliant green gaze of Ox Bruford.

"What's going on?" he asked. When Becky didn't answer, he glanced through the swinging doors of The

Green Garter. "Ah," he said. "I see Swede is at it again tonight."

Becky stared up at him in shock. She couldn't believe even a muleskinner would be so indelicate. "Again?"

"Yup. Heard he'd given it up since he got married." He looked down at her. "Swede has got the devil's own luck, you know. He claims it's because he pays attention while the rest of us drink."

"What are you talking about?"

"Blackjack. Swede's unbeatable."

"What?" Cautiously, Becky peered over the swinging doors again. Sure enough, Garrick's full attention was focused on the three cards under his hand. His face was expressionless as he looked up and shook his head at the dealer.

"He came to play cards?"

"Looks that way, though Angel will probably run him out before too long. They have an agreement. She lets him play up to a certain limit, then sends him on his way." Ox grinned. "Says it's good for business for her other customers to see someone win all the time, but she won't let him break her bank."

"What's the limit?"

"Last I heard it was five hundred dollars, but he must be close to that. He was over at the White Swan by four o'clock yesterday morning, and he started late."

"Five hundred dollars!"

"Do you want me to go fetch him for you?"

Becky looked back inside. Collette had moved to another table, but Garrick didn't seem aware she'd left. "No, I won't disturb him."

"I'll walk you home then," he said, offering her his arm. "South Pass City isn't exactly a safe place at night, or during the day for that matter."

"Thank you. I-I don't know why I came. I just..." Becky felt sick to her stomach. *"I'm trying to make a business out of the one natural talent I possess."* Garrick's words rang through her head. Her carping had turned her sweet, honorable husband into a professional gambler.

"You know, it's kind of funny about Swede," Ox said conversationally as they started down the street. "The money doesn't seem to mean much to him. He told me once he just likes to manipulate the numbers. This is probably his way of dealing with the accident at the mine yesterday. He started gambling as soon as he got here last night and never let up.

"Have you known him long, Mr. Bruford?"

"A couple of years. I met him when he was working on the transcontinental railroad. And my name is Ox, by the way."

"Is it really?"

"Close enough."

She smiled. "All right, then you can call me Becky. How is it you're still in town? Don't you usually leave the day after you unload your freight?"

Ox sighed. "I'm waiting for my army escort. I can't leave until they tell me I can. I'm hoping for tomorrow or the day after. I never know until they show up."

"That must be difficult."

"It is. They usually don't give me more than half an hour's notice."

They chatted companionably all the way to Becky's door, where Ox took his leave with an admonishment not to worry about Swede.

Once again, Becky undressed for bed, this time vowing to force Garrick to talk. Tomorrow they would discuss his plans, whether he wanted to or not.

But her carefully laid strategy came to nothing. Early the next morning, a young man came to the door with a note from Garrick. Though Becky wasn't completely sure she'd understood everything he'd written, one thing was frighteningly clear. Garrick had left town with Ox Bruford.

Chapter 13

"Cheer up," Angel said. "Swede will be back any day now."

Becky looked up from her sewing. "How can you be so sure?"

"Ox comes through about every three weeks."

"That doesn't mean my husband will be with him."

"He will." It wasn't the first time during the last two and a half weeks that Angel had wished Swede was there so she could kick his backside. Unless she missed her guess, Becky's time was near. If Swede wasn't back when that baby was born, she'd never forgive him, even if his wife did. "Let's do your cooking lesson a little early today. I have a few things I need to do later."

"All right." Becky obediently put her sewing aside, though it was obvious she took no joy in the prospect.

Angel was halfway through her explanation of making sour dough pancakes when she suddenly threw her spoon down in disgust. "Oh, for pity's sake, Becky. He's coming back."

"You don't know that."

"The hell I don't. Get your coat. I have something to show you. It really isn't my place, and I hate meddlers, but this has gone far enough.

Becky had no idea what Angel was talking about as she followed her friend outside. Within moments, they left Beer Garden Gulch behind and headed toward the middle of town. Angel turned at the meat market and continued on past the jail to the intersection of Grant and

Price Street. There she stopped and pointed to a large building.

"That's the reason I know Swede is coming back."

Becky gave her a bewildered look. "I don't understand."

"He bought it from Philip Harsh. They had to get the deed signed over before Swede and Ox left town. That's why he didn't have time to come tell you good-bye before he left. Nobody as tight with a dollar as Swede would spend that kind of money and then walk away."

Becky looked up at the structure uncertainly. The raw lumber gave the building a new, unfinished look. There was no clue as to what its intended purpose might be. "Did he tell you what he was going to do with it?"

"No. In fact, he seemed kind of reluctant to talk about it."

Becky bit her lip. Maybe Garrick hadn't told Angel because he was planning on going into competition with her. The note had said he was going to buy equipment. This building was certainly big enough for a casino.

"Satisfied?" Angel asked with a smile.

Becky nodded, unwilling to insult her friend by voicing her fears. What had she done with her childish complaining?

"Then let's—"

"Miss Angel. Thank God I found you," Molly said as she came running up behind them. "Indians... Fort Bourbon...we've got to go right now."

"Whoa now, Molly, what are you talking about?"

"They found the Sherman boy just outside of town, with an arrow through him," Molly said as she tugged on Angel's arm, trying to get her to move down the street. "Some of the men who aren't in the mines are going out to get the soldiers at Fort Stambaugh; the rest are going to stay and guard town."

"Are the Indians on the warpath?"

"Nobody knows, but the women are supposed to go to Fort Bourbon until it's safe."

"Where are the other girls?"

"They're already over there. Sam sent me to get you two."

"Fort Bourbon," Becky asked in confusion. "Where's that?"

"It's where they store extra supplies and liquor. The whole thing is underground, so it can't freeze, and there's only one door in," Angel said. "We'll be safe from the Indians there. Molly, grab Becky's other arm, and let's go."

With Molly on one side of Becky and Angel on the other, they headed toward Main Street. Long past the stage where running was easy, Becky was grateful for their assistance as they hurried along. By the time they reached South Pass City's communal storage facility on Main Street, Becky felt like she'd run a mile, though it was only three blocks.

As they entered the stronghold, Angel stepped away from her side. "Remember, you came in by yourself," she said in a low voice.

Before Becky had a chance to protest, she found herself propelled forward. She barely had time to take note of the barrels and crates stacked along the dirt walls before she passed through a doorway set in a three-foot thick rock wall. It was so low she had to duck slightly to get inside.

The inner chamber was already full of frightened women and children. Unlike the outer room which resembled a root cellar, the walls here were made of brick. Three log supports were placed at intervals down the middle of the room, dividing the women within into two distinct groups.

Becky instinctively moved toward the larger group where she saw the girls from The Green Garter. She had only taken two steps in that direction when Angel gave her a push toward the small cluster of women and children huddled near the crates of whiskey and bourbon.

"Don't be a damned fool," Angel hissed in her ear, "Get over there where you belong."

With a flash of embarrassment, Becky suddenly realized why the women had segregated themselves when she received several indignant glares from the 'decent' women of South Pass City. She pulled her coat as far around herself as she could, her steps faltering doubtfully. Just as she was thinking she'd rather take her chances with the soiled doves on the other side, a strident voice rang out in welcome.

"Mrs. Swenson, do join us. I hear that husband of yours is something of a hero nowadays. You must be very proud of him." The large gray-haired woman looked vaguely familiar, and Becky smiled uncertainly.

"Yes...yes, I am."

"I haven't seen you since the wedding. How have you been faring?"

"Pretty well." Becky suddenly realized it was Esther Morris, the Justice of the Peace who had performed their wedding ceremony.

"Excellent. Come, let me introduce you to some of your neighbors."

With Esther Morris's stamp of approval, the other women thawed immediately, and Becky soon found herself surrounded by the handful of hardy women who had followed their husbands to the mining camp.

Sam from The Green Garter appeared in the doorway. "Is everybody here?"

"Everyone from our part of town," Angel said. "Don't know about the others."

"I believe we're all accounted for as well," Esther Morris answered firmly. "You may as well shut us in."

Sam nodded. "All right then. Hans and I will be standing guard right outside, but I'll leave a shotgun for you just in case."

He started to swing the heavy metal door shut.

"No...no, wait. Don't close the door. Dear Lord, I can't do this. I just can't!" A hysterical sob rose from the back of the room. "I'd rather take my chances with the Indians."

Though the speaker didn't look much older than Becky, a toddler clung to her skirts, and she held an infant in her arms. Her pasty white face was filled with terror as she stared at the heavy metal door Sam was about to close.

"Marcia, pull yourself together," Esther Morris said sharply. "This is no time for panic."

"I can't help it," she whimpered. "I can't stand to be closed in like this. Let me go outside with the guards."

"What about your babies?"

"I...I don't know."

Becky recognized the woman's fear. One of her father's mistresses had been similarly afflicted. There had been times when even being closed in by the flimsy walls of the tent had disturbed her. "It's all right. You can go outside," Becky said to her, "I'll watch your little ones for you."

The woman stared at her for a moment then nodded. Apparently reassured by Becky's own impending motherhood, she placed the baby in her arms and knelt down next to the little boy. "Zachariah, I want you and Johnny to stay with this lady."

The little boy took his fingers out of his mouth. "Papa come?"

"No, no, Papa left with the other men. Everything's going to be fine. Mama's going to be right outside. Will you be a good boy for me?"

The youngster stuck his fingers back in his mouth and nodded solemnly.

She gave him a hug, then stood back up and faced Becky. "I'm sorry, I just..."

Becky smiled reassuringly. "I understand. Don't worry, I'll take good care of them."

The woman smiled tremulously, touched the baby once more, then hurried out.

Sam swung the three-inch thick door closed with a clang. When they heard the sound of the heavy bar on the outside being dropped into place, more than one woman wondered uneasily if Marcia hadn't had the right idea after all.

Time passed slowly. Though Becky knew very little about taking care of children, she didn't have to worry. The other women all took turns holding the baby. Little Zachariah, mindful of his mother's instructions, clung to Becky like lichen to a rock.

Far from being uncomfortable with the situation, Becky found she rather liked it. Holding the little boy on her lap, she told him all the stories she could remember from her childhood. When he started to nod off, she made him a bed on the floor out of her coat.

With the baby nestled against her breast and Zachariah sleeping by her side, she felt a deep contentment. Glancing down at the infant in her arms, she smiled. Soon she'd have one of her own. The piles of baby clothes were stacked in readiness next to the beautiful cradle Garrick had made. Becky had thought her heart would burst from pleasure when he'd given it to her. It would last through all the babies they would have together, boys with flaxen hair and girls with aqua eyes.

It was only a short hop from the thought of children to contemplation of how the little darlings were created. Surely after the baby was born Garrick would finally demand his husbandly rights. Daydreaming about Garrick making passionate love to her was much more pleasant to think of than worrying about him becoming a professional gambler or wondering if he'd left forever the way Cameron had. She was soon lost in a fantasy that made her quite warm in spite of the slight chill of the underground cellar.

"What was that?" someone asked suddenly. Instantly, every voice was still as they all strained to listen.

The unmistakable sound of gunfire echoed beyond the thick metal door, then they heard a woman's panicked scream.

"Oh God, we're going to die!" A voice inside the room rose shrilly in the stillness, followed by a sharp slap and the sound of sobbing.

"Shut up, Collette. We don't have time for that now." Angel strode forward. "Where the hell is that shotgun? No damned savage is going to take me without a fight. Everybody grab something to use for a club, the stouter the better."

"She's right, ladies," Esther Morris said, picking up an ax handle. "We'd best move all the children clear to the back where they'll be the safest. Mrs. Swenson, if you could stay with them..."

Trying not to think about what must have happened to the mother of the two boys, Becky laid the sleeping baby on the floor behind the crates of whiskey and went back after Zachariah. Though she knew her advanced pregnancy would make her more of a liability than an asset, Becky felt cowardly hiding with the seven children as the other women gathered behind Angel and Esther Morris. She looked around for a weapon, but everything that could be wielded easily had already been picked up. At last, she pulled a bottle of whiskey from one of the crates. It would make a good club the way it was, and broken it could be truly lethal.

Collette was no longer the only one crying as they heard the metal bar on the outside of the door being lifted.

"All right, you heathen bastards," Angel said, raising the shotgun to her shoulder and cocking both barrels, "we're ready for you!"

Chapter 14

Everyone held their breath. Even the sobbing stopped as the thick metal door swung open. "You just hit the end of the trail," Angel snarled as she pulled the first trigger.

"Jesus, Angel," Ox Bruford said, knocking the shotgun aside a second before it fired. "What are you trying to do?"

"Ox!"

After a glance at the hole the shotgun had blasted in the brick wall, he reached down and took the gun from her grasp. "Give me that before somebody gets hurt! Good Lord, but you women are jumpy today."

"Jumpy!" Angel put her hands on her hips. "I suppose you have some good excuse for all that shooting out there."

"It was a signal to let the others know everything's secure here. Half the soldiers from Fort Stambaugh went south looking for the Indians that killed the Sherman boy. The rest came here then headed north as soon as we found the town safe."

"I trust that means we can leave then, Mr. Bruford?" Esther Morris's imperious voice came from behind Angel.

"Yes ma'am. In fact, that's what I was coming to tell you."

"Good. Thank you."

"So, what was all that screaming?" Angel asked.

Becky was unable to hear the rest of their conversation as they stepped outside and allowed the women to leave the cellar. Becky stayed and waited for all the children to be reclaimed by their mothers. At last only Johnny and Zachariah remained. Unable to carry both children, who were still asleep, Becky sank to the floor next to them in a miserable heap.

Ox Bruford had returned, and Garrick wasn't with him. He'd walked out on her just like Cameron. What was it about her that drove men away? Sinking her face onto her crossed arms, she gave in to the tears that clogged her throat.

She didn't even care when she and the two children were the only ones left in the cellar, and silence settled over them. Then, suddenly, a long shadow fell across her, blotting out the light of the lantern.

"Becky?"

The dearly familiar voice brought her head up with a jerk. "Garrick?"

Before she even had time to register that it was truly her husband, Garrick had pulled her to her feet and into his arms. "It's all right, little one," he whispered to the top of her head. "The Indians aren't coming here. You're safe."

"I thought you weren't coming back."

"What?" Startled by her words, Garrick tipped her head back and stared down into the tear-drenched eyes. "I wouldn't leave you," he said, stroking the line of her jaw with his thumb.

The soft velvet of her eyes deepened, and he swallowed convulsively. Even with a blotchy, tear-streaked face, she was irresistible. Unable to stop himself, he lowered his head and touched his mouth to hers. His breath escaped in a rush as her lips opened beneath his, welcoming the tender invasion eagerly.

Becky breathed in his scent, glorying in the remembered pleasure of it. As his tongue tentatively explored the inside of her mouth, she decided he tasted as good as he smelled. Her hands traced the muscular plane of his back in wonder. He was so big and strong, so very male. It was as though her daydreams had come to life as her body sagged against his solid warmth and the world disappeared in a swirl of desire so intense it curled her toes.

"Mama?"

Reality returned with a rush as the plaintive little voice sounded next to them.

"Oh, Zachariah." Becky reluctantly released her husband and looked down at the little boy. "It's all right, we'll take you to your mama." She glanced at Garrick. "The woman outside the door, is she all right?"

"*Ja*, she is fine."

"We heard her scream."

Becky could have sworn he blushed. "She wasn't as glad to see me as you were. When I came through the door, she started in, and we couldn't get her to stop. Why was she out there anyway?"

"She's afraid of closed-in places. Said she'd rather take her chances with the Indians."

"Indians maybe, but not Norwegians," he said with a grin then hunkered down next to Zachariah. "What do you say, little man? Shall we go find your mama?"

Zachariah regarded him solemnly for a moment, then removed his fingers from his mouth. "Are you a good giant or a mean one?"

Garrick bit back a laugh. "Oh, definitely a good one."

"Then I go wiv you."

"All right then, up you go." Garrick stood and swung the boy up onto his shoulders. Moments later he winced in surprise as the little fingers grabbed two handfuls of his blond mane, and Becky clapped her hand over her mouth to stifle her giggles.

"It was your type that laughed when they threw the Christians to the lions," he said with mock severity.

Still grinning, Becky picked up the baby and followed them to the door of the cellar amid Zachariah's squeals of delight. Once again, she thought of the children they might have some day and smiled to herself. He would be a good father, far better than hers had been.

When they reached the door, Garrick stopped and swung the little boy into his arms. "You're such a big boy we won't fit through the door." The opening was so small he practically had to bend double to get out.

Becky came out just in time to see Marcia grab Zachariah out of Garrick's grasp as though she was afraid he'd harm the boy.

"It's all wight, Mama," Zachariah said, smiling up at Garrick. "He's a nice giant."

"Here's your baby." Becky's voice was frosty as she transferred the infant to his mother. "By the way, this is my husband."

The woman's eyes widened. "N-nice to meet y-you," she stammered, but the look she gave Becky was one of pity as she gathered her children and fled the building.

Becky stared after the other woman indignantly. "Well, I never!"

"Now I know how my Viking ancestors felt when everyone ran away from them," he said with a grin.

"They deserved it. You don't. She's probably married to some puny little...storekeeper or something."

The sound of Garrick's laughter filled the room as she tossed her head and went back to get her coat.

"She's not the first woman to be afraid of me," he said with a chuckle as he leaned against the doorframe waiting for her. "My size intimidates a lot of them."

"Only the very silly ones I'm sure."

"As I remember, you were pretty nervous at first."

"I was not!"

"You wouldn't even look at me."

"I did too."

"Nope, I remember distinctly. You ran down the stairs like your dress was on fire, skidded to a stop right in front of me, and then stared at your shoes." He straightened as she came through the door and fell into step beside her.

"All right, maybe I was a little afraid, but it wasn't because of the way you look."

"No?"

"I thought you'd be like my father."

Garrick stopped in his tracks and looked down at her in astonishment. "And you still married me?"

Becky shrugged. "I learned to stay out of his way most of the time. Anyway, it wasn't your size that scared me." She touched the thick blond hair that lay against his collar. "Of course, now that I look, you could use a shave and a haircut. I hadn't really noticed before."

"I haven't shaved since I left. I suppose I do look a little wild."

"A little."

"Bad enough to scare nervous women and small children?"

"Maybe."

They looked at each other for a moment then burst into laughter. It lay soft and warm between them like the memory of their kiss as they stepped out in to the bright autumn sunshine.

"'Bout time you two showed up," Ox said, leaning against the side of his wagon. He took one last puff off his cigarette and threw it away. "I do have other customers, you know."

"But none that offered to drive your second wagon clear from Rock Springs for nothing," Garrick said with a grin.

Ox's eyes twinkled. "I probably wouldn't have needed that second wagon if it hadn't been for everything you brought back with you. Good to see you, Becky."

"You too, Ox."

Garrick wondered with a jealous twinge when they had started calling each other by their first names. "I'll take Becky home then come back and help you unload."

"No need for that. We'll just deliver your household goods now. That window has to come out first anyway."

"All right," Garrick said. "Looks like you get to ride home, Becky."

"You bought a window?" Becky peered curiously at the back of the wagon as Garrick lifted her up onto the seat and then climbed up beside her.

"I figured we needed it with winter coming on."

"But how did you get it here without breaking it?"

"I'll have you know I've never broken a window in all the years I've been hauling freight," Ox said as he climbed up on the other side of Becky and picked up the reins. "In fact, five or six years ago I hauled three of the biggest dang windows you ever saw clear from St. Jo Missouri to Horse Creek. Brought them out for a rancher named Cantrell who..."

Becky listened to Ox's story with half an ear as the wagon moved down the street. It was difficult to pay attention when the warmth of her husband's strong muscular thigh branded her leg from hip to knee. More than anything, she wanted to reach over and hold his hand. Unsure how he'd react, she kept her hands folded in her lap.

Her heart was lighter now that he was back, but Becky was still troubled. She didn't know why he'd gone or even where for sure. Though her curiosity was about to get the best of her, she decided to wait until they were alone to ask her questions.

But when they finally reached home, she never got the chance. Garrick and Ox unloaded the window first, then a large crate. Garrick pried the lid off and insisted she unpack it. Not knowing what to expect, she dug down through the packing and discovered it was filled with new pots and pans.

Becky was busily unpacking them when the two men came back inside a few minutes later. "Thank you, Garrick! I've never had pans as nice as..." She trailed off in amazement as she realized what they were carrying. "A cook stove." she whispered. "Oh, Garrick."

Both men were grinning from ear to ear. "Told you she'd be pleased," Ox said, as they set it in the corner. "There's not a woman alive who can resist a new stove."

"I had some extra money," Garrick explained with a smile. His eyes sought Becky's and their gazes locked with silent pleasure.

"Well, Swede," Ox said finally. "What do you say we get the rest of your equipment unloaded so you can spend some time with your wife? After two and a half weeks I expect you two will have lots to talk about."

His meaning was obvious, and Becky blushed to the roots of her hair.

"*Ja*, I guess so. I'll be back as soon as I can, Becky, but probably not before supper."

"Can I come help?"

Garrick flashed her a smile. "No, I want to have everything ready before you see it."

"Oh." Her heart sank. A casino. What else would he want to keep secret?

"I'm sorry I can't take time to set the stove up now," he was saying, "but I can probably do it after supper." He dropped a kiss on her forehead, and then he was gone.

Though he'd spent the last two and a half weeks making his dream a reality, Garrick found it difficult to concentrate now that it was so close to completion. All he could think of was Becky. He'd missed her like the devil while he'd been gone, but his welcome home had almost been worth the loneliness. Her sweet kiss lay like a warm caress in his mind. As he and Ox unloaded the equipment he'd traveled so far to buy, Garrick found himself wishing he could just leave it all and go home to his wife.

The thought brought him up short. His wife? When had he started to believe his own charade? Then again, maybe it wasn't really a pretense any more. Their relationship certainly felt like a marriage, or at least what he thought a marriage should be like.

The feelings he had for her now were not the same as they had been five months ago. No longer could he complacently imagine her falling in love with another man and leaving. In fact, he found himself wanting to somehow bind Becky to him so tightly she couldn't leave. Maybe it was time to woo his wife.

"That's it," Ox said as he set the last crate down with a thunk. "You plan on stayin' here and gettin' started on this tonight?"

Garrick looked around the spacious interior of his new building with more than a little anticipation. Yet, as impatient as he was to throw the doors open for business, he shook his head. "Actually, I'm pretty tired. Think I'll just go home to supper and have a nice hot bath."

"And probably turn in early, too," Ox said with a grin. "Can't say as I blame you. If I had a woman like your Becky—not that I'm ready to settle down yet," he added quickly when he saw his friend's scowl. "Come on, I'll walk part way with you. Reckon I'll go see if I can get in a good card game at Angel's."

Garrick was suddenly tempted to ask Ox's advice. He knew his friend had been married before the war and would surely know the proper way to treat a woman like Becky. His own experience with decent women was nonexistent. The hurried, unemotional coupling with a prostitute was very different from what went on between husbands and wives.

Unlike Collette, Becky wouldn't be thrilled to the point of swooning by the very idea of bedding him. No, he'd have to go slowly. Luckily, he had plenty of time. There could be no thought of sleeping with her until long after the baby was born.

"I'll be dammed. I wonder what a federal marshal is doing in South Pass City."

Ox's voice brought Garrick out of his self-absorption with a jolt. Suddenly, his heart was pounding in his ears as he followed his friend's gaze. Even at this distance there was no mistaking the glint of a badge in the late afternoon sunlight or the familiar red handlebar mustache. The man didn't seem to have changed at all in six years. With seeming nonchalance, Garrick reached up and pulled his hat low over his eyes as though to shade them from the sun.

"Hmm, think I'll go find out what brings him clear up here," Ox said, then grinned. "I don't suppose you'd care to come with me?"

"I don't particularly care why he's here."

"At least not with the lovely Becky waiting at home. Can't say I blame you. Give her my best." Watching Swede walk away, Ox felt a flash of envy. "Lucky S.O.B," he muttered to himself. Then, with a shrug, he sauntered down the street to the saloon he'd seen the marshal enter.

"Howdy, Marshal," Ox said walking up to him at the bar and offering his hand. "Ox Bruford's the name."

"Daniel Dutton." The two men sized each other up as they shook hands.

"Join me in a drink, Marshal Dutton?"

"Don't mind if I do. My throat's full of trail dust."

Ox ordered a bottle of whiskey and two glasses. "What brings you to South Pass?"

"Just passing through. We've had some complaints of two-bit outlaws working the road between here and Cheyenne. I came to look the situation over." Dutton took a swallow of his drink. "Couldn't help but notice your friend up the street. His name wouldn't happen to be Ellinson, would it?"

"Nope, Swenson."

"Damn, I was hoping..." He sighed. "Wishful thinking, I guess. I used to know a big Norwegian who looked an awful lot like him."

"Couldn't be the same man. He's Swedish, not Norwegian."

"I think your friend's a little bigger anyway."

Ox grinned. "That's not surprising. Swede's bigger than just about everybody."

With a knot of ice in his stomach, Garrick covered the distance home in record time. How could he have forgotten even for one minute he was a wanted man?

Knowing Becky would recognize his agitation immediately, he by-passed the house and stumbled into Sophie's shed. Shaken to the depths of his soul, Garrick leaned unsteadily against the wall. With the scruffy beard and longer hair, Dutton probably hadn't recognized him, but he hadn't had such a close call in years. What was Dutton doing out of Dakota Territory anyway? Surely South Pass City was way outside his jurisdiction.

Garrick thought of Becky. This time he couldn't run. She and her child were a responsibility he wouldn't even consider shirking. A feeling of hopelessness welled up inside him. Even if Dutton's presence was a coincidence, it was only a matter of time until somebody discovered him here. He'd never be able to build the life he wanted with Becky. It would be far better for her if he maintained his distance.

For a moment he thought he would choke on the huge lump in his throat as he reached into his pocket and pulled out the ring of braided gold and silver he'd bought in Omaha. It was a wedding ring meant for a princess, *his* princess. Turning it over in his hand, he gazed at it sorrowfully. Suddenly, he knotted the hand into a huge fist and smashed it into the wall. He almost welcomed the pain as it rose in a tide from his battered knuckles to merge with the ache in his heart.

Chapter 15

"Where is he?" Becky wondered out loud as she looked out at the darkening sky. With a sigh, she threw her shawl around her shoulders and opened the door. She'd better go feed Sophie before it got dark.

Walking the short distance to the shed, she told herself Garrick would be along any minute now. After all, he'd promised to put the new stove together tonight and he never —

"Garrick?" Becky stopped just inside the shed door; surprised to see her husband crouched down next to Sophie. "What's wrong?" Becky had never seen the mare lying on her side before. With a rush of fear, she hurried across the shed.

"Shh, it's all right. Look," Garrick said quietly as he rubbed the mare's neck soothingly.

Becky followed the line of his finger and gasped. Two diminutive hooves protruded from beneath Sophie's tail. As she watched, Sophie strained, and a tiny head appeared pillowed between two long legs. With a final grunt from the mare, the rest of the body slipped out with a surge of fluid.

"Oh, Garrick, help it," Becky cried as the baby tried to lift its head then weakly dropped it back onto its legs.

"Don't worry, Sophie will take care of him."

As if on cue, Sophie heaved herself to her feet, turned, and began nuzzling the youngster.

Moving out of the way, Garrick went to stand beside Becky. "How did you know?" she asked, never taking her eyes off the foal.

"I didn't. It was just one of those times I happened to be in the right place."

"I'm glad you were here. If anything had happened to Sophie or her baby..."

He smiled down at her. "I didn't do much. Sophie took care of it by herself."

Together, they stood and watched as the mare cleaned her baby and gently nudged it to its feet.

"Look," Becky cried as the youngster took its first wobbly steps and nosed his mother's flank. "He knows exactly where to go."

"*Ja.* It's amazing how Nature takes care of her babies."

As they watched the colt locate his mother's milk and have his first meal, Garrick was achingly aware of the woman beside him. His mind was suddenly filled with the image of her within the shelter of his arms, her back pressed against him and his chin resting on the top of her head as they shared the miracle of the colt's birth. "Is supper ready?" he asked abruptly.

"What? Oh, yes. I was just waiting on you." Becky was surprised to see him turn and stride from the shed without another word. Was he angry with her for some reason? She followed him uncertainly into the house. "Is something wrong, Garrick?"

"No." The flash of hurt in her eyes as she turned away was like a knife in his heart. "I'm just tired."

"I heated water so you could take a bath after supper," she said.

"Thanks."

"I can cut your hair for you later, too."

Garrick knew he'd never be able to handle such intimate contact. "No need. I'll go to the barber tomorrow."

The small sounds that Becky made as she set the table and dished up supper were loud in the almost oppressive silence that fell between them. She felt like crying as she thought of the warm kiss they'd shared hours before. What had happened?

"You're not using your new pans."

"N-no. I thought I'd wait until the new stove is set up. They get so black in the fireplace."

"I can get everything but the chimney hole done tonight."

"It doesn't matter."

"I want to," Garrick said, reaching across the table for a biscuit.

"Garrick, what happened to your hand?" Becky was staring at his fingers in horror.

He glanced down at the bloodied knuckles guiltily. "I scraped them on a board."

"They must hurt terribly."

"It was my own fault."

"What difference does that make?" Becky scooted back her chair and went to get the tincture of iodine and a clean rag. "This won't make them feel any better, but it will help your hand heal."

Garrick sucked his breath in between clenched teeth as she dabbed the medicine on his cuts. At least the stinging pain kept him from thinking too much about how good she smelled.

"Are you going to tell me where you went?" she asked quietly.

"Omaha."

She momentarily stopped her tender ministrations and looked up at him. "What on earth for?"

"I couldn't get everything I needed in Rock Springs, so I took the train to Omaha. It only takes about three and a half days."

"When are you going to tell me what you're up to?"

He smiled up at her. "I should be ready in a day or two."

"Can't you tell me now?"

"And spoil my surprise?"

Becky turned her attention back to his hand. "I think I already know," she said quietly. "Angel showed me the building you bought from Philip Harsh."

He chuckled. "I told Ox you'd figure it out. You're the one who gave me the idea, after all."

"Are you sure this is what you want to do?"

"It doesn't really matter. I'm committed now." He smiled softly. "At least you won't have to worry about me blowing myself up any more."

"I'm glad."

"You don't sound like it."

She ducked her head even farther to keep her tears at bay. "I didn't have any business demanding you quit something you were obviously good at."

"I'm glad you did. Otherwise, I'd have never thought of doing this."

"You weren't happy with my interference at the time. You swore at me."

"I what?"

"Don't you remember? You said yay elker something."

He grinned suddenly. "*Jeg elsker deg.*"

"Yes, that's it. And you wouldn't tell me what it meant."

"It's what Norwegian husbands say to their wives when they get out of hand."

"Is that so?" Becky gave his knuckles one last swipe with the rag and stuck the cork back in the bottle. "And what do Norwegian wives say to their husbands when they feel like coshing them over the head?"

"I don't know. My mother's Irish. Anyway, Norwegian husbands are never wrong."

"Huh." She flounced over to the cupboard and put the iodine away. "Well, don't be surprised if this wife uses your own Norwegian curse on you."

"All right," he said, the twinkle in his eye belying the meekness in his voice. "If it will make you feel better."

"Yay elker Day!"

"No, no, you have the wrong accent. It's *Jeg elsker deg.*"

Becky put her hands on her hips in pretended indignation. "Oh, ya, yooo make fun of me ven my accent is not so gooood, but I never say anyting about yooors."

"That's much better," Garrick said with a chuckle. "You'll make a good Norwegian wife yet."

"*Jeg elsker deg,* Garrick!" she said, shaking her finger at him fiercely. Then she smiled sweetly. "You know, I kind of like this curse of yours. It has a very satisfying sound to it."

The last vestiges of uneasy constraint disappeared as they grinned at each other across the supper table.

For the next three days Garrick worked from dawn to dusk in the building on Price Street and Becky dreaded the day it opened for business. He was so obviously pleased with the prospect that she kept her thoughts to herself. On the morning of the fourth day, he sought her out at The Green Garter, his face shining with excitement.

"I've finally got it all set up." He took the piece she was mending from her hands and pulled her to her feet. "Come on, I'll show you."

"Right now?"

"*Ja*, you have something better to do maybe?"

"No, of course not."

"Then let's go."

Becky swallowed her protests as he led her outside and down the street. There was no way she could tell him her true feelings about his casino.

"The sign isn't finished yet," Garrick said as they came to the corner of Grant Street, "but other than that it's ready to open."

From the outside, the building hadn't changed much since the first time she'd seen it. Oddly enough, the only difference seemed to be that the entrance had been replaced by a huge set of double doors. *What in the world?*

"Close your eyes, Becky."

"But I—"

"Humor me."

Becky closed her eyes obediently. There was a moment's pause as Garrick stopped to open the door, then he took her hand and led her inside.

"All right," he said proudly, "you can look now."

Reminding herself to act pleased no matter how gaudy and scandalous she found the interior; Becky opened her eyes and gasped in shocked surprise.

Expecting crystal chandeliers and garish wallpaper, she gaped like a fool as she stared at the dirt floor beneath her feet and the vast array of tools along the walls. A large metal contraption that looked like a stove with an open firebox dominated the room. A huge set of bellows and a shiny new anvil were set up nearby. All at once, the truth hit her. "A blacksmith shop!"

"Well, of course." Garrick gave her a puzzled look. "What else?"

"I thought...it never occurred to me..." Suddenly she giggled. "Oh, Garrick, I thought you were going to open a casino."

"A casino! Whatever gave you an idea like that?"

"You said you were going to make a business out of your one natural talent. When Ox told me how good you are at playing blackjack, I thought that's what you meant."

"You thought I was planning to be a professional gambler?" Garrick was incredulous. "That's no kind of a job! Only a fool would depend on his luck at cards."

"That's all you did for three nights," she reminded him.

"It was the only way I could get the money I needed. I had an incredible run of good luck, but it wouldn't have lasted. It never does."

"I'm so proud of you," she said, giving him an impulsive hug. "You took your dream and made it a reality. Think of it, Garrick, a blacksmith, just like your grandfather!"

"Ja." His arms closed around her automatically. "And you're the one who reminded me how badly I wanted that dream." It felt good to hold her against his chest and share his excitement—too good. With a twist of regret, he set her away from him. "Do you want a tour?"

"Oh, yes. Show me everything."

For nearly an hour, they explored the smithy as Garrick explained the function of various pieces of equipment. Though Becky didn't understand all he told her, she hung on every word. There was a joyful enthusiasm about him that she'd never seen before. It was like standing in the first sunbeams of spring, and she basked in the warm glow.

"And this one is even better than my grandfather's — Becky, what's wrong?" Garrick asked in concern as she put her hands on the small of her back to ease the ache that had settled there.

"Oh, nothing. My back just hurts a little."

"Why didn't you say something?"

"It's not all that bad. Besides, I want to hear more about your smithy."

"There'll be plenty of time for that. Maybe you'd like to come back tomorrow when I fire up the forge for the first time."

"Could I?"

"*Ja*, but now I think it's time to go home."

Once outside, Becky glanced uneasily at the sky as Garrick closed the shop. Though it was still early afternoon, a cold breeze blew down the valley from the west, pushing heavy gray clouds across the face of the sun.

"Looks like we could get some snow," Garrick said, glancing up at the sky as he joined her. "Winter comes early and stays late up here."

"I know. I tried to talk Pa into moving down the mountain into Fort Brown last winter because of the snow." Becky shivered and pulled her shawl closer around her shoulders. "I'm glad we have a cabin. I never want to spend another winter in a tent."

"We should be plenty warm. I have enough wood cut to last until May if we need it."

She smiled up at him. "We'll be as cozy as a couple of hibernating bears."

The image of them cuddled together like two bears sleeping the winter away was as appealing as it was dangerous. Garrick tried to ignore it as they walked down the street together. "We better make sure everything is taken care of in case we have a blizzard."

"You think we might?" There was a touch of fear in Becky's eyes as she looked up at him.

"No, but it doesn't hurt to be prepared."

Garrick's words proved to be prophetic. By suppertime, the wind was howling around the cabin, and the snow, which had started to fall shortly after they reached home, was already piling in high drifts.

Inside the cabin, Garrick was trying to think of something to distract Becky as she flitted about. He'd never seen her so nervous. It seemed as though she'd already cleaned everything in the house three times. She even got out the stove-black to polish her new stove. She'd been chattering incessantly since he came in.

"Are you sure Sophie and the colt will be all right?"

"They're fine. The shed's tight, and Sophie has plenty to eat." Garrick paused. Perhaps this was the distraction he'd been looking for. If he got her to thinking about the horses instead of the storm... "You know we're going to have to think of a name for the foal. We can't keep calling him colt."

"That's true." She cocked her head to one side. "Any ideas?"

"How about Socks? He has four of them."

Becky shook her head. "That's fine for now, but what about when he grows up? He needs a name that makes you think of speed, not laundry."

"Like what?"

"Well...like...I don't know, something noble, like a hero in a book."

"Hmm, a hero. Lochinvar?"

"Oh, no!"

"It's not all that bad," Garrick said, a little surprised at her horrified expression, "but if you don't like it..."

"No, Garrick, it's not that. I think...I'm afraid.... Oh!"

Garrick was on his feet and at her side in an instant. "Becky, what's wrong?"

"I...I'm all wet! Angel said if that happened to send for the doctor." She looked up at him with frightened eyes. "The baby's coming, Garrick. Now!"

Chapter 16

"Now?" Garrick glanced uneasily toward the window where the blizzard howled then back to Becky. "You're sure?"

"No, But Angel said...Oh, my, God," Becky clutched the edge of the mantel as the first hard pain hit. "Garrick!"

His heart sank as he placed his hand against her abdomen and felt the telltale ripple of a contraction. There could be no doubt. Becky's labor was beginning.

"The little one is tired of waiting," he said with a lightness he didn't feel. As the tautness under his hand eased, he tried encouraging. "We better get ready to welcome him."

"What do we do?"

"To start with, you need to go put your nightgown on."

She looked up at him uncertainly. "We're going to have to do it without Dr. Caldwell, aren't we?"

"I'm sorry, Becky. I'd get him if I could."

"I know." Her voice quavered slightly as she tried to pretend it didn't matter. "H-have you done this before?"

"Ja. When the twins were born, I stayed with Mama while Papa went to get the doctor. My little brother and sister didn't wait for him to get back."

"How did you know what to do?"

"My mother told me."

"Then we'll be all right."

Garrick wished he could share Becky's confidence in his expertise. A woman's first birth was bound to be more difficult than her seventh. "*Ja*, we'll be fine. You get changed now, and I'll be right back."

"Wh—where are you going?"

"Out to the shed."

"What for?"

"I have to get something," he said over his shoulder as he headed for the door. "Don't worry, I won't be gone more than a few minutes."

But Garrick still hadn't returned by the time Becky had cleaned herself up and donned her nightgown. *Where is he? What if he's lost in the storm?*

The first fingers of panic were starting to uncurl in the pit of her stomach when the door finally swung open and Garrick came in, stamping the snow from his boots.

"I'm glad I took the time to string a rope from the shed to the house this afternoon," he said.

"It's that bad?"

"I don't think I'd have found my way back without it." He tossed a long leather strap onto the table and began to unbutton his coat.

"You went all the way out there to get one of the reins off Sophie's bridle?"

"It'll help you when the baby arrives."

"I don't understand."

"You will when the time comes." He smiled slightly. "My mother was quite insistent about it. Any more pains yet?"

"No. Do you think it was all a mistake?"

"Maybe. Guess we'll just have to wait and see."

They didn't have to wait long. Garrick only had time to remove his coat before the second pain hit with double the intensity of the first. It left Becky gasping for air and frightened half out of her wits.

"I guess that answers our question," Garrick said. "Let's get you into bed."

"Garrick?" Becky's voice wobbled tearfully as she lay down on the bunk. "Is it supposed to hurt that bad?"

"I'm afraid so."

"Sophie didn't act like it hurt her."

"She did before you came in. Besides, it seems to be harder for people than for animals."

"Why?"

Garrick shook his head as he smoothed back her hair. "I don't know, little one, but we'll get through this together."

For the next hour, Garrick spent the time between pains preparing the cradle, sharpening Becky's scissors, and doing a dozen other little chores. But the moment another pain rolled through her body, he was there holding her hand, sponging her brow, and speaking words of encouragement with that deep, wonderful voice of his. He seemed to know instinctively when every pain seized her and was always at her side within seconds.

At last everything seemed to be arranged to his satisfaction. Even the mysterious leather strap had been cut in two and each half tied to the foot of her bed. From that time on, he never left her.

She'd never seen her husband so garrulous before. He told her stories, he rubbed her back, he even sang to her. And always he was there, solid, strong, his huge hand holding hers as she crushed his fingers against the agony.

By midnight, the pains were three minutes apart and Becky was sure she was dying. "This... can't...be...normal," she panted as a particularly intense contraction finally released its grip. "Nobody would ever have more than one child if they had to go through this every time."

"I think we're almost there, little one. Don't give up."

"Fat chance of that," she hissed as another spasm wracked her body. "I'd have quit hours ago if I could!"

As Garrick gently sponged the sweat from her brow, he remembered their conversation after the hailstorm. Maybe he could distract her from the pain. "Tell me about the picnic you and your mother went on."

"What?"

"The picnic. Was it the first time you'd been to the island?"

"No, but my grandmother usually went with us. She always made me sit up straight and fussed if I got dirty."

"But not this time," Garrick said soothingly as another pain racked her body.

"No..." Becky said when she was able, "it was just Mama and me. She borrowed a boat from a friend and we rowed out to the island." Though the pains never stopped, she was able to block the worst of it from her mind. She described the day in great detail, reliving every precious moment.

When she had told him all there was to tell about the picnic, he asked her about other things she'd done with her mother and then her childhood friends. And so it went, on through the night.

Toward dawn, the contractions were so close together that Becky barely had any rest in between. No longer able to think coherently, she cursed, spewing forth every vile expletive she'd ever heard during her years in the mining camps. Her vocabulary amazed even Garrick who had spent his adult life around soldiers, railroaders, and miners.

Though Garrick never allowed it to show, he was worried. How much longer could this go on? He tried to ignore the fear as he rubbed her belly, attempting to ease the agony. He'd heard stories of women who labored for as much as three days, but surely not this intensely. Becky's face was nearly gray with exhaustion, and her grip on his hand increasingly weak. She couldn't take much more.

"Garrick..." she gasped suddenly, "it feels different...Oh, God..."

"Like you need to push?"

"Yes...I...oh...Garrick."

"I think it's time for the straps," he said with relief. Not for the first time that night, Garrick blessed his mother for telling the frightened sixteen-year-old what was going on as he delivered her twins. If he was right, Becky was in the last stages of labor, and their ordeal was almost over.

"Scoot down and put your feet on the end of the bed," he said, helping her slide to the bottom of the bunk. "Bend your knees... That's it." He wrapped the ends of the straps once around each of her hands so she could hold onto them. "Now pull on these as you push." Garrick moved around to the end of the bed and lifted Becky's nightgown up over her knees.

Becky looked up at him with bleary eyes. "Garrick?"

"It's all right, little one." He smiled encouragingly. "We're about to have a baby."

149

"God, I hope so," she gritted out as she pulled on the leather straps. "Oh my —"

"That's it, Becky, push."

Twenty minutes later, Garrick was near panic. Becky's knuckles were white where she gripped the reins and her strength was fading fast. If something didn't happen soon ... "Come on, Becky," he pleaded. "Don't give up now; we're almost there."

"I...don't...think...I...can."

"Yes, you... Becky, I see him! Just one or two more now." Garrick supported the baby's head as Becky strained one last time. With a feeling of incredible joy, he watched the baby slide from its mother's body into his waiting hands.

In less than a heartbeat, he knew something was wrong. The baby wasn't breathing. Willing himself to stay calm, Garrick turned the infant over and massaged its back with three fingers. Nothing.

Maybe there was something in the way. Garrick put one finger in the baby's mouth and removed a thick glob of mucus. Still no reaction. Desperately, he held the baby aloft and smacked it lightly on the rear.

There was a choking, gasping cry, and suddenly the cabin was filled with a howl of infantile rage as the baby sucked air into its lungs and gave voice to its annoyance. Garrick didn't think he'd ever heard a more beautiful sound.

"Garrick, is he all right?"

"*Ja,* fine," Garrick said thickly as he swallowed against the knot of emotion in his throat. There were tears in his eyes as he gently laid the screaming baby on Becky's stomach. "But I think you should know, he's a girl."

"A girl? Are you sure?"

Garrick paused in the process of tying off the umbilical cord with a piece of thread and grinned at her. "*Ja*, I'm sure. It's pretty hard to make a mistake like that."

Becky struggled to focus her eyes on the baby as Garrick efficiently snipped through the umbilical cord with the scissors and cleaned off the baby. A girl. She had a daughter.

As Garrick wrapped the baby in a blanket and placed it in her arms, Becky smiled. For the first time, she realized this wasn't Cameron's baby. It was hers...hers and Garrick's. She opened the blanket and examined her child, counting the miniature fingers and toes, marveling at the perfection of the tiny arms and legs. "Oh, Garrick, isn't she beautiful?"

"*Ja*," Garrick said with a smile, "just like her mother."

In spite of bone-deep exhaustion and the daunting prospect of all he'd have to do before he could rest, Garrick didn't think he'd trade places with anyone in the world at that moment.

The sky was a brilliant blue vault over the meadow of wild flowers. The heady smell of mountain iris and columbine filled the air as Becky twirled around, her arms stretched to the sky in joyous abandon. Without warning, Garrick was there, lifting her high into his arms, spinning with her on an invisible axis as they fell gently to the earth. The grass became a giant feather bed that cushioned them while their bodies intertwined like two vines, and the shrill wail of a mountain lion echoed around them.

Becky opened her eyes groggily. Her mind was still befuddled by her dream. It took a moment for her to understand the shrill wail that still filled her ears; then, with a smile, she rolled to her side and looked down into the cradle that Garrick had placed next to her bed. "Hello, princess."

"Is she hungry?" Garrick asked, sitting up and rubbing his hand over his face.

"I don't know. Probably." Becky glanced toward him as he rose from his bedroll and walked over to them. Garrick hadn't bothered to undress when he fell into bed. His hair was disheveled, his clothes rumpled, a day's growth of whiskers shadowed his face, and he looked exhausted. Becky thought he was beautiful.

"It's been several hours, I think." Garrick bent over and picked the baby up, his huge hands nearly covering the tiny body as he placed the squalling infant in her mother's arms. "As I remember, they eat pretty often when they're first born."

"Have you been around many babies?" Becky asked, fumbling with her nightgown.

Garrick reached over and undid the buttons for her. "I have seven younger brothers and sisters. When I look back on it, I can hardly remember a time when there wasn't a baby in the house. Well," he said, turning away, "I suppose I'd better rustle up some grub for us, too."

After parting her gown awkwardly, Becky managed to maneuver the baby into place and sighed with relief when she felt the sudden insistent tug at her breast. It was a good thing babies were born knowing what to do.

Becky smiled softly to herself as Garrick stoked up the fire in the cook stove. Leave it to him to calmly unbutton her nightgown then give her privacy as she figured out how to get the baby into the proper position to nurse. He'd shown her how to hold the baby the first time, and it was easier now.

Becky marveled at the change her feelings had undergone during the night. She had loved Garrick before, but somehow what they had gone through together had forged a deeper bond between them. As she touched the golden down of her daughter's head, a feeling unlike anything she had ever experienced flowed through her. She had this precious child and a husband she loved. Surely life could be no sweeter.

"Breakfast will be ready before long," Garrick said fifteen minutes later as he set a chair backwards next to the bed and straddled it. Crossing his arms, he leaned on the chair back and settled down to watch.

Becky smiled at him then looked back at the baby. "Can you believe how perfect she is?"

"*Ja*, she's something." Garrick couldn't tear his eyes away from mother and child. The sight stirred something deep within him, something primitive and very male. As Becky put the baby against her shoulder and patted her back, he experienced a sudden surge of protectiveness that was almost painful in its intensity.

Becky smiled as a muffled burp sounded against her shoulder. "Do you want to hold her?"

As Garrick took the baby and settled her in his arms, Becky marveled at how comfortable he looked. He acted as if holding a tiny scrap of humanity not much bigger than his hand was the most natural thing in the world.

"*Got morgen, lite barn,*" he said softly looking down at the tiny bundle in the crook of his arm.

"What does that mean?" Becky asked.

"I just told her good morning." Garrick smiled as the baby wrapped her hand around his finger. "Have you decided what to name her?"

"I really hadn't thought much about it."

"Uh-oh." Garrick grinned. "This is going to be just like naming the colt."

"I refuse to call her Socks!"

Garrick chuckled. "Then how about Dawn? That's when she was born."

"You're always so practical," Becky said with a smile. "Actually, if you don't mind, I'd like to name her after your mother."

"My mother?" Garrick couldn't have been any more surprised if Becky had said she wanted to name the baby Cleopatra. "Why?"

"Because I like the name Alaina and because you're her father. Neither the baby nor I would be here if you hadn't saved me last spring. If you hadn't known how to get her breathing this morning, she'd have died before she ever lived. You've given this baby life as surely as I did. Don't you feel it?"

"*Ja,* I feel it." Garrick wondered if Becky had any idea of the gift she had just given him. "I'm sure my mother would be flattered to have a granddaughter named after her."

"Is this her first?"

Garrick was silent for a moment then sighed. "To tell the truth, I don't know. I suppose several of my sisters are married by now, and maybe even some of my brothers."

"How long has it been since you've seen your family," she asked softly.

"A lifetime." He stood up and placed the baby in her arms again. "I guess I better get breakfast finished."

Becky bit her lip to keep it from quivering as he walked away. She'd unwittingly crossed the line once again. When would she learn not to delve into his past?

Chapter 17

"Put on your coat while I wrap Alaina up nice and warm," Garrick said, taking the baby from Becky's arms. "You've both been cooped up in this cabin for almost three weeks. It's time you got outside and got some fresh air."

"But Garrick, there's two feet of snow out there," Becky protested.

"Don't worry, I've taken care of that."

"I suppose you shoveled a path so Alaina and I can take a nice little stroll to town and back."

"No, it's easier to travel over the top of the snow up here in the mountains."

"If you expect me to get on those infernal skis of yours you can forget it!"

Garrick grinned at her as he finished putting Alaina into her new fur-lined bunting. "My skis are much too long for you."

"It's just as well." If the truth were known, Becky was more than a little fascinated with Garrick's skis. She'd viewed them as a curiosity from his Scandinavian heritage until she saw how fast he could travel on them. Instead of battling his way through the drifts, Garrick sailed over the top. Unfortunately, skiing wasn't very lady-like, so Becky kept her yearning secret. "The last thing I want to do is strap a couple of boards to my feet," she said, pulling on her mittens.

"This won't be the least bit undignified," Garrick assured her as he placed Alaina in her arms and wrapped the ends of her scarf around her neck. "In fact, you'll be the envy of all who see you."

"And who's going to see me way out here?"

Garrick's eyes twinkled as he pulled on his gloves. "Who said anything about staying here?" He opened the door and stepped to the side. "Shall we go?"

Mystified, Becky followed him outside where she gasped in surprise. The last thing she'd expected to see was Sophie hitched to the buckboard. It took her a moment to realize the wheels had been replaced by runners. "You made it into a sleigh!"

"I'm a blacksmith, you know. We do things like that."

"Oh, Garrick, it's wonderful!"

"Let's try it out," he said, grasping her around the waist and lifting her and the baby up to the seat. In a moment, he was beside her and gave Sophie the signal to start.

Unlike wheels, the runners glided over the bumpy road like silk over glass. Buried beneath the thick blanket of snow, the ruts were but a memory as Sophie pulled the sleigh through the drifts.

The main road had been packed down by the traffic, and Sophie broke into a trot as soon as they turned on to it.

Becky laughed in sheer delight as they sped toward town. "It feels like we're flying!"

Garrick just grinned, pleased by her obvious pleasure. He slowed when they came to town, carefully avoiding the places where garbage or horse dung encroached on the snow. They soon left South Pass City behind as Sophie followed the road out of town. At the top of a high hill, Garrick pulled back on the reins and brought Sophie to a stop.

"Are you ready to try it?"

Becky's eyes gaze to his face in surprise. "Me?"

"Of course, you. I think Alaina might be a little too young," he said with a grin.

Though Becky was daunted by the idea, she couldn't quite keep the excitement out of her voice. "Are you sure?"

"If you're going to use the sleigh to get around, you'll have to know how to drive it. I don't know any other way to teach you."

"You mean it's mine to use?"

"The only time I'd need it is when you and Alaina are with me. I can ski the rest of the time." He wrapped the reins around the brake lever before taking Alaina from Becky's arms and peeking under the blanket that covered the baby's face.

"She's sound asleep," he said, tucking the bundle into the crook of his arm. "You may as well get started. It's pretty much the same as driving a wagon. A sleigh just moves a little faster."

For once, Becky was grateful for her husband's stoic demeanor. No matter how bad her mistakes, he seemed unaffected. Even when she took a corner too fast and nearly wrecked the sleigh, he just told her to slow down a bit. At last, he pronounced himself satisfied with Becky's driving and took the reins back.

"How are you and Alaina doing?" he asked. "Cold yet?"

"No. With the rabbit fur you got for the inside of Alaina's bunting, I think she could stay out all day and not get cold."

"How would you like to ride over to Atlantic City and back?"

"Oh, could we?"

"I figure if enough people see us it will bring in business. Everybody will want runners for their buckboards and wagons."

Becky didn't care what the reason for the trip was; she thoroughly enjoyed herself as they flew over the snow-packed road. The small seat of the buckboard and their heavy coats forced Becky to sit with her body pressed against Garrick's side, a situation she found very much to her liking. The contact caused an odd little fluttering in her stomach and made her want to grin like a fool.

Since she was no longer pregnant, Becky was sure it wouldn't be long now before Garrick decided to share her bed. Surely he'd only been waiting for the baby to be born. Of course, it would still be a few weeks before she was healed enough, but then... She gave a happy sigh and snuggled closer against his side.

"What?" he asked looking down at her with an inquiring smile.

Becky startled guiltily and looked away so he wouldn't see the telltale blush staining her cheeks. "Oh, nothing."

"It must have been something. That was a satisfied sigh if I ever heard one."

"I was just thinking how much fun this is," she said thinking quickly. "I'm so glad you thought of it."

"So am I."

He slapped the reins against Sophie's rump, and Becky giggled in delight as they sped up. But the bubbles of joy surging through her had as much to do with the

anticipation of consummating her marriage as they did with the thrill of going so fast.

Over the next few weeks, Becky's life settled into a routine. Every morning she did the things that needed to be done around the house. Precisely at noon Garrick would come home to eat lunch and play with Alaina.

After he went back to the smithy, Becky dressed Alaina warmly, hitched Sophie to the sleigh, and drove to The Green Garter. There she spent several hours sewing and taking cooking lessons while Angel and her girls did their best to spoil Alaina. Then it was home again to fix the evening meal.

Garrick returned at dusk. He fed the horses, ate supper, then spent the evenings much as he had before, though now he devoted a great deal of time to his daughter. Alaina was a constant source of joy for both of them, one more thing for them to share.

Still, Becky was dissatisfied. Expecting a closer relationship to develop with Garrick, she found herself becoming impatient when nothing happened. She rationalized it by telling herself he wanted to be sure she was fully recovered from Alaina's birth, but she chafed at the delay. It wasn't until Christmas that she began to suspect there was more to it than that.

Becky didn't even notice that Garrick took longer than usual to feed the horses before breakfast Christmas morning. She was too busy trying to get her griddle cakes done before he came back. It was the first time she'd made them, and she wanted to surprise him.

The last griddlecake had just joined the others on the plate in the warming oven when he came in stomping the snow from his boots.

"Mmm, something sure smells good."

"Griddle cakes," Becky said, turning from the stove with a smile. "I told Angel I wanted something special for Christmas and she..." Becky's voice trailed off in surprise as he handed her a shirt and pair of trousers.

"Merry Christmas," he said with a grin.

Becky glanced at the clothes then back to his face. "I don't understand."

"You can't ski in a dress."

For the first time, she really looked at the skis leaning against the wall. She'd thought they were Garrick's, but now she saw they were much shorter. "You made me skis?"

"I could tell you wanted some."

"But how did you know? I mean, I never said anything..."

"You didn't have to. I saw it in your eyes every time I strapped mine on."

"Oh, Garrick." She went to them and ran her hands over the polished surface, marveling at how smooth the wood was. "They're beautiful. I hardly know how to thank you."

"How about by feeding me breakfast?"

"Oh..." She scurried back to her stove, retrieved the cakes from the warming oven and set them on the table. Then, with a flourish, she set a brown paper package on the table next to Garrick's plate.

"What's this?" he asked, raising his eyebrows a fraction.

"Your Christmas present," she said with a shy smile. "I hope you like it." She hovered nearby, struggling to contain her excitement as he took his time unwrapping the package.

Garrick suppressed a grin. It was times like this that she seemed very young. "A new shirt," he said, rubbing his hand over the soft wool.

"You really don't have any winter clothes."

"I do now," he said with a smile. "This will keep me plenty warm. Thank you."

Becky flushed with pleasure. "Better eat before it gets cold."

With a nod, Garrick put the new shirt aside and attacked his breakfast like a man who had been too long without food.

As soon as breakfast was over and the dishes stacked, Garrick pushed back his chair. "Why don't you leave those until later? They'll keep until after your first lesson."

"What about Alaina?"

"We'll take her with us. I'll get her ready while you change your clothes."

"All right," Becky said doubtfully as she picked up her new clothes and went behind the curtain.

By the time Becky had removed her dress and struggled into the unfamiliar trousers, she was questioning her sanity. The way they outlined her legs was downright indecent. She felt a little better when she put on the shirt. It was one of Garrick's and hung nearly to her knees. There was still a great deal of her leg exposed, but at least it covered her hips and thighs.

The thought of wearing such an immodest costume in front of her husband was daunting, but she took a deep breath and stepped out from behind the curtain.

Becky's embarrassment was forgotten instantly as she saw what Garrick was doing. Alaina was already snugly tucked into her bunting as Garrick adjusted the leather straps that held her against his chest.

"What on earth are you doing?"

Garrick didn't even look up as he tightened one strap and loosened another. "Don't worry, she's perfectly safe."

Becky eyed the strange harness dubiously. "Are you sure?"

"This is the way my father always carried the baby when we went skiing."

"Your father?"

"Mama maintained that since she carried them for the first year he could carry them the second. He never dropped a single one. Besides, Alaina likes it, don't you, min datter."

It was true. As Becky crossed the room she could hear the baby gurgling and cooing in contentment. Obviously, Alaina was quite happy where she was.

"All right," Becky said reaching over and smoothing the golden curls on her daughter's head. "I guess you know what you're doing."

She glanced up at Garrick and caught her breath in surprise. The spark of desire she saw in his eyes as he admired her outfit, sent the blood singing through her veins. Then, as quickly as it appeared, it was gone; leaving Becky to wonder if she'd imagined the whole thing.

"Shall we go?" he asked, putting on his coat.

"I'm ready if you are."

It didn't take long for Becky to discover skiing was far more difficult than it looked. With the skis attached to her feet, she was awkward and uncoordinated. She fell more than once, but Garrick, with his unending patience, was always there to get her going again.

At last, she managed to stay upright long enough to get her feet moving in the proper gliding motion. Suddenly, it seemed almost easy, and her confidence grew rapidly. Everything was going well until they came to a small incline. Garrick stopped at the top and showed Becky how to keep her skis under control.

Feeling quite bold after her success, Becky started down the hill without a qualm. She had only gone a few feet when she suddenly realized she didn't know how to stop. As she continued to pick up speed, Becky began to panic. All at once, a small tree loomed in front of her, and she tried to swerve to avoid it.

The resulting crash looked far worse than it actually was, but Becky was still floundering around in the snow when Garrick arrived.

"Becky!" he cried in alarm, as he reached her. "Are you—Oomph." One of Becky's flailing skis connected with the back of his knee, and he tumbled into the snow next to her. He twisted as he fell to protect Alaina and landed flat on his back.

"Alaina!" Becky said in alarm as she struggled to sit up.

"She's not crying..." Garrick uncovered the baby's face anxiously.

"Agoo." Alaina gave her parents a toothless smile.

They exchanged a look over her head then simultaneously burst into laughter. "I think she liked it," Becky said, giggling. "Maybe you should do it again for her."

"No thanks." Garrick flopped back in the snow and looked up at her. "Are you all right?"

"Nothing hurt but my pride. How about you?"

"I'm fine," Garrick said gruffly, as he reached up to the thick coil of hair that hung haphazardly down her neck. Though he had only meant to push it into place, his touch loosened the remaining hairpins, and it cascaded over her shoulder in a dark silky cloud. Suddenly his good intentions disappeared in a swirl of intense desire.

Almost on its own, Garrick's hand slid beneath the curtain of hair to the back of her neck. Becky's eyes closed in glad response to the gentle pressure that pulled her head down.

Her lips were cold, but the inside of her mouth was warm and welcoming as she accepted his kiss without reservation. Garrick curled his left arm around her and settled her unresisting body next to him. Even through the heavy material of her coat, he could feel the soft curve of her breast pressed against his side.

With his heart hammering in his chest, restraint was the farthest thing from Garrick's mind as Becky slipped her hand inside his coat just below Alaina's harness to rest on the hard plane of his stomach. When the kiss finally ended, it left them both breathing hard and wanting more, much more.

"Let's go home," Becky whispered huskily, lifting her hand to trace the strong line of his jaw.

Her meaning was obvious, and it snapped Garrick back into reality with a painful jolt. For a moment, all the possibilities loomed in his mind with irresistible images of the two of them together. It would be good, he had no doubt, better than good. With the blood pounding hot in his veins, it was difficult to remember he had no right to what she was offering.

Garrick released Becky and sat up. If he gave in to the urges that twisted his gut, he'd be no different than the man who had fathered Alaina then walked away. For there was no question he would have to leave and probably sooner rather than later.

"Skiing is kind of like riding a horse," he said gruffly. "If you fall, you need to get right back up and keep going."

Becky stared at him blankly as he lifted himself out of the snow and adjusted his skis. Surely he wasn't seriously thinking of continuing the lesson. Not after a kiss like that. But it soon became apparent that he was.

By the time they finally returned to the cabin to feed Alaina, Becky had become a reasonably proficient skier, and Garrick was congratulating himself on successfully diffusing the situation without Becky realizing what he was up to. He'd even managed to cool himself off, though it had been anything but easy with Becky dressed the way she was. The snug fitting trousers presented a temptation he'd never even considered when he bought them for her.

What Garrick didn't know was that Becky had decided it was time to take matters into her own hands. She didn't know quite how she was going to do it, but she was determined to seduce her husband.

Chapter 18

"**Y**ou want me to what?" Horrified astonishment was clearly written across Angel's face.

"You needn't look like that," Becky said defensively. "Surely I'm not the first to ask such a thing of you."

"You most certainly are! What do you mean you want me to help seduce your husband?"

"I don't want you to actually...you know. I just want you to teach me how."

Angel stared at her for a moment then shook her head. "I think we'd better go to my office. I have a feeling this story is one best told in private."

With the door closed against curious ears, Angel took Alaina from Becky's arms and nodded to a chair. "Sit down and start talking."

"It's all rather embarrassing," Becky began hesitantly.

"I'm sure it is, but I've probably heard worse."

Becky stared down at her hands clenched together in her lap. "Garrick and I...we don't...that is, we haven't...I don't know how to get him to..."

"Ah," Angel nodded wisely. "He's never satisfied you, has he? That isn't unusual. Men are taught from childhood that decent women don't enjoy sex, so they tend to hurry through it. All you have to do is teach him to slow down a bit."

"No, you don't understand." Becky sighed miserably. "He doesn't sleep with me at all."

Angel blinked. "You mean since Alaina was born?"

"No, I mean never."

"Never?"

"At first, I thought it was because we didn't know each other very well, then because I got so huge. After Alaina came, I thought he was just giving me time to heal, but she's three months old, and he still won't share my bed."

"Maybe he doesn't realize you want him to. Sometimes a man is hesitant to make love to his wife after a baby is born until he knows she's ready."

"He knows."

Angel sighed. This obviously wasn't going to be as easy as she'd first thought. "All right, start at the beginning."

While Becky told Angel about her life with Garrick, the older woman pursed her lips. Had it been anyone else, Angel might have suspected the man had some sort of peculiar sexual preference, but not Swede. He'd been a regular customer from the time he'd come to town last year right up until the night before his marriage. According to her girls, Swede took his pleasure in perfectly normal ways.

Nor was Swede indifferent to his pretty young wife. The night of the hailstorm when they'd slept at The Green Garter had proven that. When Angel had checked on them about midnight, they'd been sound asleep, but their positions had been so intimate she'd felt like a voyeur. Because of the pain in his back, Swede lay on his stomach, but he'd slept with a smile on his face. One muscular arm had been flung possessively around Becky, holding her close as she snuggled against his blanket-wrapped body.

"He's the one who started that kiss on Christmas day, and he got as carried away as I did," Becky was saying. "But when I suggested we go home, he acted like he didn't know what I was talking about. That night, he slept on the floor by the fireplace, just like always."

"Maybe he doesn't realize you want him to share your bed."

"I've been trying to make him understand for the last three weeks," Becky said. "I even told him it was too cold to be sleeping on the floor, that he'd be far warmer in bed. He tried to argue with me, but I finally convinced him."

Angel raised an eyebrow. "And?"

"The next day he built himself a bunk."

"Good lord. Surely the man isn't that dense."

"After yesterday, I realized I'd never get anywhere on my own."

"Why?"

Becky blushed. "It was really stupid, but I was desperate. I stood on a chair and dropped a big rock on the side of my bed. With the frame broken, I figured he'd let me sleep with him rather than on the floor."

"But it didn't work?"

"No. It took him less time to fix it than it did to break it. Oh, Angel, I don't know what else to do. You've got to help me."

"One of my rules has been to never interfere in someone else's marriage."

"I know, and I'm not asking you to. All I want is some advice. I don't have the faintest idea how to get Garrick interested."

Angel said nothing as she absently removed her finger from Alaina's mouth and handed the baby her gold bracelet to chew on. Her first inclination was to leave well enough alone. It wasn't her problem, after all. Then, the sudden image of a man popped into her head. Terence. He'd been nothing like Swede, but if he hadn't died, her life would have been very different. Usually, she congratulated herself on her narrow escape from a life of household drudgery and male domination. But today, as she held Becky's baby in her arms, she wondered if there might have been a positive side to it too.

"All right," she said. "I'll help you, but only to give advice, nothing more."

"Oh, thank you, Angel." Becky gave her a sunny smile. "I knew I could depend on you!"

Half an hour later Becky's face was the color of Angel's scarlet silk dress. "I...I don't know if I can do all that. What will he think of me?"

"The trick is to make him think you don't know he's watching. You'll drive him crazy."

Becky began her campaign that night after supper. Mindful of Angel's advice, she announced she was going to take a bath and 'accidentally' took the lamp with her when she went behind the canvas curtain.

Busy playing with Alaina, Garrick paid little attention until Becky called out to him. "Garrick, did I leave the soap out there?"

He looked over at the soap dish near the stove. "I don't see it."

"Oh, never mind. Here it is."

Garrick glanced toward the curtain and froze. With the lamp set on the shelf behind her, Becky's profile was clearly silhouetted on the canvas. As he watched, she slowly began to remove her clothing. It was sensual torture, but Garrick couldn't tear his eyes away as she stripped piece by piece, and layer by enticing layer. He'd never realized how much was beneath her dress until he watched it come off.

At last she was naked, and he thought the delicious torment was over. He was wrong. Becky put her hands on the small of her back and stretched, thrusting her breasts forward and throwing her head back. Garrick had to stifle a groan as she straightened and removed the pins from her hair before shaking it free.

On the other side of the curtain, Becky smiled as she heard the small sound. Though she felt horribly exposed and completely decadent, she was satisfied with her performance, and she climbed into the tub with a feeling of accomplishment.

Over the next few days, Becky continued her assault on Garrick's senses. She never did the same thing twice, and she was always very careful to make it appear accidental.

One day when he came home for lunch, she was dressed in her trousers. Instead of his old shirt, she had put on her own and tucked it into the waistband. Cheerfully explaining she and Alaina were planning to go skiing after lunch, she flitted about pouring his coffee, straightening the cabin and doing a dozen other little tasks that put her in his line of vision. Garrick tried to ignore the picture she made in the form-fitting pants, but his eyes kept straying to her firm little derriere and her long, graceful legs.

That evening, she put too much wood in the cook stove. It wasn't enough to burn down the cabin, but the air inside became unbearably hot. Becky unbuttoned her dress to the middle of her chest and sat on her rocker fanning herself. Garrick was his usual quiet self, but Becky noted the constant flexing of his jaw muscles with satisfaction.

The next afternoon, Garrick came home and caught her napping. Dressed only in her chemise and petticoats, with her hair all soft around her, Becky made an enticing picture. As he stood there staring at her, she stirred and opened her eyes.

"Oh, Garrick, is it that late? I hadn't meant to fall asleep." She stretched sinuously and sat up.

"You'd better get dressed before you catch your death," he said gruffly, noting the gooseflesh on her arms and chest.

"Oh!" Acting as though she had only just realized her state of undress, she grabbed her clothes and dashed behind the curtain. Privately, she wondered if that particular plan had been worth the effort; she felt frozen through.

The next night, something got caught in her stocking. With a yelp, she sat down on her bed and jerked her skirt up over her knee.

Surprised, Garrick glanced up from the set of animals he was carving for Alaina. "What's wrong?"

"Something bit me!" With apparent disregard for modesty, Becky kicked off her shoe then pulled the garter down her leg and tossed it aside. Pretending to search for the cause of her discomfort, she slowly rolled her stocking down over her calf, deliberately running her fingers over the smooth skin as she went. The stocking was about halfway down her leg when Garrick surged to his feet.

Startled by his abrupt movement, Becky looked up into his eyes. For a long moment they stared at each other. It suddenly became difficult to breathe, and she wondered how she had ever thought his eyes were cold. The look in the aquamarine depths was sending waves of heat through her whole body.

With a sound halfway between a groan and a growl, Garrick grabbed his coat and strode to the door.

"Where are you going?" Becky cried in alarm.

"Out."

"It's dark."

"It doesn't matter."

"Garrick!" but it was too late, he was gone. Becky stared at the door for a full minute before bursting into tears.

Garrick didn't even bother with his skis. Maybe a long walk over the frozen road would cool him off.

It didn't. Lately, everything Becky did inflamed him. Ever since the night he'd watched her undress for her bath, the simplest things had taken on seductive significance. When he wasn't with her, he was thinking about her and all the ways he wanted to make love to her. Lord, she was driving him insane.

After spending the better part of a week in a constant state of arousal, he wasn't surprised to find his lust hadn't cooled a bit by the time he walked into The Green Garter. He located Collette almost immediately. A smoldering look brought her straight to his side.

On the other side of the room, Angel watched the two of them. Becky had obviously been successful in her attempt to arouse him; he had the look of a man on the prowl. But what the hell was he doing here? "Damn," she muttered as Swede and Collette headed for the stairs.

Less than five minutes later, Swede reappeared alone, and Angel gave a sigh of relief. Nobody was that fast. He must have discovered only Becky could cure the fever in his blood. Angel allowed herself a small smile of satisfaction as Swede made his way to the nearest blackjack table.

An hour later, Garrick threw down his cards in disgust. It was impossible to concentrate while obsessed with the image of Becky slowly rolling her stocking down.

"What's the matter, Swede?" Angel asked quizzically.

"I'm not in the mood for cards tonight."

"How about a drink?"

"I don't think so."

"You don't want to play cards or drink, and you're not interested in any of my girls. What do you want?"

"I don't know." But he did know. He wanted Becky all soft and naked and moaning in his arms. He wanted to make wild passionate love to her until they were both so exhausted they couldn't move. Then he wanted to go to sleep with their arms and legs entwined, dreaming of each other until they woke up with their bodies clamoring for more.

"Go home to your wife, Swede. This isn't where you belong tonight."

"Maybe you're right." He pulled out his pocket watch. It was well past midnight. Becky should be asleep by now.

He toyed with the idea of having a few drinks but decided against it. Instead of blunting his carnal cravings, the whiskey would probably make him forget why he couldn't sleep with Becky. With a deep sigh, he stood up and put on his coat. "I have to open the shop in a few hours anyway. Good night."

Angel grinned to herself as she watched him leave. There was only so much a man could stand, and Swede was about at the end of his tolerance. If Becky didn't get her wish tonight, she would soon.

Becky was still awake when he came in, though she pretended to be sound asleep. She didn't need the faint whiff of perfume to know where he'd been. The image of Garrick and Collette together had haunted her since the moment he'd walked out.

So much for seducing him. All she'd managed to do was drive him straight into the arms of another woman.

Chapter 19

"You look like hell," Angel observed as she took Alaina from Becky's arms when they arrived at The Green Garter the next morning.

"I didn't get much sleep."

"From the tone of your voice I gather it wasn't your husband's attentions that kept you awake."

"Hardly. He slept like a baby." Becky sighed as she threw her coat over the back of a chair. "Apparently Collette took care of his needs quite well."

Angel's brows came together in a frown. "Swede told you he was with Collette?"

"He didn't have to. He reeked of that perfume she drenches herself with."

"Ah. So, you assumed he'd slept with her."

"Well, I don't think they played checkers."

"Nope, they weren't upstairs even long enough to set up the board." Angel chuckled. "Of course, they didn't have time for anything else either."

"What do you mean?"

"Swede went upstairs with her all right, but he didn't stay long enough to do anything but turn around and leave again."

"Why would he do that?"

"I think he changed his mind."

"You can't be sure of that."

"Ah, but I am. Collette was in a snit all night long. She only acts like that when she doesn't get her way."

"Then where was he all night?"

Angel grinned. "Losing at Blackjack."

"What? Ox says he never loses."

"No, but then Swede wasn't exactly himself last night. You've got that man so tied in knots he doesn't know what he's doing."

"Fat lot of good that does me. All I've accomplished is making a fool of myself."

"Don't give up yet. He's about to crack."

"And then what? Last night he practically knocked the door down trying to get away from me." Becky jabbed her needle through the ruffle she was mending. "We used to be comfortable with each other, Angel. We aren't any more."

"Are you willing to settle for comfortable?"

"I am if that's all he can give. I spent a lot of time thinking last night. The physical side of marriage isn't important enough to lose him over, and he obviously isn't attracted to me that way. I'd be lying if I said it didn't hurt, but Garrick Swenson is the best thing that ever happened to me. I'll be whatever he wants me to be for as long as he wants me."

"It sounds like you're in love with him," Angel said softly.

"Silly of me, isn't it? The funny thing is what I have with Garrick is a hundred times better than anything I ever had with Cameron." Becky wiped a tear away with the back of her hand and smiled shakily. "And here I am crying because I want more. At least he won't leave me with a hat full of lies and a babe in my belly."

Molly entered the kitchen just then and the opportunity to talk was lost. Angel wondered if Becky realized she'd revealed who Alaina's mysterious sire was. Cameron Price. Lord, this was getting more complicated by the moment. Belatedly, Angel remembered why she made it a policy never to get involved in other people's lives.

Though Becky no longer purposely tried to entice Garrick, he couldn't rid himself of the rampant desire she had kindled within him. The embarrassing episode with Collette had shown him no other woman would do. Only by taking long, strenuous hikes on his skis and keeping an iron hold on his emotions was he able to control it. His lust was always there, simmering just below the surface of his cool demeanor.

In the mountains, there was little difference between January and February, and the two months passed with the slow monotony of winter. But life was far from boring. Becky and Garrick both loved watching Alaina's development. They were thrilled the first time she laughed and ecstatic when she discovered her feet; she was a constant source of joy. There was no restraint where she was concerned, and both parents lavished all their affection on her. The baby was one thing they could share, and it wasn't unusual for Becky and Garrick to spend the whole evening playing with her.

Alaina was a happy baby and usually cried very little. So, when she was fussy one night in early March, they were worried. While Becky fixed supper, Garrick held Alaina, rocked her, and even sang to her. Nothing helped.

Dr. Caldwell had gone to Miner's Delight and wasn't expected back until the next day, but Garrick was ready to hitch up the sleigh and go after him when Alaina finally quieted. Even so, every time Becky tried to put her down she cried. It seemed as though hours passed before Alaina went to sleep in her mother's arms. Relieved, but still anxious, Becky took Alaina to bed with her to be safe.

Several hours later, Becky woke up soaking wet. With a sigh, she climbed out of bed and lit a candle.

"What's wrong?" Garrick asked, sitting up sleepily.

"Alaina just wet all over everything. What a mess."

"Is she feeling better?"

"I think so. Oh, Garrick, she has a tooth!"

"No wonder she was so cranky." Garrick put on his pants and crossed the room. Alaina lay at the end of the bed where it was dry, gurgling happily to herself as Becky changed the wet diaper. Sure enough, a single tooth stuck up from her bottom gum. "I forgot all about her getting teeth," he said. "Babies almost always have trouble with that."

Becky was aghast. "Are they all going to be that miserable?"

"I sure hope not."

"You're all happy now, aren't you, precious?" As Becky picked her up, Alaina snuggled down into her mother's shoulder and closed her eyes. "And now you're ready to go to sleep."

"She may be, but you aren't going to be able to."

Becky glanced down at her wet bed and made a face. "I'll just get your old pallet out and sleep on the floor."

"No, you take my bed, and I'll take the pallet."

"If anybody sleeps on the floor, it's going to be me."

Recognizing the stubborn set of Becky's jaw, Garrick sighed. She really didn't leave him much choice. "My bed's big enough for both of us."

"Are you sure?"

"As long as you don't snore too loudly."

"I don't snore!"

"Somebody who sleeps over here does almost every night."

"I'm sure a gentleman would ignore such a thing."

Garrick grinned. "Kind of hard to ignore."

"Humph, well..." She paused, obviously trying to think of a suitable retort. Suddenly, her face brightened, and she gave her head a toss. "Jeg elsker deg, Garrick!"

Garrick's smile deepened. "Same to you."

"I said it first. Do you want the inside or the outside?"

"Of what?"

"The bed. Do you want to sleep on the inside next to the wall or on the outside?"

"I don't care."

"All right then. I'll take the outside in case Alaina wakes up again."

Garrick nodded. Wishing there were some way to avoid what was sure to be an extremely unpleasant night, he removed his pants and crawled into bed.

Becky put Alaina in her cradle and blew out the light before joining him. Garrick had built the bed to accommodate his large frame, and it was quite roomy. They were achingly aware of each other as they lay shoulder-to-shoulder and stared at the dark ceiling.

"Do you have enough room?" Becky asked.

"*Ja,* sure," he lied. "How about you?"

"Just fine."

"Good night," Garrick said as he turned on his side and faced the wall.

Becky swallowed past the lump in her throat. "Sleep well."

Silence fell as the darkness closed in around them. Becky felt the sting of tears and turned away. For months, she'd dreamed of sharing Garrick's bed, but never this way. She didn't even dare reach out and touch the broad back that was so close.

Garrick lay staring at the wall, every nerve in his body attuned to the woman next to him. It was impossible to pretend she wasn't there. He could feel every inch of her, though the actual physical contact was negligible. He didn't realize he was gritting his teeth until his jaw began to ache.

If he hadn't been so aware of her, he might have missed the small in-take of breath behind him. It sounded like a muffled sob. Garrick rolled over and looked at her. All he could see was her back. "Becky?"

Embarrassed to be caught crying, she tried to pretend she was asleep, but Garrick wasn't fooled. Propping himself up on an elbow, he looked down at her with concern.

"Becky, what's wrong?"

"Nothing."

"Since when do you cry over nothing?"

"I'm not crying."

"Then what do you call this?" he asked, reaching over and brushing a tear from her cheek with a gentle finger.

"My eyes are watering."

"And I'm king of England," he said. "You don't have to be afraid of me, Becky. I won't touch you."

She rolled to her back and looked up at him. "And why is that, Garrick? What is it about me that you dislike so much you can't even bring yourself to touch me? I've asked myself a hundred times, and I can't figure it out."

CAROLYN LAMPMAN

Her words were so unexpected Garrick could only stare at her in speechless astonishment. Becky waited expectantly for several long moments. "Oh, never mind," she said at last, throwing back the blankets and starting to get out of bed.

The motion galvanized Garrick into action. Before Becky's foot touched the floor, a long muscular arm wrapped around her waist and pulled her back.

"Whoa now. I think we better talk about this."

Becky gave a humorless laugh. "Well, that's a switch."

"Whatever gave you the idea I couldn't bear to touch you?"

"I wonder. Maybe because we've been married almost a year, and we still haven't consummated it. Or maybe because you went to a prostitute rather than your own wife."

With an odd twist in his gut, Garrick realized she saw his restraint as rejection. "I thought... I mean I never realized you'd want—"

"Well, you thought wrong! It so happens I do want. Very much. I told Angel I was willing to settle for what we have, and I am. But it hurts too bad to be this close to you, Garrick. Just let me go."

Garrick felt like an utter fool. In the face of her unhappiness, his reasons seemed less important, his restraint a useless burden to them both.

"You're wrong, Becky." His voice was a sensual caress as the iron band around her middle tightened to pull her back down onto the bed and into his embrace. "I've never wanted to touch anybody as much as I want to touch you. I dream about the softness of your skin and the silkiness of your hair."

182

Becky's resistance melted like snowflakes on a hot griddle as Garrick lifted her hand to his mouth and kissed the tips of her fingers before pressing it against his chest. "And I want you to touch me; to feel how you make my heart pound; to know just how much I want you."

"Then why have you avoided me?"

"Because I was afraid I wouldn't stop."

Becky traced the hard line of his jaw with her fingertips. "Who wants you to stop?" she whispered. The last of Garrick's good intentions evaporated like so much smoke, his control disappearing in a hot blaze of desire as she brushed her fingers across his lips. "Nothing lasts forever, Garrick. I don't want either of us to look back on this part of our lives with remorse for what we could have had."

With a groan, his mouth came down on hers, branding her with his passion. His hand rode the swell of her rib cage as he adjusted his body to hers. A small moan escaped her, and she lifted her arms to circle his neck.

They kissed open-mouthed, hungrily, reveling in the feel and taste of each other. For the moment, it was enough as waves of longing rocked them both. It became too intense suddenly, and they broke apart, their breathing labored as their hearts hammered in syncopated rhythm.

"Your nightgown is still wet, Becky." His voice was like sun-warmed molasses as his lips grazed the sensitive skin beneath her ear. "Maybe we should take it off."

"Oh, yes," she whispered.

Garrick rose from the bed and held out his hand. Her brown velvet gaze locked with his as he pulled her to her feet before him.

Mesmerized by eyes smoldering with blue fire, Becky was barely aware of his fingers unbuttoning her nightgown until he slipped his hands inside to her waist. His palms traced a path of fire along the curve of her body as his lips blazed a trail of kisses down her neck.

Becky sucked in a startled breath when his fingers stopped to caress the fullness of her breasts then continued upward to the demure neck of her nightgown. Running his thumbs along her collarbone, he slid the material off her shoulders. It dropped to the floor, pooling at her feet with a soft whisper.

"That's better," he said, kissing the spot where her shoulder met her neck. His hands dropped to the small of her back and traveled down to the softly rounded derriere. "You feel so good," he whispered as he pulled her body tight against him.

"You do too," she murmured, reaching beneath his undershirt. "And I want to touch every part of you, to feel your skin against mine."

Her words fanned the flames of his desire nearly as much as the soft hands caressing him. Becky slowly made her way to the middle of his chest, stroking every square inch of him as she went.

When he could stand the sensual torment no longer, Garrick grabbed the bottom of his shirt and jerked it off over his head. His drawers soon joined it on the floor. He had to fight the impulse to take her right then. The image of them joined together on the floor in front of the fireplace was hard to resist, especially as Becky's hands continued their enticing journey up his chest to the width of his shoulders.

"Let me look at you," he said, taking a step back. He had hoped to cool his ardor a bit, but he soon discovered the error of his thinking. The light from the fireplace bathed Becky's slender body in a golden glow. Garrick found it difficult to breathe as his eyes roamed from the slope of her shoulders across the rose tipped breasts, down the curve of her belly to the long graceful legs. "You're so beautiful," he whispered, reaching out and trailing the fingers of one hand down her cheek.

She smiled. "So are you."

With a groan, Garrick pulled her into his arms. Once again, his mouth found hers, and he plundered the interior eagerly. The hard calluses of his hands were strangely erotic against her back, and she made soft sounds of pleasure as he stroked the sensitive skin. This time when they parted, Becky could barely stand. She sagged against him, her head resting on the hard plane of his chest.

Garrick kissed the top of her head. "Your hair should be loose," he murmured, touching the heavy braid that hung down her back. With deft fingers he began to unplait the thick strands, glorying in the silky softness of her hair.

Becky rubbed her cheek against the golden down sprinkled across his chest. Years of heavy work had honed Garrick's body to perfection. There was no softness in the man, only sinew, bone and muscle. Fascinated, she raised her hand to trace the rock-hard contours. He was magnificent.

At last her unbound hair fell in a thick cloud past her waist. "Has it ever been cut?" Garrick's voice was filled with wonder as he ran his fingers through it.

Becky kissed the hollow at the base of his throat. "Not since I was seven years old and had smallpox."

With his heart pounding in his chest, Garrick swept her up in his arms and carried her the three steps to the bed. It no longer seemed crowded as they settled into its welcoming confines.

With eager hands and mouths they explored each other, delighting in the secrets their investigations uncovered. And they discovered how very well matched they were. Every curve and hollow were tailor-made to fit as their bodies shifted and moved together. With an ever-increasing sense of wonder, they indulged themselves, living the fantasy that had dominated their waking thoughts for so many long torturous weeks. They both wanted it to last all night, but it wasn't long before they had pushed each other to the limit.

Their joining was as perfect as the rest had been. Becky was fully prepared to be crushed into the mattress by Garrick's bulk, but he didn't feel heavy at all as he began to move inside her. The thought barely had time to flit through her mind before she lost the ability to think at all. Her body arched to meet him as they moved in the ancient rhythm of love.

Her entire world became filled with Garrick and the incredible sensations his body was creating in hers. Becky had never experienced anything like it as they swirled higher and higher into ecstasy. Her release, when it came, was a complete surprise. It had never happened to her before, and she gripped Garrick's back as the glorious waves passed through her. She was still gasping for breath when Garrick joined her with his own earth-shattering fulfillment.

When the last shudder subsided, Garrick rolled to the side, pulling her with him as he went. He knew their time together was limited, but, for the moment at least, they'd found their own little piece of heaven.

Chapter 20

"Mmmmm." Becky woke up slowly. Gradually, she became aware of lying on her stomach and Garrick rubbing her back. It was heavenly. She opened her eyes and smiled at him. "Hello."

"Hello yourself." He leaned over and kissed her. "I wondered if I could wake you up this way."

"It's still dark outside."

"I know."

"Then why did you want me to get up?"

"Who said anything about getting up?"

She turned to her side and ran a finger down the middle of his chest. "What did you have in mind?"

"Oh, maybe some of this," he ran his hand along her hip, "or this." He kissed her neck. "Or, if you like, we could try something creative."

Becky stretched languorously. "Hmmm, creative. Now that has possibilities."

"Doesn't it though?"

She snuggled closer to him. "Why did you wait so long, Garrick?"

"It's only been an hour or so."

"That's not what I meant. Why did I practically have to force you into this?"

Garrick closed his eyes. *Because I've lied to you since the beginning, and we aren't even legally married. Because I'm a wanted man, and I'll be leaving you someday soon, probably without any warning. Most of all, because I'd rather cut off my arm than hurt you.* He couldn't bring himself to tell her any of it.

"Garrick?"

He opened his eyes and looked down at her. She was clearly frightened by his silence. "It's all right, little one," he said, running the back of his fingers down her cheek. "Those reasons aren't important now. I don't want to waste another second of the time we have."

His lips captured hers in a searing kiss that wiped everything else from her mind. It wasn't until hours later that she thought back to his cryptic words and wondered what he'd meant.

Swede's blacksmith shop was usually open for business by seven o'clock, but not that day. It was nearly noon before he arrived to fire up the forge. Even then, more than one customer thought he seemed a little distracted.

Becky and Alaina were late getting to The Green Garter, too. Molly met them at the door. "Oh, Becky, I've been waiting for you all morning."

"You have?" Becky raised her eyebrows in surprise. Molly had never sought her out before.

"Ox brought Angel a kitten from Rock Springs. Can I take Alaina and show her?"

Becky glanced toward Angel who nodded imperceptibly. "I suppose..."

"Don't worry, I'll take good care of her." Molly smiled as she settled the baby in the crook of her arm. "We'll get along just fine, won't we, sweetheart? Just wait till you see that kitten. She's the cutest little ball of fur."

"Molly's a wonder with babies," Angel commented as Molly and Alaina disappeared out the door. "She really ought to have a passel of her own." She crossed her arms and viewed Becky critically. "Well, well, I see you finally broke down Swede's resistance."

Becky turned scarlet. "H...how did you know?"

"Whisker burn."

"What?"

"That rash all over your face. Besides, you haven't stopped grinning since you walked through that door. You have the look of a woman who has spent the last few hours in bed with a lusty man."

"Oh, Angel, it was so..."

"Spare me your raptures," Angel said caustically. "That sort of thing always loses something in the telling."

"I suppose so," Becky said with a smile. Then she sighed. "One thing still bothers me, though."

"Only one? I've never met a man yet that didn't have at least a dozen quirks that drove me crazy."

"This is different. I still don't know why he wouldn't make love to me."

"So? The important thing is that he finally did. Generally, once isn't enough to satisfy a man. They almost always come back for more."

"He already did," Becky smiled softly. "Several times."

Angel rolled her eyes. "Then what are you complaining about?"

"I'm not complaining; I'm worried."

"What the hell for?"

"Maybe I'm imagining it, but he seemed almost frantic."

Angel nodded wisely. "All that teasing you did."

"No, it isn't that. When I asked why he avoided me for so long, he wouldn't answer. The look on his face was, I don't know, kind of desperate. Then he said something about not wasting any of the time we had." Becky gave Angel a bleak look. "I'm afraid he's planning to leave me."

"That's ridiculous. He'd have no reason to."

"I know, but I can't get it out of my mind."

Becky was silent for several minutes as she plied her needle through the seam she was sewing. "Angel," she said at last, "How well do you know my husband?"

"I've never slept with him, if that's what you mean. It wouldn't matter if I had. What happens upstairs here has nothing to do with anybody's marriage."

Becky blushed furiously. "That's not what I meant!"

"Then what exactly are you asking me?"

I just wondered if he ever told you anything about his life before he came here."

"Not that I remember." Angel shrugged. "But then he's not one to chatter much."

Becky smiled a little at the understatement. "What exactly do you know about him?"

"Only what Ox has told me. Swede apparently came west with the Union Pacific Railroad after the war. That's how they met. He was on the blasting crew, and Ox delivered supplies. When the railroad was finished, Ox talked Swede into coming here."

"That's not much more than I know," Becky said. "I think something awful happened in his past, something that drove him away from his home and family. Whatever it was, I'm afraid it's going to come between us too."

"Then make his life so wonderful he doesn't give a damn about what came before. Swede's a man worth fighting for, Becky. You'll never find another one like him."

"I know, but what if it's something I can't stop?"

"I'd say you'd better do as he says and make the most of the time you have."

The change in their relationship was obvious the moment Garrick came home that evening. Instead of his usual cheerful greeting, he swept her into his arms and kissed her passionately. "I thought about doing that all day long," he said when it finally ended.

"Me too." She smiled up at him. "I missed you."

He kissed her forehead. "This was the longest day I've ever had."

"You didn't go to work until noon."

"I know, but I couldn't wait to get home."

She snuggled closer. "I'm glad."

He kissed her again, leisurely this time, as though he were in no hurry. Her eager response ended all pretense of casual interaction. It intensified rapidly until they finally broke apart, breathing hard and wishing bedtime were closer. "I should go do my chores," Garrick said, touching her cheek regretfully.

"Supper will be ready in about half an hour."

Garrick bent down for one more quick kiss just as she went up on her tiptoes with the same intention. Their lips met in an almost painful collision. They backed away and grinned at each other a little foolishly.

"I'd better go feed the horses."

"And I need to set the table."

"Plan on an early bedtime."

"All right." Becky smiled to herself as Garrick walked out the door. So much for worrying about him changing his mind. He was as anxious to resume last night's activities as she was. With a little thrill of anticipation, she went to finish supper.

After supper, Garrick played peak-a-boo with Alaina while Becky washed the dishes. Becky couldn't help smiling as Alaina's delighted laughter filled the cabin. She wondered for the hundredth time how she ever got so lucky. Garrick had always been a wonderful husband and father. Now he was her lover as well.

"Time for you to go to bed, sweetling," Garrick said, kissing Alaina on the head. "Your mama and I have some important business to take care of."

"What business is that?" Becky glanced up and found Garrick's warm gaze upon her.

A hot thrill ran the length of her body as he grinned and stretched. "It's been a long day."

"Garrick, really!" Becky blushed. "You can't mean to go to bed this early."

"No, I had something else in mind."

"What?"

"Wait and see."

By the time the dishes were finished, Garrick had Alaina ready for bed. While Becky sat on the rocking chair feeding the baby, Garrick threw several pieces of wood into the fireplace before unrolling his pallet and placing it on the hearth.

"What on earth are you doing, Garrick?"

"Something I've been thinking about all day." He glanced up at her and smiled. "Looks like Alaina's asleep already."

"She is. I couldn't get her to take a nap this afternoon."

Here, let me have her." Garrick took Alaina from her mother's arms and laid her in the cradle. Becky watched uncertainly as he tenderly covered the baby with a blanket. Maybe he was trying to give her a gentle hint that it was time to get undressed.

"No," he said softly as she started toward the curtain, "I want to do that. In fact, I've been wanting to for a good long time."

The look in his eyes set Becky's heart tripping in double time as he walked around the cabin blowing out the lamps. She didn't know exactly what he had in mind, but she could tell it wasn't their usual evening of pleasant camaraderie.

The soft glow from the fireplace gave the room a romantic ambiance as Garrick turned to her. He looked almost predatory in the dim light, but it wasn't fear that sent Becky's heart thundering into her throat.

"I've imagined this a thousand times." His voice was a sensual whisper as he cupped her face in both hands and leaned down to kiss her. Becky thought he had pushed her to the limits of carnal desire the night before, but she soon discovered there were heights she'd never even dreamed of.

With erotic deliberation, he removed her clothing, kissing each bit of bare skin as it was revealed. By the time he got to her stockings, she could barely breathe and collapsed onto the rocking chair with a soft moan.

As Garrick rolled down her stocking, his lips traced the contour of her calf, and Becky wondered if it was possible to die of unrestrained lust. By the time he got to the toes of her right foot, she didn't care.

Garrick rapidly shed his own clothes before pulling her to her feet. Becky came willingly, her arms going around his neck, her lips seeking his as he scooped her up in his arms and carried her to the pallet.

The reality of making love in front of the fireplace was even better than Garrick had imagined. Not only did the heat wrap them in cozy warmth, the mellow light made it possible to watch Becky's face as he loved her. The passion and desire he saw there intensified his own. He'd never experienced anything like it.

It was the beginning of a long night of loving, the first of three such glorious nights. Though it was never put in words, both Becky and Garrick seemed determined to make up for all the time they'd lost, and to store up memories against the day when cruel fate might rip them apart.

The sound of Alaina's crying woke Becky just before dawn on the fourth morning. "Garrick," she said trying to wiggle out of his arms. "Garrick wake up."

"Huh?"

"I have to get up. Alaina's crying."

"Mmmm." He kissed her then smiled sleepily. "Come back to bed when you're done feeding her. We still have some time before we have to get up."

"You'll hardly know I'm gone," Becky said kissing the end of his nose. She slipped her nightgown over her head and went to pick up Alaina. The minute she touched the baby she knew something was wrong. "Garrick, come here!"

The panic in Becky's voice brought him out of bed like a shot. "What is it?"

"She's sick!"

Garrick touched Alaina's forehead worriedly. "She's burning up with fever. It isn't another tooth, is it?"

"I don't think so. She wasn't this hot before."

"I'd better go get the doctor," Garrick said as he pulled on his pants. He was dressed and out the door in record time.

To Becky, it seemed as though Garrick was gone for hours as she paced the floor with the baby. Nothing she did seemed to help. Alaina didn't even want to nurse. All she did was cry.

Garrick returned with Dr. Caldwell at last, and Becky breathed a sigh of relief. It was short-lived.

"Are you still going to The Green Garter every day?" the doctor asked as he examined Alaina.

"Up until the last couple of days," Becky said. "Why?"

"Did the baby come into contact with the young woman they call Molly?"

"Molly took her out to see Angel's cat earlier this week. Why, is she sick too?"

"She was. Came down with influenza two days ago."

"Is she better now?"

"I'm afraid not." Dr. Caldwell shook his head. "She died about five hours ago."

Chapter 21

"You've got to get some rest, Becky."

"Oh, Garrick, she's so sick."

"I know, but she's asleep." He gently removed Alaina from Becky's arms and laid her in the cradle. "You've had less than five hours of sleep yourself in the last two days. I can watch her for a while."

When Becky started to protest, he put his arms around her and kissed her forehead. "It's all right, little one. I love her too."

"I know." She sagged against him. "Promise me you'll wake me if she gets any worse."

He swept her up in his arms and carried her to his bed. "I promise, but only if you do what I say." He pulled off her shoes and undid the first two buttons of her dress. "Now rest, and no more argument."

"You're getting awfully bossy. Somebody ought to put you in your place," she said with a weary smile as she snuggled down into the pillow. "*Jeg elsker deg*, Garrick."

"Same to you," he said softly as he covered her with the blanket, but she was already asleep.

Garrick settled onto the rocking chair with a book he'd borrowed from Angel and prepared to sit out the interminable night. Worry curled around the edge of his consciousness making concentration nearly impossible. The people of South Pass City had hired a nurse from Miner's Delight to run the pest house where the sick were sent during quarantines like this one. Since she already had thirty patients, Dr. Caldwell had encouraged Becky and Garrick to care for Alaina at home. As he listened to the baby's labored breathing, Garrick wondered if they'd made the right choice.

Sometime after midnight, he awakened with a start. Disoriented at first, he couldn't figure out what was wrong. Then he heard it, the loud raspy breathing. Becky! In three swift strides he was across the room. His throat tightened as he knelt by her side and smoothed the hair back from her flushed face.

There was no doubt: she had come down with the influenza too. Dr. Caldwell had said it took two distinct forms, one attacked the stomach, the other the lungs. So far, the latter had proved the most deadly.

As the night wore on, Becky's symptoms progressed at an alarming rate. The conviction that he was going to lose both of them began to take possession of Garrick's mind, and a feeling of helplessness washed over him. He sank his head into his hands in defeat. If there were only something he could do.

Suddenly, a memory broke through the wretchedness. Once, when one of his sisters was on the verge of pneumonia, his father had constructed a steam bath. There wasn't time to build one outside but maybe—

It took a while to locate the large rocks he knew were within a few feet of the cabin and even longer to dig them out of the snow. By the time he'd lugged them into the cabin and buried them under the coals in the fireplace, the sound of Becky's breathing was frighteningly loud in the small room. Though Alaina seemed to be holding her own, Garrick knew she, too, could take a turn for the worse at any moment.

Desperation drove him on as he devised a tent of sorts next to the fireplace. Blankets and canvas made up the top and three sides while the mattress from Becky's bed lay on the floor. As soon as it was all finished, Garrick undressed Becky, wrapped her in a blanket and placed her inside with Alaina. Then he used the poker to uncover a few of the rocks and drag them out onto the hearth.

As the first dipper full of water hissed over the rocks, and the cloud of steam curled into the tent, Garrick began to feel hopeful. The odd contraption was working exactly the way he had planned. With any luck, the cure would be as effective. He thought he could see a difference in Alaina at the end of twenty minutes when he stopped the first steam treatment. She seemed to be breathing easier, but Garrick was afraid to believe it. He added more fuel to the fire and stripped off his shirt when the room became stifling. By the time he'd finished the second spell of steam, Alaina's fever had broken, and her breathing was nearly normal. Relief rolled through him in waves as he changed the baby out of her wet clothes and laid her in the cradle. For the first time, he began to think he might win after all.

His optimism didn't last past the third steam treatment. Becky wasn't responding, and the sound of her tortured breathing was like a knife in his heart. Garrick ignored the aches and pains that began to plague him as he doggedly continued the twenty-minute intervals of wet and dry heat.

At last, just as the first glimmer of dawn began to stain the horizon, tiny droplets of sweat suddenly appeared on Becky's brow. Hardly daring to hope, Garrick wiped them away. More appeared almost immediately, and an overwhelming sense of relief filled him as he turned to put more wood on the fire. Becky wasn't safe yet, but with her fever broken she had a chance.

"Garrick?"

Startled, he looked back over his shoulder and found her staring at him. "You're awake!"

"What's going on?"

"You caught Alaina's sickness. I tried one of my father's cures."

"Alaina—?" Becky's voice held a thread of panic.

"She responded to it much faster than you did. She's been sleeping comfortably for several hours now. Are you thirsty?"

"Very. It's hot in here."

"That's to make you sweat." Garrick propped her up and held the glass to her lips so she could drink. "The steam also relieves the tightness in your chest."

"It still hurts. I feel rotten."

Garrick smiled slightly as he set the glass aside. "I know, little one. It may be a while before you're completely well again. Maybe you'll be more comfortable if we get you undressed and into bed."

"It would be kinder just to shoot me and put me out of my misery."

"You'll be surprised how much better you'll feel in dry clothes," Garrick said as he picked her up and carried her to the bed.

"Are you sure Alaina's all right?"

"Positive. I just checked. I'll move the cradle over where you can see her."

As soon as Becky saw that the baby was sleeping peacefully, she relaxed. In fact, she was so limp, Garrick had a difficult time getting her into her nightgown. Her weakness was frightening. At last, she was settled in bed, and Garrick sank into his chair. If the truth were known, he wasn't feeling any too well himself. It was all he could do to pull off his boots.

"Garrick, you're the best husband in the world," Becky said suddenly.

He touched her cheek tenderly. "I think the angels were smiling on us both the day you fell into that creek."

"And the meadowlark sang on the way to our wedding." She reached up and captured his hand with shaky fingers. "Will you hold me?"

"You'll probably feel better if you sleep alone."

"No, I won't," she said petulantly. "I'm never going to feel better, so you may as well humor me."

"Oh, getting grouchy, are you?" Garrick said with a grin as he undressed and joined her in bed. "That's a sure sign you're getting better."

She gave a contented sigh and snuggled closer as his arms settled around her. "Now I am."

Sweet lassitude settled over Garrick. His head still ached, and he felt as if every part of his body had been beaten, but somehow Becky made it all right. He drifted off to sleep just as the sun rose in the sky and morning arrived in South Pass City.

Becky woke up several hours later to the sound of Alaina's crying. It was only when she struggled to sit up that she realized something was wrong with Garrick. Usually the slightest noise from Alaina awakened him. He didn't even stir. Even more alarming was the heat radiating from his body.

He muttered something as she touched his brow but made no other indication that he even knew she was there. Alaina could no longer be ignored. It took some doing, but Becky finally managed to untangle herself from Garrick's embrace. She didn't realize how weak she was until she tried to stand and nearly tumbled into the cradle.

It was all she could do to lift Alaina into her arms before she collapsed onto the chair. As the baby nursed, Becky carefully checked to make sure she was truly all right. Other than a slight cough, she seemed fine. It appeared that Garrick's Norwegian remedy, whatever it was, had worked. Worriedly, Becky transferred her gaze to her husband. Even if she knew exactly what he'd done, she wouldn't be able to move him over to the hearth.

Heat. Hadn't Garrick said that was what he'd used? Becky glanced over her shoulder at the fireplace. The fire had burned down to embers. As soon as she finished feeding Alaina, she'd get it going again.

Becky soon discovered the task she had set for herself was not an easy one. The floor of the cabin seemed to slant beneath her feet as she moved unsteadily across the room. Her legs were wobbly and weak by the time she reached the fireplace. The wood supply wasn't as plentiful as she might wish, but they had enough to last the rest of the day at least. After that...well, she'd worry about that when the time came.

Within a few minutes, the fire was crackling again, but the accomplishment was not without its price. By the time Becky had made her way back to the bed, she was almost too weak to climb in and pull the blanket up around herself and Garrick. She fell into an exhausted slumber almost immediately.

As the day progressed, Becky had only enough energy to feed and change the baby and make several more trips to the fireplace. The woodpile was dwindling far faster than her strength was returning, and Garrick was getting worse.

He moved restlessly, muttering incoherently, quieting only when she was next to him in bed again. Eventually, even her presence didn't help. He seemed unaware of her as he thrashed around.

Becky fought a wave of despair as she made her way to the fireplace yet again. They needed help and there was no way to get it. There was only enough wood for a few more hours, and she had no idea how to help Garrick. Alaina was safe for the moment, but for how long?

If she could think of a way to attract attention...but what? One of the things she had always liked about their cabin was the isolation. They couldn't hear the hustle and bustle of the mining camp, but no one could hear them either.

"Hello in the house. Anybody home?"

Becky's head jerked up. Was she imagining it, or had her prayers just been answered?

"Becky, Swede, you in there?" This time the voice was accompanied by a loud knock on the door.

"Angel!" Becky cried, sagging in relief. "We're here. Come in."

"Good Lord, Becky, you look like warmed-over death." Angel shut the door behind her and peeled off her gloves. "Are you all right?"

"I think so. I'm still pretty weak but—but... Oh, Angel." Suddenly it was all too much and the tears that had threatened spilled over. "Garrick made Alaina and me better, but I don't know how...how to help him and...and he j-just keeps getting worse. What...what if—"

Angel was across the room in three steps. "Shhh," she said soothingly as she pulled Becky into her arms. "Don't even say it. Swede's a big, strong man. He has as good a chance of pulling through as anybody."

"Are you s-sure?"

"Dr. Caldwell says almost half his patients are surviving." Angel glanced over Becky's shoulder at the man tossing around on the bed. "How long has he been like this?"

"He's had a fever all day, but it's only been the last few hours that he's been so restless."

"Could be he's about to hit the worst of it then. We better get him up to the pest house where Dr. Caldwell can keep an eye on him."

Becky wiped her eyes and stepped back. "How are we going to do that? Even if I wasn't so weak, you and I could never lift him."

"Ox and Sam could do it."

"Ox is back already? He was just here last week."

"He's stuck here until Dr. Caldwell lifts the quarantine. Anyway, if anybody can get Swede to the Pest House, it's Ox. He's very persuasive when he wants to be. That's why he's such a good mule skinner."

"Garrick isn't a mule," Becky said, slightly offended.

"No, but he's certainly stubborn enough. Why don't you and Alaina come with me now?"

"I won't leave him."

"Becky, Ox and Sam will be here in less than half an hour. He won't even know you're gone, and if you don't come now there won't be enough room in the wagon."

"I don't care."

"You're as stubborn as he is!" Angel sighed. "All right, have it your way then. Do you want some help getting dressed before I go?"

Becky glanced toward the bed. "No, I can manage. It will only take you that much longer to get help for Garrick. Angel, I...thank you. If you hadn't come to check on us —"

"Nonsense. If it hadn't been me, it would have been someone else."

"How did you know to come, anyway?"

"Swede didn't open his shop today. He's always there even in the worst of weather. You sure you won't change your mind?"

"No."

"Then I guess I'd better get going." Angel sighed again as she put her gloves back on. "I'll be back as soon as I can."

"I know."

It wasn't long before Becky was regretting her decision to send Angel away so quickly. Gathering the clothing she would need for Alaina sapped her strength alarmingly. She decided the baby would be all right in her bunting. That left the daunting prospect of dressing Garrick. The less time it took to get him to the pest house, the better chance he had of recovering.

Becky sat on the edge of the bed to rest for a moment before starting what was certain to be a frustrating and difficult job. Unexpectedly, he stirred against her hip. "Becky?"

Her heart leaped to her throat. "I'm here, Garrick."

"We're having beans and corn bread again."

"What?"

"Doesn't she realize I hate the stuff?"

With a sinking feeling, Becky realized he was delirious. "Garrick you need to get dressed. Sit up so I can put your shirt on."

Becky didn't really expect any response, so she was shocked when he opened his eyes and tried to focus on her. "Sit up?"

"Yes, right here on the edge of the bed. I'll help you."

It took a moment, but with Becky's assistance he managed to balance precariously on the edge of the bed.

Getting Garrick into his shirt was difficult, but his pants proved nearly impossible. Halfway through he got confused and thought he was taking them off. "I'm going to bed."

"No, Garrick, you have to get dressed."

"Dressed?"

"Yes, now pull your pants up."

"I'm tired. It's time for bed."

And so it went. They were still arguing about it when Angel returned with Ox and Sam.

"Garrick, you have to get dressed. Angel's here."

"Angel?"

"Yes, and you're embarrassing her sitting here without your pants."

"Angel doesn't care," he grumbled, but he finished pulling on his pants. Then he fell back on the bed and closed his eyes while Becky buttoned them. "So tired."

"You've been trying to get him dressed since I left?" Angel asked. She shook her head when Becky nodded.

"Well, Ox and Sam can finish the job. We need to get you and Alaina ready to go.

"Oh!" For the first time, she realized she was still dressed in her nightgown. With an embarrassed glance at Ox and Sam, she jumped to her feet. Angel caught her as she swayed dizzily.

"Steady now."

"Angel, I'm not dressed," Becky whispered as her face turned fiery red.

"Nothing Ox and Sam haven't seen before." She held up her hand as Becky started to protest. "I know, never mind. They won't look, I promise."

As Angel took Becky and Alaina behind the canvas curtain on the other side of the room, Ox and Sam managed to wrestle Garrick into his coat and boots.

"You know," Ox said, scratching his chin, "this would be a hell of a lot easier if we could get him to walk out on his own." He reached down and shook Garrick's shoulder. "Wake up, Swede."

"Huh?"

"You've got to walk, Swede. I don't know if the two of us can carry you."

"Time to sleep."

"Becky wants you to come with her."

"Becky? She's afraid of the Indians."

Ox looked at Sam and shrugged. "That's why she wants you with her."

Garrick struggled to sit up. "Got to protect Becky and Alaina."

"That's right." Together Sam and Ox managed to pull him to his feet. They positioned themselves on either side with one of Garrick's arms draped over each of their shoulders. Garrick leaned heavily on Ox who was much closer to his height than Sam. The lop-sided trio had just started toward the door when Alaina began to cry.

With a suddenness that took Sam and Ox completely by surprise, Garrick jerked himself to his full height. "BECKY!" The name came out in a roar of pure rage as he tossed Sam aside and went for Ox.

A huge fist slammed into Ox's face with a sickening thud. Belatedly, Ox lifted his hands to defend himself, but Garrick grabbed his arm and cracked it across his knee. Ox went down with a howl of agony, and Garrick turned to Sam. He had Sam suspended above the floor, shaking him like a rag doll when Becky finally reached his side.

"Garrick, stop! They're not hurting us."

Instantly, Garrick dropped Sam to the floor with a thud and pulled Becky into his arms. "Becky," he whispered, as he buried his face in her hair.

She put her arms around him and rubbed his back. "It's all right, Garrick. We're safe."

Angel knelt beside Ox. "Wish we could say the same for Ox. He's going to have a nice shiner."

"That's the least of my worries," Ox said, his face looking rather gray as he struggled to sit up. "I think Swede broke my damn arm."

Chapter 22

"**M**rs. Swenson? Your husband is asking for you." Martha Jane Canary, the nurse hired to look after the Pest House, shook Becky's shoulder.

Becky's eyes popped open. "Oh dear, not again." She sat up and rubbed her eyes. "He seemed so much calmer."

"No, you don't understand. This time he's awake."

"He is? Oh, that's wonderful."

Becky jumped up and hurried from the women and children's section into the much larger room where the male patients were. Sure enough, Garrick was wide awake, his frown relaxing into a slight smile when he saw her. "Hello," he said. "The nurse told me you were here."

She sat down next to him and felt his forehead. "Of course I'm here. Where else would I be?"

"I don't know. Home maybe. You don't seem sick anymore."

"No, Alaina and I were mostly recovered by the next morning. I stayed to help take care of you." She picked up his hand. "You haven't been a very good patient." In truth, he'd nearly wrecked the hospital two days ago when they'd brought him in. Only Becky had been able to calm him down.

He gave her a sheepish look. "I kept dreaming you and Alaina were in trouble."

"So I gathered." She smiled. "I wasn't sure for a while you were going to make it, but Dr. Caldwell kept telling me your meanness was a good sign. I'm not sure everyone would agree."

"I seem to remember something about Ox Bruford."

"Angel, Ox, and Sam helped get you here."

Garrick studied the top of Becky's head as she suddenly became interested in straightening his blankets. "I hurt him, didn't I?"

"You were out of your head with the fever."

"How bad?"

If there were only some way she could get around telling him. "One eye is swollen shut."

"And?"

She sighed. "His right arm is broken."

"Oh, hell." Garrick shut his eyes. Without the use of his arm, Ox couldn't drive a wagon. He could easily lose his business in the time it took for his arm to heal correctly—if it ever did.

"He doesn't blame you, Garrick."

"That doesn't make it any less my fault."

"Garrick—"

"Where's Alaina?"

"Angel takes care of her during the day. Ox looks after her at night."

"Ox!"

"It was Ox's idea," Becky explained. "He's staying at Angel's anyway, and all he does is keep an eye on Alaina while Angel's working. Once I feed her, she sleeps all night. If anything should happen, I'm not that far away. I've been going over five or six times a day to see how she's doing and to feed her."

"It seems we owe our friends a rather large debt of gratitude," Garrick said.

Becky was uncomfortably aware of a slightly disapproving tone in his voice. "I didn't know what else to do, Garrick. We needed help, and they gave it. I'm sorry if you don't like it, but I didn't have much choice."

"I didn't mean it to sound like that." Garrick felt small and mean as he rubbed his forehead. "It's just hard for me to be beholden to anyone. Call it stubborn Norwegian pride if you want to."

Becky smiled. "Don't worry, you'll probably find a way to make it up to them and mend your pride. In the meantime, just concentrate on getting better so we can go home."

By the following day, Garrick was ready to leave the hospital. It was said that when a patient left the pest house they either walked down the hill into town or were carried up the hill to the graveyard. As Becky waited for Garrick in the buckboard, she closed her eyes and said a quick prayer of thanksgiving. Any of them could have made the journey up the hill.

Garrick reopened the smithy two days later, and Becky went back to The Green Garter. Life had returned to normal. Ox Bruford and Angel came to dinner that night. Becky invited them to express her thanks and to help lessen Garrick's feeling of obligation. As a dinner party, it was a complete success, but Becky couldn't tell if her ulterior goal had been accomplished or not.

It wasn't until later that night when they lay in each other's arms that Becky began to think she might have succeeded. They were both drifting along in the soft aftermath of lovemaking when Garrick broke the silence.

"Becky."

"Hmmm?"

"Thank you for inviting Ox and Angel to dinner."

"It was fun, wasn't it?" She smiled and settled her head more comfortably against his shoulder. "They both seemed pleased. I don't think either one of them gets many invitations."

"I don't suppose they do."

"I thought Angel was going to cry when I asked her and Ox to be Alaina's God-parents."

"She was surprised."

Becky tilted her head back to look at him. "I can't imagine why. They're our best friends, after all. Anyway, now seemed like a good time for Alaina's baptism with Ox stuck here for almost two weeks until the quarantine lifts."

"Ah, Becky," he said as he hugged her tighter. "Do you have any idea how special you are?"

"The only thing special about me is the way you make me feel. Speaking of that, are you sure we should be...you know? I'd hate to have you get sick again."

"*Ja*, I'm sure. Maybe I'll make you feel 'special' again just to prove I'm all right."

"Now there's an idea," she said with approval.

Thinking back on their conversation the next morning, Becky was sure she'd helped ease Garrick's conscience. Still, she knew he wouldn't be satisfied until he found a way to save Ox's business.

Then she had it. All Garrick needed to do was find someone to drive Ox's wagon until his arm could heal. It seemed the perfect solution. Garrick was surprised, then pleased when she suggested it at lunch. With a quick kiss, he told her he'd look into it right away and went back to work. Becky was extremely pleased with herself as she put Alaina down for her nap. It was such a simple solution and so easily accomplished.

That's why Garrick's announcement when Dr. Caldwell finally lifted the quarantine the day after Alaina's baptism came as a complete surprise. Becky was getting ready for bed when Garrick broke the news.

"I'll be leaving tomorrow with Ox," he said with careful nonchalance."

"You're what?" Becky stared at him in disbelief. Surely, she had misunderstood.

"We figure it will only take this one trip. After that, his arm should be healed enough for him to take over again."

"I thought you were going to hire somebody to go with him."

"Experienced drivers aren't all that easy to find. It takes special skills to drive a mule team and a big freight wagon."

"Surely, there's somebody around."

"There is. Me."

Becky threw her hairbrush down in exasperation. "You could find somebody else if you tried. Why does it have to be you, Garrick?"

"It's my fault Ox can't drive himself."

"What about your shop? Who's going to run that while you're off gallivanting across the countryside?"

"John Gibbons. He's an experienced smith and said he wouldn't mind taking a break from the gold fields for a few weeks."

"Then let him go with Ox."

"He's a smith, not a mule skinner."

"I could say exactly the same thing about you." She stomped over to the bed. "And I don't suppose anything I do or say will make the slightest difference to you, will it?"

"I've made my decision." Those four words uttered in his father's no-nonsense voice had stopped Garrick's mother in mid-tirade more than once. For some reason, it didn't sound the same when he said it. Nor did he ever remember his mother looking quite so hurt.

"Fine, then there's nothing I can do about it, is there?" Becky flopped into bed, pulled the blankets up to her chin, and turned her face to the wall.

Uncertain what to say, Garrick ran his fingers through his hair roughly. When would he learn that what worked for his father didn't always work for him? Feeling like a fool, he blew out the lamps and undressed for bed. How he envied the glib-tongued Ox, who always knew exactly what to say. Unfortunately, Garrick was a man of action, not words.

Come to think of it, maybe action *was* what was needed here. He crawled into bed and cuddled up to Becky's unyielding back. Tracing the curve of her hip with the palm of his hand had no effect, nor did kissing the sensitive skin beneath her ear. Even when he unbuttoned her nightgown and caressed one warm breast with the tips of his fingers, she remained stiff and unresponsive.

He sighed in defeat. "Try to understand, Becky."

"Oh, I understand all right. Your stupid pride is more important to you than your wife and daughter."

Garrick went still as death. "Without his pride, a man has nothing."

"Then, by all means, save your pride." She pushed his hand away and tried not to notice when it fell with a soft thump behind her. "I hope it keeps you warm at night."

Her words were like a knife in his heart. Anger slashed through him with vicious intensity. Reject him, would she? Garrick threw back the covers and got up.

He was dressed in a few quick movements and headed for the door. There was no reason to stay here. He could just as easily sleep in his shop tonight. That way, he and Ox could get an earlier start in the morning. He resisted the urge to glance toward the bed as he slammed out of the house.

Becky was regretting her hasty words before he was even halfway down the path.

It was the longest three weeks of Garrick's life. Normally, he would have enjoyed the spring weather and Ox's company, but not this time. It wasn't even the scare he'd had in Rock Springs when he'd almost run smack into Marshal Daniel Dutton that kept invading his thoughts. All he could think of as they traveled the circular route was Becky and the way he'd left her. They were on the final leg of the journey at last. They would be in South Pass City by late afternoon.

"Sure hope the army's right about the Indians," Ox was saying. "Seems kind of hard to believe they're still in their winter hunting grounds with the snow melting in the high country so early this spring."

"Uh huh."

"I'll admit I like the freedom to come and go as I please, but I keep looking over my shoulder. Haven't seen sign of anybody white or red."

"Mmm."

Ox glanced at Garrick out of the corner of his eye. "Of course, I'm kind of looking forward to seeing Red Cloud next time. He said I could marry his oldest daughter as long as I promised to go to the wedding stark naked and dye my hair blue."

"*Ja.*"

Ox laughed and clapped Garrick on the shoulder. "Dammit, Swede, you could at least pretend to be interested."

"Sorry." Garrick grinned sheepishly. "Got something on my mind."

"The beautiful Becky, no doubt. Can't say that I blame— What the hell? That sounds like rifle fire."

Garrick stopped the wagon and listened intently. "It's coming from over that way."

"Indians."

"Could be. Sounds like someone's in trouble. We'd better go check it out."

"Yup."

Ox reached into the back and pulled his rifle from the scabbard as Garrick turned the wagon off the road. It took less than ten minutes to reach the spot. The rifle fire was coming from a box canyon about half a mile from the main road. Garrick secured the mules, then both men cautiously crawled to the cliff edge and peered over. A small band of Indians, obviously drunk, cavorted around a wagon, shooting rifles into the air.

"Damn, looks like a bunch of renegades." Ox said.

Garrick gave him a puzzled look. "How can you tell?"

"A war party would have posted lookouts. They're too drunk to even think of it. Besides, there's a couple of 'em look like half-breeds."

"That's an army wagon," Garrick said, narrowing his eyes against the glare of the sun. "I wonder if that's where the rifles came from."

"Good chance of it. Probably the whiskey too. It's against regulations, but occasionally a soldier sneaks it in anyway." He shook his head. "Whoever it was paid a high price for breaking the ru— Jesus, Swede, look at that."

Garrick peered down at the back wagon curiously. At first, he could see nothing unusual in the area Ox pointed to. Then his eyes focused on one of the wheels as a sudden flash of movement caught his eye. "It's a white man," he said, staring at the captive tied to the wagon wheel.

"We can't just leave the poor devil there."

"No."

Ox checked the chamber of his rifle. "I suppose you noticed we're a little out-numbered."

"*Ja*," Garrick rubbed his chin thoughtfully, "but I think I might know of a way to even the odds."

Chapter 23

"What we need is a distraction," Garrick said as they crawled back from the edge of the cliff and headed toward the wagon.

Ox looked at him as though he'd lost his mind. "Don't you think it would be better if we figured out a way to sneak in and out? Maybe we can get him out without them noticing."

"We'd have to wait for dark, and who knows if he'll still be alive by then. Can't figure out why they haven't killed him anyway. Looks like he's the only one left."

"I don't know. Some of them have a pretty nasty sense of humor. It's hard to say what they have planned for him." Ox grinned suddenly when he realized Garrick was pulling a keg of black powder out of the wagon. "Now, why didn't I think of that?"

"Probably because you're not a powder man. Grab that roll of fuses and we'll see if we can't rig up a little surprise for our friends down there."

"We'd better come up with a way to keep them from following us," Ox said as Garrick pried the lid off the powder. "There's no way my mules will ever out-run those savages."

"I think I have that figured out too. Are any of your mules broke to ride?"

"One."

"Good. He may mean the difference between this working and not."

Garrick explained his plan while he carefully measured the black powder and poured it into paper cartridges.

"By God," Ox said when he was finished, "it just might work."

"I hope so. Without my tools, I can't be positive these cartridges are accurate. Of course, with this it's the timing that's most important, and I can measure the fuses exactly."

"I'll go unhitch the mule."

An hour later, everything was in place. Garrick slunk along the rock wall at the mouth of the canyon, keeping to the shadows as he worked his way closer to the wagon. The Indians paid little attention to their captive, and none to guarding their position. Up close, Garrick could see Ox was probably correct in thinking it was a band of renegades. There were several half-breeds and even a few whites in the motley group. All of them were drunk and interested only in the whiskey and guns.

At last, he was as close as he could get without leaving the relative safety of the rock wall. The thirty-foot distance between him and the wagon was far too open for his liking. The only cover was a sparse growth of sagebrush along the canyon floor.

Without taking time to think about it, Garrick hit the ground and crawled. After an eternity of scrambling over dirt, rocks, and cactus, he reached the back of the wagon and took shelter underneath. Though he was no safer than he had been a moment before, he felt a surge of relief as the shadow of the wagon fell over him.

A few more feet and he was directly behind the prisoner. The renegades had taken everything but his drawers, leaving the man dangerously exposed to the elements. His skin was turning red from the sun, and his head had fallen forward on his chest. It was impossible to tell if he was sleeping or passed out.

If it was the latter, they were in trouble. Garrick knew he'd never be able to carry the other man and make it back through the mouth of the canyon in time. Reaching through the spokes of the wheel, he gave the captive's shoulder a slight squeeze. "Wake up," he whispered.

The man's head came up with a jerk, and Garrick tightened his grip in warning. "Shhh, don't make any sound. I'm here to get you out. Are you hurt?"

The prisoner slowly shook his head. If anyone had glanced their direction, the movement would have looked completely innocent.

"Good, I'm going to cut your ropes, but don't move yet. In a few minutes all hell is going to break loose, and we've got to be ready to run. Surprise is the only thing we've got going for us." As the man gave a nod of understanding, Garrick pulled his knife and slashed through the ropes around the wagon wheel.

Garrick winced when he saw the deep cuts the bonds had made in the man's wrists. As tightly as they'd been tied, the circulation had been cut off. If his feet were the same way, he was going to have a tough time running.

Using the other man's legs as a shield, Garrick crawled out from under the wagon in order to cut the rope around the prisoner's feet. Sure enough, the toes were slightly blue. As he cut the ropes, Garrick prayed they'd have a few minutes before the first charges went off.

At that moment, the boom of cannon fire echoed from the far end of the canyon, and revelry sounded from the rim above them.

"That's our signal." Dragging the other man along with him, Garrick scrambled to his feet and headed toward the bottleneck that led out of the canyon. As the Indians headed for their horses, they didn't even notice the two white men running for the mouth of the canyon.

Cannon fire continued sporadically behind them and Garrick thanked providence that the other man was tall and muscular. Despite the injuries from the ropes, his strong legs kept him moving, and he was tall enough to drape an arm across Garrick's shoulders. With Garrick half carrying him, the man was able to keep up with the big Norwegian's long-legged stride.

Just as Garrick began to think they were going to make it, there was a shout behind them. A glance over his shoulder confirmed his worst fear: the Indians had discovered the prisoner's escape. Five or six were giving chase while the others still milled around, looking for the army.

Though Garrick wouldn't have thought it possible, the two of them got an extra burst of speed from somewhere and cleared the canyon bottleneck just minutes ahead of their pursuers. "Hit the dirt!" he yelled and pulled the other man down with him.

The words barely left his lips before an explosion rocked the ground beneath them. A second and then a third blast erupted from different spots along the cliff wall, sending tons of rock into the canyon below. Garrick sat up and watched as the chain of detonations continued back along the bottleneck of the canyon.

There were five in all, then a pall of silence as the last of the rock settled into place.

The former captive sat up and stared back the way they'd come. "What the hell?"

Garrick held up his hand. "Seven, eight, nine, ten." Suddenly, the air was rent with an ear-splitting blast as two huge charges on opposite sides of the canyon mouth went off. Garrick shielded his face as a smattering of dirt and gravel fell around them.

"Do you think that last one was big enough, Swede?" Ox said with a grin as he joined the other two men a few moments later.

Garrick eyed the rubble that filled the mouth of the canyon nearly to the top of what was left of the cliff. "I might have over done it a little."

Ox laughed. "A little! How do you suppose the army is ever going to get those poor beggars out of there to arrest them?"

"I told you I wasn't sure about the size of that last charge." Garrick shrugged. "At least we shouldn't have to worry too much about them coming after us."

"Not this year anyway." Ox extended his hand to the stranger. "Ox Bruford's the name, by the way, and you already met Swede."

"Cameron Price," the stranger said, shaking hands with both of them. "I hardly know how to thank you."

"Swede's the one you should be thanking. I didn't do much more than light a few fuses."

"Let's wait till we get to South Pass City before we congratulate ourselves," Garrick said, heaving himself to his feet and heading toward the wagon. "It's possible they could find a way out of there."

"The army will surely take care of them if they do," Cameron said, limping after Garrick.

Ox grinned. "You're looking at the army."

"What?"

"You just saw why Swede is considered the best powder man in South Pass City. He did the entire thing with black powder and fuses."

"But I heard cannons."

Garrick shook his head as he pulled his extra shirt out of his bedroll. "Small charges set to go off at irregular intervals with lots of smoke."

"What about the bugler?"

Ox grinned. "That was me."

"That's right," Garrick said, glancing back over his shoulder. "I'd forgotten about that. For a minute there, I thought maybe we really had been rescued. I know you're pretty resourceful, Ox, but where in heaven's name did you find a bugle?"

"Under the wagon seat. I didn't think of it until you'd already left. I lit the fuses on the first charges, then high-tailed it back to the wagon and blew the reveille before getting the wagon down here to pick you both up. I was a bugler during the war, you know."

Cameron shook his head in amazement. "I'll be damned. The Indians weren't the only ones you had fooled."

"I just hope the mine owners in South Pass aren't too angry because I used up most of their powder." Garrick tossed a shirt and pair of pants to Cameron. "Here, these probably won't fit too well, but they'll come closer than Ox's will. Sorry there aren't any boots."

"It doesn't matter. Thanks."

While Cameron dressed, Garrick and Ox re-hitched the mule Ox had ridden along the canyon rim and tightened the load on the wagon. Within a few minutes they were back on the road heading toward South Pass City.

"What happened back there?" Ox asked Cameron after they were under way.

"I'm not really sure. The last thing I remember was riding into an ambush. When I came to, I was tied to that wagon. I must have gotten hit in the head some way. I suppose the others were killed outright. Did you see anything on the trail?"

"Nope, but then if they tried to run at all, the fight probably happened off the road a ways. A man might not even see something like that if he wasn't looking for it."

"That's true," Cameron said. "I'll have to send word to Fort Stambaugh as soon as we get to South Pass City. No doubt they'll send a patrol to find out what happened and take care of what's left of those renegades."

"This your first trip to South Pass City?" Garrick asked curiously.

"No, I was here the better part of the winter a year ago."

"Maybe that's why you look so familiar to me." Garrick studied him pensively. "I could swear I've seen you somewhere before."

Ox chuckled. "Probably faced him across a poker table."

"That's certainly possible," Cameron agreed. "Do you play?"

"Some."

"Some!" Ox laughed outright at that. "Swede plays poker the way he works powder. If you played him, you probably lost."

Garrick glanced at Cameron again. Had he played poker with the man? Possibly, and yet that didn't seem right somehow. He was certainly a good-looking son of a gun. With honey-blond hair and eyes the color of a summer sky, he was likely more memorable to women than other men. Ah well, it would come to him.

"So, what brings you back to South Pass City?" Ox was asking.

"Business mostly, but there's a personal reason too."

"A woman?"

Cameron grinned a little sheepishly. "How did you know?"

Ox shrugged. "There are only two things that will bring a man back to a place that isn't his home. From the tone in your voice, it didn't sound like you were thinking of revenge."

"Nope. In fact, I hope it comes to marriage."

"Sounds like you got bit pretty hard."

"A lot harder than I realized at first. I haven't seen her for over a year, but I just can't seem to get her out of my mind. When I was tied to that wagon, all I could think of were those big brown eyes and that I might never see her again."

Ox rolled his eyes. "Just my luck to get stuck with another love-sick-pup. Take Swede here. With him it's his wife. He isn't one to talk your leg off anyway, but the last three weeks you'd dang near think the man was mute."

"You talk enough for both of us," Garrick said with a grin.

225

"Maybe so, but a man gets tired of talking to himself after a while." He turned his attention back to Cameron. "Lots of coming and going in South Pass City. You sure this girl is still there?"

"No, in fact it's quite possible they've moved on. It's just her and her father. He's drunk more often than he's sober and never sticks with one job for long. It may take every cent I've got, but I'm going to pay Fenton White to get out of her life."

Garrick felt as if a giant fist had slammed into his belly. With sick certainty, he knew why Cameron Price was so familiar: he saw those features every time he looked into his daughter's face. The man he had just risked his life to save was the one person he'd hoped never to meet—Becky's mysterious past lover and Alaina's father.

Chapter 24

I'll kill him Garrick's hands tightened on the reins at the thought. *This is the bastard that got Becky pregnant and walked away without a backward glance.*

"If you love her so much how come it's taken you a year to get back to her?" Ox wanted to know.

Cameron sighed. "My...business kept me away. Besides, I'm too old for her. She was only sixteen at the time."

Garrick gritted his teeth. *You should have thought of that before you took her to bed.*

"I don't know, she's just one of those women you can't forget."

Ox nodded. "Pretty huh?"

"Yes, she's beautiful, but it's more than that. I never met a more sweetly giving person in my life. I've never been in love before. I didn't know if I was ready for marriage."

Garrick nearly choked on the urge to let the man know what his selfish uncertainty had done to Becky. Telling the pompous ass that his ladylove was already married and to keep his lecherous hands off would be extremely satisfying.

"A lot can change in a year," he began.

"Not with my lady," Cameron said with a confident smile. "When she said 'I love you' she meant it."

The air suddenly left Garrick's lungs. "She said she loved you?" He was vaguely surprised his voice worked. In all the months he and Becky had been together, she had never once told Garrick she loved him.

"All the time. Enough of that. How is it I find you two out here without an army escort?"

Garrick was barely aware of the conversation going on between Ox and Cameron. All he could think of was Becky saying she loved Cameron. And why not? He was everything Garrick was not—handsome, self-assured; he was even a good conversationalist.

It was nearly impossible for Garrick to subdue the jealous demon that threatened to overcome his good sense. Finally, though, his calm logic won out. He'd always known he was going to have to leave eventually. When he'd seen Daniel Dutton twice in less than eight months, he knew it would probably be sooner rather than later. At least this way he'd know Becky and Alaina were taken care of, and by the man who should have been there in the first place. And Becky loved him.

Briefly, the wish that he'd left Cameron to the renegades flitted across Garrick's mind, but he knew it wasn't true. Becky was right about him. Even knowing the stranger threatened everything that was dear to him, he couldn't have walked away and left Cameron to his fate.

He cast a sidelong glance at Cameron Price. To see his relaxed posture, you'd never know how close he'd come to dying. He was apparently one of those men who thrived on danger, the kind heroes were made of. And Becky loved him.

As light faded from the sky, he fought the desire to give Cameron Price some good stiff competition. If by some miracle he could overcome the odds that were clearly stacked against him, he couldn't change the fact that he was a wanted man. He would stay around long enough to make sure Cameron married her, then he'd make good his escape. The decision brought a flood of anguish, but he knew he had no choice.

Though it was long after dark when they finally arrived in South Pass City, none of them even considered the possibility of camping along the road. Leaving the other two men to the tender mercies of Angel and her girls, Garrick headed home.

For three weeks, all he'd thought about was seeing Becky again and begging her forgiveness. He'd been willing to do anything she asked of him no matter what the cost to his pride. All that had changed this afternoon. Now, instead of mending the breech, he had to sever the ties that bound them together. He'd rather cut off his arm.

The cabin was dark as he let himself in. Only the embers glowing in the fireplace lit the interior. *Home.* The familiar shadows and smells surrounded him like a welcome cocoon.

"Garrick?" Becky's voice held a note of uncertainty. He could see her sitting up in bed, holding the blanket in front of her.

"*Ja*, it's me."

"Oh, Garrick." She jumped out of bed, ran across the room and threw her arms around him. "I missed you so much."

With a groan, he dropped the bedroll he was carrying and pulled her into his arms. "I missed you too, little one."

"I'm so sorry, Garrick," she said, "I know you did what you—"

He silenced her with a kiss. All thoughts of telling her the truth and walking out of her life disappeared in a swirl of desire. Suddenly, making love to Becky became as necessary as breathing. He swept her up in his arms and carried her to the bed.

"Garrick..." Becky's whisper sounded like a caress as they settled into the welcome warmth together. She cupped his face in her hands and kissed first an eyebrow then the bridge of his nose before brushing her lips across his as though she couldn't quite believe he was really there.

They had no need for words while nimble fingers made quick work of her nightgown and his clothes. They each understood the other perfectly as they pushed each other to the limits of sensual delight.

As they made love, Garrick had the irrational desire to pull her inside himself, to make her a permanent part of him that could never be removed. The pleasure he gave her was a bittersweet reminder that it would all be over soon, and he would have nothing but memories of the special magic between them.

Afterwards, Garrick ignored the pricks from his conscience as he held her close, next to his heart. He knew he should tell her the truth about their marriage now, but this night was all he had left, and he wasn't going to waste a second of it.

"Garrick?" Becky rubbed her hands up the hard plane of his back. She could feel the desperation in him, and it made her nervous. "Did something happen on your trip?"

"Why?"

"I don't know. You just seem kind of...tense."

"Nothing for you to be concerned about."

"Ox?"

"Is pulling at the bit waiting to get that splint off his arm. He figured on seeing Dr. Caldwell tomorrow to get rid of it. How's Alaina?"

"She got another tooth and can sit up all by herself now. Last night just before bed, she rolled all the way over." Becky chuckled. "Oh, Garrick, you should have seen her. She was so surprised."

"She'll be walking before you know it." *And I won't be here to see it.* He swallowed against the sudden knot in his throat.

"Garrick, what's wrong?"

"Nothing."

"Don't lie to me. You looked so strange just now—"

"Shhh," he said, pulling her closer. "Just let me hold you." He buried his face in her hair and inhaled the fragrance of apple blossoms. Not for the first time, he wondered how she always managed to smell so good.

"You're avoiding my question." Becky's voice was panicky now. "Something's wrong!"

"I know," he murmured as his lips grazed the sensitive skin below her ear and his fingers traced erotic patterns on her back. "It's been at least a quarter of an hour since I made love to you."

"It won't work, Garrick." Her words came out in a breathless whisper, but there was a note of steely determination that was impossible to ignore. "If you succeed in distracting me this time, I'll just ask you again when we're finished. You can't make love to me all night long. Even you have your limits."

Garrick sighed. She was right, of course. Experience had shown him the futility of not telling her what she wanted to know, but a full confession could wait. There was no way he could inform her they weren't really married when she lay naked in his arms, and he certainly wasn't going to tell her Cameron Price was back. "We ran into some trouble with a band of renegades today. I guess I'm still a little shook up."

"Oh, no." A flicker of fear showed in the depths of Becky's eyes as she stared at him. "Are you sure you're all right?"

"Ja, I'm fine, and so is Ox. I can't say the same for the Indians though."

"What happened?"

"We were safe enough," Garrick said with a shrug. "I used a couple of kegs of black powder to close off the entrance of the box canyon they were in is all. They won't be bothering anyone else for a while."

"Oh, Garrick, you might have been killed."

"See, that's why I didn't want to tell you. I knew you'd get upset." Garrick silenced her protest with a finger against her lips. "Shhh, it's over, and everything's fine. Now about that challenge you issued..." He traced the curve of her cheek with the pad of his thumb.

"What challenge?"

"That I couldn't make love to you all night. Would you care to let me try?"

"Mmmm." She put her arms around his neck and settled herself more comfortably against his body. "What are you waiting for? Morning comes early this time of year."

The sky was just turning pink as Garrick leaned over Alaina's cradle. With gentle fingers, he touched the curls on her head. No matter that he wasn't her natural father,

Alaina would always be his first-born. How he wanted to pick her up and hold her close one last time. Regretfully, he turned away. He couldn't risk her waking up Becky.

Becky. Already his heart was breaking, and he hadn't even finished packing his clothes. His gaze strayed to the bed where she lay fast asleep. Garrick felt a slight twinge of guilt as he noticed the faint shadows under her eyes. She hadn't complained a bit during the long night, but she was clearly exhausted. In his desperation, he'd forgotten she lacked his stamina.

With a grimace, he turned away and finished stuffing his clothes in a bag. At the door, he paused with his hand on the latch and glanced back at the bed. What would it hurt? As deeply as she slept she'd never even know. He was across the room in a few strides. There was a suspicious prickle behind his eyes as he knelt beside her. Lord how he loved this woman. With infinite tenderness, he touched her lips in a feather-light kiss. "*Jeg elsker deg, vesla,*" he whispered.

Feeling as though his heart were being ripped from his chest, he stood and strode to the door. Now, that had been a stupid thing to do. As if the pain of leaving wasn't bad enough already.

A few minutes later, Becky opened her eyes in confusion. She didn't know what had awakened her, but she could have sworn she heard Garrick say *Jeg elsker deg* before he stomped away and slammed out of the house. Was he angry? What about? Surely not last night. She may have pushed him a little hard, but... No, of course not. That was silly. He would have stopped if he wanted to. She must have misunderstood him.

With a sigh Becky, closed her eyes again. Oh, what a night...what a long, glorious, wonderful night. She went back to sleep with a smile on her face.

"You look like something the cat dragged in," Angel said several hours later when Becky arrived at The Green Garter. "Did Alaina get another tooth?"

Becky blushed. "No, Garrick came home last night. He....uh..."

"Never mind, I get the picture. He tell you much about his trip?" Angel's voice was casual, but she watched Becky closely beneath her lashes.

"No, not really, only that they had some trouble with the Indians. Did Ox get his splint off like he was supposed to?"

"Yes, and he's probably already left town. He says even with Swede's help that quarantine set him back nearly a week."

"Miss Angel," said Sam from the doorway. "There's a problem with that last case of whiskey I opened. Do you want to come look at it?"

"Oh, I suppose so." Angel rose from the chair with a sigh. "Sometimes I wonder why I wanted my own business," she muttered as she followed Sam out of the room.

Becky smiled to herself as she plied her needle. Angel might complain about it, but she thrived on all the decision-making and responsibilities that went with The Green Garter.

"I don't care if he is about the most handsome man that ever came in here. If Collette wants him, she can have him. One man's pretty much the same as another as far as I'm concerned, and I sure as hell ain't gonna get her mad at me."

The two women didn't even notice Becky tucked away in her usual corner as they came into the kitchen to get coffee. "No man is worth her spite," the other woman agreed. "Still, it was a pretty interesting story he and Ox told."

"Sure was. That Swede, ain't he something? Imagine him setting all those charges to make them think the army was shooting at them."

"I liked the part where he went right into the Indian camp, stole their prisoner, and got them both out before the powder went off!"

"I missed the end 'cause the Thomas boy just *had* to go upstairs right then. How did Swede stop the Indians from comin' after them?"

"He blew up the cliffs all along the end of the canyon and filled the entrance full of rocks. Ain't that the dangest thing you ever heard?"

Becky sat frozen in her chair as she listened. *We were safe enough,* he'd said. Safe when he'd gone into an Indian camp by himself? What if they'd seen him? Or what if he hadn't made it back out before the powder blew? She felt sick to her stomach just imagining the possibilities.

No wonder he hadn't wanted to tell her about the Indians. He knew she'd be furious that he'd risked his life again without a second thought. Maybe he was right, too. Nothing was gained by getting mad after it was all over with.

Suddenly, she remembered her waking dream that morning. Had he really said *Jeg elsker deg*? He had never liked her interfering with what he thought was right.

Maybe her insistence made him angry. He might even still be mad about the fight they'd had before he left with Ox. It was hard to know with Garrick. He never told her what he was feeling.

It took about five minutes to get over feeling guilty and two more to become rip-roaring mad. She was his wife and had a perfect right to worry about him. Marriage was sharing, not just the good, but the bad too. They were going to get this straightened out, even if she had to back him up against the wall to do it. It was too bad Garrick disliked conflict, because right after supper tonight he was going to get the confrontation of his life!

Chapter 25

"Come on, Sweetheart, I'm not in the mood to fight with you this morning," Becky said, as Alaina giggled and kicked her feet free of the blanket for the third time. "We're going to go find Daddy."

"Daa!"

Becky stared at her daughter in surprise. "Daddy?" she said experimentally.

"Daaa." Alaina gave her mother a grin and tried to turn over on the table where Becky was dressing her.

"At least Daddy will have something to make him smile," Becky muttered as she captured Alaina and rewrapped her in the blanket. "He may need it after I get done with him."

Becky's anger hadn't abated one jot since yesterday. In fact, it had intensified. Garrick hadn't come home last night. Becky was so tired from her sleepless night that she'd fallen asleep waiting for him to come home and hadn't reawakened until this morning. It was probably just as well. If she hadn't fallen asleep, she'd have gone to The Green Garter or where ever he was hiding and dragged him home by his ear.

"It figures," Becky grouched as she finally stepped through the door with Alaina in her arms and eyed the muddy road. "Guess we'd better walk, honey. I don't want to get the buckboard stuck."

Other than the melting snow and the mud, she hardly noticed that spring had finally arrived in the high country as she followed the familiar track to town. Her mind was too busy dwelling on the upcoming confrontation with Garrick. She'd played it a thousand different ways in her mind, and all of them ended the same way—with her in his arms confessing how much she loved him. Irrational as it seemed, the fantasy just wouldn't go away.

It was possible, of course, but only if they got past the argument part first. Given Garrick's penchant for walking out in the middle of a fight, she had decided to place herself between him and the door. He wouldn't walk over the top of her to get out of his own shop in the middle of the morning...would he?

Becky sighed. With his temper, who knew what he'd do? She fully intended to tell him what she thought of his tactics before she offered a compromise to their problem. If he would let her be part of his life in every way, she would try to understand when he did what she considered stupid things like saving complete strangers from marauding Indians. Then she'd tell him she loved him, that he was the best thing that had ever happened to her, and that she reacted the way she did because she was afraid of losing him.

That's when he'd take her in his arms and say he felt the same. Oh, if only it would go that way. For about the hundredth time, she wondered why he was angry with her. She didn't precisely know what *Jeg elsker deg* meant, but the only other time he'd ever said it, he'd been mad. When she said it to him, he seemed to find it quite amusing. What had she done this time that made him want to curse at her?

He was busy at the forge when Becky and Alaina arrived at the shop. The sheriff stood nearby chatting. Garrick looked up when they entered; his beautiful smile instantly transforming his face at the sight of them. Was it her imagination, or did it falter a heartbeat later?

She couldn't be sure; the only light came from the open door and the forge. Garrick said darkness was necessary because he judged the heat of the metal by its color. Squinting into the dark interior, Becky walked in and sat on the big cottonwood block that Garrick had put there for her months ago. Becky put Alaina in the small wooden pen Garrick had built. With a sigh, the baby closed her eyes and promptly went to sleep. Becky smiled. The clamorous sounds of the smithy did it every time.

How Becky loved to come here and watch Garrick work. The gleam of sweat on his bare arms and the motion of the thick muscles as he worked the iron never failed to move her, but it was more than that. There was a quiet joy that radiated from his face as he smoothed and shaped the iron with the same loving touch he used on wood. This was his element, and he loved every inch of it, from the cinders on the floor to the acrid smell of hot metal.

As the rhythmic clang of the hammer on the metal began to soothe her, Becky fought to hang on to her irritation. The last thing she needed was to calm down. It was going to take ferocious anger to break through that Scandinavian composure of his.

"Guess I'd best be going," the sheriff said at last. "I appreciate you taking the time to do this for me, Swede."

"I should have it done for you by noon, John," Garrick said as the sheriff touched his hat to Becky and turned to go.

Left alone with Becky, Garrick knew himself for a coward. After a great deal of thought, he'd decided this would be the least painful for her, but lord, how he dreaded it.

With Cameron Price back in her life, he knew she'd come to ask for her freedom, a freedom she didn't even realize was already hers. It would be simple, a clean break, neat, and quick. For two days, he'd been consoling himself with the thought of how grateful she'd be. It would be as easy and pleasant as walking through his forge barefoot.

She surprised him by opening a window for light, then calmly closing the door.

"What did you do that for?"

"We have something very important to discuss. I don't want to be interrupted." She gave him a speaking glance. "And I don't want anyone stomping out of here in a snit before I've had my say."

He nodded and stuck the piece of metal he was working into the coals. Pumping the bellows, he waited for her to speak.

"You didn't come home last night," she said as she came to stand beside him.

"No."

"I suppose you think you had a good reason?"

"Ja."

Becky sighed in exasperation. Honestly, sometimes she was tempted to throttle him. "Look, Garrick, we both know our marriage was one of convenience. I was willing to settle for that at the time, but there are certain things a wife has a right to expect. I understand it's not your way to say much, but—"

"It's over, Becky." He winced at the baldness of the statement, but he found he really didn't want to hear about the grand passion she'd found with her one true love.

" —I can't tolerate the way you close up to m—What did you say?"

"I said it's over." He gritted his teeth as he pulled his iron out of the forge and laid it on the anvil.

"What is?"

"Our marriage, or actually the pretense of it."

"I...I don't understand."

"It's quite simple, really," he said, carefully avoiding looking at her as he struck the metal with his hammer. "We were never legally married."

"But...but how can that be? We went to the Justice of the Peace. We even had a witness and signed the papers."

"The papers say you're married to someone named Garrick Swenson. That man doesn't exist."

"Y-you're not—"

"No, I'm not. Swenson is the first Swedish name that occurred to me."

"But why?"

"It was the only solution I could think of. You needed a husband. I knew if you were desperate enough to marry a complete stranger that way, you were capable of anything." As he thrust his metal back into the fire, Garrick hardly noticed that he'd pounded it too flat for the single tree he was supposed to be fixing. "I hoped this was just a temporary measure until you got your feet under you again, but I wasn't sure until I talked to a lawyer in Rock Springs. He assured me all we have to do is walk away."

"That's why you wouldn't sleep with me," Becky said in a whisper. She had the irrational desire to cover her ears, to block out the words that pounded her as mercilessly as his hammer pounded the iron on his anvil.

"I never meant for that to happen, Becky. I'm sorry, I truly am."

"Oh, Garrick, I've been so stupid. I thought...I thought..." It was all too much. She scooped up Alaina and backed toward the door. "I'm so sorry Garrick, so very sorry. I...Oh, God." She pushed the door open and escaped into the bright sunlight.

Garrick had never felt such pain as he watched her run down the street. Where was her elation at being released from a loveless marriage? She was supposed to be happy. Instead, she seemed more anguished than before.

A horrible thought flickered through his mind. What if Cameron hadn't found her yet? He tried to remember what she'd been saying before he dropped his bomb. Something about him closing up to her? His stomach tightened into a knot as he realized it hadn't been about Cameron at all.

Suddenly, the words he'd just spoken became unbelievably cruel. She probably thought he'd talked to that lawyer this trip rather than back in October. It must have sounded like—Oh, Lord. He was out the door with the next breath.

Becky was vaguely surprised she could run with her heart shattered into a million pieces the way it was. A sham. The most wonderful year of her life and none of it was true. That's why he'd never said I love you.

Hot tears scalded her cheeks as she remembered the shameless way she had seduced him. It was only after she'd broken his resistance that he couldn't seem to get enough. He'd come home the other night to tell her he was leaving, and she'd thrown herself at him yet again. No wonder he was angry. If she got pregnant again, Garrick would think he had to marry her for real.

Her feet took her unerringly to The Green Garter. Angel might not be overly sympathetic, but her pragmatic attitude was what Becky needed right now.

Blinded by tears, Becky didn't even see the man in front of The Green Garter until she ran right into him.

"Whoa now," he said, catching her in his arms and setting her back on her feet. "Sorry ma'am, I didn't see you coming. Are you all ri— My God, Becky?"

Startled, Becky looked up and gasped in astonishment. Unable to believe her eyes, she reached up to the dearly familiar face that was still handsome in spite of the red skin and blisters across his nose. "Cameron? Is it really you?"

"Yes, my love, it's me!"

"What happened to your face?"

"Too much sun a couple of days ago." Cameron put his hand over hers where it lay on his cheek and brought her fingers to his lips. "I'd just about given up finding you," he said softly. "They said your father had died. I thought you'd be long gone."

"You were looking for me?"

"I should never have left you, Becky. I realize that now, and only hope you can forgive me."

Alaina whimpered slightly as she woke up. For the first time, Cameron glanced down. His eyes widened in shock when he realized what Becky was holding. For a long moment, father and daughter stared at each other. A man would have to be blind or stupid to miss the resemblance between them. Cameron was neither.

At long last, he looked at Becky. "Why didn't you tell me?"

"I was going to, but…but you left."

Cameron closed his eyes. "I have more to make up for than I thought."

"You didn't even say good-bye." There was a catch in her voice.

"There was no time. I was called away unexpectedly in the middle of the night."

"You've been gone over a year, Cameron. I haven't heard a word from you."

"I know." He sighed. "Stupid as it sounds, I didn't realize I was in love with you until after I left."

"But you said it every time we were together."

Cameron had the grace to look embarrassed. "Yes, but I didn't understand the difference."

"What difference?"

"I don't know how to explain it, Becky, but I never felt this way before. It's the first time I've ever really fallen in love. I thought I would forget you, but I haven't. I didn't understand how very much I cared until two days ago when I looked death in the face, and all I could think of was you."

"Death from a sunburn?"

"I was captured by a band of renegade Indians. If it hadn't been for a half-crazy mule-skinner and a very large Swede, I wouldn't be here to tell the story."

Becky felt dizzy. Cameron was the nameless stranger Garrick had risked his life to save? Did he realize Cameron was the one who—of course he did. That's why he'd picked today to tell her their whole life together was a lie.

Fascinated with the miniature features so like his own, Cameron's attention was focused on Alaina, and he missed the impact his words had on Becky. "You know I've never been much for babies, but he really is beautiful."

"Wh — what?"

"I said our son is beautiful."

"Alaina's a girl."

"A daughter?"

Cameron clearly hadn't considered such a possibility. Becky almost smiled at how like him to assume any child he produced would naturally be a boy. "Would you like to hold her?"

"Well I..." Cameron shifted uncomfortably. "Maybe later. I've never been around babies, and, to be honest, they make me a little nervous."

"Neither had I," Becky said with a touch of irritation. "You get used to them pretty fast."

"She's just such a surprise."

"I wasn't exactly prepared for her myself."

"I know. It must have been hell." He reached up and traced the curve of Becky's cheek with the back of his fingers. "Can you ever forgive me?" he asked softly.

"I'm not sure." Becky shifted Alaina to an upright position.

Her answer seemed to surprise him. "Becky, we created a child, for God's sake. You can't just turn your back on what we had."

"Why not? You did."

"I was a fool. Becky, I love you. Once, that meant something to you; or have you forgotten?"

No, she hadn't forgotten. He'd made her feel wanted for the first time since her mother's death. As she looked up at him, she remembered how very much she'd loved him, enough to do whatever he wanted. A dozen images of them in the deserted mine shack Cameron had found for them tumbled through her mind. He'd been so....wonderful. "I'm not a stupid sixteen-year-old any more, Cameron. You won't find me so easy to fool."

He sighed. "I guess I deserved that. Will you give me another chance?"

"I...I don't know."

"We were good together, Becky. What will convince you to let me try again?"

Two things occurred to Becky at the same moment. Cameron Price, the most irresistibly handsome man she'd ever met in her life, still had the ability to move her. And Garrick, whom she loved with her whole heart, had played her for a fool. She lifted Alaina to her shoulder. "You're going to have to prove to me that you can be trusted."

"I'll be the most steadfast suitor you've ever had."

Why not? With Garrick gone, she had nothing more to lose. "All right, Cameron, but if I tell you it's over, it is."

"Fair enough." He pulled her into his arms and kissed her with the practiced charm he was famous for. More experienced women than Becky had been completely swept away by his kisses. She was dismayed to discover she wasn't immune to them, either.

Neither of them paid any attention to Alaina, who looked over her mother's shoulder and smiled at the familiar figure standing at the end of the street watching the tender little scene. "Daaa!"

She wasn't the only one who noticed the man with knotted fists and clenched jaw. More than one passerby breathed a sigh of relief when Garrick turned and stalked back to his shop. It was pretty hard to ignore a Scandinavian giant who looked like he had murder on his mind.

Chapter 26

"Do you have a minute, Swede?"

Garrick paused in the process of cleaning his shop for the evening. Cameron Price was the last person he'd expected to see here. "What can I do for you?"

"I brought your clothes back." Cameron set the neatly folded pants and shirt on the cottonwood stump. "I really don't know what to say. Thank you doesn't seem quite enough for saving my life. It's a debt I don't know if I can ever repay."

Garrick shrugged. "Anyone would have done the same. How's your sunburn?"

"It doesn't hurt too bad anymore. I spent the whole day yesterday in bed at The Green Garter with Angel and her girls coming in every so often to put vinegar and some kind of lotion on it." He grinned. "Best injury I've ever had, if you want to know the truth."

Garrick thought of the salve Becky had used on his back after the hailstorm and grinned back in spite of himself. "*Ja*, Dr. Caldwell's a good one for prescribing pleasant cures for things like that. The man's worth his weight in gold."

Cameron laughed. "I was just going to get something to eat. Care to join me?"

Garrick was instantly wary. The last thing he wanted to do was spend any time with Cameron Price. "I already ate," he lied.

"Then how about a drink?"

"Too early for me."

Cameron sighed. "I guess I don't blame you. Collette told me about you and Becky."

"Collette has a big mouth."

"She has her uses," Cameron said with a shrug. "You knew the day you saved me, didn't you?"

"*Ja.*" Garrick turned away and started to hang tools on the wall. "Alaina looks like you."

"I wondered. One minute we were having a pleasant conversation, the next I thought I might have been better off taking my chances with the Indians."

"I've spent a year wondering what kind of man gets an innocent young girl like Becky pregnant then walks away without a backward glance. I wanted to tear your head off."

"If I'd had even an inkling she was with child, I wouldn't have left. I guess she had a pretty rough time."

"After her father died, she sold off everything she owned a piece at a time. When I met her, it was all gone, and she was trying to get up the courage to become a prostitute. Even though she hadn't eaten in three days, she wasn't sure it wouldn't be easier just to starve to death."

"God." Cameron ran his hand through his hair. "I deserve to be horsewhipped."

"My thoughts exactly."

"So, you married her."

Here was the moment of truth. Garrick closed his eyes and fought the urge to lie. "No," he said quietly, "I pretended to marry her. It wasn't legal. That way I could protect her but not hold her in a loveless marriage if she wanted to leave. I never had any intention of consummating it."

Cameron looked startled. "You didn't sleep with her?"

For the first time Garrick looked him straight in the eye. "That would have put me in the same category as the scum who made it necessary for her to get married in the first place, wouldn't it?"

Cameron winced, and Garrick continued. "Actually, it wasn't a problem. She was scared to death of me," he said as he hung his leather apron and sleeveless shirt on a nail. "After the way her father treated her, I'm surprised she even agreed to marry me."

"Why are you telling me this?" Cameron asked. "You obviously don't think much of me."

"No, I don't have any love for you, but Becky does, and Alaina's your daughter." Garrick dunked his head in the slake trough and came up shaking the water free. He leaned his hands on the edge of the metal tub and looked directly at Cameron. "Just remember, Price, I'll be watching. If you don't do right by them, I'll make you wish I'd left you in that renegade camp."

"Understood." Cameron watched Garrick sluice water up his arms and across his chest. "You know, Swede, if things were different, I'd be damn proud to call you friend."

Without another word, Cameron left the smithy, and Garrick stared after him in surprise. After a moment, he went back to washing. To hell with friendship. He'd rather bury the S.O.B. up to his neck in a red anthill.

"Hello, Swede. Want some company?" Angel said an hour later as she leaned on the bar next to him.

"Not particularly."

"My, my, aren't we the surly one this evening?"

"If you don't like it, leave."

Angel smiled. "Nice try. I'm not leaving until we have a little chat."

Garrick took a swallow of whiskey. "I was afraid of that."

"What the hell do you think you're doing?"

"I'm having a drink."

"Why?"

"I'm thirsty."

"Then what are you going to do?"

"Play some poker."

"I happen to know you haven't been home for two nights."

"So?"

"How come?"

"It's none of your business, Angel."

"No, I don't suppose it is, but then I feel like living dangerously tonight."

Garrick didn't bother to answer as he took another drink.

"Becky told me a very interesting story this morning." Angel surveyed the room. "Interesting hoax you set up last spring. There wasn't a one of us realized that wedding wasn't the real thing."

"It was necessary."

"Why?"

"You know very well why."

"No, actually, your logic escapes me, Swede."

"She was pregnant."

"Yes, and?"

"Come on Angel, she was desperate. I had to create a situation to protect her until she had the baby."

"So, why not really marry her?"

"I made it possible for her to leave. I knew the time would come when she'd want out."

"Or you would."

For the first time he looked at her. "Is that what you think?"

Angel shrugged. "Pretty convenient excuse if you ask me, Swede. It sounds good, but it doesn't make a lot of sense when you take time to think about it."

"Just what are you getting at?"

"For one thing, Alaina was born almost seven months ago. You didn't get around to telling Becky you weren't married until today after you've been gone for three weeks. We both know the two of you didn't part on the best of terms."

Garrick was incredulous. "You think I told her the truth about our marriage because of a stupid fight we had almost a month ago?"

"Becky does."

"How could she believe that?"

"Maybe because you spent one night with her then didn't go back."

Garrick frowned. "I had my reasons, and they didn't have anything to do with our fight."

"I know. Cameron Price is back in town."

"What's that got to do with anything?"

"I wonder," Angel said sarcastically. "Don't try to play stupid with me, Swede. I've known that baby was Cameron's since last winter."

"Becky told you?"

"Not intentionally. She doesn't even realize I know. The point is, you're letting your damned nobility get in the way of what you and Becky both want."

"Nobility has nothing to do with it. She's in love with him, not me."

Angel sighed in exasperation. "What makes you so sure about that?"

Garrick glared at her. "She slept with him, Angel. Becky would never do that unless she loved a man."

"She slept with you too."

"That's different."

"Why? Because she thought you were married? Come on, Swede. There are only two reasons a woman will try to entice a man into her bed. Either she loves him, or she wants to control him. Becky wasn't after control when she set up that very elaborate game of seduction she played on you. And yes, I know all about it. She was so desperate to have you she came to me for advice."

A look of surprise crossed Garrick's face then he sighed. "Look, Angel, I know she's not indifferent to me. I also happen to know she's in love with Price. He's the father of her child." "She *was* in love with Cameron. That doesn't mean she still is. What if her affections have changed?"

"Becky's not fickle."

"No, but the feelings between you two are very strong. Are you willing to let Cameron have her without a fight? What if she would rather be with you?"

"Come on, Angel, what woman in her right mind would pick someone who looks like me over Cameron Price?"

"All right, so he's a damn attractive man. You might not win any beauty contests, Swede, but you aren't exactly dog-ugly either. Not that it would matter if you were. There's a hell of a lot more to love than physical attraction. Frankly, I think you've got Cameron beat all hollow in the ways that count."

Garrick rubbed his face tiredly. "All right, so maybe it is possible, but there's no way to know for sure."

"You could always ask her."

"Are you crazy?"

"Look Swede, beating around the bush isn't going to work. The way I see it, you haven't got a whole lot to lose anyway." She patted him on the arm then pushed away from the bar. "It's been real entertaining talking to you, but I've got to get back to work."

Garrick stared down into his glass long after she was gone. Blast Angel and her prying. As if he hadn't had enough emotional turmoil for one day. With a grimace, he tossed down the rest of his drink before heading back to the smithy and his lonely bedroll.

Dawn the next morning brought Becky an unexpected visitor.

"Cameron!" Becky wiped her hands self-consciously on her apron as she stared up at him. "What in the world are you doing here?"

"I told you yesterday I was going to be an attentive suitor."

"It's six o'clock in the morning!"

He gave her a jaunty grin. "Are you impressed?"

Becky smiled in spite of herself. "Am I supposed to be?"

"Of course. I'm showing you how cheerful I am first thing in the morning. Aren't you going to ask me in?"

"I...don't know. I haven't even had breakfast yet."

"Neither have I. In fact, I was hoping to wrangle an invitation from you."

"That wouldn't be proper."

"We'll leave the door open." He raised an eyebrow. "Besides, I never indulge in seduction before breakfast."

Becky laughed and stepped out of the way. "Oh, all right." She'd forgotten how persuasive he could be with those cornflower blue eyes and that winning smile. Their gazes both fell on her unmade bunk at the same moment. Becky blushed and hurried forward to pull the covers up.

Behind her back, Cameron smiled in satisfaction. He'd found out what he wanted to know. There were two beds on opposite sides of the tiny cabin, and she obviously slept in the small one...alone. Swede had told him the truth then.

"I'm only having cornmeal mush."

"I love mush."

"Of course you do." Becky smiled as she went to stir the pan on the stove. "If I were having toadstools and cow dung, you'd probably love that too."

"One of my favorites," he said promptly. "Well hello, Leena. How's my little girl this morning?"

Becky glanced over her shoulder at Cameron as he stood awkwardly next to where Alaina was playing on the floor. "Her name's Alaina. Have a seat."

"Thanks."

"Coffee?"

"Yes, please."

The warmth of his gaze made her distinctly uncomfortable as she poured his coffee. Worse yet, he'd sat down on Garrick's chair. Becky had the irrational urge to pull it out from under him. She was almost relieved when Alaina fell over and began to cry.

"It's all right, sweetheart. Mama's here," she said as she put down the coffee pot and picked up the baby.

"What happened?" Cameron asked nervously. "Is she all right?"

"She just learned how to sit up a few days ago and doesn't always balance right. I think it scared her more than anything. Oh dear, I forgot the mush," Becky said as the pan boiled over. "Here, take her." She thrust Alaina into Cameron's arms and hurried to the stove.

Cameron Price had led his men into countless battles, faced the enemy undaunted, and never backed down to a challenge in his life, but he was completely unnerved by his six-month-old daughter. Unsure what to do, he held her gingerly, hoping Becky would come back before anything happened.

He looked up hopefully when she returned, but Becky was only setting the bowls on the table. She was gone an instant later to get the cornmeal mush. Used to playing with whoever held her, Alaina started to squirm, and Cameron panicked. "Becky!"

"What?"

"The baby...I don't know...I'm afraid I'll drop her," he said desperately.

Becky turned to look and giggled at the expression of sheer terror on Cameron's face. "It's all right, Cameron, she won't bite. All she wants to do is play." Becky carried the pan over to the table and set it down. "I'll put her in her bed."

Cameron gave the baby up with a sigh of relief, and Becky bit back another giggle. Honestly, you'd think he'd been asked to hold a porcupine.

Becky returned to the table and began to dish up the mush. "I hope you like molasses," she said as he smiled up at her, "because that's what I usually —"

"Daaa!" Alaina shouted from her cradle suddenly. Becky froze with the spoon halfway between the pan and Cameron's bowl. With a feeling of sick certainty, she whirled and looked into Garrick's accusing eyes.

Chapter 27

"Daaaa...Daaa." Alaina's voice was the only sound in the room as the three adults stared at each other, unable to move.

"Garrick!" Becky finally forced his name out and broke the spell that held them all transfixed.

"I...uh...I came to...um...to get my tools," Garrick stammered. "They...they're in the shed, I think." He turned and stumbled down the path to the shed. Sophie nickered a greeting as he entered, but Garrick paid no attention as he leaned against the wall and closed his eyes. How had Angel managed to convince him Becky might actually prefer him to Cameron Price?

Damn but Price moved fast. That he'd managed to charm his way into Becky's bed so quickly proved she must still love him a great deal. Garrick felt as if the air in the shed were too thin to breathe.

A slight sound outside alerted him that his solitude was about to end. Trying to get himself in hand, Garrick turned away from the door and picked up the first thing he found.

"Garrick?" Becky's voice held a note of panic as she stood in the doorway and peered into the dim interior. "Garrick, are you in there?"

"Ja." Garrick was proud of the way his voice remained steady as he turned to face her.

"I...it's not what it looks like."

"What?"

"Don't play dumb, Garrick. You know very well what I'm talking about."

"You're not having breakfast with him?"

"Well, yes, but—"

Garrick shrugged and walked over to the shelves that held his woodworking tools. "That's what it looked like."

"But—"

"Becky, don't. It's none of my business what you do anymore."

"And you don't care? Come on, Garrick we've lived together for a year."

"We shared a special part of our lives." He stared at his tools blindly. "It wasn't very long ago that you told me nothing lasts forever."

"As far as you're concerned, it's over, right?"

"Ja."

"Is that what you want, or are you just being noble, Garrick?"

"It's for the best."

"Why did you come this morning?"

"To get my tools."

"And what were you planning to do with that?"

Garrick felt like an utter fool as he looked down and realized he'd picked up one of the leather straps Becky had used when Alaina was born. "A smith can always make use of leather scraps. Why, did you want it for something?"

"No, I...I'm finished with it." She watched as he stuffed the strap in his pocket and began clearing his tools off the shelf. "I don't believe you, Garrick. There's another man sitting in your chair, eating at your table, and you don't care?"

259

"They aren't my chair and table any more. Besides, Cameron Price isn't just any man," he said quietly. "He's Alaina's father. There are those who might think I intruded on his territory."

"I was afraid you'd figured it out," she said heavily. "That's why you finally told me the truth, isn't it?"

"I should have said something sooner."

"Why didn't you?"

"You and Alaina needed me. Now you don't."

Oh yes, I do, Becky thought miserably. *I need you to take me in your arms and tell me it doesn't matter who I slept with before. That you love me and want me anyway.* "S-so what are you planning to do now?" Becky was surprised she could even talk around the knot in her throat.

"To tell you the truth, I've been thinking of moving on for quite a while now."

"Leave South Pass City?" Becky was aghast. "But Garrick, you finally got your blacksmith shop. You can't just walk away from that."

"I wasn't planning to. Most of it will load into a wagon."

"Where would you go?"

"That's the nice thing about a smithy. You can set one up in any town and have plenty of business. That will never change."

"When—" She swallowed hard. "When would you go?"

"Oh, not for a while yet. There's still a few things I have to clear up here."

"We-well, don't leave without saying good-bye."

"I won't."

Becky felt her eyes begin to fill and knew if she didn't make her escape now she was going to embarrass herself in front of the man she loved. "I guess I'll leave you to your packing then." She paused. "Garrick...I...I...thank you for everything. Without you, Alaina and I...well, thank you," she finished lamely. With one last look she left the shed and ran back to the house.

Garrick let out a painful sigh as he leaned his forehead against the shelves. He'd done the right thing. Becky and Alaina would be cared for, cherished even. He'd fulfilled his part of the bargain admirably. So, why did he feel like he wanted to die?

Becky slowed down as soon as she was away from the shed. She'd hoped Garrick had come to make amends, but he was truly finished with her. Just another of his noble causes that he'd seen to a satisfactory conclusion. That hurt almost as much as losing him.

She stopped outside the front door to wipe her eyes and straighten her apron. It wouldn't do for Cameron to see how upset she was. Maybe Garrick was right. Maybe she and Alaina did belong with Cameron. At the very least, she needed to make Garrick think she was happily settled so he could get on with his life.

Becky's eyes widened in surprise when she stepped inside. Alaina stood at the end of her cradle solemnly regarding Cameron who had hunkered down to hold the cradle still. The look on his face could only be described as awestruck as he gazed at the baby.

"Cameron?"

He looked up. "Everything all right with Swede?"

"I guess so. What are you doing?"

"Alonna was crying, and I wasn't sure what else to do."

"Alaina."

"What?"

"Her name isn't Alonna, it's Alaina."

"Oh, right." He turned back to Alaina as though he couldn't keep his eyes away. "You know, it's the most amazing thing. She looks like me, but she has your nose and your smile."

"I guess she takes after both of us."

"Isn't it incredible?" His voice was filled with wonder. "She's some of you and some of me all mixed up into a new little person. We created her together in that old shack and didn't even know we were doing it." Cameron's eyes shone as he looked up at Becky. "My daughter. I never knew how amazing it would feel to say those words."

Becky nodded and turned away. She should have been delighted, but for some reason his words made her want to cry. "I guess I better fix some more mush. This is too cold to eat."

Breakfast was a desultory meal, but Cameron didn't seem to notice. He ate as though she had set a sumptuous feast in front of him, chatting amicably the whole time. It seemed strange after sharing countless meals with Garrick, who rarely said anything. When they were finished, he took his leave. He promised to see her soon and gave her a chaste little kiss on the cheek.

It took Becky very little time to clean the cabin after Cameron was gone, and time hung heavily on her hands. Surely the special feelings she'd had for Cameron would come back now that he'd returned. It was only her disillusionment that had dimmed her intense love for him. At one time, it had been all she lived for.

Dispiritedly, Becky wandered over to Garrick's bunk. She hadn't slept in it last night, unable to face the prospect of being there alone. Now, she sat on the edge and smoothed her hand over the blanket. They'd had such a short time together in this bed, and yet it seemed somehow bigger and better than all the weeks she'd spent in one rendezvous after another with Cameron.

Becky picked up his pillow and pressed it to her face. As she inhaled Garrick's scent, a wave of loneliness swept through her. The thought of life without him was too horrible to bear.

Over the next week, Cameron made a steady assault on Becky's heart. He treated her like a fairy princess with everything he did calculated to please her. There were gifts for both Alaina and Becky, long buggy rides, evening strolls and even a play at the Variety Theater.

Saturday, Cameron took Becky and Alaina to Kidder's restaurant for an extravagant supper. Outside her door afterward, he took her into his arms and kissed her. It was warmly passionate, the sort that seductions began with, but Becky made an excuse about being tired and slipped inside the house.

Undaunted, Cameron continued to lavish her with attention, but Becky found herself curiously unmoved by any of it. In fact, she started to wonder how she'd ever fancied herself in love with him. The self-assurance she had always admired began to seem more like arrogance and conceit, his charm more practiced than sincere. He was clearly fascinated with Alaina, but really wanted little to do with her other than admiring his own stunning good looks reproduced on her tiny face.

Handsome, well-built, and charming, Cameron Price was every woman's dream. His smile was enough to melt the most ironclad feminine heart, yet all Becky could do was find fault with him. She couldn't help wondering how a man could change so much in one short year.

Deep down, Becky knew Cameron hadn't changed. He had always been as self-centered and conceited as he was handsome. The difference was that now she saw it. He no longer fit what she thought a husband should be. Truth was, he just wasn't Garrick.

It was never more obvious than the day he walked her home from Angel's. "You really should have driven," he said as he sidestepped a large pile of horse dung.

"But why?" Becky asked in surprise. "It's an absolutely beautiful day."

"What's that got to do with it?"

"Spring comes late up here in the mountains. We haven't had much chance to get out in the sunshine. Alaina and I enjoy the walk."

"I wasn't referring to the weather. These streets aren't fit for you to set foot on."

"What are you talking about?"

"You can't be serious." He stopped and stared at her. "We're surrounded by filth of every description."

Becky looked back the way they had come. Most of her life had been spent in one mining town or another. Other than when they were rendered impassable by snow or mud, she hadn't noticed the condition of the streets for a very long time. Now she saw Cameron was right. The road was liberally covered with piles of manure, garbage in various stages of decay, and other things that were best left unidentified.

"That first day, the bottom of your skirt was almost completely covered with mud and muck," Cameron was saying. "It was disgusting."

Becky looked up at him in hurt surprise. "I couldn't help it, Cameron. The streets were too muddy to bring the buckboard into town."

"Precisely why you should have stayed at home," he said, taking her elbow in a proprietary grip and turning her toward her cabin once more. "Of course, I can understand why you'd want to spend as little time as possible in that hovel. I promise you, I'll never expect you to live in such squalor."

Squalor? *Hovel*? The cozy little cabin she was so proud of? She'd have slapped Cameron for the insult if there hadn't been so many people around who might carry the story back to Garrick. How dare he criticize her home?

It was almost the last straw. Only one thing kept Becky playing the game. Garrick was watching. Even when she was with Cameron, Becky was keenly aware of when Garrick was near, as he often was. At such times, she was especially careful to appear happy. Whatever else she might feel, it was imperative that Garrick think all was well. He wouldn't do what he wanted until he was sure she and Alaina were happily settled. Becky owed him that freedom and would do almost anything to see he got it.

Still, she was glad when Cameron left town for a few days on business. It was a relief not to have to pretend for a while. The warm weather settled in to stay, and the last of the snow disappeared in a matter of two days. As the water trickled down from the mountain slopes, it filled the creeks with more than the usual spring runoff.

Becky watched the creek behind the cabin nervously. When the water began lapping at the shed, she decided to move the horses and the buckboard to higher ground. Alaina was asleep in her cradle and Becky was reluctant to disturb her. Besides, the flooded creek was so unpredictable that she was afraid of putting the baby in danger. Deciding Alaina was far safer where she was, Becky left the cabin door open and went to hitch up Sophie.

When the roar of the creek intensified, she wondered if she'd waited too long. The mare and colt were spooked, but Becky didn't know if it was the sound of the water outside or if she'd communicated her own nervousness to them. Whatever the reason, it took much longer to hitch Sophie to the buckboard than usual. At last it was accomplished, and she led the pair out of the shed.

"Come on, Sophie. You and your baby are safe now.... Oh no!" Becky stared in horror at the creek which had overflowed its banks and cut a new channel. The cabin was now completely surrounded by water. Immobilized by shock, Becky stared at the raging torrent that ran between the road and the cabin. There was no way she could cross it. She was stuck on one side and Alaina was on the other.

Chapter 28

Garrick can get her out! Becky clambered up into the buckboard and slapped the reins across Sophie's rump. By the time they got to town, the mare was moving so fast more than one pedestrian jumped out of the way when they saw the buckboard careening down the street.

Sophie had barely stopped in front of Garrick's shop before Becky was on the ground running. "Garrick, oh Garrick you've got to help me."

"Becky!" He looked up in surprise. "What's wrong?"

"I went to save Sophie only I thought Alaina would be all right where she was, but the water came up and the creek changed course and oh, Garrick, you've got to save her." Becky covered her face and burst into tears.

"Slow down, Becky," he said urgently. "Tell me again what happened."

It took several precious seconds to make Garrick understand, but he was stripping off his leather apron as he listened. "Was the water inside the cabin?" he asked, pulling a coiled lariat off the wall.

"N-no. It was still several feet from the door."

"Good, then she's probably still safe. We may need some help," he said as he strode to the door. "I don't know if I can–"

"Becky," Cameron's voice cut through the air startling them both. "What's going on?"

"Thank God. You're just the man we need, Price," Garrick said, as he lifted Becky up into the buckboard. "I'll tell you about it on the way."

By the time they arrived back at the cabin, the water had risen to the door and they could hear the faint sound of Alaina crying over the roar of the creek.

"At least we know she's all right," Garrick said, climbing down from the buckboard. "Now if we can just get to her. You ever dealt with anything like this, Price?"

Cameron shook his head. "Not really. Have you?"

"Once, and I almost didn't get back out." *It brought me the love of my life,* he added silently. "That's why I brought the rope."

"What do we tie it to?" Becky said worriedly.

"I'll hold it," Cameron said.

"Do you know what you're doing?" Garrick asked.

"Yes. I've never done it with a man, but I've helped get wagons across the Platte. It's the same basic principle. We'll use the current to get you over and back." The two men exchanged a long look. "You can trust me," Cameron said. "Whatever else is between us, I owe you my life."

Garrick nodded. "All right then, we'd better find an anchor."

Becky watched the two men in confusion as they moved up stream. *What in the world?* They hardly spoke to one another, but both seemed to know exactly what they were looking for as they studied the rocks and stumps.

Finally, Cameron stopped by a huge boulder and did his best to dislodge it. After several unsuccessful tries, he nodded in satisfaction. "This ought to hold."

"I hope so. I doubt you could hang onto me by yourself. You're going to have a tough time controlling the swing back across anyway," Garrick said as he stripped down to his drawers.

"Will somebody please tell me what you two are doing?" Becky asked. Frantic about her baby, she couldn't imagine why they were messing around so far above the cabin. "How are you going to get Alaina from clear up here?"

Garrick tied the rope securely around his waist. "The current will carry me downstream. If we start here, I should wind up fairly close to the cabin."

"Can't you just go straight across? I mean with Cameron holding the rope, wouldn't you stay in the same place?"

"It would cut him in half or at least feel like it was," Cameron said. "This way the current will be doing all the work. The rope is only there in case anything goes wrong."

"Getting back across with Alaina will be the hard part," Garrick added.

"You got me out all by yourself last year," Becky pointed out.

"Yes, but you very nearly drowned. Besides, you're an adult and Alaina's a baby. I'll have to keep her head above water. That means once I have her I won't be able to do much but keep her safe. We'll be so much dead weight on the other end. With Cameron's help, the current should swing us back over to this side."

Cameron nodded. "I just wish we could be sure it will work that way. I don't know that I can pull you back across if I need to."

"I guess that's a chance we're going to have to take," Garrick said.

Becky was silent as Garrick and Cameron continued their preparations. "What about Sophie?" she said suddenly. The men stopped and looked at her in surprise. "If we hook another rope to the one around your waist and then tie it to the back of the buckboard once you're over there, Sophie could pull you across if necessary."

Cameron and Garrick looked at each other. "You know, she just might have something there," Garrick said.

"It's worth a try, anyway."

At last, everything was ready, and Garrick stood poised on the bank. Cameron tied the rope to the boulder, then braced himself against its rough surface. "You ready, Swede?"

"As ready as I will ever be, I guess."

Becky felt as though she were being buffeted by the stream herself as she watched Garrick wade into the raging torrent. When the water was about mid-thigh, he started swimming. He seemed to make little headway as the water swept him downstream at an alarming rate.

Cameron's face showed intense concentration as he played the rope out through his hands, making sure there was just the right amount of tension. For the first time, Becky realized Cameron literally held Garrick's life in his hands. A shiver of apprehension ran down her back.

A moment later, Cameron relaxed, and Becky jerked her gaze back to Garrick just in time to see him crawl out of the water. He paused a moment in the cabin doorway, trying to catch his breath, then climbed to his feet and went inside. Alaina's cries stopped almost immediately, and Becky breathed a sigh of relief.

By the time Garrick emerged with Alaina securely strapped to his chest in her ski harness and a bundle of clothing in his hand, Cameron and Becky had the safety line tied to the buckboard. Garrick had removed the rope from his waist and tied it under his arms across his chest underneath Alaina.

"What the hell is that?" Cameron asked, his brows coming together in surprise.

"It looks like he grabbed some of our clothes."

"No, I mean that contraption he's got Elaine in."

"Oh, that's just the harness he uses when we go skiing." Becky tried to ignore an instantaneous surge of irritation. *Honestly, you'd think a man could remember his own daughter's name.*

"When you what?"

"Never mind. The important thing is that she's perfectly safe in it."

"If you say so." Cameron still looked skeptical as he headed back to his place near the rock.

With a mighty heave, Garrick threw the clothes across the swollen stream, then gave Becky a reassuring smile. The air between them fairly sizzled as their eyes locked. In that moment, they both felt the strength of their love, though neither could express it.

Garrick broke eye contact first, uncomfortably aware that his emotions were plainly visible on his face. The last thing he needed was to send Becky that kind of message. With grim determination, he directed his gaze upstream and waited for Cameron to give him the signal.

When it came at last, he stepped into the stream and walked as far out as he could. He was thigh deep before he knew he could go no farther without losing his footing. Garrick waited until Cameron had pulled in all the extra rope, then very carefully eased himself into the water and let the tug of the current sweep his feet out from under him.

He winced in pain when the rope snapped tight. It cut into his skin cruelly as he bobbed along in the water, feeling alarmingly helpless. Alaina let out a howl of protest when the cold water closed over her back, but Garrick's arms around her and the angle of his body kept her safe.

About halfway across, they were caught by an eddy that nearly pulled them under. Garrick fought to keep Alaina's head above water as he was caught in the irresistible force. Fingers of panic were beginning to claw at him when he felt the secondary rope tighten. Slowly, they began to ease out of the whirlpool and back into the regular current.

A lifetime of cold, wet fear passed before Garrick felt the scrape of mud beneath his feet. Suddenly, Becky was there, wading out to help him, her skirt immodestly tucked into the waistband of her apron. Her hands felt like warm sanity against his frigid skin, a safe haven for both Alaina and him. As he clambered to his feet, he wanted her to put her arms around him more than he'd ever wanted anything in his life.

Becky exclaimed in horror when she saw the raw strip where the rope had abraded his skin. She touched the area around the injuries with gentle fingers. "Oh, dear. I wish we had some of that salve we used on your back."

The image of Becky doctoring his hurts brought a rush of intense longing and the desire to pull her into his embrace, to imprison her next to his heart where she belonged.

Then Cameron was there, and the opportunity was lost. All three of them were nearly delirious with relief as they freed Alaina and Garrick from the straps and ropes. The mood of self-congratulations lasted clear up until they reached the edge of town. Suddenly, the constraint that had disappeared in the face of danger returned with a vengeance.

"I'll get out here," Garrick said, handing the reins to Cameron.

Becky looked up at him in consternation. "Are you sure?"

"I...uh...I have to pick up a few things at the store." He climbed down from the buckboard, then glanced back up at Becky. "There isn't much in that bundle of clothes I brought you. Go ahead and charge whatever else you need to my account at the store. Do you want me to find you a place to stay until the water goes down?"

"I—"

"That won't be necessary," Cameron broke in. "I'll take care of it from here on out. Thanks for your help with my daughter, Swede."

The words hit Garrick like a slap in the face. The risk he'd taken had been for *his* wife and child, not Cameron's. He turned away before the impulse to smash his fist into the other man's face became impossible to resist.

"Garrick!" Becky called after him, but he kept walking.

"That was incredibly rude, Cameron," she said, turning on him angrily.

"What, saying thank you?"

You know very well what I mean. Garrick just put his life in jeopardy for us, and you treated him like a hired hand or something."

"I did not. I was merely pointing out that you and Amanda are my responsibility now, not his."

"Her name is Uh-lay-nuh, Cameron! Not Amanda, or Alona, or Elaine or any of the others. Furthermore, we're nobody's responsibility but mine, and I prefer to make my own arrangements, thank you."

"I'm just trying to help."

"If you really want to make yourself useful, you can take the horses and buckboard to the livery stable over by the jail." She scrambled down from the seat. "I'll go over and pay for it later."

"Come on, Becky," he said in a pleading voice. "At least let me give you my room at the boarding house."

"I'll think about it." With a twitch of her skirt, she turned and marched down the street to The Green Garter. Her face was a mask of perfect calm until she entered the kitchen. Then her bravado crumpled as she sagged against the wall with a sob. Alaina whimpered in her arms.

"Becky, what's happened?"

The sound of Angel's voice brought Becky's head up with a jerk.

"I... I didn't know you were here."

"It *is* my kitchen," Angel said dryly. "Now, what's going on?"

It didn't take long for Becky to tell Angel of the morning's adventure and explain her dilemma. "Now we don't have any place to stay and no money."

"Money's no problem. You don't need cooking lessons anymore, so I'll pay you for the work you do. A place to stay though might be a little tougher to come by. All the boarding houses are full. Cameron just got that room yesterday."

"I guess I better tell him I'll take him up on his offer then. I suppose he'll be insufferable. He is anyway."

"Lover's quarrel?"

"Not really. He's just so darn possessive."

"Do you love him?"

The urge to unburden her soul to Angel was strong, but there was always the chance Garrick would find out if she said no. Becky was determined that he was going to have his freedom, no matter what.

"Why, Angel, how can you ask? No woman alive could resist Cameron Price for long."

Later that afternoon, Becky discovered that the 'good women' of the town who had ignored her until now were suddenly vitally interested in her life. Deciding to take Garrick up on his generous offer, she went to the mercantile to buy a few things. She planned to keep a strict accounting of all she spent and repay him before he left town.

"Swede was sayin' you might be in," the balding storekeeper said pleasantly. "You want all this on his bill?"

Becky smiled. "Yes, thank you."

"Did you hear that?" said an unfamiliar female voice. "And after the way she's been chasing after that nice Mr. Price."

"It's scandalous is what it is. Married to one man, carrying on with another, and that baby. Well, any fool can see who its father is."

"I think it's criminal the way she foisted that child on Swede, then turned her back on him as soon as Cameron Price came back to town. And Swede's still paying her bills."

"Swede's a fool if he can't see what a little hussy she is."

With tears of humiliation blurring her eyes, Becky turned and walked from the store, leaving her purchases still sitting on the counter. She didn't stop until she and Alaina were inside their tiny airless room at the boarding house. It was bad enough the old cats thought ill of her, but Garrick and Alaina were blameless.

When Becky and Alaina went down to supper, the landlady, Mrs. O'Reily, gave her the cold shoulder, and several of the men leered at her. One even went so far as to drop his hand on her knee and give it a suggestive squeeze. Becky jumped up and ran upstairs to her room. She put a chair in front of the door for good measure then threw herself on the bed. Her life with Garrick was over, a future with Cameron was uncertain at best, and the whole town was questioning her morals. Things couldn't get much worse.

Several hours later, Garrick stalked into The Green Garter, his face suffused with anger and his fists clenched at his side. He found Cameron sitting at a corner table entwined with Collette. "I've been looking for you, Price."

Cameron looked up in surprise. "What for?"

"We need to talk." He gave Collette a cold stare. "Alone."

"All right." Cameron kissed Collette and pushed her off his lap. "I'll see you later, honey," he said, giving her a pat on the behind as she walked away. "What do you want, Swede?"

"You seem pretty cozy with Collette for a man who's contemplating marriage."

Cameron shrugged. "As I told you before, she has her uses. Buy you a drink?"

"No thanks."

"At least have a seat." Cameron gestured to a chair and watched Garrick sit down. "What's the problem?"

"I want to know why you haven't married Becky yet."

"I thought she'd like to be courted a little first. Women like all the preliminaries."

Garrick gave a snort of disgust. "Seems to me you got those all out of the way last year. Are you aware that the good women of this town are crucifying her?"

"What?" The relaxed smile was wiped instantly from Cameron's face.

"My friend Tom Herman over at Herman's retail said two old bats tied into her this afternoon. They didn't attack her directly, mind you, just talked behind her back. Seems they don't think it's fitting for her to be married to one man and carrying on with another, especially when her baby looks a whole lot like the other man."

"Damn."

"I warned you once, Price. If you don't want to pick your teeth up off the floor, you'll get your priorities straight, now."

Cameron pulled a ring out of his pocket. "I was going to ask her today, but things didn't exactly go the way I planned." "By this time tomorrow we should be officially engaged."

"Good." Garrick stood up. "And I'd advise you not to mess with me."

"Don't worry. I'm not that stupid."

Garrick made his way to the bar. "Bring me a bottle of whiskey, Sam."

"Sure thing, Swede."

Becky would be safely married soon. Married, and forever beyond his reach. Garrick wondered if Cameron knew how erotically sensitive her back was, or if he ever took time to coax her into her own release. With an angry growl, Garrick pulled the cork out of the bottle with his teeth and spit it out on the bar.

Over the next few hours, Garrick broke his own rule and proceeded to get rip-roaring drunk for the first time in his life. Sometime after midnight, he staggered back to his shop and collapsed on his pallet.

The sun was up before he moved again. He awakened slowly. The pain behind his eyes was nearly as bad as the one in his side.

"Wake up, Swede."

Garrick opened his eyes slowly and blinked up at the town constable just as a boot nudged his ribs again.

"Wh-what's wrong?" he asked, his tongue thick and unresponsive in his mouth.

"You're under arrest, Swede, for the murder of Cameron Price."

Chapter 29

"Becky, open the door."

The sound of Angel's voice and her insistent knocking finally penetrated Becky's deep sleep. She sat up groggily and rubbed her eyes. "Angel?"

"Yes, now open the door."

As Becky slid off the bed, the voice of Mrs. O'Reily came through the wooden panel. "Here now, what do you think you're doing?"

"What does it look like I'm doing? I came to speak with Mrs. Swenson."

"Did you indeed?" came the indignant response. "I might have known someone like her would keep company with a...a scarlet woman. Well, I won't have the likes of you in my house, and as for *Mrs.* Swenson—"

"She won't be one bit happier about this than you are," Angel broke in. "Mrs. Swenson wouldn't give me the time of day under normal circumstances."

"Then why are you here?"

"Dr. Caldwell sent me."

"Dr. Caldwell? But—"

Whatever Mrs. O'Reily had been about to say was lost as Becky finally managed to pull the chair out from under the doorknob and fling the door open. "What do you mean waking me up at this ungodly hour?" she asked with irritation. With sleep still clouding her mind, it was the first thing she could think of that would lend credence to Angel's story.

"This...person says she has a message from Dr. Caldwell but—" the landlady began.

"Dr. Caldwell?" Becky said, opening her door wider. "You'd better get inside then, before someone comes along. I certainly hope no one saw you come in."

"No," Angel said, stepping inside. "I was very careful to use the back door."

"Just as you should," Becky said indignantly, then turned to the landlady. "And you can be sure I'll make certain she leaves the same way, Mrs. O'Reily."

"Are you sure it's safe—"

"I'll be quite all right, but thank you for your concern." Becky shut the door on the still blustering landlady.

"I'll bet the old biddy's ear is pressed to the door," Angel whispered.

Becky nodded and plopped down on the bed. Alaina woke at once with a howl. "How's that?" she said in a low voice.

"You are a sly one, aren't you?" Angel said as she joined her on the bed.

Becky grinned. "Alaina always wakes up grouchy."

Angel eyed her rumpled appearance. "And do you always sleep in your clothes?"

"No, I fell asleep last night before I got undressed." She shrugged. "Not that it would have mattered much anyway. All my nightclothes are at home. Now, what's all this about?"

"Bad news I'm afraid. Somebody ambushed Cameron Price behind my place last night and tried to beat him to death."

Becky was horrified. "Oh, no. Is he all right?"

"No, he's hurt pretty bad."

"How bad?" Becky asked fearfully.

Angel sighed. "I won't lie to you, Becky. Doc Caldwell says he hasn't got a chance in hell of making it."

"Oh, Angel," she said, covering her mouth with her hand. "I was so mean to him yesterday. If he dies, I'll never forgive myself."

Angel was silent for a moment as she rubbed Becky's shoulder soothingly. "You haven't heard the worst of it, I'm afraid," she said at last.

"What could be worse?"

"They arrested Swede this morning."

"They what?" Becky's head came up with a jerk. "Why?"

"Because he's their only suspect."

"But that's ridiculous. Garrick would never do anything like that. What made them think it was him?"

"He and Cameron had an argument at my place last night for, one thing."

"About what?"

Angel shrugged. "Nobody seems to know, but I have my suspicions."

Becky stared at her for a long moment then looked down. "Me."

"It's a distinct possibility. There's bound to be trouble when two men love the same woman."

"That isn't the case here," Becky's voice was almost a whisper. "Garrick doesn't love me, and I'm not sure Cameron knows the meaning of the word."

"Oh, for pity's sake. That's about the silliest thing you've ever—"

"Mrs. Swenson?" A heavy knock sounded on the door. "Is everything all right?"

"Just fine, Mrs. O'Reily."

"That's my cue to leave," Angel said, rising. "They took Cameron over to my place because it was close. I have an extra crib since Molly's gone. It's kind of small for a sick room, but I guess he can stay there for the time being. Trouble is, he needs someone with him all the time, and we can't do it all."

"I'll help, of course," Becky said as she picked up Alaina.

Angel nodded. "I figured I could count on you, though I really hate to ask."

"You didn't, I volunteered." Becky glanced at the door. "What do we tell Mrs. O'Reily?" she whispered.

"Not a damn thing," Angel whispered back as she took two steps across the room. With a wink at Becky, she threw open the door and watched as Mrs. O'Reily stumbled into the room. The other woman's ear had obviously been plastered to the door, and she'd been unprepared for Angel's sudden movement. "Do be careful, Mrs. O'Reily. The floor seems to be quite uneven here." With another wink at Becky behind Mrs. O'Reily's back, Angel left.

Becky caught Mrs. O'Reily's elbow with her free hand. "Are you all right?" she asked as she helped the other woman right herself.

"I think so. I wasn't expecting...I mean..."

Becky mentally blessed Angel for the diversion. If luck were on her side, she could make her escape before Mrs. O'Reily asked a lot of embarrassing questions that Becky really didn't want to answer. She reached down and grabbed several diapers and Alaina's blanket. "I have to run. See you later."

Becky left the landlady behind her as she ran down the stairs and out the door. Once she reached the street, she stopped, her mind whirling in confusion. She needed to go somewhere safe and sort it all out. With that thought, she turned and started down the street, her steps taking her unerringly to Garrick's blacksmith shop.

Balancing Alaina in one arm, she swung open the huge door and stepped into the welcoming darkness. She put Alaina in her pen and opened the window, then automatically changed and dressed Alaina. The familiar motions were comforting, but without the ring of Garrick's hammer, the smithy was horribly quiet. No fire glowed in the forge, and the tools remained in their places on the wall. It stood waiting for the smith to return. She wondered if he ever would.

Becky wandered over to the peg that held Garrick's leather apron. She reached out to touch the shirt that hung there with the apron. Sleeveless and stained, it was little better than a rag, but Garrick insisted it was exactly right for the work he had to do. As she thought of the many times she had washed it, tears welled up in her eyes.

How could this have happened? Cameron was near death and Garrick in jail. Was she the cause? Where did her loyalties lie? Though her heart belonged to Garrick, she couldn't very well turn her back on Cameron. He was the father of her child. How could she choose between the two men, especially now when she might lose either or both of them?

Becky's thoughts went around and around. Life had been simple before Cameron returned. Now it had gotten so complicated nothing made sense any more.

She wiped away the tears in her eyes. Crying wasn't going to do anybody any good. The first order of business was to visit the jail and see what she could do for Garrick. An image of what she must look like popped into her mind. She couldn't very well go to the jail all rumpled and tear-streaked.

Garrick had been living in his shop since he had left their cabin. It didn't take long to locate his things in the loft. After she washed her face and hands, she felt much better. Though Garrick's comb wasn't equal to the snarls in her long, thick hair, she finally managed to work out the worst and pull it back into a fairly respectable knot without breaking the comb.

With a deep sigh, she smoothed her hands over her skirt. There wasn't much she could do about her clothes, so they would have to do for now. The face reflecting back from Garrick's tiny shaving mirror was a bit wan but presentable, at least.

Alaina had pulled herself up in the small pen and was standing there happily chewing on the edge when Becky climbed back down the ladder. "Ma...Ma..Ma," she said.

Becky looked at her in surprise. "Mama?"

"Ma," Alaina said and promptly stuck her fingers in her mouth.

"Well, it's about time," Becky said as she bent to pick her up. "You've been saying Da for almost two weeks now." The words brought a sharp pang as Becky thought of the man Alaina thought was her father and the one who actually was.

The jail was right across the street from Garrick's shop. Inside, the newly elected town constable was asleep with his feet up on the desk, and his chair leaned back against the wall. Becky glanced around the bleak little room with disgust. Light came through two windows latticed with flat strips of metal. The desk and chair were the only furnishings except for a small pot-bellied stove in one corner. Everything was covered with a layer of dust.

If the jail was this barren here, how much worse was Garrick's cell going to be? Becky looked at the heavy wooden door set in the middle of the wall with two barred windows on either side of it and shivered. The cells that opened off the room beyond that door would be almost completely dark.

Her attention returned to the constable who slept on, blithely unaware of her presence. She cleared her throat. No response. "Excuse me?"

"Huh...what?" The man started, nearly upending his chair as he jerked awake.

"Excuse me," Becky repeated. "I'd like to visit Garrick Swenson, please."

"Who?"

"Swede."

"Oh." He scratched his cheek and glanced at the door. "'Fraid I can't let you do that."

"Why not."

"It ain't safe. He's a murderer."

"He is not!" Becky said indignantly. "Cameron Price is still alive, and it hasn't been proven Swede attacked him anyway. Besides, he's my husband. I'm perfectly safe with him."

"Not from what I hear. He near killed your lover last night. If he was that mad, can't figure he'd be real friendly toward you either."

"Are you in charge here?"

"With city prisoners."

"Oh, who's in charge of the rest?"

"The county sheriff."

"Where would I find him?"

"I dunno. Said he was going to get a shave and haircut, then ride on over to Atlantic City."

"You wouldn't happen to know where he was planning to get the haircut, would you?"

"Nope, he didn't say. In the saloon next door maybe."

"Thank you," Becky turned toward the door.

"Won't do you no good to talk to the sheriff," he called after her. "He ain't real fond of unfaithful wives, either."

Becky didn't even bother to answer. If she could just find the sheriff. John Lucien had always been friendly to Garrick. Surely he'd let her see her own husband. Becky located him in the back of the saloon just as he was climbing out of the barber's chair.

"Sheriff Lucien?"

The sheriff glanced up. "Mrs. Swenson."

"Could I speak to you, please?"

"Of course." He handed the barber two bits before turning to Becky and gesturing toward the door. "Shall we step outside?"

"I want to see my husband," she said as soon as they were out of earshot of the other saloon patrons.

"Do you think that's wise?"

"Oh, for heaven's sake. You know my husband well enough to realize he's not a violent man. Even if he were the one who attacked Cameron, he wouldn't still be mad enough to hurt me."

The sheriff gazed off across the street. "There have been...uh...rumors."

"I'm well aware of the rumors, Sheriff. There is very little truth in them, and my husband knows it."

"You haven't been living together."

"No, but not because he thinks I've been unfaithful." Becky sighed. "Sheriff, there's a lot you don't know. Has anyone told you what happened yesterday?"

"No."

He listened intently as Becky told the story of Alaina's rescue. When she finished, he rubbed his chin thoughtfully. "Do you cook, Mrs. Swenson?"

Becky gave him a startled look. "Yes, but I don't see —"

"Since the assault happened inside the city limits, the city constable's jurisdiction and mine overlap somewhat. I can't in good conscience override his decision."

"But —"

Sheriff Lucien held up his hand to forestall her. "However, there are certain rules we have to follow with prisoners. For instance, we have to provide them with three meals a day and clean clothes. For a long-term prisoner we usually hire someone to take care of both. If you were to take the job, you would at least have reason to be inside the jail three times a day."

"I'll do it."

"It won't get you inside Swede's cell, you understand. You'll have to convince Abner Stolks to allow that. If you prove you can be trusted, he'll relax. He's not unreasonable; he's just doing his job the best way he knows how. I'll let you in for a short visit now, but the rest is up to you."

"Oh, thank you, Sheriff. I can't tell you how much it means to me."

"You have to be completely honest with me. Is there anything I need to know?"

"I... I also promised to help the girls at The Green Garter with Cameron."

He gave her a sympathetic look. "This must be very difficult for you."

Becky blinked back sudden tears. "It's awful."

"I'm afraid it's going to get a lot worse before it's over."

"You think my husband did it, don't you?"

Sheriff Lucien shrugged. "It's not my job to decide guilt or innocence, only to gather all the evidence so a judge and jury can. This is a difficult situation. The Justice of the Peace has asked for the circuit judge to try the case because he feels it's beyond his expertise. Kind of too bad Esther Morris isn't the Justice any more. She wouldn't have been afraid."

Becky agreed wholeheartedly. Esther Morris had acquitted herself quite well in her eighteen months as justice. "If he's found guilty, what will they do to him?"

"The judge will pass sentence. If Price survives, Swede would probably go to the Territorial Prison in Laramie."

"And if Cameron dies?" Becky asked fearfully.

"Then it becomes murder."

"And?"

"And he'll hang."

Chapter 30

"**B**etter check to make sure she ain't sneakin' anything in to him," Abner Stolks said, eyeing Becky suspiciously.

Sheriff Lucien gave her an apologetic look. "I'm sorry, Mrs. Swenson, but I will have to search you for weapons."

"All right." Becky wasn't sure what that entailed, but she certainly wasn't going to jeopardize her visit to Garrick over a technicality. The city constable was just looking for a reason to deny her the privilege. He'd been arguing long and hard against it ever since the sheriff had told him of the plan.

"If you'll take the baby, Stolks, I'll check her."

Abner Stolks turned a little pale. "You want me to hold the baby?"

"Just until I finish the search."

It was hard to say who was more reluctant to do their part, Constable Stolks, Sheriff Lucien or Becky. Even Alaina protested when her mother handed her to the unfamiliar man. Though strangers didn't usually bother her, this one made her feel very insecure with his overly cautious grip on her.

Becky's gasp of shocked embarrassment as Sheriff Lucien ran his hands lightly over her was equaled only by the sheriff's own discomfort. In fact, his search was so unobtrusive that anything smaller than a Colt .44 would have passed unnoticed.

By the time he finished, Becky had turned several shades of red and Alaina was crying at the top of her lungs. The crying stopped the minute Becky took the baby back.

"I'm sorry, Mrs. Swenson," Sheriff Lucien said regretfully. "The baby will have to stay here."

"Why?"

He cleared his throat uncomfortably. "Considering the circumstances, I can't in good conscience let you take her in."

"But he's her father."

"Is he?" He glanced pointedly at Alaina then back to Becky.

As his meaning became clear, Becky felt herself blushing even darker. "Sheriff Lucien, my husband loves Alaina. In fact, he risked his life to save her just yesterday. No matter how mad he might be at me or Cameron, he certainly wouldn't take it out on Alaina."

"Nevertheless—"

"Oh, all right, but you better find something to distract her, or she'll scream her head off."

"Don't worry, Mrs. Swenson, I have three of my own. I know how to handle babies." To Becky's surprise, Alaina seemed perfectly content to go to Sheriff Lucien and even smiled at him when he chucked her under the chin. "See, we'll be fine. All right, Abner, let Mrs. Swenson in."

Becky followed the constable through the door and across the room beyond to the row of cells. There were four, each with a thick wooden door and a small barred window. Becky felt strangely nervous as Abner Stolks stopped in front of the middle door. Except for yesterday, she and Garrick hadn't spoken since the morning Cameron had dropped in.

Though the grating of the key in the lock sounded unnaturally loud in Becky's ears, the door swung open quietly on well-oiled hinges. She stepped through the opening and jumped as the door clunked shut behind her. The room was tiny, dark and stuffy. Garrick lay on the bunk with his arm thrown over his eyes.

"Garrick?"

"Go away, Becky."

"W-why?"

"You have no reason to be here."

"I'm your wife."

"We both know that isn't true."

Becky stiffened her spine. "I had a hard time getting in here, Garrick. I'm not leaving until we talk."

He sighed and sat up. "I don't know what to say, Becky. Cameron's dead and everyone says I killed him. Nothing I can do will bring him back for you."

Becky looked at him in surprise. "Cameron isn't dead."

"Stolks said he was."

"And Angel said he's over at her place, beat up but alive. Personally, I'd take Angel's word before Constable Stolks's. He's a little too full of his own importance if you ask me."

"How badly beat up?"

"I'm not really sure," she hedged.

For the first time he looked directly at her. "You haven't seen him?

"Not yet."

"Why not?"

"I don't know. It just seemed more important to come here first. Maybe because I can't do anything to help him."

"You can't help me either."

"Of course I can," Becky said indignantly. "I'm going to help you get out of here."

"How are you going to do that?"

"By proving you didn't do it."

"You're sure I didn't?" Garrick stood up and walked to the door. "I wish I were."

Becky stared at him in shock. "What do you mean?"

"To tell the truth, I was so drunk I don't remember a thing after about ten o'clock."

"Drunk!" Becky looked at him as though he'd grown two heads. "Since when do you get so drunk you don't remember anything?"

"Last night was the first time."

"Why last night?"

Garrick shrugged. "I felt like it."

"But surely you wouldn't —"

"Look, Becky, I don't know if I did or not. Price isn't exactly a weakling. There are very few men who could take him in a fight, let alone nearly kill him."

"But you could," she whispered. Suddenly his arrest made more sense.

"Ja, I could." He stared out the window. "Maybe I did."

"Oh, Garrick, surely you'd have some bruises or —"

"Damn it, Becky, if I were mad enough to kill him, do you honestly think I'd give him a chance to get a punch in?" He flung himself away from the window and paced across the small confines to the other side. "Why don't you just go? I really don't want you here."

Without a word, Becky turned and walked to the door and signaled Constable Stolks to let her out. She'd never heard Garrick use a swear word before, and he'd certainly never cursed at her, at least not in English.

Garrick closed his eyes as the door shut behind Becky. He knew he'd hurt her deeply when he sent her away, but he didn't want her to be part of the ugliness that was sure to come. It was going to be hard enough on her as it was. Especially when his past caught up with him, as it surely would before this was all over.

For the hundredth time that morning, he searched his mind trying to remember what had happened. The last clear image was of Cameron Price going upstairs with Collette, his hands traveling all over the curvaceous brunette as they mounted the stairs.

At that moment, Garrick had been so angry he might have killed Price if he'd had the chance. He'd definitely wanted to teach the other man a lesson about sleeping with one woman on the eve of asking another to marry him. Had he actually given in to his anger? It was certainly possible.

At least Price was still alive. With any kind of luck, he'd stay that way. Garrick lay back down on his bunk. No matter whether Price lived or died, Garrick knew his own days were numbered. There was no doubt in his mind he was going to hang for murder.

"How is he?" Becky whispered as she joined Angel in the tiny room where Cameron lay.

"About as bad as a man can be this side of the cemetery. You see Swede?"

"Yes, though it took some doing." A suspicious little quaver entered her voice. "H-he sent me away."

"Don't suppose he wants you hurt by any of this."

"It's a little late for that." Becky sat down with a sigh. "Sheriff Lucien told me I could have the job of cooking for Garrick and doing his laundry. Do you mind if I use your kitchen until I can go home again?"

"You can use it even then. Mighty long way from your house to the jail. It'd be near impossible to pack food that far and keep it hot. What did Swede have to say for himself?"

"He said he doesn't remember."

"What?"

"He was drunk. I...I think he's convinced he did it."

"Good Lord!"

"Oh, Angel, what if—"

"Don't even say it. There are too many possibilities to spend your time worrying about everything that could happen. There's plenty of heartache in life without that."

Becky gave her a rueful smile. "You're always so practical. Did you get any sleep with all the excitement?"

"Not a whole lot."

"That's what I thought. Why don't you get some rest now? I can stay with Cameron."

"What about Alaina?"

"She's sucking her fingers." Becky smiled down at the baby in her arms. "That usually means she's about due for a nap."

"In that case, I'll take her," Angel said. "She can sleep on the bed next to me, and you won't have to worry about her."

Becky gave her a doubtful look. "Are you sure? You'll wake up when she does."

"That's all right. I shouldn't sleep more than an hour or two anyway. Besides, you'll need time to cook

Swede's supper and get some rest yourself. Night is the time I'll really need you here. Everyone else will be busy."

"All right," Becky said dubiously as she handed Alaina to Angel, "but if you change your mind..."

"Don't worry, honey, you'll be the first to know."

The steady rhythm of Cameron's breathing was the only sound in the tiny room as Angel left. It was the first time Becky had ever been in one of the cribs, and she was uncomfortably aware of the opulent decadence around her. This is where the true business of the brothel went on. If not for Garrick's timely intervention, she might well have worked in such a room herself.

With a deep sigh, Becky turned her attention to Cameron. It pained her to look at him. Swollen almost beyond recognition, the once handsome face was a mass of cuts and bruises. He lay so still it was easy to believe he was near death. The thought frightened Becky clear down to her toes.

Suddenly, she was confronted with the reality of her feelings for Cameron and was surprised to discover there was a part of her that still loved him. She hadn't even realized it until faced with the possibility of his death. It was very different from the all-consuming passion she felt for Garrick but no less real. This man had given her a child; it was impossible for her to feel nothing for him.

Life was so complicated. Not only was Cameron her first lover and Alaina's father, he was the key to Garrick's future as well. Only if he lived could Garrick be released, and if he died, Garrick might hang.

Not for a moment did Becky believe Garrick was responsible for Cameron's injuries. He had the devil's own temper when he was mad, but he cooled off fast and was more likely to walk away in the middle of an argument than to actually throw punches. Whoever had attacked Cameron had waited until he left The Green Garter. Garrick would never be able to hold onto his anger that long, nor would it be like him to ambush the man instead of confronting him face to face. Then there was the fact that he didn't bear any marks to indicate he'd attacked Cameron. Even if Cameron didn't fight back, Garrick's hands would be bruised, wouldn't they?

Becky reached over and touched Cameron's hand where it lay on the blanket. His knuckles were as unmarked as Garrick's. Though he had obviously been beaten, he hadn't been involved in a fistfight. If one eliminated Garrick as a suspect, it didn't make sense. Who could have done this to Cameron? An important piece of the puzzle was missing, and there was little chance the constable would look for it.

By the time Angel returned two hours later, Becky had decided it was up to her to ferret out the truth. Whoever had hurt Cameron should be brought to justice. And it was Garrick's only chance.

Her first thought was to simply find out when the two men had left The Green Garter. It proved to be more difficult than she anticipated. Angel hadn't paid any attention; nor, it seemed, had anyone else. Sam was the only one who had seen them both leave, and he wasn't sure about the time.

"Miss Angel don't allow clocks in the casino," he said as he pondered the question, "but I reckon Swede left long about midnight."

"What about Cameron Price?"

"Seems to me it was a while later, but I ain't real certain when."

"A short time or a long time after Swede?"

He rubbed his chin reflectively. "Seems like it was pretty soon, but I couldn't tell you for sure."

Becky bit her lip in frustration. Sam's testimony was more likely to implicate Garrick than exonerate him. "Who found Cameron?"

"I did, right after we closed down about dawn. Dang near tripped over him on my way to the outhouse."

"Could you tell me where?"

"Can't miss it. Right out back by the path."

There was little hope of discovering anything the sheriff had missed, but Becky was determined to examine every possibility. She had no trouble finding the place from Sam's description. Footprints in the dust and broken weeds indicated a scuffle had indeed taken place there. Unfortunately, it was impossible to tell anything else.

Hoping to find a clear footprint, Becky skirted the edge of the trampled area. Both Garrick and Cameron had large feet. An average size boot print could help prove Garrick wasn't the attacker. Her search proved fruitless. All the prints were blurred beyond recognition.

She was about to give up in defeat when a flash of color caught her eye next to the path. Some sort of brooch lay there, partially hidden in the grass. With a surge of hope, Becky bent to pick up the unexpected clue. She stared at the pin in surprise.

It was a bronze star suspended from the talons of an eagle. An engraving depicted a woman with a shield driving her enemy before her. Though Becky had never seen anything quite like it, she was pretty sure the red, white, and blue ribbon attached to the pin at the top meant it was a military medal of some sort. Cameron had been attacked by a soldier? It didn't make any sense, but then none of it did. At least she knew where to start looking: Fort Stambaugh.

Chapter 31

"Good evening, Constable Stolks," Becky said pleasantly as she set the basket on his desk. "I hope you like venison stew."

"What?" He looked at the basket, then up at her face in surprise.

"Venison stew, do you like it?"

"I...well, yes, but—"

"Good." Becky smiled as she handed him a folded napkin from the basket. "I never thought to ask this morning."

His eyes narrowed suspiciously. "What are you trying to pull?"

She paused in the process of setting a plate and silverware in front of him. "Didn't Sheriff Lucien tell you he hired me to cook and do laundry for my husband?"

"Yeah, he told me, but he never said nothin' about this."

"Oh, dear. I thought he meant...oh, well never mind." She started to put the plate back in the basket.

"Hold on now. What exactly did you think you were supposed to do?"

"Cook three meals a day for everyone here, but I guess he meant only the prisoners. I feel so foolish—"

"No need for that," he said gruffly. "Don't reckon there's any harm done after all."

Becky hesitated. "Would you like some stew then? I made plenty, and it'll just go to waste otherwise."

"If you're sure there's too much for Swede. I can't abide throwin' good food away."

"I can't either, and I always seem to make too much," Becky said with a smile as she lifted the lid off the pot of stew. "I'm so glad you—Oh, dear." She paused with a ladle full of stew in mid-air, the tantalizing smell wafting toward him enticingly. "I just happened to think, what about your own supper?"

"I don't reckon I'll make it back to my boarding house in time for supper anyway."

"Do you mean to tell me when you have a prisoner you don't have time to eat?"

"Usually the sheriff comes by to spell me, but he's out of town tonight. "

"Of all the inconsiderate—I'm certainly glad I brought enough for both of you," Becky said indignantly. "You can just plan on eating here as long as I'm doing the cooking."

Abner Stolks gave her a dubious look as he watched her fill his plate. "Somehow, I find this all pretty hard to believe, Mrs. Swenson."

"Good heaven's, why?" Inwardly Becky winced. It was obvious she'd gone too far.

"Ain't no reason for you to be so nice to me, is there?"

"My reasons are purely selfish," Becky assured him. "A hungry man is more likely to be grouchy than a well-fed one. In spite of what you've heard, I care about my husband and would much rather have his jailer in a good mood."

"Or you could be plannin' on breakin' him out somehow."

"Are you afraid I poisoned your food?" Becky asked incredulously.

"It occurred to me."

Their gazes locked for several moments, hers plainly astonished, his suspicious. "I see your point," Becky said at last. "I guess I'd be leery in your position too." She picked up a spoon and ate a mouthful of stew from his plate and another from the pot on the table. Then she broke open a biscuit, added butter, a rare commodity in the mining town, and ate that as well. "But, as you can see, it's perfectly safe. From now on, you can dish it up, and I'll taste everything before either of you eat it."

Stolks watched her closely as she polished off the biscuit and wiped her hands on the napkin.

"I'll leave now and come back in about an hour to pick up the dishes," she said, dropping the napkin on the desk.

He didn't say a word as she walked across the room and out the door. Becky breathed a sigh of relief as the door closed behind her. Heavens, but the man was suspicious. Mindful of Joe Lucien's advice, she'd purposely set out to win Abner Stolk's confidence. The task wasn't going to be easy.

If she had planned anything truly deceitful, she'd have been caught red-handed. Of course, even if there were a way to get Garrick out of jail, he'd probably refuse to go with her. One hand in her pocket, Becky fingered the medal she'd found that morning. It was still her best chance of helping Garrick. As soon as Sheriff Lucien returned, she'd take it to him. Though he didn't necessarily believe Garrick was innocent, he'd want to check it out. Right now, she had other things to worry about.

301

If Garrick's business was going to survive, she needed to locate a smith to run it while he was in jail. It turned out to be the simplest of her tasks. John Gibbons, the man who had taken over when Garrick went with Ox, was happy to oblige. Becky's other duties were not so easily accomplished. Cooking for Garrick, nursing Cameron, and taking care of Alaina were all nearly full-time jobs, and she began to show the strain almost immediately.

Angel helped as much as she could, but with her business to run, she had little spare time. Collette turned out to be an unexpected ally, though it certainly wasn't out of love for Becky. The beautiful brunette was of no use when it came to the heavy work like changing the bedding or forcing beef broth down the patient's throat, but she was willing to sit with Cameron during the day.

Becky was so grateful for the respite that she didn't even mind the hate-filled looks she got from Collette every time they met. It didn't matter that the other woman was jealous and spiteful. Becky appreciated her help.

For the time it took to deliver Garrick's meals, Becky left Alaina with Angel when possible. Though Abner Stolks still didn't allow her inside Garrick's cell, by the second day he'd thawed enough to let her stay in the outer room of the cell block until the meal was over. Unfortunately, in the meantime, Becky didn't see Sheriff Lucien to give him the medal she'd found.

It wasn't until the third night of Garrick's imprisonment that she was able to talk to the sheriff, and then only because he sought her out at The Green Garter while she sat by Cameron's bedside.

"Sheriff Lucien's here to see you," Angel said, showing him into the tiny room. "It'll be a bit crowded with Alaina's bed and all, but at least you'll be private."

"Thank you, Miss Angel," he said with a smile. "Hello, Mrs. Swenson."

Becky was surprised to see him. "Sheriff."

"Sorry to bother you," he said, trying not to stare at the garish gold and crimson wallpaper, "but I need some information."

"Actually, I've been wanting to talk to you too."

"You have?"

Becky reached into her pocket. "I found this in the weeds next to where Cameron was hurt. It must have been dropped by the attacker."

Sheriff Lucien took the medal from her hand and studied it carefully. "It looks like some kind of military decoration."

"That's what I thought too. They'd know who'd have something like that at Fort Stambaugh, wouldn't they?"

"It's a possibility worth checking into, anyway. I'll ride over tomorrow and see what I can find out. The army has been mighty interested in this case even though it's a purely civil matter." The sheriff looked at Cameron. "How is he?"

"About the same. He'll swallow if we force liquid into his mouth, but that's about all."

"As long as he's alive there's hope. When my brother got kicked in the head by a horse, he lay there just like that for almost a week. Then one day he opened his eyes and asked what was for breakfast. Could happen this time too."

"I hope so."

Sheriff Lucien glanced around the tiny room again. It was obvious he was uncomfortable talking to her in these seamy surroundings. Becky didn't blame him. She felt a little out of place herself. "What was it you wanted to see me about?"

"The circuit judge is in town. Your husband's trial is set for the day after tomorrow."

"I see. Is that good or bad?"

"Depends. The longer we wait, the greater the chance that he'll be tried for murder. On the other hand, we haven't got a whole lot to go on right now, and things are stacking up pretty heavily against him. This judge isn't called the hanging judge for nothing."

Becky paled. "Surely he wouldn't hang my husband just for assault."

"Freeman Jones once hung a man who'd been convicted of stealing a chicken. The judge was in a bad mood and didn't like the man's attitude. If Swede is found guilty, Judge Jones could take it into his head to have him hanged the same day."

"Oh, my God."

"That's why I was hoping you'd help. This whole situation becomes stranger by the minute. This is a simple assault case, but the toughest judge around is trying it. For the life of me, I can't figure out how the army is involved. Swede won't tell me anything. I've tried until my tongue's darn near worn out. I might just as well be talking to a rock."

"He's a bit stubborn at times."

"To be honest with you, Mrs. Swenson, the way it stands at this moment, Swede looks guilty as hell, but I can't shake the feeling that I'm missing something important. I want you to tell me what went on between the three of you. I know it's personal, but it's the key to this whole mess. The last thing I want to do is send an innocent man to the gallows."

Becky looked down at her hands. She'd known she'd have to confess eventually and had been dreading it. Unfortunately, this was only the beginning, and she was all too aware that it would get much worse before it was over. It didn't matter as long as Garrick was found innocent. "You'd better call me Becky, then, because my name isn't really Mrs. Swenson," she began quietly.

Sheriff Lucien said very little as Becky told him of the circumstances surrounding her fake marriage and what had taken place after Cameron returned to South Pass City. "So, you see," she said with a quaver in her voice, "Garrick had no reason to act like a jealous husband. We aren't married and he...he thinks I belong with Cameron."

"Nobody is going to accept that after the way he's been watching you for the past two weeks. I find it a little hard to swallow myself."

"You have to understand my hus...Garrick. He always puts everyone else first. He didn't even..." Becky dropped her eyes and stared at her lap. "This is so hard. We...we weren't even intimate until I forced it on him. He married me to give me the protection of his name until after the baby was born, but he never intended it to be forever. He was glad when Cameron showed up because he didn't have to feel responsible for us anymore. There was never any love involved."

"No man is that unselfish."

"Garrick is. It was the same to him as grabbing the broken beam down in the mine or saving a total stranger from the Indians."

CAROLYN LAMPMAN

"Sounds like he has a death wish. I was in the army with a man like that. He volunteered for every dangerous mission that came up because he felt responsible for his sister drowning. Wound up getting himself killed. Could be what's going on with Swede too. It would explain a lot of things."

"I don't know of anything that would make Garrick act that way," Becky said truthfully, but she couldn't help wondering if the sheriff might have stumbled onto something. There was certainly some sort of dark secret in Garrick's past.

"At least I have a place to begin. I'll take this medal over to the fort in the morning and see if they can tell me anything. In the meantime, if you think of anything else, let me know."

"Of course."

"I know this is all very difficult for you, Mrs. Swenson...Becky. And I appreciate all your help." He glanced at the bed once more then turned toward the door with a shake of his head. "I hope it all works out somehow."

With that he was gone, leaving Becky to ponder his words. Though she usually dozed while she watched over Cameron during the long night, tonight her thoughts kept her awake. There seemed little hope of a happy resolution. Garrick's only chance seemed to lie with the medal in Sheriff Lucien's possession. If only it would identify the real culprit.

The next morning, by the time Becky had delivered breakfast to the jail and returned to The Green Garter, she was exhausted. Angel had taken one look at her face and frowned. "You best go back to the boarding house and get some sleep. I'll watch Alaina."

Becky's half-hearted protest had been easily over-ridden, and now she made her way up the stairs to her room, grateful once again to Angel.

"One moment, Mrs. Swenson," Mrs. O'Reily said from the bottom of the stairs. "I'd like a word with you."

"Yes?"

Mrs. O'Reily climbed the stairs and stood puffing before her on the landing. "Word is that you're cooking for your husband at the jail."

"That's true."

"And that you're spending your nights at The Green Garter.

"Well, yes, but—"

"I don't want the likes of you in my house."

"But, Mrs. O'Reily, I'm only helping take care of Cameron Price. I assure you there's nothing—"

"I know what you're doin' over there, and you ought to be ashamed of yourself. Your floozy ways have already nearly cost one of your lovers his life and landed the other in jail. Even that ain't enough for you, is it? You have to keep stirring the pot."

"But—"

"No buts about it. You give my house a bad name, and I want you out."

"It didn't bother you that much before today," Becky said, flushing angrily. "What happened? Did you get a better offer for my room?"

Mrs. O'Reily had the grace to blush. "It doesn't matter. You're not welcome here any longer."

"Fine," Becky said, turning and starting back up the stairs again. "I'll leave this afternoon."

Mrs. O'Reily grabbed her arm. "No, you'll go now."

"But my things are in the room."

"Not any more. I put them on the back porch."

"What for? Cameron paid for the room through the end of the week."

"My rates went up."

"That's against the law."

"Too bad. Now get out before I—"

Suddenly the door to Becky's room burst open and a ruddy-faced man peered out. "Is there a problem, Mrs. O'Reily?"

"Oh, good morning, Judge Jones."

Judge Jones? All at once, Becky understood why she was being thrown out, and it made her hopping mad. The worst of it was she couldn't do anything about it without making a scene. The last thing she wanted was to make an unfavorable impression on the man who might well hold Garrick's fate in the palm of his hand.

"Why, Mrs. O'Reily," Becky said, "you should have told me you had such an important guest."

The judge smiled at Becky. "Are you staying here as well?"

"I was, but Mrs. O'Reily was just pointing out that it's probably time for me to find other accommodations," Becky said, jerking her arm out of the other woman's grasp. "My baby really should be in healthier surroundings. I'm sorry to have disturbed you."

"That's quite all right. Perhaps we'll meet again."

"Yes, perhaps we will. Good day, Judge." She gave her former landlady a sickly-sweet smile. "I'll be sure to tell everyone just how kind you've been, Mrs. O'Reily. It should be all over town by nightfall."

Becky was proud of the way she swept regally down the stairs and out the door. It wasn't until she was outside that she remembered all her worldly possessions were in back. By the time she had walked around the building, her temper was fading, leaving behind a feeling of deep despair.

Garrick was being stubborn and silent when he should be trying to help the sheriff prove his innocence. Cameron's condition hadn't changed. The creek was still rampaging around her house, and she had no place to go. The sight of her pitifully small pile of belongings was the last straw.

Fighting the tears and trying to hold the sobs that lodged in her throat, she gathered her things. She hardly knew where she was going until she reached the blacksmith shop. It was still early, and John Gibbons hadn't arrived yet. Becky was thankful the building was deserted.

Great sobs tore at her chest as she climbed to the loft and made her way to Garrick's bedroll in the back. It lay there mussed and untidy, just as he'd left it on the morning of his arrest. Becky threw herself down on the blankets, buried her face in his pillow, and let the tears come. She cried for all the pain she had endured and for all that was to come. The tears were not just for herself but also for Garrick and Cameron and, most of all, for Alaina, who stood to lose not one father, but two.

At last, she was all cried out. The anguish was still there, but it was blunted somewhat. She felt purged.

A faint smell of leather and wood surrounded her. Garrick. If she closed her eyes, she could almost imagine he was there with her. Becky wrapped her arms around his pillow and let sleep overcome her. She slept soundly, her exhaustion so complete that she didn't even wake up when John Gibbons arrived and set to work. The sound of his hammer fit seamlessly into her dreams of Garrick.

Chapter 32

"**W**here the hell have you been?" Angel asked when Becky finally appeared at The Green Garter. "I've been looking all over town for you. Nobody's seen hide nor hair of you."

"I fell asleep."

"Not at the boardinghouse. There was a strange man in your room."

"Oh dear, did you say anything to him?"

"Only to ask him if he knew where the hell you were."

Becky winced. "I hope you didn't make him mad. He's the judge who's going to preside over Garrick's trial. Sheriff Lucien says he's very temperamental and tends to take it out on the prisoners come sentencing time."

"Don't worry, Mrs. O'Reily had me out of there before I could do any harm. I'll have to admit, though, I did give her an ear full when I realized she'd thrown you out in the street. Hope you don't mind."

"Mind! I wish I could have done it myself, the old biddy. Is Alaina all right?"

"She's fine, though she may still be a little sticky from the horehound drops Sam's been feeding her all day. I've never seen him so enthralled with a female in all the time I've known him."

"Then why were you looking for me? Mr. Gibbons said you were quite upset."

"Of course I was upset. I couldn't find you anywhere, and I was beginning to fear I was going to have to raise my goddaughter all by myself. Where were you?"

"After my little run-in with Mrs. O'Reily, I went to Garrick's shop and fell asleep. Mr. Gibbons didn't even know I was there until I climbed down the ladder and scared him half to death. What time is it anyway?"

"Close to four-thirty."

"Four-thirty! Oh no, I didn't get Garrick's lunch—"

"Don't panic. I threw a meal together and took it over. You've still got plenty of time to fix something for supper. By the way, what did you do to Abner Stolks? He was ready to go out looking for you himself. I think he would have if there'd been somebody to watch the jail for him."

"You're joking."

"Nope. I think you've made a conquest in that one."

"Do you think he'll let me in to see Garrick?" Becky asked hopefully.

"I think he'd do about anything you asked."

"Oh, I hope so."

Though Garrick's trial loomed menacingly the next day, Becky was hopeful as she carried his supper down the street to the jail. Angel's revelation about Abner Stolks had been a complete surprise. Even if he had mellowed some, she certainly couldn't imagine him actually being concerned about her. As soon as she walked through the door, it became apparent Angel had read the situation correctly.

"Mrs. Swenson," Abner said, jumping up, "we were worried about you."

"We?"

"Me and Swede."

"I fell asleep."

Stolks nodded his head knowingly as he unlocked the door into the cellblock. "Not surprising with the way you've been goin'. Too much for someone as young as you to handle."

"Becky," Garrick's voice startled her, "are you all right? Angel said she couldn't find you."

Becky could see his face through the tiny window in the cell door. She dropped the basket on the table and ran to him. "I'm fine. I went to your shop this morning and fell asleep in the loft. Nobody knew I was there." She lifted her hand to touch his face through the bars, but he pulled back.

"You look tired. Start taking better care of yourself." With that, he turned and walked away.

"I...I will," Becky said, swallowing against the knot in her throat. She went back to the table and started dishing up the supper.

"I reckon it won't do no harm for you to take his supper in to him," Abner Stolks said gruffly.

"Oh, thank you," she whispered.

Garrick lay on the bunk with his eyes closed. He heard the cell door open, but he didn't rise. Seeing Becky had been a mistake. It hurt to be so close and not be able to hold her in his arms. Knowing that her hands prepared every bite he ate, and that she touched every stitch he wore was difficult enough. All he wanted to do was fall asleep, seeking oblivion and respite from a reality that hurt.

He heard Abner Stolks come in and smelled the tantalizing odor of Becky's biscuits. Waiting for the familiar sound of the constable setting the tin plate on

313

the stand by the door, Garrick let his mind drift to happier days.

"Garrick?"

The soft voice right next to his ear startled him, and his eyes popped open in surprise. "Becky! What are you doing in here?"

"Constable Stolks let me bring your supper in."

"What for?" He jumped up and strode to the window.

"Be-because he knew I wanted to s-see you."

"You're better off if you don't."

"But Garrick —"

"Becky, just go." Garrick put his arms along the bottom of the high window and leaned his head against them. He didn't even realize Becky followed him to the window until she touched his arm.

"Please, let me stay, Garrick." Her voice was a sad little whisper that twisted a knife in his heart.

He glanced down at her. The moment he saw her brown velvet eyes swimming with tears he was lost. "Oh Lord, don't cry, little one," he groaned, pulling her into his arms and burying his face in her hair.

For a moment, they just held each other, reveling in the closeness, afraid they might never be able to touch each other this way again. Then, without conscious movement from either of them, their lips met. There was a desperate quality to it, as though they could heal their pain by losing themselves in each other. Time stood still as they shared a wildly passionate kiss, exploring the familiar with an ardor usually reserved for a new experience.

He was the first to break it off, breathing hard, his heart pounding in his chest. "I don't think Stolks would approve of me dragging you to the bunk and having my way with you."

"Maybe not, but I would." She traced the strong muscles of his back with her hands. "I want—"

"I do too, little one, but this will have to be enough."

"Your trial starts tomorrow."

"Ja."

"I'm so frightened."

Garrick closed his eyes and leaned his chin on the top of her head. "I don't suppose I can convince you to stay away?"

"No."

He sighed. "Becky, I'm not going to walk away a free man."

"You don't know that."

"Ah, little one, you're such an optimist." He kissed her forehead then dropped his arms and moved away. "The truth about Alaina's parentage and our marriage will come out almost immediately, Becky. The good people of this town will crucify you."

"I know."

"Do you? Have you thought how it will feel to hear yourself called a whore and Alaina branded a bastard?"

"It doesn't matter. My father called me that and worse all the time. As for Alaina, she's too young to understand what anybody calls her."

"People will go out of their way to be cruel."

"Angel will stand by me. I don't need anyone else."

Garrick was silent for several seconds. "I don't want you to come here any more, Becky," he said quietly.

"Wh-what?"

"You need to start putting some distance between us." His eyes were bleak in the last rays of the sun. "It's time to cut me out of your life."

"Garrick!"

"It's for the best, Becky."

"Says who?"

"Becky—"

"Now you listen to me, Garrick Swenson. We've been through a lot together the last year. Maybe we didn't always agree on everything, but you've been there every time I needed you. I'll be damned if I'll turn my back on you when I finally get the chance to return the favor." She stalked over to the door. "Wild horses couldn't keep me away from that trial. Constable Stolks," she said, knowing the man was right outside the door. "I'm ready to leave now."

Becky swept out of the cell before Garrick could think of anything to say. He heard her telling Abner Stolks she'd return for the plates later, followed by the sound of the outside door slamming behind her.

Garrick smiled reluctantly to himself. There was nobody in the world like his Becky. Then the smile faded. She didn't understand. It wasn't a simple matter of being tried for assault. Daniel Dutton could arrive any day, and Garrick's past would become an open book.

Except for Becky, Garrick really didn't care. He was tired of running, of looking over his shoulder constantly, and never having a normal life. The time had come to pay for his crime. It was impossible to keep it from touching Becky and Alaina, but perhaps he could insulate them a bit. "Will you do me a favor, Stolks?"

"Depends on what it is."

"Don't let her in to see me anymore."

"What?"

"You heard me. I don't want her in here again."

There was a moment of stunned silence. "I reckon I can see to it if you're sure that's what you want."

No, it wasn't what he wanted, but it was best for Becky.

Becky wondered what more could happen today. She decided to check on Sophie and the colt while she waited for Garrick and Constable Stolks to finish their supper. As usual, the livery stable was deserted this time of evening, and Becky welcomed the serene atmosphere inside the barn. Sophie nickered a greeting as Becky approached her stall. For once, though, Sophie's companionship didn't ease Becky's troubled mind.

Garrick was too resigned to the idea of being found guilty. All the evidence against him was circumstantial, yet he wasn't even trying to fight it. There was something he wasn't telling her; she could feel it in her bones. He hadn't even asked about Cameron. With Cameron's fate so closely tied to his own, Garrick's disinterest was odd to say the least.

And why did he deny his feelings for her? It was obvious from the kiss they'd shared that he was far from indifferent. A lump formed in Becky's throat. The trial loomed ahead, and she had no way to protect the man she loved. Her very existence provided the motive for Garrick's alleged crime, though she knew in her heart he hadn't done it.

Standing there feeling sorry for herself wouldn't help Garrick or change tomorrow's outcome. More depressed than ever, she patted Sophie on the neck and turned to go. Suddenly, she needed to hold Alaina in her arms, to embrace the one truly good thing left in her life.

But even that particular joy had to wait, for when she stepped outside, she ran into Sheriff Lucien and an unfamiliar young man.

"There you are," said the Sheriff. "Abner thought you'd come this way. This is John Simkins. He's agreed to be Swede's lawyer."

"How do you do?"

Joe Simkins was about the same height as Becky with red hair and pale freckled skin. "It's nice to meet you, Mrs. Swenson."

"Becky," she said, trying to keep the dismay out of her voice. He didn't look much older than she was. "Have you been practicing law long?"

"No, not long." He blushed and tugged at his collar as though it was suddenly too tight. "This will be my first case."

Becky kept her face carefully blank. The hanging judge and a lawyer who'd never tried a case before? Could things get any worse for Garrick? "Have you talked to my husband yet?"

"Uh—"

"We just came from there," Sheriff Lucien said. "Swede wasn't any more open with him than he was with me."

"Oh, dear."

"I was hoping you could tell Joe what you and I discussed."

"Of course. Shall we go to my husband's shop? There's no one there this time of day."

Though telling her story to Sheriff Lucien hadn't been particularly pleasant, repeating it to Joe Simkins was a nightmare. His face turned an alarming shade of red right at the beginning and never faded. Becky couldn't decide if he was embarrassed or disapproving.

"I see," he said when she finished. "So, you're not married to either one?"

"No."

"But you've slept with both?"

Becky's face burned with humiliation. He obviously hadn't been embarrassed. "I —"

"You're missing the point, Simkins," Sheriff Lucien broke in. "Swede relinquished all claim to her and the baby. In other words, he had no motive to attack Cameron Price. That's your defense."

"Oh, right. Of course. Thank you, Mrs... uh...Yes, well, I'm sure I'll be able to use this all somehow. Good night." Joe Simkins gave Becky a look that made her feel like some sort of disgusting bug, then turned and walked away.

Joe Lucien glared after him. "Damned uncivilized whelp. Somebody ought to teach him some manners. I'm sorry, Becky. If I'd had any idea —"

"Th-that's all right, sheriff. I have a feeling I'd better get used to it. Did you find out anything about the medal?"

"Yes, but you aren't going to like it, I'm afraid."

"After the day I've had, that doesn't surprise me. No one had ever seen anything like it before, right?"

"No, actually, the Lieutenant was very informative."

"He recognized it?"

"It's the medal of honor. Very few have ever been awarded, and only for bravery above and beyond the call of duty."

"Oh."

"That's what I thought too. Of course, that makes it easier to trace back to its owner."

"And it belongs to one of the soldiers at the fort?"

"No."

Becky's face fell. "Then we're no closer than before?"

"Not really, though the Lieutenant knew all about this particular medal."

"He did?" she said hopefully.

The sheriff looked grave. "I'm afraid it doesn't help Swede's case. They found it on a renegade half-breed they arrested last week. The Lieutenant returned it to its owner the morning before the attack."

"Well, for heaven's sake, who does it belong to?"

"Cameron Price."

Chapter 33

"There she is, the hussy that caused it all."

"You can tell what she is just by looking at her."

Becky stared straight ahead, trying to ignore the vicious whispers that went on around her. She felt horribly exposed where she sat in the middle of the room. Situated in the center of the unoccupied chairs, the seat had seemed comfortably anonymous when she came in. But as the courtroom filled, and no one sat in the chairs surrounding her, she became more and more ill at ease. Every person's gaze scanned her at least once. Some were merely curious, others unfriendly and condemning. She was pointed out to those who didn't know her and shunned by those who did.

Only one person didn't glance her way at all. Garrick. His eyes never wavered as he walked in with Abner Stolks. Even with manacles on his wrists, he exuded an aura of physical strength. The heavy metal cuffs pulled his arms forward and down, stretching his simple cotton shirt across shoulders that looked as wide as a barn door. The thin material did little to hide the huge biceps and powerful forearms.

Becky felt like crying. The image of Abner Stolks trying to control his prisoner should the need arise was ludicrous. Garrick dwarfed his guard. There was no doubt in anyone's mind that he was fully capable of killing a man even with his hands in chains. Irrationally, she wished she could shrink him down to the size of Joe Simkins.

Becky jumped as Judge Jones slammed his gavel down on the table. "The first circuit court of Sweetwater County in the Territory of Wyoming is now in session." He surveyed the crowded courtroom. A good portion of the town was there, their excitement barely controlled as they waited for the show to start. Judge Jones fixed them with a fierce stare. "Before we begin, I want to remind all of you this is a court of law, not a circus. If there is any sort of disturbance, you will be fined and removed. I will not tolerate rowdiness of any kind. Is that understood?"

Every head nodded, and the Judge turned his attention to a paper on the table in front of him. "The matter before the court is the people verses Garrick Swenson, alias Swede. Bailiff, has the jury been seated?"

"They have, your honor."

"Very well." As the judge studied his paper, Becky looked at the twelve-man jury. They represented a true cross section of the population of South Pass City. Over half were dressed in the flannel shirts and hobnail boots of miners, but there were several merchants in coats and vests, a mine owner in a fancy suit, and even a couple of cowboys. Becky didn't know any of them.

Suddenly, Ox Bruford was there sitting down in the chair next to her. "I just got into town, and Angel told me what was going on," he whispered, giving her hand a reassuring squeeze. "We decided to take turns staying with Alaina and being here with you and Swede."

Becky gave him a wobbly smile. "I don't know what we'd do without you two."

Judge Jones glanced up from his paper. "Is Dr. Caldwell here?"

The doctor stood up. "Yes, sir."

"It says here Cameron Price received multiple injuries as a result of a beating on the night of June twenty-second. You took care of him, right?"

"That's correct."

"What was the extent of those injuries?"

"A broken wrist, several large lumps on his head, a badly damaged knee, severe lacerations and bruises on his face and body. He had slipped into a coma by the time I saw him."

"That was almost a week ago. Has his condition changed in that time?"

"Very little. The swelling has gone down some, and the cuts are beginning to heal, but he still doesn't respond to light or sound."

"Will he live?"

"I really don't know. It's difficult to tell with head injuries."

"In your best professional opinion, will Cameron Price recover?"

"Well, I—"

"Yes or no, Dr. Caldwell."

The doctor sighed. "No, I'd say probably not."

"Thank you." The judge looked at the paper again then set it down. "Since the doctor says the man's as good as dead, the charge will remain assault until Cameron Price dies, then it will change to murder. That will allow this court to try the case now and save the territory significant time and money."

"Objection," Joe Simkins cried, jumping to his feet. "That's completely unorthodox."

"Objection over-ruled. This is my court, Mr. Simkins, and I will run it the way I see fit. Will the defendant rise and state your full name?"

The chains on the manacles clanked as Garrick rose to his full height. "Garrick Ellinson."

Judge Jones looked up in surprise. "Ellinson?"

"Ja."

"Your name isn't Swenson?"

"No."

"I see. How do you plead?"

"My client pleads not guilty," Joe Simkins said quickly before Garrick had a chance to answer.

The judge gave the lawyer an irritated glance. "Is that how you wish to plead, Mr. Ellinson?"

Garrick shrugged and said nothing.

"I'll take that as an affirmative. Mr. Breton, you may call your first witness."

The prosecuting attorney was Simkins' complete opposite, stocky, middle-aged and frighteningly competent. Becky didn't think she'd ever heard a deeper, more compelling voice as he called Collette to the stand.

Becky hardly recognized the woman who walked up to the front of the room and raised her hand to be sworn in. She wore a demure gown of black striped lavender satin. From the high neck and full sleeves to the modest bustle in back, her costume was tasteful and sedate. Even the becoming hairstyle helped disguise her full, sensuous mouth and lines of dissipation around her eyes. She sat on the edge of her chair as gracefully as any proper young lady and waited patiently for Mr. Breton to begin his questioning.

"Is it true you were the last one to see Cameron Price in good health?"

Collette dabbed at her eye with a lace handkerchief. "Yes. We spent most of the evening together."

"Was there a time during that evening that you weren't with Mr. Price?"

"Only when Swede came in and told Cameron he wanted to talk to him alone."

"Did you hear any of their conversation?"

"Some."

"Will you please tell the court what you heard?"

"Swede told Cameron he'd better get his priorities straight or he was going to knock his teeth out. Then he warned Cameron not to mess with him. I've never seen Swede so angry."

"Did you ever hear any other conversations between the two men?"

"Once, right after Cameron came to town. I was on my way home after shopping and happened to see him go into Swede's blacksmith shop. I thought I'd stop and see how he was doing since he'd been quite ill the day before. I overheard the two of them talking."

"What were they discussing?"

"Swede's wife."

"Could you tell us the gist of that conversation?"

"They were talking about Becky's baby and how Cameron was the father..."

Becky thought she might be sick as she listened to Collette's warped version of the story. She made Garrick's noble reasons for the pseudo-marriage sound like sexual opportunism.

About halfway through the sordid tale, Ox reached over and gave her hand a reassuring squeeze. It kept her tears at bay, but just barely. Through it all, Garrick sat there expressionless. Not a flicker of emotion showed, not even when Collette said Garrick had admitted Becky was afraid of him.

"Thank you," Mr. Breton said at last. "I have no further questions for the witness."

Simkins rose to his feet. "How long have you known the man they call Swede?"

"Since I came to town."

"Was that before his marriage?"

"Yes."

"And what was your relationship?"

She dabbed her at eyes again. "He was my lover."

"Little liar," muttered Ox. "One of her customers, maybe."

"During the time that you've known him, have you seen him angry other than the two confrontations with Cameron Price?"

"A few times."

"And what were the circumstances?"

"In every case he'd had a fight with his..." She paused as though not quite sure what word to use. "With his wife."

"So, in your estimation, Becky Swenson was behind every flare of anger."

"Oh, yes. He's the sweetest person imaginable when she isn't around. She's twisted the poor man into knots."

"And how do you know Becky Swenson?"

"She works at The Green Garter, the same as I do."

"Thank you. No further questions." Joe Simkins wore a self-satisfied smile as he sat down amid the shocked murmur of voices. He might not have been so complacent if he'd noticed the look his client gave him. It was the only emotion Garrick had yet shown, and it wasn't love.

"Order in the court," Judge Jones said, pounding his gavel. "You may step down, Madam. Mr. Breton, call the next witness."

Sam Collins answered the prosecutor's summons with a jaunty step. Becky relaxed as he was sworn in. Here, at least, was a friendly witness.

"I believe you were tending bar the night of the twenty-second."

"That's right."

"Were you a witness to the conversation between Swede and Cameron Price?"

"Not really. I saw them talkin', but I didn't hear any of it."

"Would you call it a fight?"

"No, in fact Mr. Price seemed real interested in what Swede was saying. He took something out of his pocket and showed it to Swede. After that, Swede seemed satisfied and never talked to Mr. Price again."

"What did Swede do?"

"Just had a few drinks."

"How many drinks?"

"I don't know for sure."

"More than usual?"

"Well, some," Sam hedged.

"Could you describe his condition as drunk?"

"I guess so, but he left without causing any trouble."

"Is it common for Swede to get drunk?"

"No, sir. Ain't never seen him do it before."

"So, his condition that night was most unusual?"

"Yes."

"Is it true that you were the one who found Cameron Price?"

"Yes, right after we closed down for the night."

"Would you describe the scene?"

"He was lying right by the trail. There was a full moon and..."

Becky watched Garrick as Sam described going for the doctor and helping the Sheriff look for clues in the scuffed-up dirt. Sitting behind him and to the side, she could only see his profile. There was no expression whatsoever on the strong-featured face as Breton established the fact that the fight had obviously been one-sided.

"And would you say Swede is capable of inflicting those injuries on someone of Cameron Price's size and strength?"

"Couldn't say. I ain't seen either one of them fight."

"I see." Breton turned and walked away from Sam; his face wore a pensive look. "How long have you known Swede?"

"A little over two years."

"And who would you say are his closest friends?"

"Why, Miss Angel and Ox Bruford."

"What the hell is he digging for?" Ox whispered to Becky. "There's no way he can use Angel and me against Swede."

"I see." Breton turned and paced back to Sam. "Would you say this Mr. Bruford is a good-sized man?"

"Well, he ain't as big as Swede, but he's got a fair amount of muscle on him."

"As big as Cameron Price?"

"He ain't quite as tall, but I reckon he's about as strong."

"Weren't you and Mr. Bruford called upon to help Mrs. Swenson last winter when Swede came down with influenza?"

"Oh, hell." Ox whispered, closing his eyes and gripping Becky's hand as Sam reluctantly agreed, then described how they'd gone with Angel to transfer Swede to the pest house.

"And how did Swede react when he heard the baby cry?"

"He uh...he got a little excited."

"How excited?"

"He pushed us both away."

"Didn't he, in fact, do more to Mr. Bruford than push him away?"

Sam shifted uncomfortably. "Some."

"Mr. Collins, would you please tell the court exactly what Swede did to Mr. Bruford? And let me remind you you're under oath."

Sam gave Garrick an apologetic glance. "He hit him."

"And?"

"He...um...he broke Ox's arm."

"What injuries did Swede sustain?"

Sam looked down at his hands miserably. "None."

"None? You mean even sick with a fever that almost killed him, Swede was able to subdue two full grown men without a scratch?"

"Yes."

Mr. Breton turned to the crowd. "Mr. Bruford, would you be so kind as to stand up?"

Ox didn't move.

"Mr. Bruford," Judge Jones said with irritation, "unless you wish to be found in contempt of court, do as Mr. Breton asks."

"He was out of his head," Ox said angrily as he stood up.

"Yes, of course," Breton said with a smile. "Much like he was the night in question, isn't that right?"

"Objection," Simkins said. "Mr. Bruford isn't under oath."

"I withdraw the question. You may sit down, Mr. Bruford. I have no further questions for the witness."

He didn't need any, Becky thought. Any fool could see Ox was built like a brick wall.

Sam gave Joe Simkins a hopeful look. It was obvious he expected Garrick's lawyer to fix the damage.

"Did Mr. Bruford try to defend himself against Swede's attack?"

"No. Swede was real sick."

"Ah, so the incident wasn't really a fair test."

"No."

"Thank you." Simkins started to walk away then stopped as though he'd just had an idea. "By the way, Mr. Collins, did Swede say anything before he attacked Mr. Bruford?"

"I think he said, 'Becky'."

Simkins switched around and looked at Sam in apparent surprise. "So, the whole attack was brought on by Becky Swenson?"

Sam stared at him in astonished horror as Joe Simkins shrugged and turned away. "Never mind, I withdraw the question."

"We'll take a short recess for lunch," Judge Jones announced, striking the table with his gavel. "Court will resume at precisely one o'clock."

Becky winced as Garrick stood up and turned to go. If she could see his face, so could the jury. Simmering rage was plainly visible as he bent down and spoke to Constable Stolks. She relaxed a little as Abner Stolks nodded in apparent agreement and Garrick's face resumed a more normal expression.

She might not have been so complacent if she'd heard how thick Garrick's accent was when he muttered, "I want to talk to Simpkins."

Chapter 34

"Did you tell Simkins I wanted to see him?" Garrick asked as he and Abner walked down the street.

"Yup. He said he had important business to take care of, but he'd meet us at the jail." He grinned up at Garrick. "I reckon he had to visit the outhouse."

The shadow of a smile crossed Garrick's face. Simkins hadn't made many friends with his self-important attitude. "Sam said you were the one he fetched when he found Price."

"That's so."

"Did you search Cameron?"

"Sure did."

"Find anything?"

"Nope, not even a pocket watch."

Garrick closed his eyes. When Sam said he'd seen Cameron take something from his pocket, Garrick suddenly remembered the wedding ring and Price putting it back in the pocket with his watch. If both were gone by the time Stolks searched him, robbery, not anger had been the motive. Garrick finally knew for certain he hadn't been Cameron's attacker. Relief flowed through him like the healing warmth of Becky's kiss.

"What's this?" Stolks said, shading his eyes with his hand as he squinted at a rider coming down the street at a fast pace. "Damn fool. He's going to hurt somebody if he ain't careful."

Garrick watched in mild surprise as the soldier pulled his horse up next to them.

"Where's Sheriff Lucien?"

"I ain't real sure."

"I have a message for him from Major McGraw at Fort Bridger."

"If it ain't secret, I reckon you could tell me. Then you'll be sure he gets the message even if you don't find him."

The soldier gave him a considering look. "I guess I could at that. Tell him Marshal Dutton will be here late today or early tomorrow. He has important evidence for the trial."

"What evidence?" Stolks asked.

"The major didn't say."

"You rode all the way up here from Fort Bridger like you had the devil on your heels, and you don't even know why?"

"Those were my orders."

Garrick's heart sank as Stolks told the young private where to look for the sheriff. Daniel Dutton was coming. By this time tomorrow, the whole world would know Garrick's shadowed past, and they'd come in droves to watch his hanging. He'd known it would happen eventually and was resigned to his fate.

But what of Becky and Alaina? Garrick felt sick to his stomach as he thought of the hell the people of this town would put them through. Already they were treating Becky like some kind of leper, and that slimy little lawyer of his wasn't making it any better. The muscle in his jaw tightened with determination. Well, that was something he could change.

"Other than that, I don't know where he is unless he rode over to Fort Stambaugh," Abner was saying.

"All right. Thanks for your help." The private wheeled his horse around and headed back up the street.

"Can't figure why the army is so interested in this case," Abner said, scratching his head.

Garrick didn't say anything. He had a pretty good idea, but he wasn't about to share it with Abner Stolks.

Joe Simkins arrived at the jail shortly after Garrick. Abner was barely civil as he opened the door into the cellblock. "I reckon if it bothers you that much, I can let you talk to him in here."

"Thanks. Those cells are just so small and dark."

Abner Stolks gave him a sardonic look as he unlocked Garrick's cell. "They were meant to house prisoners, not to hold tea parties in. Your lawyer's here, Swede," he said, his voice dripping with sarcasm. "I'm just gonna lock the two of you in the cell block for now, but I'll be right outside in the office, understand?"

Garrick nodded. "I'm not going anywhere, Constable."

"Didn't figure you were, or I'd have put the bracelets back on you." With one last disgusted glance at Joe Simkins, Abner left, locking the door behind him.

Simkins smiled nervously. "Constable Stolks said you wanted to talk to me. Did you remember something?"

"Why are you attacking Becky?"

"P-pardon?"

"You're supposed to be defending me, not annihilating her."

"But that *is* your defense. The jury has to believe it when we tell them you were actually grateful that Cameron Price arrived on the scene to take her off your hands. Once we prove you were glad to be rid of her, there's no motivation for you to attack Price. I'm just trying to make the jury see the sort of woman she is."

"What makes you think you know anything about her?"

"She told me herself." Simkins shrugged. "A baby out of wedlock, going from one man's bed to another, none of it seemed to bother her. She didn't even act guilty. Oh, she's pretty enough, I suppose, but completely unscrupulous. I wasn't surprised to find out she worked at The Green Garter. Once a whore, always a whore."

Garrick moved so fast Joe Simkins didn't even have time to blink before he found himself suspended by his coat lapels, nose to nose with his client, his feet dangling uselessly above the floor.

"That's my wife you're talking about, you little maggot. One more word out of your mouth about her, and it will be your last!"

"B-but she said you w-weren't married, th-that you s-sent her aw-way." Joe Simkins' voice came out in a frightened squeak as he squirmed in Garrick's grasp. "I didn't m-mean any h-arm."

"Didn't mean any harm! Good Lord, man, you branded her as a prostitute in front of the whole town. She's going to have to live here after both Cameron Price and I are dead and buried. Without either of us, she's going to have a rough time. You don't need to make it worse. I don't care what you say about me, but keep Becky out of it. Understand?"

"But the jury—"

"I don't give a damn what the jury thinks. If I suspect you're even considering saying something about Becky, you'll be dead before anyone can stop me."

"N-not in front of all those witnesses," Simkins said with false bravado. "You'd...you'd hang."

Garrick dropped him to the floor. "I'm going to hang anyway. It makes no difference to me whether it's for one murder or two. Now, get out of here before I lose my temper."

Joe Simkins staggered to his feet and scurried to the door. As he called for Abner Stolks to let him out, his client walked calmly back into the tiny dark cell. With a satisfied sigh, Garrick lay down on his bunk. *That should keep the little worm quiet.*

At one o'clock, the trial resumed. The minute he walked into the courtroom, Garrick saw Becky and Angel in the front with the unfriendly crowd behind them. At least she wasn't alone like she had been when he arrived this morning. Thank heavens for good friends like Ox and Angel.

Almost as if she felt his nearness, Becky turned in her seat. For a moment, their eyes met across the crowded room, and Garrick felt a warm glow deep inside. He knew what it cost her to hear herself maligned by every witness and to have everyone staring at her like a circus freak. Yet here she was, staunchly behind him, her very presence saying she believed in him. Lord, how he loved her!

"Are you sure those manacles are going to hold him?" Joe Simkins whispered to Abner.

"I reckon so. Swede made them himself when the jail was built. He's a damned good blacksmith."

Garrick turned and pinned Simkins with a cold stare. The look in his eyes plainly said the iron on his wrists wouldn't stop him.

Joe Simkins swallowed convulsively and mopped his face with a large white handkerchief.

The afternoon continued much like the morning, with Breton calling witness after witness to the stand and interrogating them with dogged determination. Time and time again, the good citizens of South Pass City testified they'd seen Swede jealously watching Becky and Cameron together, that the big man had become quiet and withdrawn since Price had returned, and how angry he'd been the night of the beating.

Through it all, Garrick sat there with an expressionless face. Every testimony was another nail in his coffin, but Garrick didn't care. It would all be over when Daniel Dutton arrived anyway. Breton, at least, left Becky pretty much alone. Simkins said nothing beyond, 'No questions for the witness, Your Honor.'

Toward the end of the afternoon, Mr. Breton finished his long list of witnesses. "The prosecution rests, Your Honor," he said, and sat down with a satisfied smile.

"Very well. Mr. Simkins, you may call your first witness."

Joe Simkins was sweating profusely as he stood up. "The defense has no witnesses."

Judge Jones sighed with irritation. "Mr. Simkins, do you know what you're doing?"

"Yes, Your Honor."

"I was expecting an interesting trial here, Simkins. You're a sad disappointment to me, not to mention all these good people who came to watch the show. Are you going to call any witnesses or not?"

Simkins gave Garrick a nervous glance out of the corner of his eye. "Not at this time, Your Honor."

The judge shook his head in disgust. "Mr. Ellinson, since your lawyer seems incapable of doing his job would you like to hire another?"

"No."

"You're sure?"

"Ja."

"All right, then. We will recess until tomorrow morning when both sides will give closing remarks. I trust you will have something to say, Mr. Simkins."

Garrick had just settled down on his bunk and closed his eyes when he heard Becky's voice in the outer office. She did not sound pleased.

"I don't care what he told you, I want to see my husband."

Stolks said something Garrick couldn't hear then Becky spoke again. "I'll take full responsibility. He's been mad at me before, and I've survived. At least he won't be able to walk out in the middle of an argument like he usually does."

Garrick grinned to himself. Once Becky set her mind on something, there was no stopping her. Stolks didn't stand a chance. Suddenly, he wanted to see her, to hold her just once more, to say good-bye in private before the hangman's noose snapped his neck. "Let her in, Stolks," he yelled through the door. "She won't leave you alone until you do."

"There, you hear that?" Becky said triumphantly. "He's changed his mind."

The outer door opened, and Becky swept in with her head high and sparks of fire in her eyes. She was quite angry, and Garrick didn't think he'd ever seen her more beautiful.

"What are you grinning about?" she snapped as Abner unlocked his door and stepped aside to let her in.

"It's nice to hear someone else get the sharp side of your tongue for a change. Poor Abner never knew what hit him." He winked at the other man as Stolks closed the door.

"Abner Stolks is not the one I'm mad at."

"Uh-oh, what did I do?"

"I wonder. How about not letting your lawyer do his job for one?"

"What makes you think I had anything to do with that?"

"Come on, Garrick, I saw the way you looked at him, and I saw the way he looked at you. You had the poor man scared to death."

"I didn't like the way he was presenting my case."

"He was defending you the only way he could, Garrick."

"Since when does destroying you help me?"

"Oh, Garrick, what do a few people's opinion of me matter when it might mean the difference between the jury finding you guilty and having you walk away a free man?"

"I'm not going to walk away, Becky. Even if Joe Simkins convinced the jury you were a scheming hussy who had trapped me against my will, and that I was thrilled to death to get rid of you, it wouldn't save me."

"You didn't do it, Garrick. I know you didn't."

"Not this time, I didn't."

She stared at him. "What do you mean this time?"

Garrick sighed. "I've been running from the law for six years, Becky."

Becky felt as though a fist had slammed into her gut, even though she had begun to suspect something of the sort. "Why?"

"I'm wanted for murder." Garrick leaned on the door and stared out the tiny window. "He was a lieutenant in the army."

"Six years ago was during the war, Garrick. Everybody kills during wartime."

"This was my commanding officer."

"Then you were framed."

"No, I'm guilty as sin, and there were a dozen witnesses."

"Wh-what happened?"

"I lost my temper and killed him with my bare hands. Then I ran." He turned from the window with a sigh. "I've been running ever since. Sometimes I wish I had just stayed and taken my punishment."

Becky closed her eyes and swallowed the tears that threatened. No wonder he didn't value his life and was always so willing to throw it away when someone else was in trouble. "That was a long time ago, Garrick. Nobody knows about it here."

"They will tomorrow. There's a Federal Marshal named Daniel Dutton on his way here right now. He was one of the witnesses." Garrick reached out and caressed the side of her face. How he loved this woman. He wanted to tell her, but a lifetime of reticence kept the words locked in his throat.

"Oh, Garrick, your poor wrist." Even in the dim light she could see the raw patches where the heavy manacles had rubbed against his skin.

As she gently touched the injury, Garrick could see tears sparkling in her eyes. With her tender heart, she'd never survive watching him sentenced and hanged. "Promise me you won't go tomorrow."

"But Garrick—"

"I don't want you there, Becky." There was no rancor in his voice, only infinite sadness. "The time we had together made my life worth something again. I don't want you to see me die."

"Oh, Garrick." She threw herself into his arms and sobbed her anguish against his chest.

He ran his hand over the back of her head soothingly. "Shhh, we don't have much time, little one. I don't want to waste it." He pulled her close and kissed her with a fervor that rivaled his forge for heat.

Becky answered fire with fire, her tongue moving with his. After a moment, she pulled him down onto the bunk and ran her palms lovingly over his body. She had his shirt half unbuttoned before he reached up and captured her hand with his.

"No, Becky, I won't make love to you here." His voice came out harsh and raspy as he fought to control his desire. "It's dirty and dark and there are bedbugs in the mattress."

"I don't care, Garrick. It's been almost a month since we...well, you know what I mean. Besides, you're the one who started this, and you know I can't resist you."

"Oh, little one." He leaned his forehead against hers "We can't, Becky. What if you got pregnant again?"

"Would you make love to me if I told you I already am?"

Garrick pulled back as though he'd been struck. "You are?"

He said it with such anguish that Becky was ashamed of herself. "No, at least I don't think so. It's a possibility after the last night we spent together, but I don't think the timing was right."

Garrick tried to ignore the spurt of joy at her admission that she hadn't slept with Cameron as he rolled from the bunk and stood up. "Then let's keep it that way. I won't take the chance of leaving you with another child, not when you're going to be alone." He held out his hand to help her up. "I think it's time you left. There's only so much a man can resist."

"I hate it when you get noble," she muttered as he called for Stolks to come let her out.

"Listen, Becky. I've arranged for Breton to come here tonight and draw up my will. I've already found a buyer for my shop, and I'm leaving the money to you. If Cameron dies, I want you and Alaina to go to my family in Nerstrand, Minnesota. My father's name is Knute Ellinson. He and my mother will welcome you with open arms if you tell them you're my wife."

"Why should they believe me?"

He raised her hand and rubbed his thumb across the horseshoe nail wrapped around her finger. "Because you wear this ring. They'll know I wouldn't give it to just anybody." He pulled her into his arms for one last kiss. "Don't forget me, little one," he whispered against her lips.

Abner Stolks had to clear his throat three times before they heard him.

Chapter 35

"**W**here are Angel and Alaina?" Becky asked Sam when she got to The Green Garter.

"I heard her movin' around in her room when I went by a while ago. Wait..." he called out as Becky headed toward the stairs. "Miss Angel don't allow no one in her room when..." he sighed as she disappeared around the corner. Oh, well, she'd find out soon enough when Angel bounced her right back down the stairs. Sam shrugged and went back to his coffee.

"Angel—" Becky was so upset, she burst into Angel's room without even thinking to knock. "I just have to talk to someb..." She trailed off. The young woman seated at the vanity with her hairbrush frozen in mid-air was a stranger. "Oh, excuse me, I was looking for..." Again Becky halted in confusion. "Angel?"

"Didn't anyone ever teach you to knock?" Angel sighed. "Come in and shut the door, Becky."

"I'm sorry...I didn't mean... Is it really you, Angel?" Becky could hardly believe her eyes. With her hair falling around her in soft waves, and without the usual layer of heavy makeup, Angel looked a good fifteen years younger.

"Yes, it's me. In fact, it's the real me, and as soon as you walk out that door you'll forget you ever saw me like this."

"But why do you do it? I don't understand."

"We all have our secrets, Becky, and quite frankly mine are none of your business."

Becky flushed and dropped her gaze. "I'm sorry, Angel. I didn't mean to intrude."

"I know you didn't." Angel sighed again. "Look, it's Ox I'm upset with. I didn't mean to yell at you. If the truth be known, you're about the only person in this cesspool I trust."

Alaina chose that moment to wake up from her nap, and Becky went to pick her up off the bed with a flicker of relief for the distraction. Of course, if she thought about it, she'd always known there was something unusual about her friend. A glance around the room proved that. How many successful madams had a rag rug and a patchwork quilt in their bedroom, not to mention a bookcase full of books?

Angel turned back to her mirror and began the long process of applying her makeup. "What's happened to get you all upset?"

As usual, Angel was right. Everyone had a right to their secrets, and Becky had no business sharing Garrick's with anyone else. She'd just have to figure out how to save him by herself. "Garrick said he didn't want me at the trial tomorrow."

"He told you that before."

"I know, but this time was different." As the more familiar Angel began to appear, Becky felt more comfortable with her. "Oh, Angel, I just said good-bye to him. It hurts so bad I want to die."

Angel stuck her curling iron into the lamp chimney and deftly pinned her hair on top of her head. "He hasn't been convicted yet."

"I know, but he's sure he will be."

Angel gave Becky a sympathetic look in the mirror as she pulled her curling iron out of the chimney and began the long process of curling her hair. "I learned a long time ago to live for the moment. My advice to you is don't start mourning him until he's gone. Anything can happen between now and then."

Angel's words stuck with Becky all through the long night as she sat with Cameron. She even felt more hopeful about him. Not only had he more readily swallowed the broth, his color seemed better and his breathing easier.

Mostly, though, her thoughts were for Garrick. Anything could happen, especially if she took matters into her own hands. She toyed briefly with the idea of breaking him out of jail. It didn't take her long to realize the futility of that, and she turned her mind to other options.

Nothing had occurred to her by the time she delivered the breakfast that might well be Garrick's last meal. She wasn't even surprised when he refused to see her. With some notion of improvising as the opportunity arose, Becky retrieved Garrick's revolver from its hiding place in the shop and had the livery man hitch Sophie to the buckboard before he left to get a good seat at the trial.

She had no real plan when she returned to the jail to pick up the breakfast dishes. Her heart jerked when she realized the building was empty. Abner and Garrick had already left; she'd missed them. A huge knot formed in her throat.

"Hello in the jail."

Becky lifted her head. *Who in the world?* Almost everyone in town was at the trial. She peered out the door. There were three men on horseback. Two were dressed in an odd combination of Indian and white clothing and appeared to be prisoners of the third, who led their horses.

"Hello." The man in charge swept the hat from his head and smiled when he saw Becky. "Is Sheriff Lucien around?"

Becky noticed two things at once. The man had the longest red handlebar mustache she'd ever seen, and he was wearing a badge. "Marshal Dutton?"

"That's me."

"Sheriff Lucien isn't here right now. He...uh...he asked me to stay here in case you rode in."

"I see." Marshal Dutton scratched his head, then put his hat back on and swung down from his horse. "Is there room in the jail for my prisoners?"

"There are three empty cells."

"I'll only be needing two."

Becky hoped Abner hadn't taken the keys with him. He usually did, but with the jail empty maybe...

Luck was with her. She found the keys hanging behind the desk. It would buy her time to come up with a plan.

As the marshal transferred his prisoners to the cells, Becky tried desperately to think of a way to keep him from the trial. Nothing came to her.

"Did Captain Price contact the sheriff before his accident?" the marshal asked as he locked the door to the cellblock.

It was a good thing his back was to her because Becky would have given herself away with her expression of shocked astonishment. Cameron was a captain in the army? Dutton was after Garrick for killing an army officer! What was the connection? Whatever it was, she had to get Dutton away and fast.

Almost at once a devious plan began to form in her mind. "Hadn't you heard the good news?" she asked as he turned around and handed her the keys.

"What news?"

"Cameron regained consciousness last night."

Marshal Dutton raised his eyebrows. "Now, that *is* good news. Is he all right?"

Remembering Sheriff Lucien's story about his brother, Becky nodded eagerly. "Oh, yes, in fact, you'd never know there'd ever been anything wrong with him."

"Well I'll be damned...uh... Excuse me, ma'am. I was just a bit surprised."

"I know how you feel. It's like a miracle. Cameron left you a message, by the way."

"He did?"

"Yes, he said he'd found where the other man you were looking for has been hiding and asked me to bring you out."

Marshal Dutton looked skeptical. "Why you?"

"He wasn't sure he could trust anyone else."

"Who are you, anyway?"

"M-my name is Becky."

"Becky." The marshal relaxed and smiled. "You're Price's fiancée. He talked about Becky all the time. It's a pleasure to meet you at last. You're fully as pretty as Cameron said you were."

Becky blushed. This man was obviously a friend of Cameron's. She hated to deceive him, but Garrick's life was on the line. "This is my buckboard, so we can leave right now."

"Might as well."

Within minutes, Becky was driving the buckboard out of town with Marshal Dutton riding his horse alongside. Garrick's pistol holster was tucked out of sight beneath the seat where Becky could just touch it with the heel of her foot.

She was taking him to a deserted miner's shack several miles from town, though she really wasn't too certain what she'd do once she got there.

Marshal Dutton turned out to be a pleasant companion, chatting comfortably about a variety of topics. Becky fought the urge to like him. After all, he was here to see Garrick hang.

"There it is," Becky said as they topped the rise above the cabin. She was relieved to see it was still deserted.

Marshal Dutton looked surprised. "Are you sure?"

"This is where Cameron told me to meet him." That much was true, for this had been their trysting place for six weeks. Alaina had been conceived within its moldering walls.

"It doesn't look like he's here."

"He probably hid his horse somewhere."

Dutton gave her an odd look. "Why would he do that?"

"In case there's any more of the gang around. It's safer that way."

"Would he really want you to come out here if it was dangerous?"

"He knew I'd be with you."

"That's true." He rubbed his mustache pensively as he surveyed the situation. "It looks safe enough from here. Shall we go on down?"

Becky nodded, and they started down the hill toward the cabin. In the bright morning sunlight, it looked as though a good strong wind might blow it down. Surely it hadn't been this dilapidated when Cameron brought her here eighteen months ago, or had she just been too starry-eyed to notice? One thing for certain, Cameron had no business calling her tidy little cabin a hovel!

"Maybe I'd better go in first," Marshal Dutton was saying as he dismounted. He tied his horse to what was left of the hitching rail outside. "I'll be right back."

As soon as he was out of sight, Becky clambered down from the buckboard and pulled Garrick's gun out of its holster. Clutching it nervously, she followed the marshal inside.

It was obvious no one had been here in a long time. Light filtered in through a hole in the roof, and dust mites danced in the sunbeams as they fell across the rumpled bed in one corner. Marshal Dutton was staring at the empty wine bottle and guttered candles on the dusty table. Becky winced as she noticed the faded stocking hanging from the head of the bed. Had she really been so mesmerized by Cameron that she'd left her clothing behind?

"Marshal Dutton."

He didn't turn as he shook his head in amazement. "This looks more like a love nest than a hideout. Can't think why Captain Price would want to come here."

"To seduce an extremely naive sixteen-year old, I'm afraid. However, this has nothing to do with Cameron, Marshal Dutton."

He looked at her for the first time, his steely gaze traveling from the gun barrel pointed at his chest up to her face. As their eyes locked, Becky felt a shock of horrified comprehension. She'd have to kill him if Garrick was to go free. Nothing else would make any difference. Suddenly, the gun felt as if it weighed twenty pounds.

"Do you really want to shoot me?"

"N-no, but I don't have any choice."

"Why?"

"So...so you can't hang my husband."

"They'll hang you instead."

An image of Alaina flashed across her mind, and she faltered. That moment of hesitation was all Daniel Dutton needed. In two strides, he crossed the room and wrested the pistol from her two-handed grasp.

"Never was any good at talking when I was staring down the barrel of a gun," he said. "Now just who the hell are you?"

Becky slumped against the doorframe and closed her eyes. It had all been for nothing. "I didn't lie about that."

"Then where is Cameron Price?"

"He's still at The Green Garter in a coma. I'm sorry I gave you false hope about him, but I didn't know how else to get you away from town."

"To save your husband?"

"That's right."

"If you have a husband, how are you involved with Captain Price?"

"He's the father of my baby."

There was a moment of silence. "I don't suppose you'd consider explaining all this to me?"

She opened her eyes and looked at him. "What for? You'll just go back to town and tell them to hang Garrick anyway."

"Garrick! Not Garrick Ellinson?" Suddenly he was staring at the gun in his hand. "My God, it is! I sat and watched him make this very pistol grip from a chunk of wood he found on patrol one day." Dutton ran his fingers reverently over the smooth surface. "It's bigger than normal to fit his hand. I thought I saw him in South Pass months ago, but they told me the man was a Swede."

"So, you do know him."

"Know him! Garrick Ellinson is the closest thing to a brother I ever had."

"Then why do you want to see him hang?"

Daniel Dutton looked at her as though she'd sprouted two heads. "Whatever gave you an idea like that?"

"Garrick told me so last night. He said he—he killed a man during the war, and you were one of the witnesses." Tears welled up in her eyes. "It happened six years ago, Marshal. Garrick hasn't seen his family or used his real name in all that time. Isn't that enough punishment? Can't you just forget you know where he is?"

Daniel looked sick. "All this time he thought he was wanted for murder?"

"He's not?"

"Hell no...uh pardon me, but I just can't believe... Lord, he saved my life!" He looked at the pistol again. "I guess I should have known he'd feel that way. God never made a gentler soul than Garrick Ellinson."

"Then he didn't kill anybody?" Becky asked hopefully.

"Oh, he killed a man all right, but the rest of us considered him a hero, not a murderer."

"For killing his commanding officer?"

Daniel took off his hat and ran his fingers through his hair. "It was right at the end of the war. The Union army was getting short on officers and made some questionable promotions. One of them was Lieutenant Graverson. The man had no sense at all. He made one stupid mistake after another, and every one of them cost us a man or two."

He paced to the table and back again in agitation. The memory obviously still had the power to affect him. "We'd been moving east to join Grant's troops for several days. There were signs of enemy activity in the area, but Graverson refused to stop and reconnoiter. He led us right into an ambush. We lost three quarters of the men we had left. When it was all over, Graverson started looking around for somebody to blame."

"Garrick," Becky whispered.

"No, Jan Ellinson and me. We'd been the scouts."

"Ellinson? Garrick's brother?"

"His cousin. The three of us grew up together, and were closer than brothers. Anyway, Graverson ordered Jan and me executed for treason. Nobody would follow the order, and he went berserk, yelling he'd do it himself. When Graverson pulled his pistol, I figured I breathed my last, but I reckoned without Garrick Ellinson. I'll never forget it. He was only nineteen years old, but he looked like an avenging angel as he came crashing across that clearing and slammed one of those big fists of his into Graverson's jaw."

"Garrick beat him to death?" Becky was horrified in spite of herself.

"Nope, never hit him again. That one punch broke Graverson's neck. About that time, the Rebs found us, and we all scattered into the underbrush. Those of us who made it to Grant's camp didn't even have to discuss it. Lieutenant Graverson's death was reported as a casualty of war. Since Garrick's body was never found, I've always held the hope that he was somehow still alive, though I couldn't imagine any reason he wouldn't come home." He stared at the gun in his hand. "All this time, he thought he was a wanted man."

Becky closed her eyes. "Poor Garrick." All at once her eyes popped open. "So how does Cameron fit into all this?"

"Price? Not at all, as far as I know. He's been working with army intelligence for the last couple of years. Lately he's been assigned to help me clean up a band of renegades that have been stirring up trouble with the Indians and terrorizing folks on the Overland Trail. He captured about twenty of them a few weeks ago in a box canyon."

"Cameron did?"

"I heard a couple of civilians had a small part in it, too. At any rate, I just brought in the last two today. They haven't confessed yet, but I'm pretty sure they were involved in the attack on Captain Price. I found his watch on one of them."

Becky clapped her hands over her mouth. "Oh, my God, the trial. Marshal Dutton, you've got to get on your horse and ride back to town to save Garrick!"

By the time Becky had the story told, Daniel Dutton was in the saddle and heading out. "You're sure you'll be all right by yourself?"

"Yes, now hurry."

All right? It was laughable. For six weeks, she'd come to this cabin by herself to meet Cameron. How could she have been so utterly stupid? With one last glance at the inside, she turned her back and climbed into the buckboard. Much as she'd like to destroy the evidence of her seduction, Becky had more important business to attend to. Garrick was still on trial for his life.

Chapter 36

"I'd like to call Ox Bruford to the stand." Joe Simkins scanned the crowd expectantly. He smiled confidently as Ox came forward to be sworn in.

Garrick resisted the urge to look at the door again. Where was Daniel Dutton? He'd been expecting the marshal all morning and still no sign. If by some miracle he didn't show up soon, the jury might come back with an innocent verdict, that is if his lawyer would shut up and let them go out. For the first time in days, Garrick had hope.

Sometime during the night, Simkins had apparently come up with a new strategy. Judge Jones had grudgingly granted him permission to call his witnesses, and he'd been at it all morning. One after another, he'd brought people up to testify about everything from the mine disaster to the fact that Swede paid his bills on time.

Simkins had painted the picture of a do-gooder philanthropist that frankly made Garrick a little ill. It probably had the same effect on the jury, besides having absolutely no relevance to the case. Garrick wished Simkins would shut up and sit down.

"Would you consider yourself a close friend of the defendant, Mr. Bruford?"

"Yes."

"What do you do for a living?"

"I'm a freighter."

"We already heard testimony that Swede accidentally broke your arm and made it impossible for you to run your business. Will you please tell the court what retribution he made for that after the quarantine was lifted?"

"He drove my wagon for four weeks until my arm healed."

"What about his own business?"

"He hired someone to work in the shop while he was gone."

"In other words, he put the success of your business before his own?"

"That's right."

"Did anything out of the ordinary happen on the last day of that trip?"

"Yes. We heard gunshots as we were coming up the mountain from Rock Springs and went to investigate."

"What did you find?"

"A bunch of renegades holed up in a box canyon. They'd apparently captured an army wagon. They were drunker than the devil and acting crazy. We were just going to leave 'em alone till we noticed they had a prisoner, a white man. Couldn't very well walk away then."

"So, you decided to save the man even though you were grossly outnumbered, and he was a stranger?"

"That's right. Swede had a plan."

As Ox retold the story of Cameron Price's rescue, Garrick wondered if Ox and Angel had been responsible for Simkins changing his presentation. If this kept up, he'd probably be nominated for sainthood just before they hanged him.

"If Swede hadn't cut him loose and carried him out of the canyon, could Mr. Price have escaped by himself?"

"No."

"So, three weeks ago Swede actually saved the life of the man he's accused of assaulting?"

"That's right."

"Thank you, Mr. Bruford, I have no further questions."

The prosecutor rose ponderously to his feet and walked forward as though he were deep in thought. "A most impressive tale, Mr. Bruford. I assume Cameron Price was properly grateful for his timely rescue?"

"He seemed to be."

"And did either of you know the identity of the man you set out to rescue before Swede brought him out of the canyon?"

"No."

"I see. Was the name familiar to either of you after he introduced himself?"

"No."

"So, Swede had no way of knowing he'd saved his wife's former lover?"

"Objection, Your Honor. It hasn't been established that Cameron Price and Becky Swenson were lovers."

"If he's the father of her baby, I think it's pretty obvious that they were lovers at some time or other," Breton pointed out.

"That hasn't been proven either."

"That's true," Judge Jones agreed. "Rephrase the question, Mr. Breton."

"Fat lot of good that will do when the jury already heard him say it," Ox grumbled. "The answer is no, we didn't know who he was."

"Mr. Bruford, you will kindly keep your observations to yourself," Judge Jones snapped. "Mr. Breton, you may continue."

"Thank you, I have no further questions."

"Fine. Mr. Simkins, do you have other witnesses?"

"No."

"Very well, then. We'll hear closing statements."

After a day and a half of endless testimony, the closing statements by the two lawyers were surprisingly short and to the point. Simkins concentrated on Swede's many sterling qualities, the fact no one had ever seen him in a fight, and that he had saved Cameron Price's life a few short weeks before. Breton admitted Swede was a truly nice man, but even nice people could react with violence when jealousy and whiskey were involved.

"Gentlemen of the jury," Judge Jones said when both lawyers had finished. "You have heard the testimony. Consider it well before you reach your verdict. This court stands adjourned until the jury returns."

The twelve men stood and filed solemnly out of the schoolhouse to the saloon next door. No one else left the makeshift courtroom for fear they wouldn't get their seats back when the jury returned. Everybody had their own opinions and were so busily discussing them that the sound of a horse and rider thundering up to the door went unnoticed.

It wasn't until a strident voice rang out over the noise of the crowd that any of them paid attention. "Your Honor, I have important evidence for this trial."

Garrick flinched when he heard the familiar voice. Daniel Dutton had arrived.

Judge Jones gave the newcomer an unfriendly look. "Who are you?"

"Daniel Dutton, U.S. Marshal."

"The jury is already out, Marshal."

"Yes, sir. However, you may want to recall them after you've heard what I have to say."

"Are you sure it's relevant to the matter at hand?"

"Yes."

"All right, you may approach the bench."

Suddenly, there was dead silence in the room as he walked to the front. Every ear strained to hear what the stranger had to say.

Vitally aware of his friend sitting there waiting for the ax to fall and the crowd listening intently, Daniel spoke loudly enough for everyone to hear. "Your Honor, I have reason to believe that the two men I have in custody are responsible for the attack on Cameron Price."

The Judge raised an eyebrow in surprise. "On what do you base that?"

"They're the last of the gang Captain Price and I have been tracking for eight months."

The other eyebrow went up. "*Captain* Price? Marshal, I think you'd better start at the beginning."

Becky had never pushed Sophie so hard. The mare was starting to lather by the time they reached the outskirts of town, but Becky hardly noticed. She had only one thought in mind, to get to the trial before the jury went out. She'd been halfway to town when she remembered her conversation with Garrick the night before. Something that had been said during the trial had convinced him he was innocent. If she could just get Joe Simkins to put Garrick on the witness stand and tell the jury what that was, maybe he could convince them as well. After he realized Marshal Dutton wasn't there to arrest him, Garrick should be willing to talk.

Becky was so intent on getting to the schoolhouse that she almost missed the pair emerging from The Green Garter.

"Becky," Angel called as the buckboard came down the street. "Thank heavens you're here. Come give us a hand."

Turning to see who was calling her, Becky almost fell out of the buckboard. Angel stood in the doorway, supporting a very weak Cameron Price. Even with his arm around Angel, he was swaying unsteadily.

"Cameron?" Becky could hardly believe what she was seeing as she stopped the buckboard and jumped to the ground. "What are you doing out of bed?"

"Got to tell them... Swede didn't do it," he said. "Good thing you're here, Becky," he said. "Those stairs about did me in."

"Damn fool wouldn't listen to reason," Angel said with disgust. "He insists on going up to the trial. Said if I didn't take him, he'd go on his own."

Becky moved in on the other side and propped him up. "Killing yourself won't help him, Cameron. Can't one of us just go?"

"No, not with Freeman Jones as the judge. I wouldn't trust him as far as I could throw a bull moose. Get me into the buckboard."

It was quite a struggle, but with Angel pulling him up, and Becky pushing from behind they finally managed it. "Just don't fall out, Price," Angel said as she clambered into the back of the buckboard. "You aren't exactly a featherweight."

Panting slightly, Becky climbed into the driver's seat and picked up the reins. "That's right. We'll just leave you in the dirt."

"I want to know how you woke up knowing what was going on, Cameron," Angel said as they jounced down the street. "It was plumb spooky the way you opened your eyes and said 'Is the trial still going? Swede didn't do it.'"

"I heard Becky talking to somebody. When they mentioned Jones, I knew Swede was in trouble."

Becky gave him a startled glance. "But that was two days ago, and you were unconscious."

"Two days? I knew I'd been trying to wake up for a long time, but I didn't realize it was that long."

"You could hear us talking?"

"Bits and pieces. You were with me a lot, weren't you, Becky?"

"Every night and some of the day," Angel told him. "You should be grateful to this young lady."

"Oh, I am, believe me, I am."

The warmth in his voice made Becky distinctly uncomfortable. She was quite relieved when they arrived in front of the schoolhouse.

"Uh-oh. Unless I miss my guess, the jury is just coming out of the Grecian next door," Angel said.

"Then we best get moving." Cameron grimaced as he moved to the edge of the seat.

"Here, Cameron, put your good arm around my shoulder," Becky said as they helped him out of the buckboard. "There, can you walk?"

"I think so." A good four inches taller than Angel, Becky was much closer to Cameron's height and was able to support him better. In fact, with his good arm around Becky's shoulders he could walk almost normally except for a slight limp. "Let's go."

Inside the schoolhouse, no one noticed the odd trio struggling through the door. All eyes were focused on the front of the room.

"Do you have any proof of what you say, Marshal Dutton?" Judge Jones asked with more than a hint of irritation in his voice. "I'm not about to let the defendant go just because you come in here with some cock and bull story and tell me he isn't guilty."

"Just the two half-breed renegades in the jail house."

The judge made a rude noise. "You'll have to do better than that, Dutton. Those prisoners could be anyone. I want someone who can prove Cameron Price is in army intelligence."

"I have proof, Your Honor." Everyone turned to look as Sheriff Lucien stood up and walked to the front of the room. "This Medal of Honor was found in the weeds near where he was attacked. When I took it over to Fort Stambaugh, they told me it belonged to Cameron Price. The Lieutenant in charge said—" As one, the crowd leaned forward to hear his words as the loud tromping of hobnail boots heralded the arrival of the jury through the door behind the judge.

"We have reached a verdict, Your Honor," said the jury spokesman.

"Fine. Just wait a minute." Judge Jones directed his attention back to the two lawmen in front of him. "That still doesn't prove he's in the army now, let alone that there's any truth to Dutton's story."

"Your Honor." The jury spokesman's voice was a trifle louder than before. "We've reached a verdict."

"I know. Is there anyone here who has irrefutable proof that Cameron Price was working for army intelligence at the time of his attack?"

"I do, Your Honor. In fact, I can identify the two men who did it."

Every head in the audience swiveled, and a communal gasp went up as they saw who stood in the doorway at the back of the room.

Freeman Jones glared at the stranger angrily. The judge was a man who liked things orderly, and this trial had become anything but. "Who the hell are you?"

"Captain Cameron Price, United States Army."

"*Your Honor.*" The jury spokesman was practically yelling now. "We have reached a verdict."

"Oh, all right, what is it?"

The spokesman drew himself up importantly. "After due consideration of all the evidence put before us, and because we all know Swede pretty well anyway, we find the defendant" — he paused to make sure he had everyone's attention— "we find the defendant not guilty."

Pandemonium broke out as members of the audience thumped each other on the back and swarmed to Garrick, congratulating him on his good fortune, assuring him they'd never doubted his innocence for a moment.

Her heart filled with glorious shining joy, Becky sought Garrick's eyes across the room, wanting to share his victory with him. His gaze locked with hers for a long moment then slid away in dismissal. When he turned his shoulder, Becky felt her heart shatter into a million pieces. He was free, and he still didn't want her.

Garrick didn't think he could bear it. The words he'd prayed for but had given up hope of hearing suddenly meant nothing to him. All he saw was Becky standing in Cameron's embrace, her arms wrapped around his waist, a smile of pure happiness lighting her features.

Even when he couldn't see her anymore, the pain was horrible, an unbearable agony no man should have to endure. The hangman's noose would have been kinder.

Chapter 37

"Are you sure you know what you're doing, Garrick?" Daniel was troubled as he watched his friend load his belongings into the buckboard.

"*Ja*, I'm sure," Garrick grunted. His muscles knotted with the strain as he lifted his anvil to the bed of the small wagon. The buckboard, Sophie, a few of his tools, and the clothes Becky had made for him were all he was taking from his life here.

"Does Becky know you're leaving?"

"No."

"Don't you think you should tell her?"

"No."

"For God's sake, Garrick, she's in love with you."

Garrick wedged his hammers into an empty corner. "She's in love with Cameron Price."

"Horsefeathers! That sweet little lady damned near shot me with that hog leg of yours and —

"Daniel," Garrick said quietly as he leaned his arms on the anvil, "you're one of my oldest friends —"

"And brother-in-law, don't forget."

"*Ja*, that too, but if you don't shut your mouth, I'm going to dump you in the horse trough."

Daniel grinned. "What would your sister say?"

"Kirsten would probably say *mange tasen takk*. That husband of mine talks too much any way."

"What does that mean?"

"Many thousand thanks."

Daniel laughed. "I guess you know your sister pretty well at that." Then he sobered. "I know we've discussed it to death, Garrick, but at least promise you'll go tell Becky good-bye."

"If I promise, will you drop it?"

"Yes."

"Good, then I promise." Garrick went back in to pick up a box of tools. As far as he was concerned, they'd said good-bye in his jail cell a week ago. Nothing that happened between them now could equal it.

"Wish I could be there to see your parents' faces when you show up at home," Daniel said when Garrick came out of the shop again. "They never gave up on you, even after all these years. Your whole family has missed you."

"No more than I've missed them."

"No, I suppose not." He glanced up the street. "I guess it's time to leave. Here comes Joe Lucien."

"Are you sure it's safe for the two of you to transport those prisoners west to Fort Bridger?"

Daniel grinned as he untied his horse. "Yup. Thanks to you, the rest of the gang is already there. You accomplished more with three kegs of black powder in one afternoon than the whole army did in dang near a year."

"What about Indians?"

"Most of the activity seems to be to the east. You'll be in more danger than I will."

"And I'll have an army escort. Guess I'll see you in a month or so, then," Garrick said, reaching over and gripping his friend's hand.

"If you aren't there when I get home, I'll come looking for you."

"Don't worry, I'll be there." He gripped harder. "Thanks, Daniel, you gave me back my life."

"It's only fair. I wouldn't be here if it weren't for you." A wealth of unspoken emotion flowed between the two men as they shook hands.

"You ready to go, Marshal?" Joe Lucien asked as he rode up.

"Sure am." Daniel swung up into the saddle. "Give my best to your folks, Garrick."

"I will, and I'm going to tell your wife you chattered like a magpie for almost a whole week."

Daniel chuckled. "Somebody in the family has to. Your mother and I have to make up for all the rest of you. Don't forget that promise," he said over his shoulder as he rode away.

Garrick's smile faded as he watched the two lawmen leave. Even the anticipation of seeing his family again couldn't erase the ache in his heart. For the dozenth time that day, he reached into his shirt pocket and pulled out the ring of braided silver and gold. Becky's wedding ring.

Should he give it to her or not? Two days ago, he'd found the horseshoe nail ring on his pillow with a note. The childish scrawl was difficult to read but easy to understand. Becky heard he was leaving town and knew he'd want his grandfather's ring back.

It hung from a rawhide thong around his neck just like before, but now it meant so much more. Now it meant Becky. He could feel it against his chest, branding his skin, twisting his heart.

Abruptly, he knew he *had* to give Becky the braided ring.

Her husband might be clever and handsome, a bona fide army hero, but as long as Becky had the ring she'd never forget Garrick. It was pure selfishness, but Garrick wanted her to think of him as often as he thought of her.

Before he had a chance to change his mind, he headed down the street to The Green Garter. *I'll just give the ring to Angel and leave,* he told himself, trying to pretend he didn't know Becky was usually there this time of day.

The kitchen was cool and dark after the hot sunshine outside. Garrick couldn't see much when he stepped inside, but he could hear.

"Da, da, da, da." Alaina's excited chatter was music to his ears.

"Oh, sweetling, how I've missed you," he said, scooping her up in his arms and giving her a hug.

Alaina put her chubby little arms around his neck and mouthed his cheek before making a little popping noise with her tongue.

"Consider yourself kissed," Angel said with a grin. "Becky just taught her that."

Garrick smiled at the baby in his arms. "Is that what that was? Does my little darling want a kiss, too?" He gave her a loud smack on the cheek, and she giggled.

"I wondered if you were going to come say good-bye," Angel said.

"No, I hate goodbyes. It's too final."

"Fine with me. I don't much like sad farewells myself."

He looked around, then sat down with a disappointed sigh and started tickling Alaina. The little girl squealed in delight. "I never thanked you for all you did while I was in jail, Angel, but I want you to know I appreciate it."

"That's what friends are for. She isn't here, Swede. Cameron took her on a picnic."

"Good."

"Damn it, aren't you even going to give him a run for his money?"

"Becky made her choice."

"What choice? You've avoided her since the trial like she had a case of rabies."

"The first thing I did when I got out of jail was build her a bridge across the creek so she could go home."

"Right, and you moved all of her things out of your shop. It was pretty obvious you didn't want her around."

"I wanted her to know she was free to follow her heart."

"She got the message she was free, all right. You were about as subtle as a buzz saw."

"She's never once said she loves me."

"Maybe she's not the kind that does."

"Drop it, Angel."

Angel threw her hands up in the air dramatically. "Fine. I wash my hands of the both of you. I've never seen two people so bent on being miserable in my life. Damn stubborn Swede anyway."

"Will you do something for me?" he asked quietly.

"Sure, why not?" she said sarcastically. "I live to please."

The corners of his mouth quirked slightly as he reached into his pocket. "I know you do." He looked at the ring for a moment before handing it to Angel. "Will you see that Becky gets this? I bought it for her last October and never found the right time to give it to her."

"It's beautiful." She took it from his hand and looked at it curiously. "What's this engraved inside?"

"*Jeg elsker deg.*"

"What in the world does that mean?"

Angel thought at first he wasn't going to answer. His entire concentration seemed focused on the baby as Alaina held onto his fingers and stood balancing herself on his thighs. "It's Norwegian," he said softly. "It means I love you."

"You've become quite a cook," Cameron said as he sat back on the blanket with a satisfied sigh. "That was the best meal I've had in a long time."

"Thank you, Cameron." Becky seemed unaffected by the compliment as she calmly packed away the remnants of the picnic.

"You're not the same girl you were when I was here last year."

"No, I grew up."

He reached out and touched her hair. "You're even more beautiful than the first time I ever saw you."

"So are you."

He smiled. "Ah, Becky that's one reason I love you so much. You're always so refreshingly honest."

"Actually, Cameron, I'm just too ignorant to know what I'm supposed to say."

"That's all right." He brushed her mouth with the tip of his finger. "I can think of several things I'd rather do than trade compliments." His voice was husky as he leaned forward and kissed her.

Becky closed her eyes and allowed him full use of all his expertise. There was no doubt about it, Cameron Price was truly an artist when it came to kissing. He knew exactly how much pressure to exert, when to open his mouth, and where to put his tongue. Becky was pleased to find herself completely unmoved.

"Becky my love—" His beautiful eyes smoldered as he folded her hand into his and kissed it. "—marry me."

"I don't think so, Cameron."

"Wh-what?" He stared at her blankly.

"No, I won't marry you."

"But I love you."

"I know, you've told me a thousand times." She pulled her hand free of his. "You even said so just before you left me alone and pregnant."

"I didn't know you were pregnant."

"Didn't care, you mean. Come on, Cameron. I might have been too naive to realize what could happen, but you knew where babies came from. It didn't matter to you if I conceived. You weren't planning on being around."

"You make me sound like a selfish bastard."

"Yes, you were, weren't you?"

"I didn't hear you complaining at the time."

"I was sixteen years old, Cameron, starved for love and willing to do anything you asked. I thought I'd found my hero."

"Then this has all been a sham?"

"No, not all of it. I truly thought I still loved you when you came back. I soon discovered most of it died long ago. To be honest, I'm not sure it was ever much more than infatuation."

"Then why all this elaborate playacting?"

"Because Garrick deserves his freedom, and he'll never take it as long as he thinks we need him. Now that he's leaving, I don't have to pretend anymore."

"You're in love with that big, dumb Swede," Cameron said in astonishment. "You actually prefer him over me?"

"That's right, Cameron. He's worth at least ten of you."

"What about Alaina?"

"Congratulations, you finally got her name right."

"You can't keep her from me. She's my daughter."

"No, Cameron, she's *my* daughter."

"I'm her father. I gave her life."

"She may have come from your seed, but Garrick's her father. He breathed life into her the day she was born, and he's been there for her ever since. The most important part of being a father is living up to your responsibilities. You gave up your rights the day you walked away without a backward glance." She stood and picked up the basket Angel had lent her for the outing. "It's been a pleasant morning, but it really is time I was getting back. Good-bye, Cameron."

Becky was amazed how good it felt to walk away and leave Cameron Price sitting there in total shock. It was probably the first time a woman had ever refused him anything. She was still smiling when she walked into The Green Garter.

"Must have been some picnic," Angel said.

"Cameron asked me to marry him."

"So, when's the big day?"

Becky grinned. "The twelfth of never."

"You turned him down?"

"I left him sitting there with his mouth hanging open."

"Good for you. Maybe there's hope for you yet." Angel gave her a shrewd glance. "Swede was here while you were gone. He's leaving today."

Becky's smile disappeared. "Oh."

"He left you something." Angel handed Becky the ring and watched her face sympathetically as the tears gathered in the dark brown eyes. "He said he hadn't ever found the right time to give it to you."

Becky reached up to brush a tear away. "No, I suppose not. It's a wedding ring. Look there's something written inside. I can't tell..."

"It's Norwegian. *Ja elsker* something."

"*Jeg elsker deg?*"

"Right."

Becky wrinkled her nose. "Why would he put a Norwegian curse inside a ring?"

"A curse? Damn funny thing to say for a curse if you ask me."

"He told you what it meant?"

"Yes. I love you."

"It means I love you?" Becky couldn't believe her ears. No wonder he thought it was funny when she used it to put him firmly in his place. Suddenly, the full impact of it hit her.

"Oh, my God. Angel, when did he leave?"

"About fifteen minutes ago. Why?"

"I've got to catch him."

"It's about time."

"But you don't understand. He loves me."

"No fooling! I'd never have guessed," Angel said as Becky ran out the door. "You know, Alaina," she said to the gurgling baby on her lap, "I love them dearly, but your parents really aren't too bright."

He loved her! Becky's heart sang as she ran down the street to his blacksmith shop. She'd been sure of it that night in his jail cell. But when the not guilty verdict came in, Garrick had turned away without so much as a smile. Then he'd moved her things out of his shop, and she hadn't seen him since.

When Angel told her he was leaving town, Becky had taken the horseshoe nail ring to the shop as an excuse to talk to him. After two hours of waiting, she'd given up and left it on his pillow with a note. The gesture had been futile. She'd given up her one solid tie to him for nothing except the certain knowledge that he was glad to be rid of her.

It had all been a ruse. *Jeg elsker deg.* He'd said it even when he was angry. Garrick loved her as much as she loved him. Darn his nobility anyway.

Becky was breathing hard by the time she reached the shop. It was deserted. His clothes were missing from the loft and the peg where his leather apron always hung was empty. He was gone.

"No!"

She ran out of the shop and looked around frantically. The army's weekly convoy east out of South Pass City was just winding up the hill. The familiar black buckboard was last in line.

"*Garrick!*"

The distance was too great for him to hear her desperate cry. Becky knew it was hopeless, but she lifted her skirts and started running. Clear through town, she raced. Panic lent her speed and stamina, but it wasn't enough. She reached the bottom of the hill just as Garrick arrived at the top.

Winded and unable to run anymore, Becky slowed to a stumbling walk. Tears coursed down her cheeks while she watched him drive out of her life. She was too late.

As the buckboard jounced over the last of the washboard ruts at the top of the hill, Garrick heard the familiar song of a meadowlark. The sound brought a bittersweet pang, and he turned back for one last look at the town. The taste of defeat stung the back of his throat.

A movement at the bottom of the hill caught his eye. Focusing on the figure so far below, his heart seemed to jump out of his chest. Becky!

With fear pounding through him, he didn't even take time to turn the buckboard around. Something was very wrong. Garrick tied the reins to the brake lever, jumped to the ground and sprinted back down the hill.

Tears were streaming from her eyes, and her breath was coming in great sobbing gasps when he reached her. "What's wrong, Becky?" he asked, grabbing her upper arms.

"C-can't...t-talk..." she gasped, trying to catch her breath.

"Has something happened to Alaina?"

Becky shook her head.

"Angel, then?"

Again, she shook her head. Still struggling to speak, she lifted her hand and put her fingers on his lips. "T-take us ...with you, Garrick. I...love...you."

He stared down at her, incredulous hope shining from his eyes. "What did you say?"

"*Jeg...elsker...deg*, Garrick. I love you."

"Oh, little one." He pulled her into his arms and kissed her passionately. It wasn't practiced or technically perfect, but it came straight from his heart, and Becky thought she might go up in smoke from the sheer power of it.

He broke it off at last and searched the velvet brown of her eyes. "Do you really love me?"

"Oh, *ja*. Every stubborn Norwegian inch of you."

"Why didn't you ever tell me?"

"One of my father's mistresses once told me a smart woman always lets the man say it first. That way he doesn't feel trapped. Only, you've been telling me for months, and I didn't even know it."

"Where's Cameron?"

"Probably somewhere feeling very sorry for himself."

"Why?"

"I told the arrogant windbag exactly what I thought of his marriage proposal."

"You turned him down?"

"Yes, and it felt wonderful."

"Are you sure that's what you want? Cameron Price is every woman's dream."

"Not mine." She smiled up at him. "My dreams are all tied up in a big blond blacksmith who has more courage than sense. I don't want to live without my dreams, Garrick."

"Neither do I, little one."

He hugged her so tightly, she thought her ribs would crack. It felt wonderful. "So where are we headed, Garrick?"

"How would you and Alaina like to go to an old-fashioned Norwegian family wedding?"

"I'll go anywhere with you, Garrick. You don't even have to ask." Becky gave a blissful sigh and tried to snuggle even closer into his embrace. "Who's getting married?" she asked as an afterthought.

Garrick gave her one of his beautiful smiles as he lifted her high in his arms. "We are, little one," he said as their lips met in a kiss filled with magical promise. "We are."

Author's Note

As with all historical romances, Meadowlark is a blend of fact and fiction. Gold was discovered in the Wind River Mountains at South Pass in 1868. By 1870, South Pass City, Miner's Delight, and Atlantic City were booming gold towns. The town in Meadowlark is a composite of all three.

Between seventeen and twenty-eight saloons, brothels, and casinos flourished in South Pass City during its heyday. Many were similar to the fictitious Green Garter. The liquor storage facility, facetiously known as Fort Bourbon, really was used as a refuge for women and children during Indian attacks, and more gold probably changed hands in Beer Garden Gulch than ever came out of the Carissa mine.

South Pass City is considered by many to be the home of women's suffrage. It was the city's representative to the Wyoming Territorial Legislature that introduced the historic bill giving women political equality. When it passed, and women gained the right to vote, R. S. Barr protested by resigning his office as Justice of the Peace contingent upon the commissioners being able to find a woman who could replace him.

Esther Hobart Morris, the world's first female Justice of the Peace, was duly appointed and served for nine months, presiding over twenty-six cases fairly and with great dignity. As part of her duties, she may well have performed weddings like Garrick and Becky's. Had she still been in office, I'm certain she'd have done a better job with Garrick's trial than the fictitious Freeman Jones.

Martha Jane Canary, better known as Calamity Jane, was occasionally hired as a nurse for the pest house, though placing her there as late as the spring of 1871 may not be accurate. Tom Ryan truly was the owner of the Goulden Curry mine, and probably employed a powder man for each shift. Philip Harsh had a prosperous blacksmith shop at the corner of Price and Grant Streets. There is no record that he sold his building to a big Norwegian known as Swede, but I like to think he could have.

About the Author

Carolyn Lampman has won several industry awards for her previous novels, including the Reader's Choice Award and the Coeur Du Bois Heart of Romance award. She was also a finalist for the coveted RITA. Carolyn lives in a small town in Wyoming with her husband, a Welsh Corgi, and a herd of grandchildren who come and go.

Made in the USA
San Bernardino, CA
03 December 2018